WHISPERS
IN THE NIGHT

WHISPERS
IN THE NIGHT

MOLLY TABACHNIKOV

iUniverse, Inc.
Bloomington

Whispers in the Night

iUniverse books may be ordered through booksellers or by contacting:

iUniverse
1663 Liberty Drive
Bloomington, IN 47403
www.iuniverse.com
1-800-Authors (1-800-288-4677)

ISBN: 978-1-4759-3654-4 (sc)
ISBN: 978-1-4759-3656-8 (hc)
ISBN: 978-1-4759-3655-1 (ebk)

Library of Congress Control Number: 2012912388

Printed in the United States of America

iUniverse rev. date: 07/30/2012

For those who made this possible:
Sharon Mack, who gave me the idea;
The Coral Springs Writers Group,
whose encouragement kept me going;
and for my writing buddy, Jhena Plourde,
who never let me give up.

CHAPTER 1

The whispers in the night started when Fox Monroe was six years old. They woke him up while it was still dark. Were Papa and Daddy talking? It didn't sound like them. The soft noise sounded like voices, but he couldn't make out any words, and the sound faded in and out. Maybe if he tried real hard and reached for them . . .

He fell asleep again before he could finish the thought.

He told his fathers about it the next morning at breakfast.

"It was weird," he said, his thin face serious. "Like these voices in the back of my head."

"Did the voices tell you to do something?" There was a frown on Papa Gerry's usually smiling bearded face.

"Oh, they weren't words," Fox replied, looking thoughtful. "It was like—Y'know how when we're at Avery Fisher and before the music starts everybody's talking but you can't hear—" He hesitated, then brought out a grown-up word. "—sepisufistic things."

"You mean specific," Daddy Pete corrected, but his slender face was worried, too.

"Yeah, that," Fox said, shoveling oatmeal into his mouth.

Even though he was intent on his breakfast, he noticed the concerned looks his fathers exchanged.

That afternoon Daddy Pete made an appointment with Doctor Spinner. Fox liked Doctor Spinner, because he joked about Fox's name, and he was gentle, and Fox always got a lollipop after the examinations. He didn't even mind the needles because Doctor Spinner distracted him with jokes or stories when the needle went in.

"Am I real sick?" Fox asked, worried at the fuss.

"Nah," Doctor Spinner answered, looking Fox in the eye.

"Then can I go get a lollipop?"

"Sure. Go tell Susie I told her to give you a red one."

Fox smiled and jumped down from the table. He could hear the conversation as he walked to the waiting room.

"Well?" Papa Gerry asked. Fox glimpsed how he and Daddy Pete held hands tightly, the way they did when they were worried.

"I can't find anything organic," Spinner replied. "He's perfectly healthy, and judging from this examination, there's nothing overtly wrong behaviorally. We could put him through the battery of tests, MRI, CAT scan. But I don't think it's necessary. I'll refer you to a good psych person I know."

"Yeah," Papa Pete said. "I don't know whether to be relieved or more worried."

"I know," Spinner sympathized.

Fox didn't understand most of the words. He decided to forget about it and went in search of Susie and the red lollipop.

The psychiatrist was a young man whose pony-tailed blond hair was shiny and clean. Fox liked him right away because his eyes smiled as much as his mouth, and Fox felt good in the office.

"So," Dr. Katz said when they were sitting on the couch in the playroom. "Why do they call you Fox?"

"I got this pointy nose," Fox said. He pointed to his nose. "An' red hair, kinda like a fox. An' I got these yellow eyes. Foxes got yellow eyes, at least some of 'em. Daddy looked it up onna innernet and it said so!" He grinned. "I'm a fox," he said gleefully.

"I guess so. Why do you want to be a fox?"

He thought a minute. "They're smart. An' they're fast. An' they play with each other but they don't hurt each other."

He played with the toys and talked to Doctor Katz, and afterward announced that he liked the new doctor and wanted to go back.

So when his fathers told him he had to see the doctor again, probably a few times, Fox smiled. Then he saw that Daddy's eyes were kind of scrunched up, the way they got when he worried, and Papa's mouth was a thin line. He hated to upset his dads. But what could he do?

During the next session, the doctor asked, "So, do you still hear the voices?"

Fox wanted to say that the whispers had stopped, but he sensed somehow that no one would believe him. He pretended to think hard, like he was remembering something.

"Not all the time," he said slowly. In that same strange way, he knew what to say to the doctor. "And it's like they go in and out."

"Are they telling you anything?" the doctor asked calmly.

One of the wheels had fallen off the truck that Fox was playing with and he concentrated on trying to put it back. "Nah. It's just noise. You can't hear one voice. Just noise."

After a couple of visits to the office where he played and talked, Fox told the doctor that he didn't hear the whispers any more. He told the same thing to his fathers. He hated to lie, but the worried frowns on his fathers' faces upset him more. He still heard the whispers every night, but they didn't bother him.

At the end of the last visit, Dr. Katz shook hands with Papa and Daddy. "He seems fine to me, just an active imagination. If you feel the need for another appointment, call me. But for now, he seems to be functioning in a normal way. I can understand your worry, but remember, every kid has a unique way of viewing the world. This is Fox's."

Fox couldn't understand most of the words, but he saw the way Daddy's eyes relaxed, and Papa's frown disappeared. Everything was back to normal.

Sort of. Because Fox knew he could never tell anyone about the whispers. It had to be a secret.

Fox's bedroom was large enough for him and his toys and books, and it looked out from the second floor over the back yard where a huge oak tree grew. Of course, he could never go into the back yard to play. The super's apartment was the only way to get there, and Mr. Lee guarded his privacy. But the tree was beautiful. In the warm afternoons, the sun filtered green through the leaves. In the winter, the snow gathered on the branches, and it was pretty.

One rainy Saturday, he and Daddy Pete played on the dark parquet floor in the living room.

"What's our story gonna be about today?" Fox asked.

"You decide," Daddy said, smiling.

"Yeah! Okay, these two guys land their spaceship. It's on a new planet. And they have a robot, but there's a problem with it. They go outside."

Fox glanced up. His father nodded, his eyes shining.

"So they don't know there are dinosaurs on the planet. But they go out anyway."

The story grew more and more fantastical until, by late afternoon, both of them were laughing and gasping for breath.

When the story was finished, Daddy said, "You know this is just fiction. Do you remember what fiction is?" Daddy always said that after one of their story times.

"Sure," Fox responded. "It's make-believe. You can't touch it or anything. 'S not real."

Daddy Pete hugged him and went off to make dinner.

A few minutes later, Papa Gerry came home. Papa Gerry was kind of the opposite of Daddy Pete. Where Daddy was small and thin, like Fox, but with blonde hair and blue eyes, Papa Gerry was big and strong, with a dark brown beard and warm brown eyes. Papa was a nurse at St. Vincent's Hospital in the pediatrics wing. He told Fox that meant that he worked with children. Fox liked to hear about the children. So Papa would tell Fox about the kids leaving the hospital with their parents, everyone smiling and waving good-bye.

But today Papa Gerry wasn't smiling. He looked sad and tired.

"What happened?" Daddy said when he came out of the kitchen. He led Papa over to the couch and settled him against the cushions.

Tears ran down Papa's face. "Carrie." He choked. "Carrie died."

Daddy put his arm around him and cradled the larger man's head against his shoulder. Fox watched them, silent, as they stayed motionless for a while. He hated it when his fathers were upset, and when they cried his stomach felt tight.

Then Papa sat up and wiped his face. "I was in her room to give her an injection. She was so brave," he said quietly. "Her parents were there. They were watching TV, the way they did most afternoons. Then she turned to them and said, 'I love you,' and then she—she flatlined."

He put his head down, and Fox could see the tears flowing again.

Daddy cupped his partner's face in his hands. "You made her time easier," he said firmly. "You helped her."

Papa Gerry just nodded.

"I'll make some coffee." Daddy kissed Papa's cheek and got up.

Fox watched Papa for a minute, then crawled into his lap. Papa put his arms around him and Fox snuggled into his father's shoulder. He always felt so safe in Papa Gerry's arms.

"C'n I ask you something?" Fox said.

"Um."

"What happens to you when you die?" Fox knew about dying. Jeremy's great-grandma had died last year. Everyone was sad, and they buried her in a big coffin.

Papa Gerry took a deep breath. Fox leaned back and rested his temple against Papa's soft beard. "No one knows, hon. Some people think you go to a beautiful place called heaven. Others think you get born again in another body. Some believe your energy just goes out into the world."

"Wadda you think? Do you think heaven is what happens?"

"I wish I could, Fox. I really wish I could."

Fox squirmed around and put his arms around Papa Gerry's neck. "I love you, Papa Gerry. I don't want you to die. Ever!"

"I love you, too, son," Papa Gerry whispered.

And for a while, Fox felt comforted.

But that night he couldn't fall asleep. The whispers got louder, and he thought he could hear crying. He was afraid Papa was sad again.

He got up and walked to the door, as quiet as he could be, and crept down the hall to his parents' room. He stood outside for a while, but he couldn't hear anything coming from inside except Papa's soft snores.

Suddenly he looked around because he felt as if someone was watching him. Not like Daddy or Papa, when he caught them watching him play and felt their love surround him like a warm towel. It was scary, like the watcher wasn't a nice person. And what made it more frightening was that there was no one there.

Fox ran back to his room, his bare feet making no noise on the wooden floor. He jumped into bed and pulled the covers up to his nose. He lay there for a long time, his eyes open, feeling the unseen watcher. When he finally fell asleep, his sleep was fitful, and his dreams were filled with images of people crying.

CHAPTER 2

"So that's how babies are made?" Eight-year-old Fox looked at his fathers from where he sat, cross-legged on the living room floor, the big book of pictures in front of him. He was doubtful about the whole business.

They glanced at each other; smiles played around their lips.

"Yup," Papa Gerry answered.

"It's yucky," Fox said, gazing at the pictures again. "Why would anyone want to do that?"

"Because it feels good," Daddy Pete explained. "We know you don't like to hear this, but you really will understand it when you get older."

"Y'mean like when I'm nine, or ten?"

Now both men grinned.

"I think you'll have to wait a little longer than that," Daddy said. "Maybe until you're sixteen or seventeen."

Fox nodded, thoughtful. He knew his fathers wouldn't lie to him, even though this sounded too silly. Besides, he could always tell when someone was lying, and both of them were telling the truth.

Then he asked, "If it takes a man and a woman to make a baby, what about me?" He looked up at his fathers, waiting for their answer. They could explain anything.

Papa Gerry answered him. "We really wanted a baby, but we knew we couldn't make one. Your mother was a very good friend of ours." He looked at Pete, smiling fondly.

"Your mother didn't always live in Wyoming," Daddy said, turning back to Fox. "Wait a minute." He got up and went to the yellow oak bookcase that held the photo albums. He selected one, then came back and sat down on the couch again, leaving a space between him and Papa.

"C'mere." He patted the empty cushion between the two of them.

Fox climbed up on the couch as Papa Gerry opened the album.

"Maybe you remember we showed you this picture before. We were in college," he explained, pointing to a small, slender woman smiling out at the camera from between Papa and Daddy. They looked a little different in the picture. Papa didn't have a beard, but Daddy did.

"I dated her for a while, before I met Papa Gerry," Daddy said. "I loved her as a friend, but not like a wife."

"Something else I'll understand when I'm older," Fox muttered good-naturedly.

Papa turned the page. "And this is after we moved to New York, right here in this building. She lived on the fourth floor, and the three of us saw each other all the time."

He put the open book on Fox's lap before he continued the story.

"She knew we wanted to have a child, and, as you just learned, we couldn't do it ourselves. So she gave one of her eggs." He pointed to the drawing Fox had left on the floor. "We both gave our sperm, and they created you. Since we don't really know whose sperm actually went into the egg, you belong to both of us."

Fox glanced at Papa, frowning.

"So why isn't she here now?" he wanted to know.

"Your mom isn't like anybody else we ever knew," Daddy Pete explained. "She's an artist—a painter. And very good. She could've been famous. After you were born, the three of us took care of you. It was like we were a family of four."

Daddy sounded kind of sad. Fox slipped his hand under his father's.

"But when you were—oh, about a year old, she said she had to move away. New York was too busy for her, too noisy. She needed somewhere quieter. You probably got your exceptional hearing from her. You certainly got her eyes."

Fox ran his finger over the picture. He never wondered about his mother before. All of a sudden, it was like she stood in front of him, a real person.

"Her eyes . . . They're kind of gold, like yours," Daddy explained. "I've never seen anyone else with eyes like that. Like someone put gold sparkles in them."

Did she hear the whispers like I do? Fox wondered, looking down at the picture in the album. His mother stared out at the world with confidence. Her hair was the same auburn color as Fox's, and it grew straight and smooth, like his. But he couldn't make out the color of her eyes. Everyone's eyes looked red.

"She loves you very much," Papa Gerry said. "And you'll meet her, soon. For now, how about writing her a letter?"

"A *letter*? Y'mean like on paper in an envelope?" Fox looked at his fathers in dismay. "Why don't we just email her? Or call her?" He had never written a letter in his life. It would take days for a letter to get there. He couldn't imagine doing it. Even Gamma Rose, Daddy's mom, had email.

"Your mom lives far out in the country," Papa said. "She hates computers and even telephones. The only way to get in touch with her is to write a letter."

Fox considered this for a moment. How could anyone live without a computer? Without a phone, even? Well, Papa and Daddy knew a lot of strange people. His mom wasn't the weirdest. And she sent him really cool presents, mostly wooden toys or books about animals.

"Okay," he said. Then he looked around. "What should I do?"

                        —

"Hey, Fox, c'mere. Lookit this." Big Wally's voice was pitched low so the teacher in the middle of the yard couldn't hear. He held his big, beefy hand out in front of him. The crowd of boys around him stared at it.

Fox walked slowly over to the group huddled around Big Wally. He knew he was safe with these guys. Even though he was the smallest one in the second grade, they respected him because he always knew when a grown up was nearby who could ruin whatever trouble they had planned. It was just a knack, but it earned him a safe place in the pecking order.

"Waddaya got, Big Wally?" Fox asked as he walked to the group.

He had been hanging out with the guys since the beginning of the school year, and he had learned that sometimes Big Wally didn't think before he acted. Fox had learned to be cautious.

Wally opened his palm as Fox approached to show a flat, square plastic package. "Ever seen one a these before?" he asked gleefully.

"Yeah, sure," Fox answered. "It's a condom. A rubber. Guys put it on their penis before they have sex with a girl to keep from having babies. And to keep from getting sick."

Fox knew that Big Wally was going to talk about sex and he was probably going to get it all wrong anyway. Wally always did. Besides, Fox's fathers had already explained it. So, while Big Wally was messing up the facts of life for the other boys, Fox's gaze wandered into the schoolyard.

A new girl stood shyly in a corner of the yard. Her skin was the color of coffee with extra cream, the way Daddy Pete liked it. Her black hair, a curly cloud around her head, moved slightly in the breeze.

Fox's heart stopped.

She was the most beautiful girl he had ever seen, but more than that, he felt a sweetness inside her. A joy that she wanted to share with the world.

Leaving the boys, he walked over to join her. Feeling shy himself, he said softly, "Hi. I'm Fox."

"I'm Sonia." She turned to him. Her eyes were deep black, and they seemed to glow. "You got weird eyes." But her tone wasn't mean.

"Yeah," Fox said. "Everyone says so."

"I like them." She smiled at him.

And just like that, Fox fell in love.

⁓

Fox felt like he was having the best time in the world. He had his dads, their apartment (a safe place when the world was too mean or confusing), a fascinating neighborhood, and every year there was the Pride Parade. Riding on Daddy Pete's shoulders, or standing with Papa Gerry's arms around him, he would shout out to the friends and neighbors—Rickie's mom and dad holding hands, Noriq's mothers with their arms around each other and Norrie smiling up at them. The feelings of those evenings washed over him like a warm, comforting tide.

He was also getting letters from his mother every couple of weeks or so. He looked forward to them. They were full of news about her painting, and the horses she took care of. She had sent him a present for his birthday, too. It was a scene painted on wood, and a friend of hers had cut it up into jigsaw pieces, so it was a puzzle. He and his fathers put it together, but it had taken them days. When it was finished, Papa Gerry put varnish on it so it would stay. Fox hung it in his room.

Then there was Sonia.

He and Sonia were in the same class in school. Their buildings were in the same direction and only a couple of blocks apart, so they walked home together. They did their homework either at Sonia's house or at his, and most weekends they played together. They had the same birthday, but she claimed to be older, since she was born two hours earlier and Fox never argued. They both loved black and tan ice cream sodas, the difference between the taste of the coffee and the sweetness of the chocolate soda. They discovered Harry Potter together and read aloud from the books for hours. Sometimes Fat Joey would join them, or Sid, or Norrie. Twigs in the park became wands, and they chased each other around yelling, "Expelliamus" or "Protego." Fox was often Harry, with Sonia being Hermione, but whenever Sonia wanted the lead role, Fox gave it to her. Keeping Sonia happy was that important, and when she smiled at him, he felt as though he was standing in the warm sun of early spring.

Fox felt as comfortable with Sonia as he did with his dads. Maybe even more, because he could tell her about the whispers in the night. He didn't want to tell his dads. They worried so much. But Sonia didn't worry. She thought it was neat.

When he was nine, Fox found Lucky. It was a sunny spring Sunday, the first really warm day of the year. He was cruising the neighborhood, alone this time, when he became aware of a weak cry for help. It wasn't like he actually heard it. More like he felt it.

The tiny kitten crouched behind a garbage can. She was obviously hurting—she couldn't breathe. Instinctively, Fox's thoughts reached inside her body. It was really complicated, but slowly and carefully, he followed the pain signals.

There! He found the problem. Very gently, he helped her small lungs pull in air. Suddenly, he had that creepy feeling, the one he'd had before, that he was being watched. He looked around. No one was there.

Quickly, Fox picked up the kitten and walked out of the alley, into the street. As he walked through the crowds of people, the sense that he was being watched grew weaker. He looked up, expecting to see a shadow in the sky or a thin cloud in front of the sun. There was nothing there.

"Hey, Pops," he called to his fathers as he walked in the door. They were relaxing in the living room, reading the paper. "Look what I found. Can I keep her?"

Fox carried the kitten, barely larger than his palm, to the center of the room and knelt on the floor. He looked at his fathers, pleading.

Papa Gerry, so huge and so gentle, got up and squatted next to Fox. He ran his forefinger delicately along the animal's spine, then looked up at Daddy Pete. They nodded.

"Okay," Daddy Pete said.

Papa Gerry added, "But you have to remember that she's your responsibility. That means you take care of everything—litter box, food, everything. You have to be very mature about it."

"Oh, I will," Fox responded eagerly.

He never stopped to think about what had happened. It was a natural reaction, like an instinct. He had felt the pain, and he had to do something to cure it.

Of course, he didn't tell his fathers what he'd done. He always tried not to worry them, or make them unhappy. But he did talk to Sonia.

"So what am I, Sonia? Am I, like, a mutant? Y'know, like the X-Men?"

She thought for a minute. "No, it's more like in the Harry Potter books, the Healers. It's way cool. Like a healing talent."

When she described it like that, Fox had to agree that it was okay. A healing talent—cool.

Every night, Fox snuggled into his covers, warmed by a *sense* that was getting stronger all the time. It was as though he had another way of experiencing things, different from touching or hearing. It went directly into his mind. He *felt* his fathers' love for each other, and their love for him, like another blanket surrounding him. Sleepy thoughts slipped into his mind from the other apartments, soothing him.

But one question he couldn't escape, *Why me? How come I can hear people's thoughts? And how did I cure Lucky?*

The questions kept him awake, until Lucky's thoughts floated lazily from food to warmth as she drifted off to sleep next to him. He was safe. He was home.

CHAPTER 3

Fox liked being ten, but fifth grade was hard. There was so much to learn. And he was in a different school, middle school. On the first day of the term, a lot of kids said something about his eyes. They teased him about having cat's eyes, or freaky eyes.

Maybe I can go into them, Fox thought. *Get them to change their minds, stop teasing me.*

He tried to find a way in, but it was too complicated. It wasn't like Lucky's mind that was so simple. All it did was give him a headache.

And it brought back that feeling of being watched by that same dark presence he'd felt before.

Fox pulled his thoughts back and stared at his tormentors. When they saw he didn't react, but just looked at them like they were crazy, they stopped. Now he knew everyone, and it was cool.

Also, the whispers in his head were getting louder. They didn't only come to him in the night, but during the day, too. Sometimes he could almost make out the words.

One night he lay in bed staring at the shadows cast on the wall by the streetlights shining through the tree outside his window. The noises in his head gave him a headache. As he stroked Lucky trying to calm himself, his mind wandered, memories springing up. A particular Sunday afternoon when he, Sonia and Kim ran through Washington Square Park. Sounds of guitars and singing following them. A cold snowy evening spent huddled under a comforter, while Daddy Pete read aloud from *David Copperfield*. An exciting spring afternoon when he and Fat Joey had watched workmen build a brick wall behind—

Fox sat up abruptly. Lucky meowed in protest.

Walls could dim the noises from the street, he knew. Why couldn't a wall dim the noises in his head? So he imagined a wall thick enough to keep out the whispers. He built the wall inside his mind, laying it brick by red brick, the grayish mortar thrown down on the lower course, then a brick added and everything evened off. Soon he had a mental barrier that kept out the loudest whispers. He was proud of the result.

He also built a door—a thick, wooden door, like the door to his classroom at school. When he opened the door, the voices washed over him. He quickly closed it again, and they faded. They didn't quite leave, but the noise was low enough.

Now he could keep them out.

One day in January Fox walked home from school alone. Usually Sonia walked with him but today she had an errand she had to run for her mom.

It was a cold, gray day. The slush in the streets was brown, and the buildings looked dirty and sad. People walked with their heads down against the damp wind that blew loose papers around. Fox hated days like this. The usual bright colors of his world had disappeared.

The guys were standing at the opening of an alley, where the wind wasn't so bad. As usual, Big Wally was in the center, his small piggy eyes visible above the heads of the others, his thin blonde hair plastered to his head by the damp. They were all laughing.

"What's so funny?" Fox asked, approaching them. He was cautious. He hadn't been hanging with the boys much, and he wasn't certain about how they were going to act.

Big Wally looked at Fox, the sneer he always wore on his lip even broader today. "It's something about your *gi-i-i-r-r-rlfriend*." The last word was said in a mocking drawl.

"I don't have a girlfriend." Fox kept his voice level. He didn't want a fight.

"Oh, yeah? Then why d'you hang with her all the time?"

Fox fought to keep his temper. "Maybe because she's better company than you are."

"I bet she is. And y'know, yesterday she let me see her pussy. And feel it." He paused, staring at Fox to see the effect his words would have. "And she felt me, too!" he crowed.

The strange *sense* he had warned Fox that Wally wasn't telling the truth.

"No." He didn't shout. He had to stay cool. "She wouldn't do that."

"You callin' me a liar?"

"Yeah, 'cause that's what you are."

"No, I ain't."

"Yes, you are. You're a dirty liar."

Fox knew he had gone too far.

Wally's eyes narrowed and his mouth opened wide. Then he pulled his hand back and punched Fox square in the mouth.

Fox fell to the ground. The physical pain was horrible.

Even worse was the picture Fox glimpsed at the moment Wally's fist connected: Sonia standing there yelling at Wally, that he better get away or she would kick his tiny balls up through his head.

"Take it back," Wally threatened, his fist ready to swing.

"Why?" Fox said, not caring about what would happen. He wanted to hurt Wally. "Y'think I can't kick your tiny balls up through your head?"

Wally hit him again. And again. Fox curled up in a ball, trying to stay away from the punches. When the other boys dragged the bigger kid away, Fox sprawled on the damp ground. He couldn't move. The others left him and wandered off into the cold. Fox lay there, trying to get his strength back.

Then he felt it again, the shadowy, evil presence. It was floating in the air, high above him. It seemed to be moving back and forth, searching for something. For him?

Suddenly it disappeared, as though a cover had been dropped over him. Fox breathed in relief, and struggled to stand.

He managed to get to his knees. Very slowly, he got his feet under him and staggered upright. As he leaned against the brick wall a woman rushed over to him.

"Are you all right, dear?" She looked worried.

"Yeah. I'm fine." Fox pushed himself away from the wall and almost fell.

"No, you're not. Where do you live? I'm going to help you get home. Here, lean on me."

He looked up at her. A scarf covered her short brown curls and a trick of the light made her glasses seem gray. She was a stranger, and he had been warned against strangers. But she *felt* nice, the way his fathers did.

She put her arm around him and he rested his weight on her. Soft leather gloves covered her hands stroked his face gently. She spoke as they walked in a soothing voice like the kind Papa used when Fox was sick. She told him her name was Francine Rigby. She was a writer for a magazine and just happened to be passing by.

"What happened to you?" she asked. "I saw a bunch of boys walking away, laughing. Did they have anything to do with you?"

Fox didn't answer. He was having enough trouble just walking.

"Well, anyway, I'm glad I'm here to help. Oh, watch this step up. Is this your building?"

"What happened?" asked Daddy Pete, alarmed, when he answered the door.

The woman said, "I found him not far from here. I think he was beaten up."

Daddy took Fox into the living room and sat him down on the couch. Then Daddy tenderly placed a cold compress on his throbbing nose and mopped the blood and tears from Fox's face.

When he finished tending to his son, Daddy turned to the woman who was still waiting anxiously near the door. "Thank you," he said quietly.

"It was the least I could do. I think I saw the boys who did this. If you need me to testify or anything . . ." She reached into her purse and took out a card.

Daddy nodded.

"I don't want to keep you from your son," she said smiling. "I can let myself out."

Daddy turned back to Fox and laid his hand gently on his forehead. "Can you tell me about it?"

Fox closed his eyes, the fear and pain coming back to him.

Slowly, he described what Wally had said.

Daddy searched Fox's face. "It must have been a shock to you," he said. "I know how you feel about her."

"But that's just it. He was lying."

"How do you know?"

"I just do," Fox answered. "I always know."

Somehow Fox couldn't bring himself to tell Daddy what he had seen when Big Wally hit him. Fox even doubted himself. How could he have seen it? Was it something he imagined?

But Wally had reacted as if it was true.

Daddy Pete guided Fox to his bed and helped him to lie down. "And he beat you up for calling him a liar?" He sounded angry.

Fox nodded. "He wanted me to take it back, to say he was telling the truth. But I wouldn't."

Fox closed his eyes, not crying any more. He felt safe now. He was home. Daddy stayed with him, stroking his hair, until Fox fell asleep.

He felt safe behind the strong wall he had built. The whispers didn't bother him that night. And, in spite of the pain, he slept very well.

When he woke up, he saw that Daddy had put a new letter from his mother on the table next to the bed.

Fox had to stay home for two days after that. When he returned to school, Big Wally kept away from him, and so did the boys. Daddy and Papa told him that the boys wouldn't bother him again, and they were right.

When he walked into the apartment a week later he heard sounds of conversation and laughter coming from Daddy's office. "Hi, I'm home," he called.

Daddy came to the office door. "Hi, Fox. Come in here. There's someone I think you'd like to see."

The lady seated in the gray arm chair looked familiar, but Fox couldn't quite place her. He nodded hello.

"Maybe you don't remember me," the lady said.

Her voice triggered the memory. "You helped me," Fox said. "After I got . . ."

"Yes," she said. She seemed to understand that he didn't want to say the words.

"This is Ms. Rigby," Daddy said. "You were lucky she was passing by. And I was lucky, too, in a different way."

Fox looked at him, confused.

"Ms. Rigby is a journalist. She writes the book review column for a magazine. And—"

"And I was pleased to see that Peter Monroe is your father," Ms. Rigby interrupted. "So I was able to get an interview with him. Looks like it was good luck for all of us." She laughed, shaking her brown hair, the light glinting off her glasses.

Fox couldn't see her eyes and that made him uncomfortable. He had the ability, though, to *sense* if someone wanted to hurt him, or help him. Ms. Rigby wanted to help. He was certain.

"Cool," was all he said.

"Isn't there something else you need to say to Ms. Rigby?" Daddy prodded.

"Oh, yeah," Fox said brightly. "Thank you. I couldn't of made it home without you."

Ms. Rigby smiled. "You're very welcome, Fox Monroe. It was my pleasure."

—

After his fight with Wally, Fox looked at Sonia in a different way. Oh, he knew that boys and girls were not the same, but Sonia wasn't just a girl. She was his best friend, his mate, the one he could always rely on to listen and understand.

Now he noticed that her waist was narrower than his, and her hips were a little bigger. She was even starting to think differently. Like when they read in *The Order of the Phoenix* that Harry kissed Cho, Sonia sighed and said she thought it was wonderful.

"Oh, what's so wonderful?" Fox thought it was silly.

"It's romantic," she explained. "Maybe they'll really get together."

"Huh?"

"You know, be boyfriend and girlfriend."

Fox couldn't understand what was supposed to be so great about that, but he knew better than to say so. He played it safe and said nothing.

"I wonder who will be Harry's girlfriend," Sonia said. "Maybe Hermione. I think they have a thing for each other."

"Mph. I bet it's Ginny." He was being contrary.

"Ginny!" Sonia exclaimed mockingly. "Ron's little sister? You gotta be kidding!"

Sonia seemed to be growing up, going somewhere Fox couldn't follow yet.

Fox was having fun. He was perched on a rock in Central Park with Sonia, the August heat and humidity pressing down on them. The shade of a tree offered only a little relief, but they didn't care.

He was scanning people as they walked by on the path, just on the surface of their minds, and telling her what they thought. It was a game they'd made up at the start of the summer. Fox was getting good at it.

A young man in a brown suit, his tie straight and tight in spite of the heat, hurried past. He looked prim and proper.

"His underwear is itching him," Fox whispered to Sonia.

They giggled.

A pretty woman jogged along, her blonde pony tail swaying with her pace. Her green shorts and matching sports top were dark with sweat.

"Oh, man, she's thinking about her boyfriend," Fox said. "X-rated ideas there."

He turned to Sonia. Her eyes were glinting mischievously.

"Go in deeper?" she suggested.

"No way!" He wasn't shocked exactly, but he didn't want to share thoughts like that.

The blacktop in front of their rock was empty for a while. Fox and Sonia sat in friendly silence. He started thinking about school, about being in sixth grade next year. A new program was starting. Every Friday afternoon would be "club time." The principal, Mrs. Hoffman, sent a letter to all the parents telling them "it would be an opportunity for students to explore their talents and interests." Whatever.

There were a lot of different clubs, and he was unsure about which one he wanted to join.

"Hey, Sonia," he said, keeping his eyes on the path below them. "Which club are you gonna join next year?"

"I dunno," she said. She turned her gaze from the overhead leaves to his face. "How about you?"

"The writing one sounds good. I could write stories. Like Daddy."

She nodded. "The science one sounds okay, too."

"Or y'know which one would be really cool. The ecology one. The letter says it's gonna do things like start recycling programs and write petitions. How about that one?"

"Yeah, that sounds good. If we get the right teacher, it could be awesome."

They smiled at each other, glad to have a plan in place. They were interrupted by the sight of a man entering their space. He looked like one of the walking wounded in the city. His pants were dirty gray, too loose at the waist, and his shirt was stained and torn.

"Well?" Sonia said.

Fox hesitated. "I don't know if I want to. I bet his mind is nasty."

"Oh, go on. It'll probably be more fun than the suit. Or Miss Jogger."

Shrugging, he tried. The guy's mind was a mess, thoughts all jumbled. And it was dark. He couldn't get a clear picture of anything except—

"Oh, my god. He has a knife!" Fox hissed, pulling out of the other's mind abruptly.

At the sound, the stranger turned to them. His eyes seemed to burn in his grimy, bearded face. The man took one stumbling step toward them.

Fox jumped up and pulled Sonia to her feet, prepared to run.

Suddenly, the man collapsed, foam coming out of his mouth.

People ran from both directions, crowding around the fallen figure, shouting directions at each other or calling for help. A policeman ran up. He started talking into his shoulder communicator.

Fox stood on the rock. He was shaking. *I was inside his mind*, he thought. *Did I do that? Did I make him collapse? Did I kill him?*

Sonia put a hand on his arm. "Are you okay? Fox, talk to me!"

For a moment he couldn't speak, couldn't even turn away from the scene below. Then, "D—did I do that? Did I make him—"

"No! You weren't even in his mind for that long."

"But what if—"

Sonia grabbed his chin and forced him to face her. She stared into his eyes. "Fox Monroe, you didn't do anything."

"I should talk to the cop down there." Tears were forming in his eyes.

"And tell him what? That you were reading his mind and all of a sudden he fell down? That somehow with your mental powers you made him do that?"

When she put it like that, Fox had to admit it sounded crazy.

"You do that, they'll put you in the loony bin and throw away the key."

He took a deep breath and tried to bring the shaking under control. But he couldn't shake the guilt.

CHAPTER 4

"I'm gonna spend the summer in Canada!" Sonia announced after the last day of the seventh grade. She was so excited she couldn't stand still, but bounced from foot to foot. "Mom called her cousin last night and it's all arranged."

Fox was stunned. Spend the summer without Sonia? They had spent every summer together for the past five years, ever since second grade.

But she was so excited and happy. Fox pasted a smile on his face. "Hey, that's great, Sonia. You'll have an awesome time," he managed to get out.

She chattered on. "My cousins live in Montreal. It's kind of an old city, and hilly, and my cousins are just our age. Ralphie is our age, twelve, and Danton is fourteen. They're really my second cousins or something. I don't understand all that stuff."

He didn't know what to say. He wanted to be happy for her, but his disappointment was a weight in his stomach.

"But Canada, Fox!" she squealed. "I've never been outside the country before. And they're gonna take me to Niagara Falls for a special trip."

Sonia went on describing her plans, but Fox couldn't pay attention. The summer stretched in front of him like a desert. He counted on Sonia to be a companion in traveling the streets, or going to the movies. The regular Harry Potter birthday party was in July, he realized. Was he going to have to there alone?

"I'm leaving day after tomorrow. It's real quick. I'll hardly have time to get ready and there's *so* much to do." Sonia's words penetrated his gloom. "I promise I'll send you loads of post cards, and take about a gazillion pictures. And we'll have so much to talk about when I get home."

"Yeah," Fox mumbled.

Sonia turned around and danced off to pack. Fox walked slowly back home.

How could she do this? Fox asked himself. *Leaving in just two days. She never even told him. How could she go away and leave him on his own?*

A voice inside his head that sounded like Daddy Pete's told him to stop being selfish. But Fox didn't feel selfish. He always did everything he could to make Sonia happy. Why couldn't she do the same for him? Was that selfish?

Then he remembered the look on her face, her dark eyes glowing, her cheeks flushed. The memory of the sweet happiness coming from her bathed him in a soft warmth. He couldn't step on that.

Yeah, he was being selfish. He quickened his pace. He had to tell Papa and Daddy the news and figure out what he was going to do without Sonia for the summer.

The path around the Sheep Meadow in Central Park baked in the July heat. Fat Joey was already lagging as the two of them walked around the amphitheater where the Shakespeare plays were staged. But the path up to Belvedere Castle was shady. The overhanging trees blocked out some of the sun. Fox looked over at Fat Joey who was panting on the slight incline.

"C'mon, Joey. We're almost there."

"Yeah, I know." Sweat dripped down Joey's face and he gasped. "I just. Wish. I never. Came. How. Did you. Talk me. Into this?"

"It's been a long time since you were here, that's how come." Fox turned around to walk backward in front of Joey. "Remember two years ago, we went up to the castle and flew paper airplanes down on the guys rehearsing? Then we ducked down so no one could see us? And they got all mad, and we ran away?"

Fox smiled, remembering how scary and funny it had been. He and Sonia had led the group down the path away from the stage. Even Fat Joey ran with them. At the bottom they collapsed on the grass to catch their breath, but they were still laughing so hard it took them a long time.

"You know you like the view from the top. You can rest when we get there. Just a little more," Fox encouraged.

They turned the corner and they were at the top. Joey leaned against the wall, breathing in gasps.

Fox turned around, admiring the view. Down below, the small lake sparkled in the hot sun. Fox knew the water was too dirty to drink, or even wade in, but from up here it looked beautiful. The trees and grass of Central Park spread out on all sides, so different from the fancy apartment buildings in the distance on Fifth Avenue, or the Museum on Central Park West.

The sun was hot. It beat down on Fox's head and reflected off the light colored stones of the Castle. A slight breeze dried the moisture on Fox's forehead as he turned to look at Joey.

Fat Joey continued to support himself against the wall, but his breathing was more normal. He was still sweating a lot. Fox got a little worried.

"Hey, Joey, you okay?" he asked, walking over to the larger boy. He put a hand on Joey's shoulder to reassure him. And then it happened.

Pictures appeared in his head, fuzzy and unclear. Two grown-ups, he recognized them as Joey's parents, were standing in a shabby room yelling at each other. He saw them across the room, but he seemed to see them from a lower point than usual, and his eyesight wasn't as good.

He realized he was seeing a memory in Joey's mind, seeing through the other boy's eyes. The yelling got louder. He/Joey ducked around the door as quietly as possible, because he knew if made any noise and they realized he was there they would start in on him. He went into his room and opened a drawer filled with chocolates and candy, his pudgy hand reached in and—

Fox pulled away, afraid Joey could feel his confusion. He was scared by what he *saw*.

It was like what had happened three years ago when Big Wally had punched him, and he saw the scene with Sonia. But this time there was no pain to cause those pictures. Were the pictures real? Did the pictures come from Fat Joey?

If he could *see* into Joey's mind, maybe he could change things, too. Make him not feel so bad about his parents, or not want chocolate so much. He tried it, tried to go *behind* Joey's eyes, like he'd tried to do with those boys in the fifth grade.

Fear held him back. The image of the stranger in the park two years ago, collapsing on the pathway, still haunted him. He didn't want to risk it. But this was his friend. He might be able to help.

Slowly, he dipped into Joey's mind. It was complicated and dark, memories piled on top of each other, worries and fears and old hurts swimming in the dimness. He couldn't *see* what he was doing, couldn't find his way around. Afraid he would hurt his friend instead of help, Fox pulled back.

On the way home, he tried to talk to Joey about it.

"You eat a lot of candy, huh Joey?" Fox asked.

"Yeah, candy makes me feel good," Joey answered. "Everyone likes to eat candy."

Fox hesitated. "But don't you ever think maybe you shouldn't eat so much?"

"Nah, it's okay. I got big bones. That's what my Aunt Winnie says. She says it's big bones and baby fat. She says I'll grow into it."

That night, as he lay in bed, Fox went over the day's events. Fox knew Joey had a problem. He wanted to help, to go into Joey's head and fix it. But he didn't know how and he couldn't ask his dads. They would just get worried and send him to a doctor, like when he first told them about the whispers.

And Sonia wasn't around now. He could've told her. He couldn't put it in a letter. He would have to wait until she came home.

Sonia returned in the middle of August. The phone call came on a hot, humid afternoon when Fox was debating whether to go somewhere air conditioned, like a movie, or just drown himself in a bathtub full of ice cubes. Usually he liked his room, but this was one of those times he wished they lived in a more modern apartment building so that they could have air conditioners in every room.

"Hey, Fox," Daddy called into his room. "Phone call."

Fox got out of bed slowly, his tee shirt sticking to his back. "Coming," he said grumpily.

As soon as he heard Sonia's voice, he forgot about the heat.

"I just got in this morning," she said. "Oooh, Fox, I have so much to tell you."

"I'll be right over."

He walked to Sonia's, the hot, damp air forming a barrier in front of him. He thought about how to tell her about Joey. Then the anger he'd had during the summer returned, along with a sense of being abandoned. *Why wasn't she there when I needed her?* he thought. *She went away and left me when it was important.*

His anger grew as he walked.

He rang the bell. Sonia opened the door and threw her arms around his neck. He hugged her back, his arms stiff.

"Welcome home," he muttered.

She stared at him, her head cocked to one side. "You're angry at me."

"No."

"Yes, you are. I can tell. Now give."

You left me, he wanted to say. You deserted me for some people in Canada you don't even know, and I needed you. He tried to get the words out as he looked down at her—

Down? They used to be exactly the same height. He had grown during the summer, he knew. His jeans were shorter and he could reach things on shelves more easily. He hadn't even realized how much.

But Sonia had grown also. Not taller but more mature. Her hair was different, too, slicked back and neat. She was beautiful.

He couldn't stay mad at her. He smiled.

"Oh, Fox, it's so good to see you. I have so much to tell you," she said, hugging him again.

This time he hugged her back. As her arms went around his neck a second time, Fox *saw* it. Sonia's cousin Danton leaning in closer to her, his eyes closed, his mouth parted . . .

He pulled away from her. "You let him kiss you!" he said, shocked.

Sonia looked at him, her eyes wide in confusion.

"What—? Who—?" She shook her head. "How did you know? I never told—"

Fox caught the change in her expression as she figured it out. "You read my mind?"

Fox looked at his feet. "Yeah. I didn't mean to. It just happened."

He explained what had happened that summer with Fat Joey, and then about seeing into Big Wally's mind two years before. When he got to the part about kicking his tiny balls up through his head, Sonia giggled.

"Yeah, you shoulda seen him," she remembered. "When I started screaming that he just turned around and ran away like a scared little girl."

She laughed again, and Fox joined in.

When they stopped, Fox looked at her.

"So what am I?" he asked, suddenly serious. "Am I a freak?"

Sonia looked Fox up and down and posed, her chin cupped in her hand as if in deep thought.

"Yeah," she said, nodding. "Definitely."

Fox frowned, upset by her words. "Really?"

"Yeah," she smiled. "A really cool freak. My freak."

They smiled at each other. But Fox kept thinking about the pictures he had seen, and the tug he had felt to help Fat Joey.

CHAPTER 5

"W ell," Sonia said a few days later, "I think it's time."

"Time for what?" Fox looked up from the interlocking stack of twigs he was building in the grass. At the same time he was concentrating on trying to control the ants that swarmed in the grass. He first attracted them so they all gathered around the small fort, then he forced them away.

It was fun playing with them, until he noticed that some of them stopped moving. They were dead. He'd killed them. Disgusted with himself, he took his attention away from the insects and turned to Sonia.

The weather had finally turned pleasant. It was cooler and dryer; the sun was warm and the grass was soft. It was a perfect morning to laze. He didn't want to move.

"Ground Zero," Sonia answered.

Fox groaned. For the past three years they had made a pilgrimage, as Sonia liked to call it, to the site of the former Twin Towers. They always went at the end of the summer.

"Let's go tomorrow," Fox offered.

"If we wait any more, it'll be too crowded. You know it's always a zoo down there in September." She stood up, swatting Fox on the shoulder. "Come on. Let's round up the others."

They always went there in a group, Fox, Sonia, Fat Joey, Norrie, Kim, Mercedes, Dennis, and any of the others they could find. They needed the support of numbers, Fox thought. It was weird, the effect that place had on you.

Fox got to his feet, grumbling about bossy women. Then he play-punched Sonia and took off running. She scrambled to catch up.

They played tag all the way to Fat Joey's house, grabbed him, and collected the others. Norrie, Kim and Mercedes were sitting on the stoop of Norrie's building. They had to search for a while for Dennis, and finally found him heading into the corner bodega.

"Perfect!" Norrie exclaimed. "We need supplies."

They loaded up on chips and sodas, and candy bars for Joey, then headed downtown in a straggling group. Fox and Sonia were in front, the way they always were. Joey, as usual, brought up the rear.

"Do any of you remember 9/11?" Sonia asked.

The others looked at her, puzzled.

"Hey, I wasn't born in the city, like you guys were. I didn't come here from New Jersey 'til I was seven. Okay?" She turned around, walking backward, so she could see everyone. "So do you remember or not?"

They all shook their heads.

"Wait," Fox said. "I don't know anything much. I was only about three. I just remember Daddy packing real quick, and Papa rushing off—I think to the hospital. He was still working at St. Vincent's then." He frowned in concentration. "Daddy and I went to the Bronx, I think. To Aunt Georgia. Yeah. And Papa came up there a couple of days later."

He shook his head. "That's all I remember. I asked Papa about it, years later. He said the teams at St. Vincent's waited all night for survivors."

"What happened?" Dennis asked.

"There weren't any," Fox said quietly.

The kids walked without talking for a while. Even if they didn't remember it themselves, they'd heard grown-ups talk about it. They knew how serious it was.

Then Mercedes asked, "How long they been building there?"

"Nine years now," Kim answered. "And still not done. They were supposed to be finished next year, in time for the ten year anniversary."

"Maybe by the time we're in college," Joey said.

They laughed, and talk turned to school. They were all excited about starting eighth grade, and graduating from middle school. Then there'd be high school.

There was also talk about Fox and Sonia's birthday. The party this year was going to be spectacular, a real blow-out. Fox and Sonia just smiled when their friends asked about the plans. The preparations were secret.

The site was crowded, as always, but not as bad as it would be in September. They made their way to the viewing platform, but there the

27

crush of people separated them. Fox found himself standing next to a woman. She was shorter than Fox, and slender. A dark pony tail, flecked with gray, lay straight against her back. She was dressed in black, which made her seem even smaller. Her eyes were sad and her mouth turned down.

A sudden surge in the crowd pushed Fox against her. He turned to apologize. Then—

He was in a large sunlit kitchen, gleaming steel appliances reflecting the light. The pictures were clear and sharp this time, not like the other times. A man, old, probably about thirty-five or forty, stood beside the kitchen island, gulping a cup of coffee.

He felt his eyes look down at a dark granite counter where his hands (but smaller than his real hands) were cutting an apple. A girl, about ten, and a boy, about eight, sat at the table eating oatmeal.

"Gotta run, honey," the man said. He put the cup on the table and walked quickly in Fox's direction. Fox felt a kiss on the cheek. "See you at supper."

The man turned to the kids and gave each one a kiss on the head. "Be good," he said, and walked out the door.

Then Fox was staring at an answering machine, the red light blinking. The voice coming from it was the man's.

". . . trapped in the office. We don't know which way to go. Maybe we'll try going up."

There were noises in the background. People were shouting and there was the distant sound of sirens. Then the man was coughing and talking again. "I love you, honey. I love the kids. Good-bye."

Suddenly Sonia was next to him, tugging on his arms.

"C'mon, Fox," Sonia whispered. "C'mon away from here."

Fox allowed himself to be pulled into a corner away from the crowd. He was trembling, and his wet shirt stuck to his body.

"What's the matter?" Sonia sounded panicked.

"I—I *saw*—In her mind." Fox gulped in air. "It—It was horrible, Sonia. Her husband—In the Towers. He—She—" Fox couldn't talk for a moment.

"Calm down, Fox. Breathe."

Sonia grabbed his hands. He tried to control himself but the images in his mind wouldn't go away.

"Please, Fox. You're scaring me."

He took a deep breath. Then another. His heart slowed, his breathing became regular. When he could talk, Fox described to Sonia what he had *seen*.

"And she keeps remembering it, over and over again," Fox said. His voice sounded strange to him, like he was choking.

"I know, it must have been horrible. But you gotta pull yourself together," Sonia said, looking over her shoulder. "You don't want the others to see you like this."

Fox nodded, and gulped air a few more times. Then he grabbed Sonia's hand and they went looking for their friends.

"What's the matter, Fox?" Norrie asked when they met up. "You look like you've seen a ghost."

"Yeah, I did," Fox answered, twisting his face in what he hoped was a really scary way. "And it was all burned and nasty."

He lifted his arms and made his hands into claws and walked slowly toward the others. They all laughed, and Fox felt relieved. He hadn't had to explain himself.

"Hey, it was seriously spooky there today," Joey said. "Maybe they don't want us there anymore."

"Who doesn't?" Mercedes asked.

"The people who died," Dennis said, his voice low. The others nodded and there were murmurs of "yeah" and "right".

But Fox was more concerned with the ones who were alive, who suffered every day of their lives, like the woman he'd *seen*, and like Joey. The people whose past he would see every time he touched them.

The visions were getting stronger, clearer, and they happened when he didn't expect them. He felt the familiar resentment. It wasn't fair that he was saddled with this talent. It didn't do anybody any good. He couldn't help anyone. All it did was torture him.

He couldn't live like that.

CHAPTER 6

"After all, it's not every day yer young man—or woman—turns thirteen," Papa Gerry said in a raspy imitation of Hagrid's voice.

He walked into the living room where Fox and Sonia were sprawled on the floor, crumpled paper scattered around them. They were trying to make invitation lists, and the job was going slowly.

"That's eleven, Papa Gerry," Sonia said without looking up.

"In the Harry Potter books it's eleven," Papa replied in his normal voice. "Eleven years old is important to the Brits. I think thirteen is much more significant."

Fox looked at his father and raised an eyebrow. He knew Papa was about to go into one of his explanations, and he felt bothered by the interruption.

Papa looked down at them, frowning in mock seriousness. "In some cultures you would be adults next month. Responsible for your own lives and your own sins. And some of the initiation ceremonies are not fun. Some of them involve minor surgery, ritual tattooing, the giving of blood—"

"Okay, okay," Fox said, raising his hands in surrender. "We get the picture. We'll get the lists finished. Will that do for a painful initiation?"

"But it's only September," Sonia complained. "Our birthday isn't until the end of October. Why do we have to do this stuff so early?"

"Extra special birthday, extra special preparations," Daddy Pete said, joining them in the living room.

"Why not just invite everyone?" Fox said in disgust, throwing his pencil on the floor and standing up. "I have homework to do."

He clomped into his bedroom and slammed the door. He stretched out on his bed, trying to relax. He heard Sonia trying to calm his fathers with explanations of schoolwork load and extra classes. He knew he should be out there, but he didn't care enough to make the effort. And she wasn't wrong. It was just the beginning of September, and already he was behind. As well as all his regular classes, club time was a prep course for the exam for the special high schools. Ms. Greenwald taught the after-school class, and made them memorize vocabulary, Greek and Latin roots, math formulas, and a couple of billion other things. It was a lot to do.

Besides all that, he had other things on his mind.

Chief among them was figuring out how to block out the pictures that forced themselves into his head whenever he touched anyone. His regular shield, the brick wall, didn't work. He and Sonia had spent weeks trying out ideas, but nothing worked. He wasn't looking forward to the party with this hanging over his head.

There was a timid knock on his door, and Sonia's voice saying, "C'n I come in, or will you bite my head off?"

"Okay."

"What happened out there?" she asked, sitting down next to him on the bed.

"Oh, the usual." Fox sighed. "I can't sleep, I'm worried about what I *see*. D'you have any idea what it's like in school? I walk through the halls, and I'm afraid to touch anyone. It's even worse in gym."

He looked away. The visions he'd *seen* came back to him. Like Tony whose mom worked two jobs, who ate supper alone in front of the TV and couldn't think of a way to help her. Like Corinda whose parents demanded perfect grades from her and who cried herself to sleep because of the stress. "What'm I gonna do?" he asked. It was hopeless.

"We'll figure out something, Fox. We always do." She stood up. "Meanwhile, get your ass back in there and help me with those lists!"

Caught up in schoolwork, after-school exam prep and planning for The Party—everyone talked about it in capital letters—time flew by. He and Sonia worked on the problem of his mind pictures whenever they could. Finally, two weeks before the party, she burst into his room, her eyes shining. "I think I've found it!" she exclaimed, producing a DVD from behind her back.

Fox looked at it. The movie was *Forbidden Planet*. Fox remembered it very well. A spaceship from Earth landed on a planet to rescue a research group that had crashed there. The crew was threatened by a horrible monster that couldn't be stopped by the usual means.

"*Forbidden Planet*? What'm I supposed to do—haul out that disc whenever I'm close to anyone?"

"No, dummy. Look."

She slipped the disk into the player, then skipped to a scene halfway through the movie. Fox remembered it. When danger threatened, impenetrable metal screens automatically flicked over the windows of the Professor's house.

Fox looked at Sonia, grinning. "You're a freakin' genius!"

He built it in his mind, carefully imagining the super-tough metal big enough to cover the brick walls that were already there. He imagined the slabs of metal slamming into place and locking, with a double thickness for the door. He sat with his eyes closed for a long time. Then he looked up.

"Okay," he said.

Sonia walked over to him and gently put her hand on his cheek. He could sense images, but they seemed far away and fuzzy.

Fox smiled. "I think we got it."

"Ready to take it for a test drive?"

They walked out onto the street, Fox feeling better than he had in weeks. He put himself in positions where he would touch other people. First he stopped to look in store windows in the middle of a group of five tourists. The shields went up immediately. There were no visions.

Fox turned to Sonia, grinning broadly. He stuck his thumbs up. He was free!

They walked to the street corner where the light had just turned red. A crowd had gathered waiting to cross. Fox pushed into the middle of the crowd.

Suddenly the shields failed. Words and scenes crashed in on him, too confusing for him to separate them. He backed out sweating and shaking.

"It failed," Fox told Sonia as his heartbeat slowed. "It failed. Now what?"

"It worked at first," Sonia comforted him. "Maybe you just have to practice some more."

For the next week Fox went out every afternoon looking for groups he could join. On the first day he had to replace the shields three times. The second day he lasted for a solid hour, but by the end he was exhausted.

He worked at it every day. It was like lifting weights, something he had tried briefly a year before. He had to build up to it, he thought. It was hard.

Two days before the Party he and Sonia took off for a final run-through. Fox was pleased with his progress. School had been totally bearable during the week before. His shields had held up for three days in a row.

The two of them strolled down the street. Fox was nervous. This had to work, it just had to. He purposely brushed against someone on the street. No problem. Then he tried waiting at a street corner in the middle of a crowd waiting to cross.

Every time, the shields slammed into place. No images invaded his mind.

He was free.

"I think you just saved my life," Fox said as they walked back home.

With his new shields in place, Fox knew he would enjoy The Party. It was going to be awesome.

Their friend Cyril had offered his restaurant, a large bistro just off Waverly. Blue and white Christmas lights were strung up over the bar and wrapped around the exposed beams in the ceiling. Turquoise and white streamers draped the walls. The place looked like something out of Hogwarts at Christmas.

Sonia looked fantastic. She wore a long silky dress with swirls of blue, white and turquoise. The scooped neck was low enough to hint at the shape of her small breasts. Fox could see the slim gold chain around her neck. Her shiny black hair was caught up on top of her head, the curls spilling over and tumbling around her face.

Fox was proud of his appearance, too, with his new white shirt and black chino pants with a crease so sharp he was afraid he would cut himself. He wore a special bolo tie that his mother had sent him as a birthday present, and the turquoise in it matched the color of Sonia's dress. He knew his outfit was cool, but not as awesome as hers.

Fox joined Sonia and their parents in a receiving line at the entrance of the restaurant. Huge butterflies in his belly threatened to get out and terrify the guests. Fox swallowed hard and smiled.

The group greeted the guests, who then deposited their presents on a table near the bar. There were seventy-five people coming, the largest party Fox had ever been to.

When all the guests had arrived, Cyril put on special music, a baroque sort of march, and the receiving line formed a procession. Fox and Sonia proudly led the way to the long table in the front of the room. They sat there, like a king and queen. It was a signal for the party to start.

The wait staff, dressed in their uniforms of black shirts and gray pants, served the meal. There were five different kinds of burgers, including Cyril's specialty that had jalapeno peppers and chili powder and burned your mouth if you weren't careful. They were Fox's favorite. There were veggie burgers for the vegans that used no animal products at all, as well as the standard cheeseburgers with garlic and cumin, turkey burgers for those who didn't eat beef and "plain" beef burgers with a secret ingredient that Cyril wouldn't divulge to anyone. Fries, mashed potatoes, and rice pilaf, fresh veggies of all kinds—the food seemed limitless.

Fox and Sonia were excited, and talked as they ate, sometimes with their mouths full. Their parents mostly just grinned, looking proud and happy. Every few minutes, someone would come over to congratulate the two of them and their parents, often when Fox had just taken a bite of burger. He got used to just smiling and nodding. In spite of the interruptions, Fox felt that he was in a dream.

The dream didn't last.

When the dinner plates were cleared away, Cyril put on the dance music. He had all the latest sounds. When the music started, Roger walked over to Sonia.

Roger was fourteen, a freshman at Bronx Science. His wavy blonde hair fell down below his ears, framing a pale face with bright blue eyes.

"Wanna dance?" he asked Sonia.

Her cheeks darkened slightly and she nodded.

Roger led her to the dance floor. Fox looked on, a funny feeling in his stomach. Sonia seemed to be having a good time, waving her arms and shaking her hips.

Then the music slowed. Roger's arms went around Sonia's waist and her arms went around his neck. They swayed close together to the beat of the music.

Fox turned away. He couldn't look any more. Sonia had deserted him, the way she had during the summer. He felt angry.

He walked over to the table where Fat Joey, Norrie and Kim were sitting and found an empty chair.

"Hey, great party," Joey said. "The food is the best."

"Yeah," Kim joined in. "It's the coolest party I've ever been to. Sonia's folks and your dads really went all out."

Fox curved his mouth in a small smile that he didn't feel, glad he didn't have to talk. He kept glancing over to where Sonia and Roger were dancing. It felt like sticking his tongue in a place where a tooth had been removed, to test whether it still hurt.

The conversation around him shifted to school, and the familiar complaints started. Too much work, too hard. Norrie brought up the subject of the prep class for the special exams.

"Which school d'you want?" Norrie asked, turning to Fox.

"Stuyvesant," Fox answered.

"I really wanna go to Science," Kim said.

"Not me," Fox disagreed. "Don't wanna bother with the subway, y'know?"

"D'you think you'll make it?" Joey asked. He wasn't doing well in the test prep class and Fox knew Joey was afraid he wouldn't make it into any of the special schools.

Fox was going to give a flip answer when Sonia came over to the table.

"C'mon," she said to Fox. "Let's dance."

He turned his head to look at her, but he didn't get up. He was mad at her, and he didn't like the feeling. He blamed her for making him angry.

He looked at his three friends. Fat Joey shrugged, and Norrie and Kim smiled as if they knew something he didn't.

Why do girls always have to act like that, like they can see everything, Fox thought. *Like they're so superior.*

"I don't know how to dance," he said sullenly.

Sonia smiled and nodded at the others at the table, ignoring what Fox said, and took his hands. She pulled him up from his chair and led him to the dance floor.

35

"Its easy. Look, like this." She placed Fox's hands at her waist, and put her hands on his shoulders. "Now you just kind of move back and forth."

They moved together to the music. Fox found it was fun, in a weird sort of way. Other couples crowded onto the floor, forcing Fox and Sonia closer together.

Fox's shields slammed into place. He didn't want to see what Sonia was thinking. He didn't want to *see* what Sonia had felt when she was dancing with Roger.

Then the music ended, and Cyril's voice sounded on the speakers.

"Ladies and Gentlemen, I give you—" A drum roll echoed out. "—the birthday boy and girl, Franklin Jefferson Monroe and Sonia Castilla Barkowski."

The others cleared the floor, leaving Fox and Sonia alone in the middle. The lights went down, and Cyril wheeled out a metal table with a huge sheet cake on it. It was frosted in chocolate and decorated with a boy and girl on broomsticks to acknowledge their love of Harry Potter. Twenty-six birthday candles burning brightly on top, thirteen for each of them.

Fox looked at Sonia, her eyes shining brighter than the candles. He smiled back. He couldn't stay mad at her. She was his best friend. He would do anything for her.

CHAPTER 7

With the party over, and his shields in place, Fox could devote himself to schoolwork. It was a good thing the excitement had died down when it did. The load of work was frightening.

He had a report on city government for Social Studies, a novel to read for English, pages of translation for Spanish and a lot of math and science he didn't understand. Sonia helped him with the Spanish. She was outstanding in the class, partly because she was so smart, and partly because her grandfather was Puerto Rican and spoke Spanish to her all the time.

The after-school exam prep club was work, too, especially since the exam was coming up at the end of the month. The whole gang signed up for it. Fat Joey had a lot of trouble, especially with the math, but Kim helped him. Sonia seemed to sail right through all the Greek and Latin roots and math short cuts. Fox was sure she would pass the test.

Until the day she didn't show up.

Ms. Greenwald looked around as she took attendance.

"Anyone know where Sonia is?" she asked. A little frown showed between her brown eyes.

The whole class looked at Fox, but he shrugged and shook his head. He had no idea.

After first period the next day, Fox caught up with Sonia in the hall.

"So what happened yesterday?" he asked, matching his step to hers.

"Nothing." Sonia wouldn't look at him. "Had stuff to do. You know."

"Like what?"

"Just leave it, okay. It has nothing to do with you." Sonia hurried away down the hall. She didn't look back.

That afternoon, Ms. Greenwald didn't call Sonia's name. But she asked Fox to stay for a minute after she dismissed the class.

"Why did Sonia decide to drop out?" she asked. She wasn't accusing or angry, just curious.

"No idea, Ms. G.," Fox answered. "I tried to talk to her, but she wouldn't say anything."

"Okay. Thanks, Fox." Ms. Greenwald started to turn away, then stopped. "If you do hear anything, please let me know."

"Sure. And if you hear anything . . . ?" He let his voice trail off as a question.

"Yes, I will."

Fox walked home in a daze. Sonia had quit the class, and she hadn't even told him. Something must be wrong. But what could be so wrong that Sonia wouldn't tell him? They told each other everything.

At least, he thought they did.

He considered scanning her mind, as he had done to others. No, that felt wrong.

He called Sonia that night, but her mother said Sonia wasn't feeling well and couldn't come to the phone. Fox got the feeling it wasn't true, that Sonia just didn't want to speak to him. He couldn't figure out why.

"What happened, Fox?" Mrs. Barkowsky asked. "Did you two have a fight or something?"

"No. I don't know why she doesn't want to talk to me."

"Well, I'm sure you'll settle it. You've been friends for such a long time."

"Yeah," Fox said, sounding more sure than he felt.

He clicked the phone off feeling very unsatisfied. He couldn't figure it out. Had he done something? Was there something wrong with Sonia that even her mom didn't know about?

Maybe he could ask Ms. Greenwald the next afternoon if she had learned anything new. Ms. G. was cool. She wasn't real old—maybe twenty-five or so, and she had a great way of explaining things. Yeah, she might tell him.

During the next day Fox tried to talk to Sonia in home room or in the hall between classes. She ignored him.

After three o'clock, Fox walked to Ms. Greenwald's room. She was putting on her coat, but stopped when Fox walked in.

"Ms. G., could I talk to you a minute?"

"Sure, Fox. Take a seat." She gestured to one of the student desks at the front of the room.

He sat, and Ms. Greenwald sat at the desk next to him.

"What's the matter?" she asked.

Now that Fox was here, he wasn't sure exactly how to start. He sat there, not speaking, for a moment.

"I know you're worried about something," Ms. Greenwald said. "Your eyes become cloudy, almost gray."

Surprised that his teacher had noticed it, Fox took a deep breath and plunged in. "It's about Sonia. I was wondering if you heard anything more."

"No, I haven't. I was hoping you could fill me in. What's the problem?"

"That's just it. I don't know what the problem is. Sonia won't tell me."

"Sorry, I can't help you there. I wish I could. All I know is that her mother called and said that she isn't interested any more."

Fox sighed. He was more worried than before. "Thanks, Ms. G." He got up and turned to go.

"Have a good weekend, Fox," Ms. Greenwald called.

"Oh. Yeah. Thanks. You too."

Okay, Fox thought on the way home. No school tomorrow or the next day, so no chance to accidentally run into her. He'd have to search her out.

Saturday was windy and chilly, but not cold. Fox walked the streets of the neighborhood looking for Sonia's black curls, or the striped hat with all different colors she liked to wear. No sign of her.

At noon, he came home.

"Did Sonia call?" he asked Papa.

His father was getting ready to go on shift at the hospital, and he was busy. He shook his head. Fox heard the door close.

Fox wolfed down the spinach pie and fruit salad Daddy had prepared for him. Daddy sat across the table, pen in hand and a pad of paper next to his half-empty plate.

"No work at the table," Fox joked.

"That's at the dinner table," his father said, smiling. "This is lunch. Different rules."

"Dad, c'n I talk to you a minute?"

39

"Sure, son. What's up?" Daddy put down the pen.

"I'm worried about Sonia," Fox said. "And I don't know what to do about it."

Then he explained about Sonia dropping out, and not wanting to talk to him. Saying the words made him feel a little better.

"It may be nothing," Daddy said. "We've talked about this, about how changes in your body make you act differently—"

"Yeah," Fox interrupted. "It just seems like this is more important than that."

He couldn't describe the connection he felt to Sonia, the way he sensed her feelings even when they were apart. He knew she was upset, just didn't know about what. He was never able to talk to either of his fathers about his strange ability. How could he explain this?

The next afternoon he decided to wait for her in front of her building. She would have to go out sooner or later, he reasoned.

But hours passed with no sign of her. It was a chilly day and as the sun started to go down it got colder. Fox walked a short distance up and down the street to stay warm. He wanted a cup of hot chocolate or tea or soup.

Where is she? he thought. *What's she doing? Who is she with?*

He got angry as the time passed. Here he was, worried about her, and she was avoiding him. It wasn't fair.

Finally when the sky was getting dark, he saw her. She walked slowly, her head down, as if she was thinking, or sad. She didn't see him.

Fox stepped in front of her. "I've been waiting for you all afternoon. Where have you been?"

"None of your business," Sonia answered irritably.

For a minute Fox couldn't speak. Then he found his voice. "Okay, Sonia. You *have* to tell me. What's wrong?"

"Nothing," she said, turning her head away.

"Yes, there is," Fox answered. He reached out to turn her face toward him. He purposely kept his shields down.

When he touched her cheek, he *saw* it.

Thoughts and memories that weren't his crashed into his brain. Lying in bed. Sonia's bed. Her father coming into the room. Streetlight shining through the window onto his white, white skin. And then—

Pain, fear, humiliation filled every part of him.

And Fox ran.

CHAPTER 8

Fox ran home and slammed into his apartment, thankful that no one else was there. The light in his room was dim. With the door closed, it was quiet and restful. He needed that.

He took a deep breath. What was he going to do about Sonia? He had to help her, but he didn't know how. He was only a kid. He needed an adult to figure this out.

He had to tell someone, a grown-up who would know what to do. He could ask his fathers. A teacher, maybe, like Ms. Greenwald. Or the guidance counselor. Or—

Wait. He couldn't tell anyone. What would he say about how he found out? Could he tell a grown-up that he *saw* it in Sonia's mind? They would never believe him. Even if his fathers believed him, they'd be more worried about him than Sonia.

He'd have to convince Sonia to tell someone. It might help her. *He* usually felt better when he told his fathers about something that was bothering him. Yeah, that's what he'd do. Tomorrow.

Satisfied that he had a plan, Fox turned over and closed his eyes. He set his shields very tight. He would need his sleep. Tomorrow wouldn't be easy.

⌒

Fox always hated Mondays. Mondays meant returning to school, getting back into the routine. This Monday was worse than most because he also had to talk to Sonia about something so horrible, so painful, that he could hardly bear to think about it.

The morning was slow torture. He couldn't talk to Sonia during classes, and in between them she kept in a crowd of her friends. She was doing it on purpose, Fox decided.

In the middle of lunch period he walked over to the table where Sonia was sitting with Fran, Mercedes and Jo. For a moment, Fox was surprised. Sonia usually ate with Norrie and Kim, but they were nowhere around. Fran and Jo were talking and giggling, while Mercedes looked on smiling, but Sonia was sitting a little apart. Her eyes were downcast; her shoulders were slumped.

"Hi," Fox said, forcing his voice into a cheerful tone.

The three girls looked up at him.

"Hi, yourself," said Mercedes.

Fran and Jo smiled at him. Then they looked at each other and giggled. Fox's face warmed, and he knew he was blushing. He didn't let that stop him.

"Sonia, c'n I talk to you a minute?" he said.

Fran and Mercedes smiled, in that secret way girls seemed to have, then the three turned to Sonia. They expected her to do something.

"Oh, all right," Sonia said angrily.

Fox led her to the corner of the cafeteria. When they were far enough away that no one else could hear, he turned to Sonia.

"I *saw* when I touched you yesterday," he said. "I didn't mean to, but I did. And . . ." He groped for words. "I think you have to tell someone."

"What?" Sonia said in a high pitched voice. "No. Never."

"You gotta do it. You can't let it continue. You could tell Mrs. Grolnick. She'd know how to help."

"I'll never tell that nosy guidance counselor. No. Please, Fox," she moaned, "leave it alone."

For a minute Fox was quiet. "Then I'll tell her."

Sonia took a step back. "Fox Monroe, if you ever tell anyone about this I will never speak to you again." Her words were short, as if she was biting them off, but there were tears in her eyes. "Understand?"

And she turned and walked away.

⚯

"Mr. Monroe!" Mr. Foswell's voice broke through Fox's reverie. "Mr. Monroe, will you please join us here in the classroom."

Fox jerked his head up to look at his math teacher. He felt the usual flush creeping up his cheeks. He had been trying to figure out what to do about Sonia and he hadn't heard Mr. Foswell's question.

"Sorry," Fox muttered.

He was glad this was the last period of the day. He could go home and give the problem the attention it needed. He still had no idea of a solution. He *couldn't* tell anyone. Sonia had made that clear.

The last period ground to a halt and Fox hurried out of school. On his way home, bundled up against the cold, Fox decided. He *had* to talk to his fathers, in spite of what Sonia said. Somehow, he had to get a possible solution from them, but without telling them the truth. It would be tricky.

That evening he was sprawled on the couch watching the news with Papa, while Daddy made supper. Fox usually liked when Daddy cooked. He was a lot better at it than Papa. But tonight Fox was so on edge, looking for an opportunity to start the conversation without giving it all away, that even the wonderful aromas of baking chicken and roasting potatoes coming from the kitchen didn't make him feel good.

The scene on the TV changed. A man was being led away in handcuffs while the reporter's voiceover told the story of a father sexually abusing his daughter. Fox hadn't been paying attention, but now he focused on the screen.

Papa sat up straight, frowning. "Bastard oughta be strung up," he muttered. Then he looked at Fox. "I'm sorry you heard that."

Fox was shocked. Papa was always so opposed to violence, hated the thought of harming another person. He stared at his father. "But why? I mean why should he be strung up?"

"You don't see the kids who come in after one of these sons of bitches gets through with them." Papa Gerry took a deep breath. "You know the mechanics of sex, even if you've never actually done it, right?"

Fox nodded. "Yeah, I know." Seeing the alarm on Papa's face, he added, "Not first hand, of course."

"Good. You're too young. Anyway," he continued, "when an adult forces a kid, there's a lot of tearing and bruising. A child's body just can't handle it. I don't want to go into too much detail. It's too horrible. And that's not the worst."

Fox stared. He wanted information, but this seemed to be too much.

Papa took that as a sign to continue. "It's the psychological damage that's the most painful. See, the girl—or boy, it could be either—think *they* did something wrong. They feel guilty."

Fox could feel that it was hard for his father to talk about this. But he had to know. It was important.

"Then the parent tells the kid it's an expression of love. Like you could hurt someone you love like that."

Fox had never seen Papa Gerry look so angry. But he wanted his father to keep on talking. "So why is the psychological damage so much worse?"

"The physical stuff—the cuts and tearing—we can fix. But what it does to the kid's mind we can't fix that easily. It takes years of therapy, if it works at all."

Now the central question, the one that was really bothering Fox. "What'll happen to the kid? Y'know, the one we just saw?"

"Oh, she'll probably be taken out of the home. Put in foster care." A pause. "And that kid's pretty lucky—they put a stop to it early. The longer it goes on, the worse it is."

"What'll happen to the father?"

"He'll go on trial. Hope he goes away for a long time."

Fox looked back at the TV, trying to imagine what would make a man do something like that to his own daughter. "And then after the trial he'll go to jail, right? That's good."

Papa sighed. "Yeah. Except the trial is another hardship. The kid has to testify."

Fox was stunned. "Y'mean, after all that, the kid has to tell the story to a bunch of strangers?"

"Sometimes it's just to the judge."

"But aren't there psychiatrists and doctors and people like that? Can't they tell the story?" Fox's voice was high with disbelief.

"Of course. But usually the kid has to tell it. Well, has to tell it to somebody. The psychiatrist, the doctor, the lawyer." Papa shook his head. "And if the therapy is going to work, the kid has to talk it out."

Fox started to protest. "Isn't talking about it worse? I mean if—"

Papa interrupted. "You remember when I told you that you have to lance an infection, drain the pus out, before it can heal? Same thing here."

Daddy Pete walked in, wiping his hands on a towel. "This is not very cheerful dinner conversation," he said. "And the food's ready."

Dinner was very quiet that evening. Fox was thinking hard, and his fathers were upset by what they had seen on TV.

"I'm sorry I laid that on you, Fox," Papa Gerry said over dessert.

"No, Papa, it's okay," Fox said. "I needed to know that stuff."

His fathers looked at him, identical frowns on their faces. They obviously were going to ask more questions, and Fox didn't want that. "Norrie's cousin had a friend who went through that. We were all freaked out when she told us about it. So I just wanted to know."

The two men looked at each other and their shoulders relaxed. Fox muttered something about hitting the books and walked to his room.

Instead of studying, Fox lay on his bed worrying about Sonia. Papa had said that the longer it went on, the worse it was. He *had* to do something soon. He couldn't tell. He'd lose Sonia's friendship forever if he did. But he had to protect her.

He couldn't see a way out.

CHAPTER 9

The exam for the special high schools was getting close. Fox was nervous. He knew he had to find a way to push Sonia's problem to the back of his mind. He needed some sleep. His connection with Sonia kept him on edge most nights. He could *sense* when her father came to her room, and *hear* her crying even when the man left her alone.

All the time, his anger at her father grew.

One night he lay in bed and fantasized that he could burst into her apartment and stab her father. She'd be so grateful to him she would—no, she wouldn't. She'd be horrified.

The thought made him angrier.

After a week of this, the shadows under his eyes made Papa Gerry check his forehead for fever, and Daddy Pete started to talk about an appointment with the doctor.

"It's okay, Pops," Fox said for the twentieth time. "It's just the exam. That's the day after tomorrow. I'll be all right then."

"You sure?" Daddy asked.

Fox nodded, hoping he could solve it by then.

⟋

"That was a bitch," Norrie said as the gang walked out of the exam.

Fox agreed. It had been the hardest test he had ever taken. What was even harder was keeping his mind on the test questions, and keeping his shields tight so he wouldn't be tempted to *see* anyone else's answers. At least now he'd have more time to figure out what to do about Sonia.

"Hey," Joey interrupted his thoughts. "Hard day. Let's go get ice cream."

The late afternoon air was crisp and cool, but Fox felt drained. He could tell by the expressions on the others that they felt the same. He'd finally been able to get some sleep by slamming his shields tight before he went to bed. Problem was, keeping the shields tight took energy, so even the sleep he got wasn't that restful. It was better, but far from perfect.

As they walked, the kids exchanged comments about the test. They tried to match answers as they remembered them. It depressed Fox even more. He was convinced he had failed, and would have to go to Hughes or one of the other regular high schools.

Sonia hadn't taken the test. Not that Fox expected her to. After dropping out of the prep class, she hadn't even responded when the group spoke about meeting up and walking to the test together. She was spending more and more time away from her old friends and sometimes she didn't hand in assignments. Fox felt the familiar anger rising in him. Her father was ruining her whole life, not just now, but forever.

"I know I didn't make it," Joey said as Fox forced his attention to the present. "That test was too hard."

"C'mon, Joey," Kim said. "None of us will know for months yet. You don't know for sure. Don't get negative."

Joey smiled, but Fox could tell he didn't believe what Kim said. If he was being honest, Fox didn't think Joey stood a chance either. But he wasn't going to say that. He wasn't even sure about his own chances.

The corner ice cream store was filled when the gang trooped in. They clustered around, shouting their orders at the girls behind the counter.

"We know, we know," Gisella, the tall slender blonde, shouted back. "You've only been coming in here for three years, after all."

Mercedes picked up her strawberry sundae, and Fox heard Kim lean over and whisper to her, "How do you eat that shit and stay so skinny?" They both smiled at each other. The warmth of their friendship seeped in behind his shields and cheered him a little.

When it was Fox's turn, his voice caught as he ordered the black and tan soda. Sonia should have been next to him, ordering the same thing. They should have sat at one of the fragile looking metal tables and grinned at each other and compared answers. It wasn't fair, he thought.

The group around him continued their chatter about the test, and which school they would go to if they passed. He smiled and gave one-word answers, not paying attention, allowing the *feeling* of the group wrap around him like a comforter. The group had its own identity that was obvious to his regular senses as well as his telepathic ones.

Every individual had their own *feeling*, too, he had noticed. It was like a unique scent, a perfume. Joey, for instance, was sweet, but fragile, like those lacy chocolate cookies in the bakery. Kim was strong and bright and lemony, and Mercedes was soft, flowery.

And Sonia was . . . But Fox couldn't define Sonia's *feeling*. He knew it as well as he knew the features of her face. He could find it even at a distance.

An idea began to form as he thought about this. He couldn't concentrate on it, though.

That night he tried to make the idea clearer. He could find Sonia anywhere, he knew that. He could *feel* her now. If he lowered his shields a little he could *hear* her.

His shields came down and he focused. It was as if he was right next to her. She was in bed, her muscles rigid with fear, worried that her father would come into her room again. That he would do it to her, and then whisper to her that it was something for just the two of them, that no one could know, that he loved her.

Fox felt nauseous. He wanted to pull away, to slam his shields into place again, but he knew he had to stay there.

He did. He *felt* with Sonia, felt her father's weight on her. He shared her sick shame as the man lifted her nightgown and felt the sharp pain as he entered her.

"I love you so much, darling," her father whispered softly as he pushed into her again and again. "Don't cry, my love. You're my little angel."

A final push and he was finished. He lay on top of her for a minute, then pulled himself upright. "Remember, this is just for us. No one else should know."

Fox *heard* the words, and then *felt* the wetness on her cheeks. His anger burned hotter.

But he had also *felt* her father's identity. It was like a fingerprint, or DNA. Now he could track the man. He could follow him.

Fox caught the *scent* of Sonia's father. The man walked into the room he shared with his wife, and climbed into bed. Fox lowered his shields all the way and *heard* him.

He watched as Mr. Barkowski settled into bed. He caught a *sense* of his feelings of righteousness and what he considered love. The man turned over once and fell into a deep, dreamless sleep. Meanwhile Fox also *heard* Sonia's weeping as she tried to ease her aches and dry her tears.

Fox couldn't control the rising anger. That bastard was sleeping peacefully while Sonia tossed and turned in pain and shame. Sonia's sweetness, the light that came from her that this man had extinguished with his actions and his lies, fueled the rage. It wasn't right.

It. Wasn't. Right.

The fury built up in Fox's chest, a white-hot ball that enveloped his whole body. Finally it stabbed out of Fox's head, into Sonia's father.

Fox felt the man's muscles tense, and then start to shake. A rattling breath squeezed out. Then nothing. Fox couldn't *sense* any thoughts or sign of life.

The old pervert was dead.

CHAPTER 10

F ox lay on his bed, drenched in sweat. He was weak, physically and mentally. Reaching into Mr. Barkowski's mind, the force it had taken to kill him, had drained Fox to the point of exhaustion.

His thought processes were slow and muddy. I . . . killed . . . a . . . man. He searched for some feeling of guilt, but couldn't find any. His action had been spontaneous, uncontrolled. All he felt was revulsion and fear.

What was he?

The sensation of being watched returned, and this time the shadowy presence seemed to be aimed right at him. Fox tried to pull his shields tight. He couldn't secure them, but he felt the shadow pass over him. Then he just lay there, his eyes wide open.

The phone call came all too soon. It woke Fox from dreams of death.

"Oh, my god," he heard Papa exclaim. "We'll be right over."

The phone slammed down. Fox heard drawers opening and closing, and low voices from his fathers' room.

"Fox, you need to wake up right now. There's been an emergency," Papa called to him.

Fox got out of bed and went to his door. "What happened?"

Papa put his hands on Fox's shoulders. "This is going to be difficult for you, son. Sonia's dad died last night, very suddenly, no warning. That was her mom on the phone. We're going over there to see if we can help."

He squeezed Fox's shoulders.

"I know you're shocked," Daddy said when Fox didn't speak. "Take a minute."

Fox took a deep breath. He had tried to prepare for this but now he found that he couldn't speak. He nodded.

"Throw some clothes on," Papa said. He and Daddy hurried to their room.

They walked to the Barkowskis without talking. The deserted streets looked strange. The shadows felt threatening and every streetlight seemed to point an accusing finger at Fox. It was as though a shadow was following him, shouting his guilt to the world.

Papa kept his arm around Fox's shoulder, comforting him. Fox was grateful for the security. He knew facing Sonia would be rough.

Even with his shields tight, Fox sensed the confusion and sorrow in the apartment as the three of them entered. Mrs. Barkowski sat on the pea green couch, sobbing. Sonia sat next to her. Her arms were around her mother. Her eyes were dry.

The next-door neighbors, Harriette and Marjorie, stood to one side looking solemn. Papa, Daddy and Fox nodded to them. Then Papa walked to Mrs. Barkowski's side while Fox went to Sonia and tried to hug her. Sonia flinched. No one seemed to notice.

"I'm so sorry, Yolanda," Papa said softly. Then he looked up at the two women. "Did anyone call the authorities?"

Marjorie nodded. Harriette said, "They took—him away."

Papa nodded and Daddy turned to Mrs. Barkowski. "What do you need, dear? Who shall we call?"

She continued to cry into her handkerchief, giving no indication that she had heard. Sonia pointed to a small black book on the table next to the phone. Daddy picked it up and murmured to the neighbors, "Coffee? Might be a good idea."

Marjorie turned to go into the kitchen, and Harriette followed. Papa walked back into the master bedroom, while Daddy started making phone calls. Fox took advantage of the action to whisper to Sonia, "C'n I talk to you?"

She jerked her head to the side and, kissing her mother, walked toward the far corner. Fox followed.

When they got to the relative privacy of the hallway, Sonia spun around. "It was you," she hissed, a statement not a question. Her voice was quiet but the accusation was strong. "You did it."

Fox stopped walking, stunned. He couldn't speak.

"Well, no answer, Mr. I-Can-See-Into-Minds?" she said scornfully.

"But—What? I—" Fox sputtered. He glanced at Sonia's face, then looked down, afraid the guilt in his eyes was obvious. He longed for a trace of their friendship, their indescribable closeness, but even through his shields he *felt* her hurt and betrayal. How could she think he would ever do anything to hurt her?

"Why do you think *I* did it? You know my powers," he said plaintively.

Sonia remained silent. Fox knew he looked guilty and raised his eyes. She glared at him with that impenetrable stare.

He couldn't hold out against that look. "'It was an accident! I didn't mean to," he finally admitted. But that was no excuse. He looked at the grown ups gathered in the living room to check if they noticed the low-toned interchange. "I did it for you!" he blurted.

Sonia's eyes narrowed, and she spoke in a harsh whisper. "You're a yellow-eyed freak, Fox Monroe. I never want to see you or speak to you again. Ever!"

"Sonia," Fox pleaded quietly.

She turned and went back to her mother.

And Fox ran.

CHAPTER 11

An hour later, Fox found himself wandering the streets of the neighborhood. He had a hazy memory of muttering something to his fathers about needing to get away and then rushing out the door.

He felt his life was over. Sonia hated him. He had done it for her, he had *killed* for her. Yet there was that questioning voice inside his head. Had he done it for her or for himself, so he wouldn't have to feel the same horror she endured? Selfish, again?

No. No. He did it for her, the person who meant more to him than his own life. The one who had just told him she would never see or speak to him again. He wished he could take back everything, that he could rip this terrible ability out of his mind.

I'm never doing anything like that again. I'm never going to even look into anyone's mind. I wish I was dead.

He didn't know how long he walked. He had a hazy memory of the sun rising, yet even the light didn't banish the shadows that seemed to pursue him. He found himself looking over his shoulder, even turning around. There was never anyone there.

It was late afternoon when he came home. His parents were there. Lunch was on the table.

Daddy Pete met him at the door and led him into the dining room. "Sit down Fox. You look exhausted. Have something to eat. You'll feel better."

Fox sat, but he couldn't eat. There was a dense, hard rock in his stomach.

"We know you're feeling bad, Fox," Papa Gerry said. "Do you want to talk about it?"

Fox sat with his eyes on the table. He was afraid if he spoke he would tell everything, and that would be horrible. The rock in his stomach turned to lava. He thought he would throw up.

When Fox remained silent, Papa continued. "It's better to talk. Remember, you have to lance the infection or it festers. It makes you sicker."

Fox didn't look up or say a word.

"Okay," Daddy sighed. "Why don't you go lay down, rest for a while. We'll be here when you're ready."

But Fox didn't talk, not that day or the next. In school he was like a robot, going through the motions but somehow separated from the world. He was in a bubble surrounded by a fine gray mist that kept him from feeling anything.

And at night . . . When he closed his eyes he *felt*, once again, the twitching of Mr. Barkowski's muscles, the stiffening of the body. He *sensed* the dying thoughts, and he knew he was the cause.

At dinner a few nights later Papa said, "The autopsy revealed that Victor Barkowski died of a brain aneurysm. A cluster of them, actually. Rare, but not unheard of."

"So no evidence of foul play or anything?" Daddy asked.

"None. And since it wasn't suicide either, it means that Yolanda and Sonia will get the insurance money, no problem," Papa said.

The conversation went on about what Sonia and her mother would do now, whether the money was enough, the long-term effects of a tragedy. Fox let the words flow over him. He knew the truth, that he was a murderer, just as he knew he couldn't speak.

He liked the numbness. He didn't want to feel Sonia's absence, or the terrible weight of what he'd done. There was no remorse in his thoughts, but there was a horror at his actions. He walked to school, did his homework, answered questions in class in one word. During lunchtime he sat at a table with his friends, but he didn't talk to them. *Just the way Sonia sat*, he thought.

At home he spent a lot of time in his room lying in bed. Lucky curled on his chest, a comforting warm weight. He lowered his shields to go into the cat's mind. He liked being in her head. It was so uncomplicated. Eat, shit, play, sleep. That's all there was. Sometimes "play" and "eat" were the same thing. He wanted to stay in there forever.

Sonia came back to school the next week. In class, she looked at her notebook and never raised her eyes. The teachers didn't call on her, as though they were giving her time to recover from an illness. She wouldn't look at Fox, or talk to him. There was always a group with her, but she didn't speak. She never even smiled.

One chilly, gray December day Fox came home from school dragging his feet. He heard the chair scrape against the floor as Daddy got up from the computer to come into the living room.

"How was school, Fox?" Daddy asked.

"Fine."

"Are you okay? You're acting like you're sick—"

"I'm good. Just tired." Fox could see the worried look on Daddy's face, but couldn't summon the energy to do anything about it. "I'm gonna lay down."

"There's a letter from your mom. Over there, on the table." Daddy gestured.

Fox picked up the envelope as he walked to his room. He wanted to read the letter, but he couldn't summon the strength. He set it on his desk and fell into bed.

When he woke up it was dark. The alarm clock next to his bed read five thirty. Fox decided to get up and wash for dinner.

The meal was slow torture. There was very little conversation. Papa and Daddy watched Fox as he lifted every mouthful of fish stew and chewed it. His arms felt heavy and achy. Maybe he was coming down with something.

As the meal ended, Papa Gerry confronted him. "We're worried about you, son. We think the whole business with Sonia's dad has really thrown you. We've made an appointment for you to see someone, a doctor. Maybe you can talk it out."

Fox just nodded and walked to his room. He didn't have the energy to argue. What good would a shrink do anyway? A shrink couldn't make it so he didn't see into people's heads. No doctor could erase the memory of murder. Besides, he knew he could find a way to lie to the doctor, and that would be that.

The envelope with the letter from his mother sat on the desk. He lay on the bed to read.

My darling Fox, it started.

> *I got your letter. I wish I could be there, to hold you and comfort you the way I did when you were a baby. I think I know how you're feeling, so I realize there's nothing I can say that will make it all better.*
>
> *I also got a letter from Pete. Your fathers are very worried about you and they want you to see a doctor. Sweetheart, listen to me. I've been there and I can say you have to be honest with anyone who's trying to help you. But there are parts that you have to keep private.*
>
> *Just as you learned to deal with the whispers when you were younger, you can cope with this. I know about that because I heard the whispers, too, and I learned to handle it. Not everyone understands about the whispers, so be careful what you say. Don't tell anyone!*
>
> *You're a strong person. You can do this. You will get even stronger, and someday soon you'll come out here to see me and I can explain everything to you. I wish we could be together now, but I can't be in the City.*
>
> *I love you, dear.*

And then just her scrawled signature.

Fox looked up at the ceiling. He suddenly realized that he really missed his mother, even though he didn't remember her. He loved his fathers, and he knew they loved him, but it wasn't the same. Especially since she knew about the whispers.

And how *did* she know about the whispers? What would she explain? Fox was baffled and confused by her words. He might try to figure it out if he didn't feel so tired. But he didn't have the energy. And now he had the added problem of a shrink poking into the situation. He closed his eyes.

The biggest problem would be keeping the secret.

CHAPTER 12

D
r. Marji Smallwood was a plump woman whose graying hair was pulled back into a bun at the nape of her neck. There was a small smile on her round face when Fox and his fathers walked into the waiting room. She shook hands with all three of them, then turned to Fox. "Would you wait out here, Fox? I'm going to talk to your dads for a few minutes, then you and I can talk."

Fox nodded disinterestedly and walked to one of the chairs that lined the room. He took his iPod from his pocket, and didn't even look up from it when the three adults went into the office. The chair wasn't very comfortable. There wasn't enough padding, and the arms were too high. He hoped the wait wouldn't be long.

By the time the second song on his playlist was ending, his fathers walked out of the other room. The doctor waited at the door. She gestured for him to come in. Fox took the earbuds out and stood up.

As he started to walk toward them, they each reached out to him. Papa's fingers brushed his shoulder, and Daddy's touched his hand. He knew it was meant to be comforting.

The office was a pleasant room. Large windows let in the sun. Two easy chairs faced each other in front of the windows and a couch stood against the far wall. There were three bookcases filled with frightening titles like *Adolescent Psychosis* and *Clinical Diagnosis of Childhood PTSD*. A small, birch desk with neat piles of paper was tucked into a corner.

The doctor followed Fox into the room, closing the door, and gestured at the chairs. "Why don't you sit down and make yourself comfortable." She gave that small smile again and said, "Or as comfortable as you can be under the circumstances."

"I thought I was supposed to lay down on the couch."

"You can, if you want to. Most of my patients seem to prefer the chair." She paused while he made up his mind.

Fox sat in one of the chairs and stretched his feet out in front of him. "So what do I call you?" he asked, trying to sound casual.

"Dr. Smallwood. Later on, you might want to switch to Dr. Marji. We'll talk about that at a future time." She paused. "And you're Fox. Why do they call you that?"

Fox looked straight at her. There was no bullshit about her. Her gaze was honest and unembarrassed. She gave off the feeling of calm interest that he could *sense* without *looking*; she had seen it all, and nothing could shock or disgust her. He liked that.

"My real name is Franklin. But that's too stuffy for a kid. And my dads didn't like the name Frank."

"So they just chose Fox?"

"Well, my kind of red hair. And my pointy nose." He looked down at his hands, clenched in his lap.

"And your gold eyes?"

Fox nodded.

"Do you know why you're here, Fox?" Her tone was calm, not accusing or worried.

"Sort of."

"Can you tell me?"

Fox squirmed in the seat. "My dads are worried."

"Yes, they are. Are you worried?"

Fox shook his head.

"Are you acting differently?"

"I guess."

"Are you hanging with your friends?"

Fox considered a minute, then shook his head.

"What do you do during the day?"

Fox shrugged. "You know, go to school, do my homework."

"Who do you eat lunch with?"

He thought, then realized he hadn't had a real conversation with any of his friends for days. He jerked his head up. "How'd you know—? Why are you asking me all this?"

"It's a rather common problem, called depression, and it's something I think I can help with. I want you to know, Fox, anything you say in here is just between us. I won't tell anyone, unless you give me permission." She paused. "Or unless it involves you hurting yourself, or someone else. Deal?"

"Yeah." Fox sat up straight in the chair. He noticed that his hands weren't clenched any more.

They spent the rest of the session talking about school and his fathers. He mentioned Sonia, but didn't go into any detail. Fox found it was easy to speak to Dr. Smallwood. He looked forward to more talks with her.

At the end of the hour, they walked into the waiting room together. Papa and Daddy stood up and joined them.

"We'll schedule weekly meetings for now," Dr. Smallwood said. "As well as the talk therapy, I think Fox would benefit from some medicinal therapy, too. I suggest a very small dose of Zoloft. It's been shown to be effective for people his age, and, if his doctor agrees, he can start taking it immediately. Just give me about an hour to talk to his doctor."

She turned to Fox. "The pills should help with the tiredness. But you have to promise me that if you have any strange feelings, if you feel sadder or feel like hurting yourself, you will tell your fathers at once." She turned to his fathers. "You have to monitor him, watch for signs of strange behavior. Teenagers can have reactions to antidepressants. They can have thoughts of suicide or their depression can get worse. So watch him."

She walked with them to the outer door. "It usually takes a while for the pills to be effective—a few weeks, at least. So don't expect miracles."

Papa nodded and Daddy said, "Thanks." They left the office without speaking to each other. His parents still wore worried frowns.

"Let's stop off and eat something while we're waiting for the pills," Papa suggested.

The nearby diner wasn't crowded and the three of them got a booth right away. They studied the menus without speaking as though afraid that any conversation would blow up in their faces. The waitress took their orders. Fox didn't feel like eating anything, but he asked for a burger and fries. He would have to make the effort.

"So what do you think of her?" Daddy asked, sitting back in his seat.

"She's okay, I guess." Fox took a sip of water to give himself time to think. "To tell the truth, I'm a little scared. I mean about what she said, like I might hurt myself or someone else."

Papa looked at him seriously. "It doesn't happen often, but she had to warn us about it. Look, Daddy and I, we're here, and you can always tell us if you feel strange. You know that, right?"

Fox nodded, and was saved by the arrival of their orders. He ate even though he wasn't hungry, just to give himself an excuse not to speak. The whole situation frightened him.

At the end of the meal Papa got a call on his cell. The prescription was ready at their pharmacy. They could pick it up immediately.

The walk home was quiet. Fox heard the rustle of the pills in his pocket and felt the weight pulling him down. He was afraid of the medicine, in a way, especially after the warning the doc had given him.

In the kitchen, Papa handed him a pill and a glass of water. "Take this before dinner every day. And try to drink all the water."

"It probably won't be for a long time. You just have to get your head straight about Sonia's father," Daddy said.

"Yeah," Fox murmured.

He was sure there was more to it than that.

CHAPTER 13

For the first few weeks, Fox didn't feel any different. Then, gradually, he started feeling more energetic. He looked forward to school, to seeing his friends. The memory of what he'd done was no longer a needle digging into his heart, but more a dull ache, a constant reminder.

His sessions with Doc Smallwood were going well, too. They talked about the same things, school, his friends, his parents, his friendship with Sonia. He told the doctor about how he had met Sonia, how they had played together, even about the Birthday Party. But not the important stuff. He remembered the letter from his mother, and he kept any talk away from his special ability.

Then one night, four weeks after he started taking the pills, he had trouble falling asleep. He heard the whispers, and they were louder than usual. He tried to strengthen his shields, but he couldn't. He concentrated on slapping the heavy steel shutters over the brick walls. The whispers didn't stop. They didn't even get softer.

Fox panicked.

He counted on his shields to protect him from the voices and the visions. How could he live without them?

The next morning he was quiet. Daddy Pete was sleeping in. Fox and Papa faced each other across the table.

"You okay?" Papa frowned.

Fox shook his head.

"Why not, dear? What's the matter?"

"Couldn't sleep," Fox answered. His voice sounded scratchy, even to him. "Funny dreams."

"Funny strange, or funny haha?"

"Strange." Fox decided to risk something close to the truth. "Like someone was trying to get into my head."

"I don't like the sound of that," his father said, getting up. "I'm calling Doc Smallwood."

Fox didn't object.

That afternoon, Papa and Daddy took Fox to the doctor's office.

"So what's the matter?" the doctor asked. It was like she was asking about the weather.

"I couldn't sleep last night. I—There were these voices in my head."

"What did the voices say?"

His words sounded shrill. "I couldn't tell. There wasn't just one voice, there were a million, all talking at once."

"Did they tell you to hurt yourself? Or anyone else?" Still so damn reasonable.

"No. They just—I couldn't sleep. They were there. I couldn't get rid of them." Fox didn't like it. He was being managed, for crissake. He hated that. She was trying to get into his head, just like the whispers, and he couldn't block her out. The anger mounted—

Oh, my god, he thought. Just like with Sonia's dad. He couldn't get angry, couldn't let his feelings get the better of him. His head was pounding, so he lowered his head to his hands and closed his eyes.

"Okay, Fox, this is what we're going to do. You're going to go back home and lay down. Try to get some rest. Your fathers will take care of you. But if you feel that you might hurt yourself, or anyone else, you *have* to tell them. Will you promise me?"

Fox nodded. He was too upset to speak. She didn't understand about the voices, and he couldn't explain.

In the waiting room, the doctor had a private conversation with his fathers. They both looked worried as the three of them walked back home. Papa Gerry led Fox to his room and helped him get into his pajamas, just like when he was six. He was strangely thankful. Being treated like a little child was what he needed right now.

Papa kissed him on the forehead. "Get some sleep. It'll be better in the morning."

But it wasn't. Fox woke up in the gray light of very early morning. He couldn't breathe. His chest felt tight, his temples were throbbing, he was nauseous. He staggered to his parents' room.

"Papa—Daddy," he gasped, unable to say more.

Papa was awake immediately. "Oh, my god. Pete, wake up!"

The memories of the next few hours were hazy. Fox remembered being bundled in blankets, then an ambulance with Papa on the cell phone to Beth Israel. Familiar faces, people Papa worked with, clustered around him. Then nothing. Sleep.

Fox spent the night in the hospital. He hated it. The mental cries of the other patients were everywhere, and the regular hospital routine of blood pressure checks and visits from the nurses kept him unsettled.

He had never been sick before, not even chicken pox or the flu. When he had been hurt there was a definite cause for it, something that could be treated quickly. He had no experience with this.

The next morning, Doc Smallwood walked into his room, with Papa right behind her.

"You had a panic attack," she explained. "We're going to take you off the Zoloft and try something—"

"No," Fox interrupted. "Please, nothing else." He was embarrassed by the weakness that made tears appear in his eyes. He looked directly at Papa. "Please, no more meds."

The doctor started, "I don't know—"

"Can we talk outside for a moment." His father's tone was more of a command than a question.

They walked out, closing the door softly behind them. Fox tried to filter out the other noises so he could *sense* their thoughts.

"—not psychotic before he started Zoloft." Papa Gerry's deep, rich psychic *voice*.

"I still don't know—" Doc Smallwood's *signature* was lighter.

"We can monitor him—"

Fox exerted all his energy to keep the connection. He started to sweat and lost their thoughts.

Soon they came back into his room. Papa was smiling.

"You're going to have to stay here for a few days," Papa said. He smoothed Fox's hair from his damp forehead. "But you're going to be okay."

"No more meds?" Fox asked hopefully.

"No more meds," Papa agreed.

Fox stayed in the hospital for three days. They were the most boring three days of his life. Papa stopped in whenever he was able to, when things slowed down in the wing. Daddy came by three times a day to talk and bring him books. But there were endless hours with nothing to do but read or watch TV. And at night, there was the routine of nurses.

Doc Smallwood had agreed that while Fox was in the hospital he didn't need the antidepressants. But she had made them all promise that the final decision would be made when he returned to school. Fox didn't like the idea, but he had no choice.

He could feel the damaging medicine leaching from his body, and his shields grew stronger. On the day he went home, closely guarded by Papa and Daddy, he felt almost like himself.

"You'll stay out of school for a week," Papa said. "Then we'll see."

"But I want to go back now," Fox complained.

"We'll talk about it," Daddy said firmly.

Fox stayed home for a week. His fathers told everyone he had the flu, a rather bad case, very contagious. That way he didn't have to answer any embarrassing questions or even have any visitors. That suited him fine. Slowly his strength returned.

"Wow," he said at breakfast the day he returned to school, "I feel much better." He still felt a little shaky and not quite as strong as before the hospital. But he had slept well for the first time in weeks, and he felt more energetic and positive than he had felt in a long time. The pain of memory was duller, although the horror remained. Even the prospect of seeing Sonia again, of suffering her anger, didn't seem as terrible as before.

"I'm really glad, Fox," Papa said. And Daddy added, "Ready to go back to school?"

"I am *so* ready." Fox wolfed down the Cheerios.

His parents smiled. They ate in friendly silence for a moment.

Then Daddy said, "What would you think about going back on meds? Just to be safe."

Fox shook his head. "I really don't think I need it."

"But what if you start feeling depressed again? It could happen." His worry was so powerful Fox could have sensed it even without his talent.

"I don't think it will," Fox said, pushing his cereal bowl away. It was empty anyway. "Look, I was really bummed out about Sonia's dad. She's like . . ." He fumbled for a description. "She's like a sister. More than. What happens to her sort of happens to me." Well, that came very close to the truth. "And then when she wouldn't talk to me, never gave a reason, I got really weirded out. But I feel strong now. I got you guys, and I got Doc Smallwood. I'll be okay."

Papa and Daddy looked at each other. Fox could *sense* the desire to do what was best for him fighting with their need to comfort him. And if he could *see* their conflict, maybe he could influence it a little.

Carefully, Fox lowered his shields, a little at a time, until he could *see* clearly into Papa Gerry's mind. Daddy always went along with Papa in medical decisions. All he had to do was change one mind.

He was distracted at first by the feelings of love for him and each other. He tore away from that comfort and searched for the thoughts about him and his meds. There. He could *sense* the path, more clearly than he'd ever been able to *see* before, could almost *see* two different roads. All it would take was just a little nudge, a gentle tap.

Then he slammed his shields back in place. No. He couldn't do it. He couldn't reach into another mind. What if he did it again, killed someone just with his thoughts?

"Well, we'll see," Papa Gerry said, and Fox came back to the discussion. "We'll talk to the doctor when we see her. That's today, by the way. Right after school."

"Yeah. I remember. I'll be there."

CHAPTER 14

They all welcomed Fox back to school—Kim, Norrie, Fat Joey, Mercedes, Dennis, even Jo and Tommy, who didn't usually hang out with them.

"You look like shit, man," Joey said to him as they walked into the building. "Your eyes got circles on the circles. You look like a raccoon."

"Thanks," Fox said drily.

"That must've been *so-o-o-me* flu," Kim said.

"Yeah, it was fierce," Fox said. "Had stuff coming out of both ends!"

"Yuck," Mercedes said, wrinkling her nose.

There was no sign of Sonia.

"Where *is* she?" Fox asked Kim during homeroom.

"Dunno," Kim answered. "She's been out for two days."

Norie leaned over from her seat two desks back. "I heard that her Mom wants to move to New Jersey. Her brother lives there—somewhere in Hackensack, I think. And Sonia's mom wants to be near her family."

Kim nodded. "Yeah. I can understand that."

"So are they leaving right away? I mean, before the end of the year?" Fox was scared. She'd been his best friend, the only one he could talk to. Was she going to leave before he had a chance to make up with her? The thought was horrible. "She'll miss graduation and everything," he added, trying to hide his feelings.

The girls shrugged. The bell rang and the class got up to go to first period. Fox didn't have a clue about Sonia, and he didn't know who to ask. He knew Sonia wouldn't talk to him. In the crowd of kids walking through the hall, he felt alone.

That afternoon he walked in the chilly air to Doc Smallwood's office. The gray clouds overhead threatened rain, or maybe even snow. It was early for snow, Fox thought, trying to distract himself. Only November. Early winter. Snow. Snowball fights with Sonia in the park, chasing each other home to hot chocolate and—

It was no good. He couldn't keep thoughts of Sonia out of his head. Maybe it was lucky he was going to see a shrink.

Inside the office, Fox dumped his book bag on the couch and plopped into the chair near the window. "Doc, am I crazy?" He couldn't keep the desperation out of his voice.

"I prefer not to use that term—"

"You know what I mean. Am I loco? Bats? Gone?"

The doctor looked at him for a minute without speaking. "No. You're definitely not loco." She smiled. "You have a problem at the moment, you're depressed, and I can help you overcome that if you let me."

Fox could *see* that this was something the doctor had been waiting for. He *sensed* the thought that now he would "open up" and talk about what was "really bothering him." Well, he knew he couldn't do that. But he *could* come close.

So he told her about Sonia, about how they were best friends for years and he loved her so much and now she wouldn't talk to him and maybe there was something more he could have done to help her after her father's death . . .

"Fox, you couldn't have done anything. Her father died. It was a tragedy, but something that you couldn't prevent." She leaned over and handed him the box of tissues so he could dry the tears on his face.

Fox was amazed at how well he could act. Oh, the tears had been real, in a way. He was very upset about losing Sonia, and he felt guilty that he couldn't have done anything to prevent the hurt she suffered. He could *sense* that the doctor was pleased with the session.

"So what do I do now?" he sniffed.

"You can't *make* her talk to you. You have to give her space and you have to realize it isn't your fault . . ."

Fox tuned her out, while nodding to show he understood. The more he pretended this was helping, the greater the chance he wouldn't have to take any more meds. It was worth the effort.

"I don't think you need meds any more," the doctor ended by saying. "The death of your best friend's parent, and now the possible end of that friendship—these are life-altering events. You're suffering grief, and you have to work through it. Meds won't help now. They only dull the emotion. We'll keep on talking, though. That will help."

He made his way home that evening feeling better than he had been. He was off the meds. Fox smiled.

There was an even better surprise for him at home. As they sat down to dinner, Papa said, "How'd you like to meet your mother this summer?"

Fox looked from one parent to the other. "Honest? Y'mean go out there and really *see* her?" A huge smile spread over his face. "Wow! More than like it. I'd love it."

Daddy's grin answered his, and Papa smiled through his beard.

"Daddy will go with you, 'cause I can't take that much time from work. He'll stay for a week or so. But your mom says you can stay as long as you like. The whole summer, if you want."

"There's lots to do there," Daddy said. "Horseback riding, fishing, hiking. And she's not too far from town."

Fox didn't care. He was going to meet his mother at last. The person who had the same eyes he did, and maybe the same—what? Talent? Ability? Curse? She might be able to understand what he was going through.

Then he thought of Sonia who always understood and helped him. He quickly sat on those feelings before they betrayed him. If he seemed to be sad again, his dads would get worried and start him on meds. He couldn't risk that.

So he smiled as they made plans for the trip. He forced himself to ask questions and offer suggestions. While the three of them laughed and planned, Fox almost forgot his heartache.

Sonia didn't return to school that week, or the week after. When Fox saw her again, she looked pale and there were smudges under her eyes. She seemed to have lost weight. She looked like a ghost. When Fox tried to talk to her, she avoided him.

Fox spoke about it to Doc Smallwood.

"I dunno. It's like a part of me is gone. Like my arm was cut off or something." He lowered his shields slightly and *sensed* that this was the right thing to say.

"And . . . ?"

"I don't know what else to do," Fox said, allowing a touch of desperation to enter his voice.

"What do you want to do?"

What did he want to do? What he wanted to do was get inside Sonia's mind and change it, erase the bad memories, make her happy again. Like he wanted to get inside the minds of everyone who had problems, and fix things.

Just what he could never do. He could never risk it.

More than that he wanted to get rid of this ability that was making his life a hell.

"I just want to be friends with her again. Make it like it was," he answered.

"It can never be like it was, Fox. The death of a parent changes a person. And, let's face it, the experience changed you, too."

Fox nodded. It sure had.

In April, winter finally released it grip on the city. The days grew longer, the sky wasn't continually overcast. Fox left his parka at home. He walked outside into the sunlit street, his sweatshirt and windbreaker protecting him from the gentle breeze. The sky was a softer blue, no longer hard and glaring. He took a deep breath. The familiar odors of car exhaust and damp cement combined with a slight tang of salt air and rotting garbage. It was the smell of home.

Norrie and Kim were walking with Fat Joey toward the bodega. They waved for him to join them.

"Hey, guys," Fox said.

"Hey, yourself," Joey answered. "Nice day, huh?"

Fox nodded. They walked along the street, chatting about school and friends.

"We should be hearing about the special high schools soon. My moms have been double-checking the mailbox for weeks," Kim said.

"Yeah," Norrie said. "My folks have been bugging me for months. I hope I get in."

Fox nodded. In his world, it was a small worry.

"Hey," Kim said, "didja hear about Sonia?"

Murmurs of "no" or "uh-uh" answered her.

"Her mom decided to move them to New Jersey right after graduation. At least she's gonna wait 'til then. I was afraid she was gonna . . ."

Fox lost track of the conversation. The huge stone lodged in his stomach again. He was going to lose her completely and he wouldn't even have a chance to say good-bye.

CHAPTER 15

The next three months were a roller coaster. The special high school results came in, and Fox made it into Stuyvesant, just like he wanted. He was on top of the world. Then he saw Sonia and wanted to share the good news, but she still avoided him. The plans for his summer vacation were a frequent topic of conversation at home, which gave him a lot to look forward to, but at the back of his mind was the knowledge that he was going to have to tell his mother about what he'd done.

In May, Osama Bin Laden was executed. The news leaked late at night and people drifted into the street. At first there were just a few, but as the hours passed, crowds gathered. Fox tried to keep his shields tight, but even so feelings of relief and joy seeped in. He wanted to go outside and join in the celebration. His parents nixed the idea.

"It's inhuman to celebrate a person's death," Papa said.

"But this guy was responsible for the deaths of thousands," Fox said. He remembered the woman he'd bumped into at Ground Zero. He relived the memory of the phone call and he felt the anger rise. He jumped on the emotion, crushing it. He couldn't allow himself to get angry. It was too dangerous. "He was like a modern Hitler."

Daddy joined in. "He was an misguided man and, granted, he murdered thousands of innocent people. But no one should rejoice in his killing."

Shit, Fox thought. *I can never tell them about Sonia's dad. They'd hate me forever, even worse than Sonia does. They can never know.*

Even so, Fox rode the tide of celebration alone in his room. The emotion was too powerful to resist, as though everyone was recovering from an illness at the same time and waking up to see the sun shine. It made him feel like he belonged to the world, something he hadn't felt in a long time.

But in a few days the euphoria died down and Fox's world returned to normal. Once more, he felt unconnected. He was lying to everyone. He had to keep secrets from his fathers, something he was good at, but hated. In the school lunchroom he often looked at his friends joking around or gossiping, and he felt so much older. He'd lived a lifetime in the past months. He would never be the same.

He was still seeing Doc Smallwood. "It's weird, Doc. Like I'm happy and sad at the same time. I'm proud that I'm graduating, but I'm gonna miss my old school."

He *sensed* that the doctor was pleased with how he was "opening up," as she phrased it. He still told her he was sad about Sonia, and she agreed that it was a natural reaction. But knowing he could manipulate her was another brick in the wall of his isolation.

At the end of May, she said, "Fox, you seem to be much better. Stronger. Not as sad."

Fox nodded.

"How would you feel about stopping our sessions?"

"Wow, Doc. D'you think I'm ready? I mean, I feel much better. I'm not tired all the time, and I'm doing a lot more."

"It's up to you. If you feel you're ready, we can stop. Just remember, you can come back any time, even for just one session if you need it. Okay?"

Of course it was okay.

~

One hot humid Saturday in June, Fox took the bus to Stuyvesant High. He had to attend something called "Camp Stuy" for people who would be entering the school in September. The building was three times bigger than his old school, but he followed the other kids through the doors trying hard not to be scared. Even without his talent, he could see that they felt as nervous as he was.

There were tests to determine what classes he would take like math, science, reasoning skills—after three hours, Fox's head was buzzing. It wasn't just that the tests were tough. He also had to stifle any impulse to *look* into the minds that surrounded him.

There was even a swimming test. He flunked that one. He'd have to take swimming class in the fall. For the results of the other tests, he would have to wait until school started to find out what his schedule was like.

The two weeks between Camp Stuy and graduation day dragged by, but finally it arrived. The sun shone from a clear, robin's egg sky, and a soft breeze blew through the small trees that stood at regular intervals along the street. Fox clipped his tie to his collar and shrugged into the navy blue suit jacket. He stared at his reflection, surprised that his appearance hadn't changed, except that his eyes were darker, more gold than yellow. He thought his face should be older, sadder, but it was the thirteen-year-old face that he had seen in the mirror on the day of the Birthday Party, less than a year ago.

Papa and Daddy walked with him to Washington Irving High School where the larger auditorium could hold all the graduates and their families. Papa carried the neatly pressed blue graduation gown, and Daddy carried the matching blue cap. At the entrance, they solemnly handed the apparel to Fox, and wished him good luck. Then they went to find seats in the auditorium.

Fox followed the stream of students to the classroom where the boys were putting on their caps and gowns.

"Hey, Fox," Dennis greeted him, grinning. "We're really gonna do it! We're movin' on."

Fox could *feel* the happiness and pride of his friends even through his shields. He, too, felt happy that a new world stretched out in front of him. For a moment, excitement about the summer with his mother and high school overshadowed the horrible memories and the loss of his best friend.

The ceremony was long and boring. But when it was finally over, Fox saw Sonia standing by herself near the wall outside the auditorium.

"Sonia, please," he said, rushing over to her. "Can I talk to you?"

She looked right and left, but the hall was crowded. There was no easy escape route. She shrugged.

"I . . . I just wanted to say . . ." His voice faded away. Now that he had the chance, he didn't know how to begin.

"Say what? Say you're sorry? Like that's gonna make everything better?"

73

"No. I mean yes. I mean . . . You were my best friend. You still are my best friend. And after this we might never see each other again. I've just got to know you don't hate me." To his embarrassment, Fox felt his eyes prickle with tears.

Sonia's expression softened. "I don't hate you, Fox. But you did a terrible thing. And I don't know if I can ever forgive you for it."

Fox hung his head. He didn't want Sonia to see the tears. "C'n I at least write to you?"

"No. If I *do* forgive you, I'll write to you. Until then, there's nothing more to say."

She turned away and made her way down the hall.

Then the same-sex marriage bill was signed into law. The sound of a huge cheer came through the open window at the news. Papa and Daddy jumped up and hugged, then lifted Fox bodily off the couch and pulled him in. Tears were running down the faces of the adults, and Fox was surprised to find tears on his own cheeks.

Daddy broke away. "C'mon. We're going out!"

They joined the crowds on the streets, everyone cheering and hugging. His fathers kept hold of Fox as they moved slowly through the packed sidewalks to Sheridan Square. They made their way toward the Stonewall Inn where, as Papa kept saying, "it all started forty years ago."

The celebration went on all night, but Fox and his fathers gave up around four in the morning. Exhausted, they walked back home, still smiling. Daddy and Papa were high on happiness.

They walked through the door and collapsed on the couch.

"So," Fox said, "are you gonna make honest men of each other?"

"What?" Daddy yelped.

"Are you gonna get married?"

"You impudent little fox!" Papa said. He and Daddy jumped on Fox, ruffling his hair and making him laugh until he gasped for air.

"And with that, scoundrel," Daddy said, "you go to bed. We'll talk in the morning."

"It *is* morning," Fox said.

Papa swatted him playfully on the shoulder as he walked to his room. He didn't think he'd be able to sleep, but he fell out as soon as he hit the bed.

The parades and parties went on for days. So did Fox's preparations for his trip to Wyoming. Fox tried to imagine what Wyoming would be like. His mother's descriptions make him picture a rugged landscape, an area surrounded by mountains in the distance. But the images were hazy.

Even his mother's face wouldn't come clear. Now that the actual meeting was drawing near, he found himself impatient, and a bit scared. How would she react to him? Would they be able to communicate mind to mind, and did he dare go *into* her head? What could she tell him about his strange ability?

He was so busy he hardly had time to think about Sonia, but when he did a lump formed in his throat.

CHAPTER 16

They spent the next two weeks buying new clothes, packing, getting the airplane tickets. When he and Daddy said good-bye to Papa at the airport that morning, it was like he was coming out of a dream. Now all he felt was impatience, and the journey seemed endless.

Finally, as evening was coming on, they stood in front of the yellow clapboard house in the middle of desolate scrub and buttes. The door opened. For a moment Fox couldn't move.

He stared into eyes that were exactly like the ones he saw in the mirror every morning. His mother. His mom. He was finally standing face to face with her. He could hardly believe it.

Then his mother swept him into a fierce hug and held him close for the longest time. When she released him, they stared at each other, memorizing faces they hadn't seen in a lifetime.

Fox looked down at his mother. *I'm taller than she is!* he thought. Her hair was pulled back in a ponytail that was mostly auburn but had some traces of gray. The eyes that held Fox's were gold, just like his, but there were fine lines around them. Her skin was darker, like she spent a lot of time outdoors. She wore jeans and a large denim shirt. Her cowboy boots were broken in. She must wear them a lot.

Fox liked the look of her.

"What *am* I thinking," she said. Her voice was a bit hoarse, as if she wasn't used to speaking. "Come in, come in."

She ushered them into a large room that seemed to take up most of the house. A wood-burning stove sat on a slate platform in one corner. Two comfortable looking couches and two easy chairs were grouped in the center. Blankets draped over the couches were an Indian design in grays, blacks and reds. The pictures on the ivory colored walls were also Indian. A staircase went up from the back. Fox liked the serenity of the room and he relaxed.

"Here, let me take your coats," Marta said.

Fox didn't want to take off his coat. He had been chilly ever since they landed in Cheyenne. But he didn't want to appear soft in front of his mother, so he slipped it off and handed it to her.

"It *is* kinda chilly in here," Daddy said. "I didn't realize Wyoming would be so cold."

Marta looked at him, frowning. "This isn't cold. It must be all of fifty-two out there." Then she smiled. "You'll get used to it. It'll just take a while. I'll light a fire."

She went to the stove, put in small bits of wood, and lit them. When they were burning, she added larger pieces. "We're not used to having a fire in the middle of the summer. You really do get used to the temperatures."

Fox smiled at her, drinking in her appearance. He didn't know what to say or do. Part of him wanted to start talking right away, to tell her everything that had happened to him. He wanted to ask questions and find out how she handled her ability. Another part of him didn't want to say anything, ever. He'd have to admit what he had done to Sonia's father.

Marta turned and put her arm around Fox. "Let's get you settled. This way." She led them upstairs.

Fox's room was smaller than his bedroom at home, but it felt cozy, not closed in. Wooden bed, bookcase, small closet. He unpacked quickly, eager to get back to her. To his mom. He savored the word.

When he came out, he heard voices, and followed them to a small kitchen behind the great room. He recognized Daddy's, and his mother's. They were speaking quietly.

"He really needs you right now," Daddy said. "He's been through some rough times, and I think you're the one who can help him."

"What do you mean rough times? Is there something you haven't told me?"

"Maybe it's better if he—"

Fox cleared his throat and Daddy broke off.

"You guys hungry?" Marta asked. "I bet you are. Probably haven't eaten anything decent all day. Let me get something."

Daddy stayed for a week while Fox settled in. They went for hikes around the prairie and the buttes. At first, Fox thought the landscape was desolate, like you would see on the moon or Mars. Then he started to see the beauty of it. It wasn't splashy and green, but quieter. The colors were like the Indian blankets, almost dull. It let you appreciate the outlines of the hills against the sky, the shapes of the scrub, the occasional tree.

He understood why his mother loved it here. It was quiet. Nobody lived nearby—the nearest neighbor was two miles away. He could relax his shields without getting the static he *heard* in the city.

When Daddy left, he made Fox promise to call from the drugstore in Chugwater every week since there was no reception at his mother's house. Then life settled into a routine and the tension Fox hadn't even been aware of drained out of his body. Keeping his shields up at full strength took energy. It was like he was standing at attention all the time even though he didn't realize it.

There were two horses in the barn behind the house named Tango and Jose. The animals were older, Marta told him, left there by a dude ranch fifty miles away. They weren't used often, so the owner, Mr. Taunton, boarded them with her. She cared for them, the ranch gave her the feed, and she could ride them whenever she wanted.

Fox wanted to learn to ride in spite of the horses' size. On his first try he couldn't even make it into the saddle. He fell to the ground, and the air was driven out of him.

"C'mon, chicken, get up!" Marta teased.

He levered himself off the ground and dusted off his jeans. "How come there's no parachute with these things?" he asked ruefully.

Marta laughed and helped him mount.

After his second time on Tango's back, he felt more comfortable. The first few days were an agony of stiff muscles, but in a few weeks he was riding like a pro.

On his first solo outing on Tango, Fox *felt* a different presence in his mind. Feelings of joy at being in the open country. Carrying a slight weight. It took a moment for Fox to realize he was *hearing* the horse's thoughts.

They were different from Lucky's. The cat's thoughts raced from one thing to another, because she was constantly on the lookout for food or danger. Tango's images came more slowly. His head was filled with the feelings of running with the wind in his mane, or eating sweet grass and good hay.

He pulled his thoughts back quickly. He had promised himself he would never go into another mind again.

But the temptation was too great, and it didn't seem to do any harm. Fox learned that he could go inside Tango's mind and *suggest* what the horse should do, where they should go, how fast. Fox learned to lean into the muscular surge when Tango changed pace or went uphill. They went out almost every day. Fox *directed* Tango to go slow most of the time. After all, the horse was old and Fox didn't want to strain him.

There was a lot of work to do around Marta's house. The small vegetable garden needed constant attention, and the chicken coop had to be cleaned out. In the back yard greenhouse, Marta grew herbs that she made into medicines which she sold or exchanged for food or services. Fox enjoyed caring for the animals and watching the plants grow and the vegetables ripen.

On the first day, Marta had to supervise Fox closely, showing him the difference between a weed and a useful plant.

"But that's a pretty flower!" he protested.

"Yeah, and if you were planting corn because you needed to eat, and a rosebush started growing in the middle of the cornfield, that rose bush would be a weed!"

Fox shrugged, making the muscles in his shoulder protest. All his muscles protested, the way they had when he was learning to ride. That evening his muscles hurt even more. He decided he hated the garden and he would never go back to it.

The next day was easier. He muscles warmed and he got used to it, even enjoyed it. More than that, he liked helping his mother. Working outdoors helped him adjust to the temperature, too. He mucked out stalls and weeded the garden shirtless, feeling the sun warm on his shoulders.

On his first Saturday in Wyoming, his mother woke him early.

"C'mon, sleepyhead. We're going into town," she called.

Fox was up, washed and dressed in record time. He was eager to go into Chugwater.

"You're moving easier," Marta said as he entered the kitchen.

"Yeah. It's amazing. I didn't think I'd ever walk like a normal person again!"

She laughed softly. "Sometimes hard work is the best medicine."

"And I feel better all over. Like I can relax here." He couldn't tell her about the memories that haunted him, but now were a little less painful, like a slow-healing wound. He knew they would never disappear completely, didn't think it was a good idea if they did. His actions taught him a lesson, like falling off a horse made him learn the right way to mount.

Marta nodded as she placed the dish of eggs in front of him. "Don't you miss TV or your computer?"

Fox thought for a moment and was surprised to discover that he didn't. "The only thing I miss is my cell. How come you don't have reception here?"

"Too much area. Too difficult to put in enough towers. I'm just as happy, though. I like being far away from things here, and it's quieter."

Fox looked at her face and envied the calm he found there. He wanted to feel like that, but he didn't think he ever would.

When they got into Chugwater, Marta led him to the Chugwater Soda Fountain. She had an arrangement with the owner that allowed her the use of the landline in exchange for herbs and medicines. Marta waved to Mrs. Dayton as they walked in, and led Fox to the back room.

"Hey, Daddy," Fox said when his father picked up.

"Fox! How are you?" At the sound of Daddy's voice, Fox realized how much he'd missed his fathers.

"I'm fine. Marta's been keeping me real busy, working in the garden and stuff." He went on to explain what his days were like.

When he finished, Daddy handed him over to Papa. "Fox, son, we miss you."

"I miss you, too, Papa. But I really like it here." He repeated what he'd told Daddy. He knew he could have just told Papa that Daddy had all the information, but he wanted to keep Papa as long as he could.

"I'm glad you're having a good time," Papa said when he finished.

"I am. But you sound tired, Papa. Is everything okay?"

"Just busy at work. You know how it is."

Fox nodded, even though he knew his father couldn't see him. They spoke for a few more minutes before hanging up.

"I'm going over to the library to check out the computer," Fox called to Marta as he walked out of the back room.

The library was a small building that contained a small assortment of books. *My school library probably has more books*, Fox thought. But the room was quiet and welcoming. He introduced himself to the elderly lady behind the desk who explained to him about the computers.

"It's dial-up," she said. "The connection might be slower than what you're used to." She smiled to show she meant no insult.

Fox checked his email. He hoped for some word from Sonia, a sign that she had forgiven him. But there was none. He answered his other mail, assuring his friends that he was having a great time and would tell them everything when he got home. Then, disappointed, he signed off and walked out into the sunshine.

This routine made three weeks pass quickly, and Fox realized he had never really talked to Marta. He wondered if she was keeping him busy purposely to avoid the conversation. He had to admit that he felt almost relieved that he didn't have to tell her everything. But he didn't want to wait any longer. If he had to force it, he decided, he would.

That evening, as they sat on the porch after dinner watching the sunset, Fox spoke up. "Can we talk, Marta?"

"Sure, sweetie. But . . . why don't you ever call me Mom?"

His face felt warm. "Dunno."

"Is it because I left you so many years ago?"

"It's not—Yeah, I guess so."

"Do you understand why I had to do it?" Her voice was soft.

Fox fought an impulse to *look* into her mind. "Y'mean because it was too noisy in New York."

"That's what I told your fathers. Or it's what they *wanted* to hear. But I think you know the truth, Fox."

They both turned from looking at the sky and stared into each other's eyes. Fighting the resolution about never going into anyone's mind, he dropped his shields and he *saw*. In her mind was the same knowledge he had. She could read minds, share thoughts.

He reached over and took her hand. *You can do it, too,* he thought at her.

Of course. It was driving me crazy.

Why didn't you build a shield wall?

I never learned how. I didn't begin to hear thoughts until I was almost thirteen. Much older than you were when the whispers started. Open your shields.

81

Fox hesitated. Now that the time was here, he felt nervous. He *saw* his mother's shield, fragile, paper-thin. It wouldn't have kept out anything. But he waited until she lowered the barrier before he jumped into her thoughts.

It was like going back to a half-remembered place, a home he could barely recognize. He'd been here before.

Marta caught his thoughts. *Of course you were here before. You were inside me for nine months.*

Fox *felt* her amusement.

Now, let me show you my life.

She's a normal kid, growing up in Chicago, going to school in the mid-eighties. Suddenly, when she's thirteen, she starts hearing voices in her head. She feels fear and confusion.

She tells her parents, a couple of reformed flower children who are convinced the drugs they took in the seventies have totally messed up their kid's head. People in white lab coats shine lights in her eyes and talk at her. She's never been to doctors before, never been sick. Now they drag her to one doctor after another who all put her on meds that do nothing at all. She overhears the words "schizophrenia" and "bipolar" but she doesn't know what they mean. And all the time she's suffering and convinced she's going to die—

Oh my god, you were terrified. Why did they do that to you?

They thought they were doing the right thing. They were about to throw me in the loony bin when I realized what was happening.

Is that why you don't want me to tell anybody about my mind reading?

Yes. But there's more. You'll see later.

Now it's been six months of meds and doctors, and no one knows what's wrong. She's lying in a bed in the hospital disoriented by the meds.

Yeah, I know about that.

A friend hands her a book, *Psion* by Joan D. Vinge. It's about a telepath. She devours it and searches for more. Slowly, she develops her ability until she can make out people's thoughts. Once she realizes what the doctors want, it gets easier. She says what they want to hear and they take her off the meds.

She starts to paint because that way she can spend a lot of time alone in a studio, away from people. Her parents set up a studio for her. She is happy and proud of the beautiful things she creates. She's a small young woman, shy, keeps to herself. Others leave her alone. She's lucky she's not picked on. Maybe it's because everyone at school knows she's crazy.

She begins to feel something following her, watching her. Maybe she's going crazy again. But she holds tight to the shield she created and after a while the feeling goes away. She graduates and goes to Michigan—

No, don't look at that.

Why not?

It's very private. And I don't think you're old enough.

Yes. Very firmly. *Yes. I am.*

She meets Peter Monroe, a wonderful young man, an English major, who writes beautiful stories about star ships and robots. Daddy is a young man with a reddish beard and rimless glasses. They are lovers for a while. When they're juniors he meets Gerry and it's all over.

She's very sad for a while. She retreats into her painting, producing strange stuff. It has jagged lines and very little color.

I don't like those paintings. They're too angry.

After a while she emerges. She still hurts, but the pain is less as she realizes how much Peter and Gerry love each other. She comes to love Gerry, too.

They stay friends, mostly because Peter and Gerry are the only people she is able to be with. Being with other people gives her a headache after a few hours. But these two are different. Their love is protective and gentle, and they provide a barrier between her and the rest of the world.

They graduate and Pete and Gerry persuade her to move to New York. For three years it's great. The men make an island of quiet for her. But then the whispers come back. She starts to get headaches again. She doesn't say anything, but she needs to leave.

When Peter and Gerry tell her they want to have a baby and ask for her help she is doubtful. She feels the two men are family, that they belong together. But living in the city is so difficult. She finally agrees, reluctantly.

Images of cold operating room tables, injections, Papa and Daddy standing on either side of her each holding one of her hands. Some bad news, all flashing very quickly. Then the positive pregnancy test, the doctor smiling telling them everything is alright. Feelings of contentment and happiness rush through her. Soon the headaches begin to fade, then stop completely.

It was like you were shielding me while you were inside me. You were protecting me. I was supposed to protect you, but you protected me.

I don't remember that, Fox sent.

Marta continued in thoughts, not images. *Yeah. After you were born, the whispers came back, and so did the headaches. Besides that, I began to feel that someone was looking for me. It was like this dark shadow that disappeared when I turned around. No, don't look at those memories. They're not pleasant. I loved you and your fathers, but I couldn't stay. So I left and found this place.*

I can help you! Fox interrupted her thoughts with feelings of rising excitement and happiness. *I can show you how to build walls inside your mind and keep out the noises. You wouldn't have headaches any more. You could come live with us—*

NO!

The denial was so absolute, so loud, it broke the contact between them. Fox looked around, disoriented for a moment, shaken by the strength of her refusal. He saw his mother, tears on her cheeks, looking away from him and back to the sunset.

Needing a moment to get his thoughts together, Fox dragged his eyes to the horizon. The sun had barely moved. It felt like they were communicating for hours, but it was really only seconds. He took a deep breath.

"Why not?" His voice sounded scratchy, as if he hadn't spoken for hours.

"Look, Fox, I know you're very mature for your age, and you understand a lot about this—this thing. But I've made a life for myself here. It's quiet, no one bothers me. I can paint, or mix medicines from the herb garden. Every once in a while I go to Cheyenne or Denver to sell some paintings, once a year maybe to Santa Fe or Dallas. I never have to stay for long. It's a good life. I'm used to it. I like it."

"But you could come live with us."

"It wouldn't work, sweetie. Just trust me. It's better this way."

They watched the sunset for a while and then went to bed. For the past month Fox had fallen asleep as soon as he hit the bed, but tonight he lay awake staring at the moonlight coming through a chink in the curtains. There was so much to think about. He wasn't alone, and that was comforting. But it still didn't tell him why they had this ability. And sooner or later, he had to tell his mother about Sonia, and he dreaded it.

CHAPTER 17

T he next day Jack, one of Mr. Taunton's men, rode to the house. The dude ranch needed the horses. Fox asked if he could bring the horses over and then take them back when they were done. So he rode Tango with Jose's reins attached to his saddle.

"Hey, Fox, wanna earn a coupla bucks?" Mr. Taunton called as Fox dismounted.

"What do I gotta do?"

"Just lead some kids around the ring on the ponies. It'll get you twenty."

Fox grinned and nodded. It would be an easy twenty. The kids were so excited to be on a horse. He liked acting like an older brother who could explain about how to mount and keep pressure on the knees. And of course he could mentally *control* the horses so they walked at a slow, easy pace.

The afternoon passed quickly. Fox rode home as the sun was starting down with twenty dollars in his pocket and a smile on his face. He understood why his mother liked this life.

His mom was in her studio packing pictures into wooden crates. She didn't look up when he came in.

"What's up?" he called from just outside the door.

"Oh, Fox, I didn't even hear you. I'm glad you're here. I got a call from my friend in Denver. The gallery is doing a special show on shamanistic painting, and he wants some of mine. He thinks there's a real market for them right now."

She sat down and mopped her smiling face with a bandanna. "Only problem is we have to leave day after tomorrow. That doesn't give us much time."

They spent the rest of the afternoon packing up paintings and nailing crates. Fox was exhausted by the time dinner was finished, and fell into bed, asleep before he had a chance to stretch out.

The next morning they finished crating the paintings, and loaded the minivan. There were ten paintings in all, one of them Fox's favorite. It showed a shadowy face in clouds turned red in the sunset. He recognized the butte as the one behind Mom's house. He loved the muted gray and sand slashed with vivid red and black.

Mom closed the back of the car. They stood smiling at each other for a moment. Then she frowned. "I think we have to buy you some new clothes."

Fox followed her eyes. The bottom of his jeans were now above his ankles and his shirt felt tight around his chest. He was surprised that these clothes had been loose on him at the beginning of the summer.

"I guess I've grown some, huh?" he said with pride.

That afternoon they went to Cheyenne where Fox got jeans, shirts—and a sportcoat. "What do I need that for?" he protested.

"We're going to a real city. Just shut up and enjoy it."

He had to admit it looked good on him. It emphasized his broader shoulders and trim waist.

"You're not a little kid any more," his mother commented.

"Sometimes I think I never was," he answered quietly.

The next day they woke up early. Marta was quiet as she dished out breakfast.

"What's the matter, Mom?" Fox asked, worried.

She glanced up. "That's the first time you called me mom."

He looked down, embarrassed. "Yeah, well, I guess I did some thinking. And learning." Then he brought himself back. "But what's wrong?"

"Nothing, really. I just hate going into big cities, and Denver is pretty big."

Fox nodded. Her thin shields would never keep out the *noise* of so many minds.

Marta shrugged. "But we won't be there for long. Oh, and you'll want to put your strong shields up again."

They started on the three hour trip right after breakfast. As they drove southwest, the buttes gave way to hills, and then mountains. Fox stared out the window, overwhelmed by the size of the Rockies.

As they pulled up at the loading dock behind the gallery, his mother said, "Okay, kid, we're here."

They unloaded the crates carefully, and carried the first one into the building. A man stood inside the door. "Marta, darling, you don't have to do that! We have workmen, you know."

"Julius!" Mom exclaimed. "Great to see you. You look wonderful. This is my son, Fox." She turned to her son. "Fox, this is Julius Langdon, the owner of this wonderful gallery."

The older man shook hands with him. It pleased Fox to be treated as an equal like that.

She was obviously glad to see him, but she didn't hug him or even shake hands. It puzzled Fox for a moment. Then he put it together. Any physical contact would mean the intrusion of the other person's thoughts. Suddenly the loneliness of his mother's life became clear to him.

Julius turned to Marta. "Come to the office. We'll get the paperwork out of the way."

Fox asked, "C'n I look around?"

Marta glanced at Julius, who nodded. "Okay. Just be careful. Don't touch anything."

Fox had never been in a gallery before. The entry room was large, the plain white walls hung with eight paintings by different artists. He looked closely and saw various signatures, proving he was right. A doorway off the right opened onto a slightly smaller room. A hand-lettered sign said, "Marta Freemont." This was the room his mother's pictures would hang in.

A second doorway led to another room, this one with nine paintings on the wall. All of them were signed by "Valerie Bitsui." These pictures were mostly of medicine wheels, dream catchers or shields. He'd seen dozens of similar pictures, but these had a surprising magnetic quality that he didn't understand.

He wandered through a doorway to the third room and was struck by a blast of color and light. The painting that hung on the opposite wall was about six feet long and five feet high, and showed a cluster of reddish adobe houses outlined against an intensely blue sky. He felt as though he should know the place, but he didn't remember ever being there.

He walked slowly toward the painting and leaned close to it. He wanted to enter the scene, be a part of it.

"If y'get a grease smudge on it y'gotta buy it," a hoarse voice said from behind him.

Fox started, feeling he had been shaken from sleep. He turned to look at the owner of the voice.

The man was huge, bigger than Papa Gerry. Curly gray-black hair fell to his shoulders and a long beard the same color covered the bottom of his face. He wore sunglasses. Fox thought this was strange because the light in the gallery was not very bright. A pungent almost sweet odor hung about the man that Fox recognized as marijuana.

Fox managed to speak. "Sorry. Didn't mean to hurt anything. But it's really cool."

The man stared at him. "Cool, huh," he snorted.

"I mean I really like it," Fox hurried to say, afraid he had offended the man.

"Yeah, you should. Took me long enough to paint it," the man said gruffly.

"So you're—" Fox looked quickly at the signature on the painting. "—Joshua Williams."

The man nodded.

"I'm Fox Monroe. Marta's son."

Joshua Williams nodded, then turned away. Fox was surprised that he hadn't even offered to shake hands.

When he returned to the front he found his mother had finished her business with Julius. Fox and his mother left to check into their motel and Fox had the chance to ask Marta about the strange man.

"Joshua's strange, all right," she told him. "He's a sort of hermit, lives somewhere south of Santa Fe. But he paints beautiful pictures."

"He smelled of marijuana," Fox said, "and he wore sunglasses!"

Marta smiled. "Yeah, Joshua smokes marijuana. Says it helps him create."

"But you don't need that stuff," he said to his mother.

"Tried it. Don't like it. It's a matter of taste." She glanced hastily at her son. "At least if you're an adult. If you're a kid, you stay away from it. Right?"

Fox agreed. His one experience with meds that had destroyed his shields was more than enough.

The next day they returned to the gallery early. The men who worked for Julius were going to hang her paintings and she wanted to be there to supervise.

"I trust Julius," she told Fox. "But I just want to make sure."

It was interesting. As the installation went on, Marta told Fox why one painting was hung above eye level, another below, and why two were hung next to each other. He also got to meet the other artist, Valerie Bitsui.

He liked Valerie. She was a Navajo. Her uncle was a medicine man, she told Fox, and also explained to him what that meant. When he asked her about the power he felt coming from her works her eyes crinkled with delight.

"Many members of my family have been medicine people," Valerie explained. "My uncle is a shaman. We have been that way going back generations. For some the gift takes the form of healing. I use it in my paintings."

Joshua stood apart from everyone. He would grunt or motion with his hands to indicate where he wanted something. He still wore the sunglasses, and he never spoke.

Fox could see his mother getting more and more nervous as the hours passed. He guessed that being around so many people was torture for her. She put a brave face on, and he admired her for it.

In the evening when the work was done they went out for a quiet dinner. The next day they would rest and go to the gallery in the evening. He hoped the day off would make his mother feel better.

Marta seemed to be more relaxed as they headed down the main street. At the opening Fox wore his new sports jacket and drank seltzer with a piece of lime in it He felt very sophisticated. Julius made a short speech introducing the artists who spoke about themselves briefly. Even Joshua said a few words.

Then the artists and Julius circulated, answering questions and talking about the paintings. Fox was included. Guests clustered around paintings or in corners of the gallery and as he passed a group they asked him about his life. He told them that at first he thought life in Chugwater was desolate, but his opinion had changed. Now he saw the beauty in it. He liked the people, too.

After two hours, Marta came over to him. "I sold a picture, right off! You must be good luck."

She was smiling and seemed happy. Looking closely, though, Fox saw the tension in the lines around her eyes and mouth. It was obvious that she wanted to get out of there, and away from Denver. He wanted to do something to help her.

Maybe he could enlarge his shields, make them cover her as well as him. Working quickly, Fox pulled his shields in tight. Then he pushed hard against them. The shields budged a little. Encouraged by his success, Fox tried harder.

He imagined himself as the Incredible Hulk and set his shoulder against the metal wall. He strained, digging in his imaginary heels, heaving with all his might.

It gave him a headache. Not just a little one, but a full-blown monster. He retreated to the bathroom to give himself time to recover.

Half an hour later, Fox found Marta in the middle of the crowd. "I'm real tired, Mom," he said, trying to look young and pathetic.

She smiled, but Fox thought her smile looked forced. "Sure, hon." She turned to the group around her. "I've got to go. You know how it is. Growing young men need their sleep."

She thanked them for coming, and for their attention. Then the two of them escaped to their hotel.

⌒

The next day they were on their way back to Chugwater. As the miles passed, Mom's shoulders relaxed.

"It was a good show," she said. She spoke more slowly, her voice not as high as it had been in the gallery. "I sold three pieces, and Julius said several others were interested. And you—you were terrific! You really wowed those people."

"Huh?"

Mom giggled, sounding like a little kid. Fox was glad that she seemed so relaxed. "You don't know the effect you had on them? For real?"

"No. What effect? Waddaya mean?"

"The way you talked about my paintings. Explaining about the colors and the light. Even the subject matter."

Fox frowned in confusion. "But I was just saying what you told me when we talked about your pictures. It was nothing."

"Well, they were impressed. I could tell. Couldn't you?" She glanced at Fox. "Well, couldn't you?"

"My shields were up. Otherwise it would have been—" He stopped. He had been about to say unbearable, or something like that. But for Mom it *had* been unbearable.

"Yeah. Anyway, you were a hit. And the way some of the women looked at you! I'll tell you, kid, if you were a few years older, you could've had your pick. Must be your gorgeous gold eyes."

Fox felt the familiar warmth on his face. When was he going to grow out of blushing? To cover his confusion, he said, "Hey, Mom, I'm getting hungry. Could we stop for lunch?"

She smiled and settled back in her seat. "Sure."

Fox was tired by the time they got home. They ate an early dinner and went to bed.

In spite of his fatigue, he had a hard time falling asleep. He *had* to tell his mom about Sonia. They were so busy with the animals, the garden and then the show that he hadn't been able to find the time.

He was going to have to force it. Fear and guilt tightened his stomach, making him feel queasy. Would she love him after what he'd done?

CHAPTER 18

Two nights later they were sitting on the porch again, looking at the reds and oranges spread out against the sky. Fox was nervous. For two days he had been planning a speech, deciding how to tell his mother about Sonia and her father and everything.

Well, he decided, now was a good time. "Mom, c'n I talk to you?"

"Sure, hon, what's up?" She was leaning back in her rocker. She looked so peaceful that Fox hated to ruin it.

"Remember the letter you sent me last spring? Where you told me not to tell anyone about what I can do?"

Mom nodded, but she sat up straighter.

"Well, it came too late."

"What?" Her surprise and concern penetrated Fox's shields.

"Like you said last time, it's easier if I show you."

He's back in second grade, seeing Sonia for the first time. He feels the love for her. Scenes flash by. He's playing Harry Potter with Sonia. They're running through the park waving wands. He's sharing an ice cream soda with Sonia. They're doing homework together.

She sounds like a wonderful girl. Marta's thoughts interrupted.

Yeah. We had fun together. But then things started happening.

He's in Central Park with Fat Joey. He *sees* inside Joey's head. Then he's at Ground Zero and the images from the unknown woman replay in their minds. He *shares* his fear and despair.

He *shows* his room, before the Party. Sonia gives him the video. He demonstrates how he builds his shields.

See, it's easy. You could do it, too.

Leave it.

Images of the Birthday Party. He relives the joy, the jealousy, the belonging. He stops for a moment, because he has to warn her.

This part is very ugly. Are you sure you want to continue?

Yes.

He's in Sonia's head as her father comes to her in the night. The hatred and anger grow stronger, uncontrollable, until—

His mother pulled out of his mind so fast it was painful. Fox was so ashamed that for a moment he couldn't speak.

"You must hate me now," he finally got out. He felt paralyzed, encased in a block of ice.

"I could never hate you, dear." Her voice was choked. "But what you did . . ."

They sat in silence for a few minutes. When she spoke again, his mother's voice was low and intense. "What you did terrifies me. I never thought the power could be used like that. Oh, Fox, why did you do it?"

"I didn't mean to, Mom," he protested. "It just . . . kinda happened."

He looked at Marta, but she was staring at the horizon. She wouldn't turn her head.

"I couldn't control it!" he blurted.

"That's what worries me."

Marta was silent for a while as she rocked back and forth. It seemed to Fox like she was gathering her thoughts. Finally, she spoke. "Fox, you have to promise me you'll never go into anyone's mind like that again. Promise me!"

"Don't have to. No way I'll ever do that again. It was horrible, Mom. I can't stop thinking about it. And now Sonia hates me and she won't call me or even write to me and I'll never see her again." There were tears in his eyes. The weakness added to his feeling of shame.

Marta finally turned to face him. "I can't talk about this any more tonight. We'll hash this out tomorrow. Okay?"

Fox nodded. He felt like shit. He had disappointed his mother, the only person in the world who really got what he was going through.

~~

The next day dawned bright and warm. Fox woke to the smell of coffee and bacon. His stomach growled, surprising him. He didn't think he'd ever be hungry again.

He washed quickly, but hesitated before going to the kitchen. How could he face his mother after admitting to murder? He *felt* that she didn't hate him for it, but he was ashamed of his actions. He didn't want to see the shame echoed in his mother's eyes.

Marta turned around when Fox entered the kitchen. She smiled. "Hi, Sweetie. Hungry?"

Fox loosened his shield. All he *felt* was love, and comfort. "Y'know, you're great, Mom!"

"What prompted that?" she asked, spooning eggs and bacon onto his plate.

"I was afraid you'd be mad at me. Or at least . . . I dunno. Maybe scared of me, or disappointed."

"I told you yesterday, you could never do anything to make me stop loving you. But, Fox . . . you *killed* somebody."

"I know," Fox said miserably.

"And you're going to have to live with that for the rest of your life."

He nodded, tears forming in his eyes.

She walked to him and hugged him tight. "I know why you did it, and maybe it was for the right reason." She breathed deeply. "I've just never seen anything like that, never heard about it. It . . . it terrified me."

He couldn't say anything. She gently pushed him toward a chair.

"You can't change the past, darling. All you can do is control how you act from now on. Just remember, you always have me and your fathers. We'll always be here for you."

"There's one other thing, Mom. After . . . that thing. I was walking the streets for hours, and I kept feeling that there was something searching for me. I was looking over my shoulder all the time, but I couldn't see anything."

Marta was silent.

"Was that the shadow?" Fox asked, fear in his voice.

"Probably," Marta said slowly.

"It's just . . . to me, it felt like a sort of searchlight. Y'know, the kind the cops use on helicopters when they're looking for criminals."

"Yeah. It might be the same thing. But if you're careful you don't have to worry about it."

He took a deep breath. The horrible coldness eased. For the first time in months Fox thought that maybe the worst of it was over.

They sat down at the table. Marta gestured to his plate. "Eat the eggs before they get cold."

"But how can I be careful?" he asked between mouthfuls.

"Keep your shields tight, I guess. Don't go *into* anyone's mind."

He nodded.

"But most of all," she said forcefully, "control your emotions!"

Suddenly his stomach tightened and he couldn't eat. "But what am I gonna do, Mom? What's in the future for me?"

"Well, for the rest of the summer you're going to work hard. Physical labor is always a good way to get your head straight. And we'll talk more. Mostly you're going to feel your way, just like the rest of us."

"But—" Fox started to protest.

"There's no answer, love. No one knows the future. In the past month I've gotten to know you. You're a good person, Fox."

He looked at her, surprised. "Really?"

"Yeah, really," she smiled. "You'll find your way. I know it."

Fox spent the rest of the summer doing just what his mother suggested. He worked hard and he found that gradually the fear and darkness receded.

Marta let him sit in the studio as she painted, as long as he promised to be quiet. While she was working, he *scanned* her gently, trying to figure out how she decided what colors to choose, what objects to paint. He couldn't get a handle on it though.

"C'n I try, Mom?" he finally asked.

She set him up with a blank canvas and an easel at the opposite side of the studio. "Try these water colors first," she suggested handing him a tray. "It's a little easier."

"What should I paint?"

"Paint what interests you. Or what you feel. Don't worry about being perfect. Experiment."

He tried. He wanted to paint the grassland near the butte where he and Tango liked to stop and rest in the sun. He got the shapes right, the flat-topped butte and the meandering river. But the colors were all wrong and it looked fake.

After a week of trying to get it right, Fox decided that painting was not for him. "I think I'll stick to writing," he told his mother. "Like Daddy."

He left Wyoming at the end of August. As soon as he got on the plane the noise of other people's thoughts slammed into him. He got his shields in place just in time. He had forgotten how hard it was to maintain them all the time.

When he landed in New York, Papa and Daddy were waiting at the exit from the gate. He was so happy to see them that he almost dropped his carry-on as he ran over to them.

His fathers stared. "You've grown so much!" Papa exclaimed, and Daddy just stared, his eyes shining.

Fox grinned at the two of them. "Fresh air, farm work—y'know. Mom worked me like a field hand." He laughed to show he was kidding.

"Well whatever it was, it was good for you," Papa said.

"So tell us everything," Daddy said, picking up Fox's bag.

He described the ranch and his duties there, the horses, the freedom. The conversation carried them all the way to the apartment. As he went on, his fathers started looking worried. Finally his talk ground to a halt.

"What?" he demanded

"You sound so enthusiastic," Papa said. "You really liked Wyoming, didn't you?"

Fox nodded.

"Do you want to live there?" Daddy's voice sounded anxious.

"Hell, no!" Fox's vehemence surprised even him. "I mean, it's a great place, and I love Mom, but I couldn't *live* there. Do you know what the wintertime temperature is?"

They sat down to dinner. Papa and Daddy gave each other meaningful glances, then stared at him. Fox stared back.

"What's up?" he demanded at last.

"Do you remember the question you asked us last spring?" Papa asked.

Fox looked at them blankly and shook his head.

"Y'know, about making honest men of each other?"

For a moment Fox couldn't figure out what they meant. Then a huge grin spread over his face. "You mean you're gonna—"

Both men nodded, their grins matching their son's.

"At the end of October—on your birthday, in fact. A double celebration," Daddy said. "We didn't want to tell you in a letter, or even over the phone. Is it—Is it okay with you?"

"Okay!" Fox shouted. "It's the coolest thing that's happened *ever!*"

For a moment he felt a sudden pain as he remembered the last double celebration. But even that couldn't diminish the happiness.

"Edie insisted on doing our star charts," Papa said, grinning sheepishly. "She said that was an auspicious day. There was another one at the end of June, but we didn't want to wait."

"So," Daddy said, "you up for being best man?"

"For both of us," Papa said.

Fox nodded. His fathers were so happy he could *feel* it even though his shields were tight. *What a great day*, he thought. *The perfect ending to a perfect summer.* Except Sonia wasn't there. He stomped down on the hurt. He wasn't going to let it spoil this moment.

When all the questions were answered, Fox asked about the thing that had bothered him all summer. "Did Sonia call?"

There was a pause. Then Papa shook his head.

"No, hon," Daddy said. "No word at all."

Fox nodded and pretended he didn't care.

CHAPTER 19

F ox stared at his new school. Stuyvesant High School. After a year of dreaming and planning, he was finally here. The plain façade of the ten story red brick building was intimidating. So was the thought of being with so many smart people.

"There's no black hole in there."

Fox jerked his head around, startled out of his contemplation. The speaker was a tall kid with dark brown skin, wide dark eyes and close-cropped hair. Very good looking, Fox thought. Very confident, too. I bet he's brilliant.

"Huh?" was all he could say.

"It won't suck you in. You have to walk."

"I know. I was just—"

The older boy grinned. "Yeah, it's pretty scary at first. I'm Mark Chambers."

"Fox Monroe."

They shook hands. Fox felt this was an excellent beginning, even if he had sounded retarded at first.

"It'll take a while to get used to it. C'mon, I'll show you where to go."

The school was *huge*. There were escalators between floors, specialized labs for the various sciences, computer rooms, drafting rooms, regular classrooms. Fox worked hard at keeping his shields firmly fastened. He didn't want to be tempted to use his powers. Not in school.

"How do you find your way?" Fox asked breathlessly after the tour.

"You'll do okay," Mark answered smiling. "Just give it time."

That evening at dinner Fox gushed to his fathers about his first day at school. "It's totally awesome. It would be easy to get lost. And the courses they offer! Y'know," he said, turning to Daddy, "they give a class in science fiction. I can't take it 'til I'm a junior, but it's there."

They took a few moments to eat. The table was silent except for the sound of chewing.

Fox paused, his fork halfway to his mouth. He admitted his fear in a small voice. "The kids are all so smart. I don't know if I can keep up."

"They wouldn't have accepted you if they thought you couldn't," Papa said. "You'll have to work harder than you did in middle school, though. Not as much time for goofing off and hanging out."

"When I first got to Michigan," Daddy said, "I was scared that I couldn't make it. But I did. And you will, too."

The first week went by on fast-forward. Fox's teachers proved to be very patient with the newbie ninth graders. The work was difficult, especially the math, but math had always given Fox a hard time. History was fascinating, though, and so was English. He began to think he could do this.

The following Tuesday, Fox walked into the cafeteria, bought lunch, and looked around for someplace to sit. He didn't recognize anybody, and he walked to a table that was half empty.

"Hey, Fox, over here," he heard.

He turned around. It was the boy he'd met his first day. Mark waved him over to a group of kids. Fox stood, undecided, in the middle of the huge room.

Mark got up and walked over to him. "C'mon, kid. Don't be shy. We're all fellow geniuses around here."

"I don't know—"

"We're just talking science fiction. You said you were interested. Something about growing up with it . . ." Mark trailed off.

"Yeah. My dad, Pete, he writes—"

Fox didn't have a chance to finish. Mark stopped short and Fox almost bumped into him.

"Wait a minute. Your dad, Pete. Your last name is Monroe, right? Peter Monroe? You're Peter Monroe's son?"

Fox nodded.

"Holy shit!" Mark grabbed Fox's sleeve and unceremoniously dragged him to a table where seven students sat. "Hey, guys, you'll never guess. This is Peter Monroe's son."

They stopped talking and looked up at Fox. The four boys and three girls regarded him curiously. He glanced around at them, too embarrassed at being the center of attention to take a good look. He was only a freshman, after all.

"Peter Monroe is really your father?" one of the boys asked skeptically.

"The science fiction writer?" a girl said.

"Yeah," Fox answered, confused.

"Hey, let the kid sit down," Mark said.

They cleared a place for him. As soon as he was seated, they all started talking at once. Fox caught bits of the conversation. They thought Pete Monroe was a great writer, up there with Asimov and Heinlein, not like the bozos who wrote fantasy but a real writer of the hard stuff. Between bites of food, Fox tried to answer questions about his father. He described the afternoon games they played, making up stories on the parquet floor. He talked about book signings at the stores in the neighborhood, although he'd never been to the out-of-town events.

Mark made the introductions all around, but Fox knew he would never remember all the names. A girl with long brown hair asked, "Do you write?"

Fox admitted to "scribbling" a few things. He had tried to turn some of the adventures he had made up with his father into real stories. He wasn't satisfied with any of them.

When the questions finally stopped, Mark turned to him.

"I know it's a lot to ask," he said hesitantly, "but do you think your father would be willing to meet us? I mean, just for a little while?"

Fox thought. Daddy Pete was a generous man. He always had time for Fox's friends, and Fox knew he always tried to answer the fan mail he got. "I could ask him."

There were replies of "great" and "awesome." Fox and Mark exchanged numbers, and Fox promised to text as soon as he could arrange something.

He walked away feeling taller and more mature. He had friends, and some of them were seniors. Life was definitely improving.

Fox asked Daddy Pete that afternoon.

"Sure I'd be glad to meet them," his father answered. "Fans are fun, especially the younger ones. Let me look at my calendar and we can set up a time. Think they'd object to coming here?"

Fox shook his head. "Thanks, Daddy. You're great!"

But inside he was concerned about how the kids would react to his two fathers. He knew they were all intelligent people, but he had read enough to realize that not everyone was cool with his arrangement.

He texted Mark that evening. Mark sent back the message that the whole group would be available at any time. Daddy cleared his appointments for the following Saturday afternoon, and it was good to go.

By Saturday morning, Fox was so excited he could barely sit still. Daddy organized snacks and drinks, and Papa arranged his schedule so he could be home. Fox was proud of his parents. They were so willing to accept his new friends, to open up their home and their lives. Fox was sure it would be a stupendous afternoon.

When the doorbell rang, Fox smoothed down his tee shirt. He knew he looked good. Participating in "swim gym" kept the muscles he built up over the summer. His jeans were old enough to be slightly worn and comfortable, but not raggedy. Yeah, he was doing okay.

He opened the door to see Mark standing there with a shy smile on his face. The others were grouped behind him. Fox smiled back and ushered them into the living room.

"Dad, this is Mark." Fox thought saying Dad instead of Daddy made him sound older. He liked it. His father glanced at him quizzically but didn't say anything, just accepting the new name.

Mark held out his hand to shake. "Mr. Monroe, I can't tell you what an honor this is. We've been reading your works for years. We think you're one of the best."

"Thanks," Dad said, shaking hands. "An author always likes to hear that his work is appreciated."

Mark introduced the rest of the group. Each one stepped forward and shook hands with Dad, then they took seats around the living room. No one spoke for a minute, and Fox was afraid that the afternoon was going to be a bust.

At that moment, Papa walked into the room. Fox stood up. "Everyone, this is my father Gerald Jefferson." He held his breath.

Mark stood up and held out his hand. "It's wonderful to meet you, Mr. Jefferson. Do you think we could pick your brain, too? Help us find out more about Mr. Monroe's creative process?"

Papa smiled. "Sure. But I don't know how much I could help."

"Sometimes even the writer doesn't recognize where inspiration comes from," Amy said. She shook back her long, curly hair and glanced at Dad. "Right?"

"Yes. Sometimes it's a puzzle," Dad agreed.

Fox let out a breath he didn't even realize he had been holding. Everything was going to be all right.

Papa brought out the snacks, and the conversation started. The questions the kids asked showed that they really had read Dad's works. Where did the idea for the aliens in the second book come from? Just what was the trans-dimensional hyperdrive? In *Robots Underground*, why did Alec react to Frankie the way he did?

There were specific questions, like how did he organize his day? How did he start writing a novel? Did he outline first, or just start writing?

Then the conversation steered to more abstract matters. How did he see the future? How could the human race save the planet? Did he really think there were aliens out there?

Fox sat back listening to the interchange. It was exhilarating. Dad considered each question seriously, and Papa chimed in with stories of his partner's schedule and writing habits. Fox felt a glow that started in his stomach and spread throughout his body. He was part of a family.

Then Chung asked whether Dad really believed that telepathy was possible. The wall that separated Fox from the rest of the world thunked into place, the closely-guarded secret that set him apart.

"Yes. It's possible, just like I think it's possible that there's life on other planets. I think telepathy exists out there. Of course, we haven't seen any real proof of it, nothing verifiable, anyway. But, yes, it's there."

The seven kids looked at him, questions in their eyes.

He continued his explanation. "We know that identical twins sometimes have . . . unquantifiable methods of communication. They occasionally can sense when the other is in pain or in trouble. And sometimes parents can know things about their children, like when they're hurting, or even when they're lying about something."

He paused and looked thoughtful. "Of course, all the evidence for that is anecdotal—no hard data. But it is interesting."

"You sound like Mr. Spock," Keisha said, and everyone laughed.

"I said interesting, not fascinating," Dad corrected.

There was more laughter and they refilled their plates. Dad asked the kids about their attempts at writing. Amy and Brad, both blushing, told about stories they had written. Dad listened carefully and offered suggestions. He even agreed to read the stories when they were finished. The group was obviously impressed.

Finally the conversation wound down. The kids got up to leave, thanking the men profusely. Even without his ability, Fox could tell that the afternoon had been a success.

He walked them to the door. Amy, Keisha and Miranda hugged him, while the boys shook his hand. They all told him how grateful they were for the opportunity, what a great apartment he had, how they enjoyed meeting both his fathers.

"Your dads are super cool," Mark said as he stood outside the door. "And so are you. You're a great addition to our group."

Wow, Fox thought as he closed the door. *What a welcome to high school. The cool kids like me, Pop and Dad are getting married. I'm the luckiest person in the world.*

CHAPTER 20

The wedding arrangements were even more elaborate and difficult than the birthday plans a year before. The guest list was longer, because it included friends of Papa's from the hospital as well as a whole gang of people Dad knew through his writing. Fortunately, Cyril insisted on having both the ceremony and the reception at his restaurant.

They wanted to keep the guest list to under a hundred and fifty, but that was proving difficult.

"Pop, how come you have only a few relatives coming? Dad has lots," Fox asked, looking up from the list.

Papa sighed. "You know that not everyone approves of . . . us. Of Dad and me."

Fox nodded.

"Well, my parents are like that. Most of my relatives are the same. They don't like the way we live."

"And that's why we don't visit them? Like we go to Gamma and Dad's people all the time?"

"Yeah."

Fox didn't have to *see* into Papa's mind to know that the situation hurt him. The pain was obvious. He walked to Papa's chair and hugged his shoulder. "Well, *I* approve," he said. "So does Dad's family. And you have so many friends who want to share this with you that you can't even make up a guest list!"

The three of them laughed, and the mood lightened.

Fox was glad that Papa and Dad were taking on the responsibility for the event. School was hard, even more than he'd imagined it could be.

He was up late most nights finishing assignments and his weekends were filled with homework and projects.

He was lucky to hang with the science fiction crowd. They were all hyper-bright in his eyes. Sometimes one of them tutored him or explained a difficult point. He wondered why the teachers couldn't explain it as well as these students. Maybe the students remembered the difficulties more clearly.

Sometimes Fox was sorely tempted to *look* into the teacher's mind, especially during exams. He resisted. He knew it wouldn't be fair, and it wouldn't give him a good idea of whether he was learning. In school he kept his shields tight even though it took a lot of energy.

Mark was especially helpful when it came to math. The older boy was a whiz. He showed Fox short cuts to solving algebraic problems. Fox felt guilty because there was no way he could repay Mark for these efforts.

Except for one.

One evening at dinner he said, "Hey, Pops, could I invite someone to the wedding?"

"Of course," Dad replied. "But I thought we'd made a list of your friends."

"There's one more. I want to invite Mark. He's been real good to me, helping me in school. I kind of want to thank him."

Papa and Dad looked at each other and smiled. "You really like this guy, don't you?" Papa asked.

"Yeah," Fox said enthusiastically. "He's way cool."

Dad nodded. "You want to mail the invitation, or hand it to him in person?"

Fox stared at his reflection in the three-way mirror of the tuxedo rental store. "I look like a doofus," he muttered.

Papa's image appeared in the mirror. "No, you don't."

"Do I *have* to wear a tux?"

Dad's reflection joined Papa's. "Yes. You're the best man. The best man wears a tux. So do the husbands. We have to, you have to. End of conversation."

Fox had to admit that Papa looked handsome. The suit emphasized his broad shoulders and slim waist. Papa had trimmed his beard so it lay close to his cheeks, coming to a point under his chin. Dad looked every bit as good as Papa in a different way, slender and wiry next to the larger man.

Fox stood back and admired his fathers. "Well, I just hope I look as good as you do. And I don't embarrass you. Or myself."

Both men laughed. "You couldn't possibly," Dad said, kissing the top of Fox's head. Fox squirmed, embarrassed. He wasn't a little kid anymore.

When the day of the wedding came, even Fox had to admit that he didn't look too bad in the tux. He stared at his reflection. He still looked more like his dad than his papa, his body slender. But his shoulders were broader than they had been a year ago. His face was losing the baby-fat roundness, his pointed chin becoming a bit more square. With his auburn hair slicked back, he still looked like a fox. Foxier, he thought, smiling.

Dad knocked on the open door of his room. "C'mon, Narcissus, time to get going."

They walked to the back entrance of the restaurant, avoiding the people beginning to crowd into the front. Cyril was there, smiling a greeting.

"Everything's all ready," he assured them. "It's gonna be another awesome event brought to you by Monroe and Jefferson."

But this time without Sonia, Fox thought. God, he missed her.

The ceremony went flawlessly. As Papa and Dad held hands and recited the vows they had written, Fox felt the prickling in his eyes that meant tears. He refused to hide his head. He was proud of the tears, and proud of his dads. It was a glorious day.

Cyril's promise lived up to their expectations. The decorations were gorgeous, the food delicious, and the music totally cool. As soon as the party started and he saw they didn't need him, Fox looked around. He saw Mark standing by himself near the door.

"Hey, Mark. Glad you could make it."

"Wouldn't have missed it for anything," Mark answered, shaking his hand. "I've never been in this place. It's awesome."

"Yeah," Fox said dismissively. "C'mon. There're some people I'd like you to meet."

He led Mark to the table where his friends were sitting and introduced them. Mark was polite and seemed enthusiastic, but Fox could *sense* that Norrie, Joey, Kim and the others didn't have Mark's full attention. Fox didn't know why. Maybe his friends were too young.

They made their excuses and walked toward the head table. The newly married couple were standing behind it, busy talking to friends and colleagues. Fox waited until there was a break in the conversation.

"Papa, Dad, you remember Mark," Fox said when they got his parents' attention.

"Of course," Papa said, shaking hands.

"I'm glad you could come," Dad said. "There are some people here I think you'd like to meet." He gestured at a group of men and women talking animatedly in a corner. "Do you mind if we steal him away?" he asked Fox.

"Would it be okay?" Mark asked.

"Sure. No problem."

Dad ushered Mark to the group. Fox recognized them as science fiction writers, colleagues of his father's. He knew Mark would be interested in meeting them, and they would like talking to him. Everyone liked talking to Mark.

Fox wandered back to his friends. Their conversation hadn't changed in ten years. Complaints about school, parents, bands that had split up, songs that rocked, songs that sucked. The separateness he had felt before, the feeling of alienation, came back. He had been through so much more than any of them. No one could understand.

But he joined in the good-natured grousing, pretending to be normal. Eventually he brought up something he needed to know.

"Anybody hear anything from Sonia?" he asked, trying to seem casual.

"Got an email from her last week," Kim answered. "She started high school down there in Camden. She said it was okay, but the kids are kind of cliquish. She's having trouble making friends."

"Gee, that's too bad," Fox said, struggling to keep his voice neutral.

"Yeah. She sounded real sad," Kim continued. "I wish she'd move back here."

"So do I," Fox whispered.

At that moment the dance music started, and Cyril's voice came over the speakers. "Ladies and Gentlemen, in their first dance as a married couple, let's welcome Mr. Gerald Jefferson and Mr. Peter Monroe!"

The guests applauded enthusiastically as the two men made their way to the dance floor. Fox stood up and walked closer to get a better look. His fathers wrapped their arms around each other as Roberta Flack's voice sang "The First Time." Fox drank in the sight of his parents swaying gently to the music. They were so handsome, and they looked so happy. For a moment they leaned back and looked at each other, the love obvious in their faces. Then they leaned in, kissed and held each other tightly.

Fox felt an arm slip around his shoulders in a friendly hug. "They look really good together," Mark said.

Fox could only nod. He couldn't speak around the lump that had formed in his throat. He never thought you could cry for joy. If only he could find someone to love him like that, someone he could love.

Other couples were making their way to the floor. Swallowing the lump and turning to Mark he said, "Hey, why don't you ask someone to dance?"

"Okay," Mark answered and looked at him. "Wanna dance?"

Blinking in surprise, Fox was speechless.

"I'm sorry," Mark said. "I thought—I mean it's just—"

"No." Fox smiled. "I mean, yes, I want to dance with you."

They walked to the dance floor. Mark put his arms around Fox's waist and Fox circled the older boy's shoulders. They stood close together and danced slowly. Fox glanced over to see his fathers looking at him and smiling. He smiled back.

CHAPTER 21

"Mark wants me to come over to his house to study on Saturday," Fox said as he and Dad set the table.

"Where does he live?" Papa called from the kitchen.

"Just over in the Mews." It was only a few blocks away. They couldn't say no because of distance.

"How old is Mark?" Dad asked.

"He's a senior. He's seventeen. Why?"

Papa came into the dining room with the baked salmon and asparagus and they all sat down.

"He's quite a bit older than you," Dad answered as they picked up their napkins and silverware.

"So? It's only three years."

Dad took a forkful of salmon. "That's a lot at your age."

Fox could *sense* the worry in his parents' minds but he couldn't understand why they were objecting. "Look, Mark's really brilliant. He could help me a lot. He explains things so I understand them." Fox sighed. "I just don't know why *he* wants to study with *me*."

Papa raised one eyebrow. "Really?"

Fox glanced up in time to see the smile on both men's faces. "Whadaya mean?" It came out angrier than he had intended.

Papa put down his fork. "Fox, you're a handsome kid. You're smart and have a good personality. We saw you dancing with Mark at the wedding. We think maybe you're attracted to each other and we're . . . concerned."

Fox looked from Papa to Dad. Is that why were they worried? Oh, yeah, *he* was attracted to Mark. Mark was handsome, intelligent, kind—he was wonderful. But Mark? Attracted to him?

"We don't want to see you hurt, or forced into anything you don't want to do," Dad said. "I don't know if it's a good idea for you to be in that kind of situation with Mark."

Fox felt exasperated. "I get that you're worried. But remember, I've heard the lectures about 'inappropriate touching' since second grade." *So had Sonia.* "I know how to avoid it. I mean, even a couple of the boys in my old school . . . Well, anyway, Mark wouldn't do anything like that. He's too . . . cool."

He wanted to add that he hadn't *sensed* anything like that in Mark, but he couldn't say it.

Papa and Dad looked at each other and seemed to reach an agreement. "Okay," Papa said. "But you keep your cell on you all the time, and call us if *anything* happens that you don't like. Promise?"

"Okay," Fox said. He was sure he wouldn't have to.

On Saturday, Fox gathered his books and called to his parents that he was going. He had given them Mark's address and phone number, his parents' names. He figured he was lucky they didn't ask for a DNA sample.

They were worried about nothing, he decided. He had danced a couple of times with Mark at the wedding. But Mark had asked other people, too, both male and female. And Fox had danced with some of his friends. He even asked one of Dad's friends. She told him that he was a "smooth dancer" and added "almost like you could make me read your mind." He had lost a step.

Mark didn't feel that way about him. Sure, he had to keep his shields tight at school, and at the wedding, so he couldn't detect anyone's hidden feelings. Still . . .

No, it wasn't possible.

Conflicting images formed in his mind. Sonia's father on top of her. The pain and self-hatred. The blackness inside her mind.

Then he remembered the drowsy, peaceful thoughts from his fathers that drifted into his consciousness at night. The sight of them dancing at the wedding. The thoughts he had picked up from his mother about her and Dad.

If that's what it was like, he wanted it. But the only *feelings* he got from Mark were friendly.

He walked to the entrance to the Mews. It was a tiny street, barely more than an alley. The trees that arched overhead had lost most of their leaves, but the street itself was clear.

The people who live here wouldn't allow anything else, Fox thought.

He knew the residents of the Mews were wealthy. Each house was owned by one family. The oak doors were stained a dark brown, the steps leading up to them clean. It looked like a picture out of a history book, a street preserved as it had been for centuries.

He rang the bell. The door was opened by a pretty woman wearing a simple black dress.

"Hi," he said. "I'm Fox Monroe. A friend of Mark's?"

"Yes," the woman answered. "Mr. Mark is expecting you. Please come in. I'll tell him you're here."

Mr. Mark? Fox was taken aback for a minute, but he managed to recover. He followed the woman into an entryway the size of his living room. The floor was marble tile, and an antique mirror and table holding an elaborate flower arrangement stood against one wall. A staircase wound up to the right. A crystal chandelier hung from the ceiling. It was overwhelming.

The woman turned to Fox. "May I take your coat?"

Fox shrugged off his jacket. He felt like a country hick in the middle of all this splendor.

The woman led him to a room on the left. It was lined with bookshelves from floor to ceiling. Two leather chairs as well as a comfortable looking couch faced each other in the center.

"Please sit down. Mr. Mark will be with you shortly." With that the woman left.

A few minutes later there was a clattering on the stairs and Mark burst into the room. "Damn. I told Felice to send you up as soon as you got here," he said breathlessly. "I'm sorry you had to wait."

Fox smiled. "No problem."

"Well, c'mon up." Mark led the way.

"This is some house," Fox said. "I've never been to the Mews before."

Mark looked around as if seeing it for the first time. "Oh, yeah. It's okay I guess."

They walked through a door at the top of the stairs. The room reflected Mark's personality. All the furniture was dark wood. The king size bed took up half the floor space, the square headboard rising up six feet. Books and an open laptop were scattered across the blue bedspread. A tall antique chest of drawers was in one corner.

Bookshelves, filled with works about engineering, space flight and, of course, science fiction, lined the walls on two sides. The heavy velvet drapes that covered the two tall windows were pulled back to let in the fading autumn daylight.

"You take the desk." Mark pointed to a table along the wall. "There's an outlet for your laptop and there's wi-fi. Anything you need, just ask. Oh, and are you hungry? I could get us some snacks."

"I'm good," Fox answered. He was intimidated by the expensive furniture in the room and by the way Mark took it all for granted.

"I'll just finish this, then I can help you with your math," Mark said. "That okay?"

"Yeah, sure." Fox set his stuff down on the desk and started to sort it out. Then he stopped. "Mark, I just gotta ask. I really appreciate this. I need the help. But—" He stopped, unsure how to go on. "I mean, why are you doing this? I can't help *you* with anything."

Mark smiled, his teeth brilliant against his dark skin. "It's nice to have someone here in the room. It helps me concentrate. Besides, when I explain something to you, it makes it clearer to me. It's good for me to review this stuff. That make sense?"

"Yeah," Fox smiled back. He turned to his work.

Fox came home as it was getting dark. He walked into the apartment humming.

"So?" Daddy said, looking up from the newspaper. "How'd it go?"

"It was *great!*" Fox answered. "Mark explained quadratic equations and showed me how to do this thing in mechanical drawing. He knows so *much*. He's awesome."

"Hm," Dad said. "And he didn't—y'know, try anything?"

"Of course not," Fox said, scowling.

Every Saturday after that, Fox went to Mark's house to study. After that first time Felice didn't stop him at the door but told him to go right up to Mark's room. For two months, Fox worked hard. With Mark's help he did well on his midterm exams. He was happy, and so were his dads.

After exams, Mark invited him to continue the study sessions. Fox was overjoyed. He loved being with Mark, and he was learning a lot. Nothing "happened," as his fathers kept asking, even though Fox secretly wished it would.

One clear, cold day in early January, Fox was at the desk while Mark lay on the bed curled around his laptop. The afternoon was drawing to a close. Mark turned the lamps on. The light made the room feel isolated and cozy.

When the assignments were finished, Mark called to him. "Hey, Fox, look at this!"

Fox walked over to the bed and sat down next to Mark. The open laptop showed swirls of intense color on the screen.

"It's beautiful," Fox said.

"It's called a fractal. It's a representation of chaos theory," Mark explained. "That tells us that even in chaos there's a pattern, if you know how to look for it."

Fox didn't say anything. He was mesmerized by the constantly changing hues. It was like a kaleidoscope but better.

He turned to Mark to say so. The older boy leaned toward him, slowly and gently, and their lips met.

The surge of pleasure made Fox's shields weaken for a second, and he flinched back.

"I'm sorry," Mark said, lowering his eyes. "I just—I thought maybe you wanted it, too."

"I do," Fox answered, surprised at how much he wanted it. "But—Well, I've never done this before."

"No. No, of course you haven't." Mark shook his head. "I keep forgetting how young you are. You always act so—"

"So mature," Fox finished for him, and grinned. "Everyone tells me that."

"Yeah, well. Maybe we should go slowly," Mark suggested. "I never want you to do anything you're not ready for."

CHAPTER 22

"Hey, Pops, I'm going over to Mark's to study," Fox called to his parents as he walked through the living room.

Papa looked up from his book and raised an eyebrow. "Study, huh?"

"Yes," Fox said a little too forcefully. "We really *do* study, y'know."

"Don't tease him, Ger," Dad interrupted. He looked at Fox. "Just don't be home too late."

"Yeah, yeah," Fox said under his breath, closing the door behind him.

They didn't understand, he thought. *They couldn't. They're old. They're both almost forty. They don't remember what it was like to be young.*

The March skies were gray and a bitter wind whipped his coat. Fox didn't like the idea of going out into the cold but he enjoyed the afternoons with Mark. The older boy's explanations made things fall into place.

And then afterwards . . .

Fox reached the house in the Mews and rang the bell. He liked the house in the secluded cul-de-sac. Even in the middle of winter the street was kept clean of snow, in spite of the storms that had covered the rest of the city.

Felice answered the door and ushered Fox inside. She took his coat just as Mark came running down the curved staircase. They said hello and went upstairs.

With the door closed, they were more enthusiastic. They leaned in to kiss. As their tongues touched Fox felt the familiar tingle that started in his knees and went to the top of his head. He wanted to stay like that forever.

"I love your eyes." Mark pulled away and pretended to be stern. "But we got work to do."

"Slave driver," Fox said.

Mark pushed Fox into the chair next to the desk while he flopped onto the bed. His books and laptop lay open on the dark blue bedspread. He picked up one of them and started reading.

Fox looked at him for a moment. He loved the look of Mark's lean body sprawled nonchalantly against the pillows.

With a sigh Fox turned to the books on the desk. He had math and biology homework to finish. He was going to need help with both.

"And that's how you do it," Mark said as they finished the problem. He stood up and stretched.

"Why can't the teachers explain it like that?" Fox said, exasperated. "It's so clear when *you* show me, but when *they* do . . ." He trailed off.

Mark smiled. "I think they forgot what it's like to be our age."

Fox smiled at the echo of his own earlier thought. He followed Mark to where he stood in front of the window and leaned his head on Mark's shoulder. Together, they gazed out onto the cobblestone street.

Both boys turned their heads at the same time. Fox relaxed into the kiss, savoring it, feeling the rising excitement. Kissing Mark was the most enjoyable thing Fox could imagine. So far, things hadn't gone beyond kissing and touching. Fox knew there was more, but Mark wanted to go slowly. Then Mark pulled back.

"What's the matter?" Fox asked.

Mark held Fox's gaze for a moment. "I like you a lot. I just . . . feel sort of responsible for you. I'm afraid that if I let myself go I'll end up forcing you into something. I don't want to ruin this."

Fox smiled, brushing Mark's brown cheek. He felt the slight roughness of a beard. It always surprised him and made him realize how much older Mark was. Shaking off the feeling, he said, "I'm hungry."

"C'mon, let's get some food."

They raced down the stairs to the kitchen where Gloria, the cook, was cutting up vegetables. She was a large woman who obviously ruled her kingdom with an iron hand. A white apron covered her ample breasts and belly, a black dress showing behind it. She was an awesome sight, especially holding a large knife.

"Hey, slow down, you two!" she ordered.

They laughed and Gloria looked offended.

"Oh, no, Glory," Mark sputtered. "Not you. Just something we were talking about upstairs."

"Hmph," Gloria responded.

"Y'got anything we could eat?" Mark asked. "We're just two starving students getting weaker by the minute." He pulled a pathetic face.

"Do I got anything to eat," Gloria grumbled. "Do I got—Waddaya think goes on here? 'Course I got stuff." She walked to the refrigerator still clutching the knife and pulled out a tray of cut-up fruit. "Here. Now go away and don't bother me."

"But, Gloria, I love you!" Mark joked. "I can't live without you. Don't banish me."

"You don't get outta here I'm gonna do more than banish you," Gloria said pointing the knife. A smile softened the words.

"Oops," Mark said, jumping back in mock fright. He grabbed the tray and turned to Fox. "Let's go."

They ran up the stairs arriving at Mark's room breathless.

Mark collapsed onto the bed, still laughing, and Fox walked around to the other side to join him. They put the tray of fruit between, wolfing down half the watermelon chunks and grapes before they spoke.

"Hey, Fox, look at this," Mark said, pulling his laptop closer to them.

"Another fractal app?" Fox asked, raising an eyebrow.

Mark slapped him playfully on the shoulder. "You have a one-track mind, child. No, this is something they're gonna hit you with next year when they start trying to cram geometry and trigonometry into your head."

Fox made a face.

Mark laughed and started to explain the equations that filled the screen. Fox looked at Mark's face more than at the computer. He admired the older boy. Mark was smart, handsome and made friends easily. All the things Fox wanted to be.

Each time Fox came to study, Mark was conscientious about spending most of their time doing schoolwork. But when they finished, they always ended up on the bed making out.

Every week Fox longed for more. He loved to kiss Mark. The older boy's lips were soft, his tongue delicate in its exploration of Fox's mouth. He felt the pleasurable building of pressure in his groin until Mark pulled back with the *take things slowly* agreement preventing them from going further.

Fox wanted to end that agreement.

Now, they wiped the fruit juices from each other's faces and smiled. Fox felt an intense attraction to Mark, and even with his shields at full strength, he felt Mark's desire. "Let's forget the rule today," he said suddenly.

"Are you sure?" Mark asked, his tone serious.

"Completely." Fox kissed him.

As the sensation grew more intense, Fox's shields vibrated, threatening to come down altogether. He lowered them a little, and some of Mark's feelings *seeped* in. He *felt* Mark's pleasure just as he felt his own. He could *sense* what Mark was going to do, what Mark wanted him to do. Their pleasure mounted until Fox lost track of what he was feeling or what Mark was feeling and it all resonated together like fractals swirling in his body and all he could do was ride the tide of sensation to the end.

Afterward they lay in bed, the sweat drying on their bodies. Mark turned to Fox. "I thought you'd never done this before?"

"I guess you're just a good teacher," Fox said.

"Ready for another lesson?"

Fox nodded.

Mark reached over and grabbed a piece of watermelon. He bit off a piece and fed the rest to Fox. Then he leaned over and they shared the watermelon taste in each other's mouths.

It was even better the second time.

CHAPTER 23

I n April, the weather swung from frigid to mild, and the wind became a pleasant breeze. Fox was doing well in school. His grades were good, and he even enjoyed his classes. His relationship with Mark was a wonder. He couldn't believe that Mark found him attractive and wanted to be with him. It was a constant source of amazement and joy.

The only thing missing was Sonia. He still hadn't heard anything from her. As he walked the streets of his neighborhood, he flashed on memories of playing with Sonia, walking home from school with Sonia, lazing in the park with Sonia. Her absence in his life was like a hunger.

Fox walked quickly along the sidewalk on his way to school. The early morning light shone on the tops of buildings, and the wind whipped away the scents of pollution and spoiled food that lurked in alleyways. He lifted his head and jogged the rest of the block, his backpack thumping rhythmically.

Mark was walking down the street as Fox approached the school. Fox smiled. Usually he didn't get a chance to see Mark until lunchtime. The electric tingle he felt every time he saw his friend made his stomach lurch in a pleasant way.

Mark grinned as he saw Fox. "Hey, I have some *great* news!" he called.

"Well. Give," Fox said as he caught up.

"Let's get out of the wind."

Inside the lobby, Mark put down his bookbag and fished out an envelope. He handed it proudly to Fox. "Stanford University" was printed in large letters on the upper left hand corner.

Fox took the letter from inside the envelope and opened it. "We are pleased to inform you that you have been accepted—" He looked up at

Mark. "You got in!" Fox didn't know how to react. He was happy for Mark because he knew the older boy really wanted to go to the California university. But California—It was so far away.

Suddenly the wave of emotion weakened Fox's shields and he *saw.* Images of warm sun, trees, other students. Bustling activity. And an intense happiness and sense of belonging.

The only thing Fox didn't see was any sign of himself.

"Look, I *gotta* go tell Mr. Tenneford about this. He's the one who—I have to run. We'll talk about this on Saturday, okay?"

Mark ran off, leaving Fox standing alone in the lobby.

He won't even think of me, Fox thought. *Everyone deserts me—Mom, Sonia, now Mark.* Everyone except Papa and Dad, said a small voice in the back of his head. And the others didn't desert you. Stop being selfish.

Fox ignored the voice. Didn't he deserve some consideration? He'd been through so much in the past year, so much that nobody knew about. And he'd toughed it out. He was being left alone again, and it wasn't fair.

They would talk on Saturday. Maybe he could change Mark's mind. Not go *inside* or anything, but just talk to him.

Selfish. The word echoed in his mind as he walked to his first class.

＝＝

As if it were mocking his feelings, Saturday was a warm, bright day. Fox could even see the beginnings of buds on the trees as he walked into the Mews to Mark's house. *It should be raining,* he thought. *Or at least cloudy. Don't I ever catch a break?*

Mark was laying on his bed as usual, surrounded by his books and laptop. He smiled happily as Fox walked in. "Hey, love. How's it going?"

"Horrible." Fox sat down at the desk and faced away from the bed.

"What's up, Fox? Something bad happen?"

"You mean besides you going away?"

"Wait a minute." Mark sat up in the bed. "Are you *upset* with me? For this?"

Fox turned around. "You're leaving, aren't you? Going clear to the other side of the country. As far away as you can get. Yeah, I'm upset."

Mark got up and went to the desk. He sat down in the extra chair. "You knew I applied. You knew how much I want to go there. Fox, they have the best artificial intelligence people in the country. I could learn so much!"

"But it's so far away!" As soon as he said it, Fox realized how childish it sounded, how whiny. He hated the sound of his own voice.

"I'll be back for vacations. We can still see each other. And we can email and text." Mark smiled. "I can still help you with your *homework*." He wagged his eyebrows suggestively.

"I don't want to joke," Fox said harshly. "I want to be with you. I—I love you."

Mark's face got very serious. "You knew when we started this that it couldn't be permanent. Jeez, Fox, you're fourteen years old! You're going to change in a billion ways by next year."

Fox turned away so Mark wouldn't see the tears in his eyes. He didn't speak.

"I never should have started this," Mark said bitterly.

"Damn straight," Fox said, finding his voice. He scooped up his bookbag and headed out the door.

"Fox!" Mark called after him.

He didn't look back.

~

Fox walked into the apartment and dropped his keys on the hall table. Dad came out of his office, a surprised look on his face.

"You're early. Everything okay?" The surprise turned to concern.

"Yeah," Fox answered brusquely.

"Uh-huuuuh. Want some tea? I'm ready for a break anyway."

Fox followed his father into the kitchen and collapsed into a chair next to the small table.

"Um, didn't you have a study session with Mark today?" Dad asked hesitantly.

"Cut it short." Fox really didn't want to talk about it now.

"Okay. You know if you want to talk I'll be here. Oh, and there's a letter from your mom. It's on the hallway table."

Fox felt Dad's eyes follow him as he trudged back to his room, detouring along the way to pick up the letter. He *would* talk to his fathers about this later. First he had to get his thoughts in order, figure out how he felt about the whole problem.

He loved Mark. Needed him. Not just for help with schoolwork, but for the special warmth and support Mark gave him. It was different from the way he felt with his fathers. He loved them, too, and needed them. But with Mark it was different.

Sort of like it had been with Sonia.

He pushed that thought away. He couldn't deal with that now. All he wanted to do now was lay in bed and think about Mark, about what he would do without the love and closeness they had shared. Part of him wanted to hate Mark for going off to California and leaving him.

The small voice in the back of his head whispered, *selfish*. He ignored it.

~~

Dinner that evening featured grilled Fox. He told his parents everything. At first they were angry.

"What did he mean, having an affair with you? You're just a kid." Papa had trouble keeping his voice down.

"He's so much older than you," Dad said. His tone was quieter, but harder. He was really angry. "He had no business making you do—"

"He didn't *make* me do anything," Fox said loudly. "*I* was the one who started it. *I* wanted it. Don't you understand? He wouldn't have—"

"I understand he wanted you to think that way." Papa Gerry's voice was loud. "He's old enough to know—"

Fox got up from the table abruptly and threw down his napkin. "You don't understand anything!" he yelled. "You're not listening to me!"

Fox ran into his room and slammed the door, tears streaming down his face. He fell down on his bed and angrily wiped his cheeks. He had never felt so miserable. Except after he lost Sonia.

And now even his fathers didn't understand. Isolation and loneliness washed over him again. He turned over, his eyes burning.

Lucky jumped up onto the bed and curled up on the pillow. Gently the cat rubbed his face against Fox's cheek as though reassuring him, then padded silently down the bed and settled on Fox's stomach. The warm weight helped steady his breathing and gave him a measure of comfort.

Well, he thought, *at least I have a letter.*

He picked up the envelope and tore it open. His mother's scrawl brightened his mood a little. He loved her letters. He read about Tango and Jose, about what was going on in Chugwater, about her paintings. It made him forget about himself for a few minutes. He was even happier when she said that she looked forward to seeing him this summer.

He hoped his fathers would let him go. He needed it.

CHAPTER 24

Fox settled into Tango's saddle. He smelled the warm earth and fresh grass, and he felt almost happy for the first time in weeks. He was grateful his fathers had let him come to Wyoming. Somehow the huge, desolate landscape made him feel better.

Sitting up straight again, Fox urged Tango forward. His muscles were still a bit sore so he sent a mental command and *nudged* the horse to go slowly. He had been helping Mr. Taunton put out hay for the horses all morning. It was hard work, but the forty dollars in his pocket made Fox forget about his shoulders. The warm sun felt good.

Maybe later he'd go into town, see if any new magazines had come in, go to the library and email his dads. He wanted to tell them how the first week back had gone. Unbidden, the picture of Mark lying on the bed rose in Fox's mind. He waited for the sharp pain that usually accompanied these memories. It wasn't as raw as it had been when Mark left three weeks ago.

His parents had been right. They told him the hurt would never go away. His mother added that the misery *did* get less in time. Maybe grownups weren't completely clueless.

He *urged* Tango into a trot, ignoring the aches, and got home quickly. After he took care of the horse, he banged open the screen door. "Hey, Mom, I'm home," he called.

"I'm back here," she answered from her studio. "And don't—"

"I know. Don't bang the door."

"Yeah, so don't." Mom turned around as Fox walked into the studio. "I swear, kid, you get better looking every day."

"Sure," Fox said. He grabbed his mother around the waist and planted a kiss on her cheek. "Look who my parents are."

She swatted him playfully on his backside.

"Listen, Mom, is it okay if I take the bike and go into town this afternoon?" Marta had bought a bicycle in the spring just for his use when he came out.

"Okay," she said, turning back to the easel. "Just be home before dark."

Fox turned to go, then paused to look carefully at the painting. Most of her work showed the countryside around Chugwater, sometimes with faces in the clouds above the hills. This one was different.

A dark cave with stalagmites and stalactites filled the canvas. In the center a girl huddled, lit by a brilliant light that fell from a hole in the roof of the cavern. The details of the cave were painted in, but the girl was just sketched.

She looked like Sonia.

Fox was shaken. "Where did you get the idea for this?" he asked, trying to keep his voice level.

"From you. I *saw* it last year, and I've been planning it out ever since. Do you mind?" Fox *felt* her concern even before she turned a worried glance on him.

Fox thought for a moment before he answered. "No. No. I really don't mind. It's just the way it should be. But—"

"What?" she said when he didn't continue.

"Could you make it a little more hopeful? Like maybe she's looking up at the light, maybe reaching for it? Like she thinks she can find her way out?"

"Sure, hon. Makes it a better picture that way." She smiled and went back to work.

Fox left whistling.

Fox thought about the town as he rode the bike along the deserted road. The Chugwater Soda Fountain boasted a wooden bar, supposed to be from England. The soda equipment was the oldest in Wyoming. According to the signs, it was from a dead railroad town called Rock Creek. The place was supposed to be a real tourist attraction.

It also had a really cute waitress. Her name was Lilah. Her long blonde hair was pulled back in a ponytail so you saw her slightly round face and bright blue eyes. She didn't look like the pictures of models that he had seen, or like actresses in movies. She was rounder. Not fat, but more solid. Her legs were shorter, her waist and hips fuller. And her breasts . . . Fox appreciated her looks. He just wasn't sure what he wanted to do about it.

Lilah was sixteen, a junior at the local high school. She earned spending money working behind the counter at the Soda Fountain. Whenever Fox came in, she had a pleasant word for him. They would chat about school. She was shocked to learn about the size of Stuyvesant, and Fox was amazed that her school had a total population of 60.

"But how'd you get that name?" she asked one day.

"Huh?" Brilliant answer.

"How come people call you Fox?"

"Well, y'know, my kinda red hair. And my pointy nose. Even my eyes."

"I like your eyes," Lilah said, smiling up at him. "Never seen any like 'em."

Fox *sensed* that Lilah wouldn't mind if he asked her out. He felt shy, though. After all, she was more than a year older than he was, and her life was so different. Considering the way most people in Wyoming felt about homosexuality, he wasn't sure if he could tell her about his dads.

He braked to a stop in front of the store and leaned the bike against the wall. When he walked into the cool dimness he spotted Lilah relaxing in one of the booths.

"Hi, Lilah," he called.

Her bright smile greeted him. "Hi, Fox. What can I do for you?"

"Usual," he answered, sliding onto a stool at the counter.

Lilah walked behind the bar and started making the black and tan ice cream soda. Fox had introduced her to the treat at the beginning of the summer. She had tasted it and proclaimed it "okay," but it was obviously not something she loved. There was only one other person who ever appreciated this combination.

"So how ya doin' today?" Lilah asked. She placed the ice cream soda in front of Fox and leaned across the bar opposite him.

"Good. Did some work for Taunton this morning." He stirred the soda with his straw and shoveled a large spoonful of ice cream into his mouth.

"Hey, y'don't have to finish the whole thing in one bite," she laughed. Her nose crinkled in a delightful way.

Fox blushed and choked slightly. Then he laughed, too. "It's real warm out there, and I worked hard this morning."

They were silent for a minute. Then Lilah said, "There's a new picture in Cheyenne tonight. *Sherlock Holmes 4*."

Fox nodded, but he didn't say anything.

"It should be good. I'd like to see it. Wouldn't you?" she asked, looking up at him through her lashes.

Fox knew what she wanted him to say. He had trouble finding the words. "Yeah. But I don't drive," he finally managed to get out.

"I do. I even have my own car." The invitation was obvious, even to him.

"Um. Well, if you drive, c'n I take you to the movies tonight?"

Lilah grinned. "Yeah, that'd be nice. I'll pick you up at six thirty, okay?"

"Cool," he answered. Inside he was shouting.

As he rode home, the elation vanished. He'd never been on a real date before. The study sessions with Mark weren't the same thing. How was he supposed to act? What should he say?

Why did he ever get himself into this?

Fox opened the door as quietly as possible. It was after midnight and he didn't want to wake his mother. He wished it was morning so he could tell her all about it.

The light in the great room was on, turned down to low. Marta was sitting on the couch. She put down the book she was reading as Fox walked into the room.

"Mom! You waited up," he said, surprised.

"Of course. I had to know how your first date went." She patted the couch next to her. "Tell me."

Fox sat down. "It was great. I mean, the picture was kinda lame. Y'know, a lot of fake fighting and bad English accents. Lots of explosions and stuff. But it was fun. And Lilah's really cool. She's easy to talk to."

He didn't say anything about the kiss on the cheek Lilah had given him before he got out of the car.

"Oh, and, Mom." He hugged her. "Thanks for all the tips about how to act and stuff. It helped a lot."

She smiled. "What're moms for? Well, I'm going to bed. It's been a long day. Don't stay up too late."

Fox watched his mother walk to her room. She was pretty, for an older woman. He understood why his fathers loved her. He got a glass of milk from the kitchen and came back to the couch. The events of the day crowded his mind. He needed to think.

He liked Lilah, liked being with her. He felt attracted to her. Was he betraying Mark? The memory of Mark's lips and hands came back to him, but didn't overwhelm him. That shocked him. Was he forgetting Mark already?

So was he gay, or was he straight? Or bi? It was too confusing. The thoughts swirled in his head, making him feel dizzy.

At least he didn't have to keep his shields tight, he thought as he relaxed on the couch. That was one of the great things about living here.

He stood up and stretched. The problems could wait until tomorrow.

⌐——

Over the next month and a half, Fox took Lilah to the movies every weekend. He figured that meant they were boyfriend and girlfriend, even though they didn't talk much. Usually just a few words about the movie, or what they did during the week. Not like it had been with Mark. They had talked for hours about schoolwork, science fiction, their families, what lay out there in the stars.

Lilah seemed happy to be quiet. Sometimes, after the movie, they stretched out on the hood of her car and looked at the sky.

One clear night, Fox tried to start a conversation. "So waddaya think is out there?"

"I dunno." She shifted on the hard metal. "An' I don't care much."

"But wouldn't it be cool to find out? I mean, to really see other planets and stuff?"

"The Bible says God created the Earth. It doesn't say anything about other planets." That finished it as far as she was concerned.

Their kisses became more passionate. Fox enjoyed kissing her and liked the feel of her small, soft hands on his back and arms. She allowed him to put his hands under her blouse and over her breasts, a sensation that pleased him and left him wanting more. As he kissed her and ran his hands over her body, he felt the mounting pressure he had felt with Mark. He also *felt* her response.

Lilah always stopped him before it went too far.

"I like you a lot," she said one night, pulling back. "But I signed a pledge in school that I wouldn't—you know—go all the way until I'm married. Almost all of us did."

Fox straightened his clothes before he answered. "Why?"

"It's a sin. And we don't want to get pregnant, of course!" Lilah's tone of voice showed that she thought he was a dummy.

"There are ways . . ."

"Oh, we learned all about that in Sex Ed. Condoms don't work all the time. Neither does anything else." Lilah fished her comb out of her pocket and turned the rear-view mirror so she could see herself. "Did you know that girls who get pregnant and get abortions are so depressed they commit suicide? Yeah, we learned about that, too. Anyway, abortion's a sin against God."

Fox was speechless. He had never heard that kind of nonsense before and he couldn't figure out how to start answering her.

The next day he had the arguments in place. Fox rode into town to the Soda Fountain. Lilah was behind the bar looking at the old TV set perched in a corner. The newscaster was talking about the possibility of getting rid of the Defense of Marriage Act, and the new push in California to pass a law allowing same sex marriage.

She turned around as Fox walked in. "Did you see this?" Her voice was shrill with outrage. "They want to make this kind of sin *legal!*"

"Huh?" He never talked about his family, worried about the reaction of the people in a state that had witnessed the murder of Matthew Shepherd.

"Queers marrying," Lilah went on. "Can you imagine? It shouldn't be allowed. It's—it's an abomination in the sight of God. They're perverts, that's what they are."

Fox was shocked for a moment. How could she say things like that? What kind of person was she?

He finally pulled himself together enough to say, "Uh, I'm sorry, Lilah. I just came in to say I can't see you this Saturday. My mom has stuff she needs me for." He was amazed at how easily the lie came.

"Oh, sure, Fox. I understand. I'm sorry you can't come to the movies. It's gonna be a good one. I'll ask Sarah or someone."

Fox barely kept himself from running out the door.

As he rode home, her words circled in his head. He couldn't understand it. Her ideas were—wrong, outdated, stupid . . . He ran out of descriptions.

He skidded into the yard, but he got himself under control enough to put the bicycle away in the barn. It was supposed to rain tonight, and he didn't want it to be ruined.

Marta was in the kitchen when he came in. "Hi, sweetie. You're home early. What—"

Fox slumped into a chair breathing hard.

"What's the matter, hon? What happened? Are you okay?"

"I'm fine, Mom," he reassured her.

"No you're not. Something's wrong. Tell me."

Fox repeated the conversation he'd had with Lilah, including what she told him on their last date. "Mom, how can she be so stupid? I mean, she's not a bad person, but her ideas are so—" He shrugged in disgust and frustration.

"She's not stupid, Fox, just brainwashed. She believes what she's been told. What everyone around her believes."

"How can you live here with these people?" Fox stood up suddenly and started pacing, unable to contain his anger. "They're so . . . narrow. They don't *think*!"

Marta sighed. "I've learned not to talk about certain subjects."

Both of them were silent for a moment. Then Fox said, "Well, I can't see her any more. It's just too weird."

"Then you have to tell her. Make up an excuse if you have to, but you can't just leave her."

"I can't see her again. She's like a monster in a beautiful body. I can't—"

Marta came around and stood in front of her son. She grabbed him by the shoulders and shook him. "Yes, you can. You have to. What're you gonna do, drop her without an explanation? Mark didn't do that to you."

Fox dropped his eyes. He remembered his last meeting with Mark. The older boy had been so kind, so understanding. Fox pleaded with him not to leave. Mark folded Fox in his arms and kissed him, then just held him while he cried.

He figured Mom was right. He had to tell Lilah. He didn't know how, but he would figure it out.

Fox looked up at his mother. "She said that queers were perverts." He snorted on the last word. "What does she know? Norrie's moms would never do what Sonia's father did. A fine, upstanding married man."

"Yeah," Marta agreed. Fox *felt* her disgust as she remembered what he had *shown* her. "He was a real pervert. A real—"

"Bastard? Son of a bitch?" Fox knew how much his mother hated using that kind of language.

"Too mild for him," she said, turning to leave the room.

"Shit head? Cocksu—"

Marta swatted him on the back of his head before he could finish the last word. "See? You haven't run out of words."

Yeah, Fox thought, *except when it came to saying good-bye.*

He'd never been good at that.

Lying in bed that night, Fox knew that he could do it the easy way. He could go inside Lilah's head, plant the idea that she didn't love him, or even like him that much. That *she* wanted to break up with *him*. It would be so easy. Just a bit of a nudge, a small change—

No! He had decided he would never do that, never go inside anyone's head again. It was too dangerous.

He would have to rely on words. But which ones?

Fox reached for calm so he could sleep, but his thoughts were too riled. At home, he would stroke Lucky and share her mind, but she wasn't here. But maybe, if he could find another mind . . .

He checked for the shadow before he relaxed his shields. He *sensed* his mother's sleepy thoughts as she drifted off. He *felt* her love for him, her satisfactions with her paintings. Then her thoughts turned to his Dad, to Pete, and the thoughts and memories were too personal. He pulled away in a hurry.

He pushed his mind out to *feel*, very faintly, the animals that inhabited the nighttime landscape outside. There was a coyote on the hunt, alert to any movement that could indicate prey. It was tense, wired. His mind jumped to a vole, the tiny creature quivering with awareness of anything that might be a threat.

He had never been able to stretch his power that far before. It was exciting. He knew he was growing up, and his ability was growing as well. How far would it go? How much power could he have?

Fox turned over, trying to get comfortable. The combination of his problems and the minds he had shared made him feel awake. He *reached* to the barn, to the slow, contented thoughts of the horses. Tango's thoughts were full of sun and running in the grass. The barn was warm, there was soft hay all around. Tango's thoughts grew hazier.

Feeling more relaxed, Fox pulled his shields tight and fell asleep.

CHAPTER 25

The next morning Fox rode out to the bend of the river on Tango. He needed to calm his mind and focus his thoughts so he could decide what to do about Lilah.

I can't go on with her, he thought. *She's bizarre. I can understand the aliens in Dad's stories more than her. But how do I do it? What do I say?*

He stopped at a spot near the water, but far enough away from it so there were no trees. He could see for miles, right up to where the buttes outlined the sky. It was isolated, no houses, no dudes on horseback, no one.

He sat back in Tango's saddle and lowered his shields. He was getting better all the time at keeping them up. It took less energy than it had at the beginning, but it was still a relief to bring them down. He *felt* the life of the high plains, the small animals scurrying fearfully from home to food source; the mind of his horse, slow moving and contented. If he allowed himself to go deeper, he could *sense* the grass and small trees whose thoughts were the slowest of all. He breathed deeply.

Now he could plan. Fox searched his memories of books he'd read and movies he'd seen. What examples of break-ups could he copy? How could he phrase—

Suddenly he became aware of the presence searching the emptiness. Like a searchlight. He slammed his shields into place, and the ghost-like feeling passed by. Fox dismounted. He had to walk around for a while to shake off the fear that had enveloped him.

It felt like a living creature, but somehow slippery, and Fox was sure it was looking for him. Only his shields kept him protected.

He had felt that shadow before, like the time he cured Lucky or the night that Sonia's father died. Maybe there were too many other minds in the city, too much distraction. He hadn't felt the thing in Wyoming until he used his powers to *see* his surroundings. Maybe if he kept his thoughts inside his own head he would be safe.

He had to talk to his mom about it. He jumped onto Tango and galloped home.

———

"So you don't feel it, Mom?" Fox asked after he told her what had happened.

"No," Marta replied slowly. "I don't. But then I don't use my ability, and I was never as strong as you. I try not to *see* into other people, let alone animals or plants."

They sat for a moment, listening to the silence.

Finally Fox said, "So I should chill for a while."

His mother nodded but the worried crease in her forehead didn't disappear. Fox got up and walked onto the porch. He had a lot to think about, and he still didn't know what to say to Lilah.

Yet the next week, there he was, riding the bike into town to talk to her. He had collected as many phrases and sentences as he could remember, and cobbled together something like a speech. His mouth was dry and his stomach was jumpy.

He tried to calm himself. All he had to do was make sure his shields were in place. And remember everything he'd read. And keep his temper in check.

He never learned to juggle.

Lilah was sitting at a booth reading a book. The picture on the cover showed a pirate holding a swooning girl whose filmy white negligee was ripped open revealing an expanse of pale flesh. She looked up as he walked in and smiled.

"Hi, Fox. I missed you."

"Yeah, me too." He found it difficult to look her in the eye, so he gazed at the book in her lap. "Whatcha reading?"

"Oh, it's real exciting, about pirates and girls getting kidnapped and stuff. I enjoy these historical stories."

"But doesn't it go against—" He stumbled. "I mean, your pledge and all."

"Oh, it's no problem *reading* about it."

Fox nodded. "Look, Lilah, we gotta talk. You got a minute?"

She nodded. "Mrs. Dayton, I'll be right outside," Lilah called into the back.

They walked out the door and sat down on the bench. Lilah turned to Fox. "What's up, Foxy?"

"I've been thinking a lot. About us"

Lilah was silent. She scratched her knee absently.

Fox noticed a mosquito bite right next to the dimple just below the thigh that he liked to—Tearing his thoughts away, Fox took a deep breath and looked down at his hands. "I like you, Lilah. A lot. And I like when we kiss and everything . . ."

"Yeah. Me, too. So?"

"But I know you took an oath that you wouldn't, y'know, go all the way. And I—" He pulled out one of the lines he'd found. "I don't want to make you do something you'll regret. Something you'll hate me for." Now he looked up. He stared into her eyes, projecting earnestness. "I respect you too much for that."

Her tone got harder. "So-o-o-?"

"So I think it'd be better if we didn't see each other any more."

Lilah looked at him, her blue eyes narrowed. "Are you breaking up with me?"

Fox looked down again. "I guess so."

"Because I won't sleep with you?"

"No," Fox began. Then he reconsidered. "Well, yeah, in a way. Look, Lilah, you have really strong ideas, and I understand that. It's not you, it's me." What a cliché, he thought. "I can't trust me. Do you see? You're just too beautiful."

"Hmph." Lilah turned away. When she turned back, her eyes were hard. "Fox Monroe, if you're just saying that to get me to—"

"No, I'm not! Honest. It's just—" This had gone a lot better in his head. "You're a good girl. I would never want to—you know, hurt you."

"I can't decide if you're the best guy I ever knew or just the best liar," she said, shaking her head. "But I'm gonna give you the benefit of the doubt."

"Thanks." Fox smiled.

"It's not like you're the only fish in the sea. There're lots of other boys out there, y'know."

"I know, Lilah. And you'll find the one that's right for you." God, one cliché after another. "I—I'll always remember you." That much was true, anyway.

"Good-bye, Fox. I'll never forget you, either." She smiled.

Fox kissed her on the cheek and mounted his bicycle. All he felt was relief.

~

The next three weeks passed quickly. Even though he didn't feel the shadow didn't appear again, Fox was careful not to use his talent. He felt that part of him was missing. He had become so used to *sensing* the thoughts of people and animals around him that not doing it was unnatural.

On the plane ride home he thought long and hard about how much had changed in the past two years. He was glad the whole story would never be told. Everyone would think it was one of Dad's science fiction novels.

His mind drifted from there to the big news he had gotten on his last phone call home. One of Dad's books was going to be made into a movie. It was one of the robot stories about mechanical people who grow beyond their programming and fall in love. Fox always liked that one. It was so beautiful. Of course, he would never admit it. That'd be too uncool.

It's gonna be a good year, he thought. *Dad's movie is gonna be great, I just know it. I'm gonna be a sophomore, all kinds of new classes—*

Without Mark.

The familiar sadness. Fox knew it would always be there, like the thoughts of Sonia. The emotions were growing less painful, even the memory of Lilah was fading. Damn! Did grown-ups always have to be right?

CHAPTER 26

Fox turned fifteen that October. The family celebrated with a small dinner at Cyril's, just his dads and him. Of course, Cyril went a little over the top with the cake—three layers with intricate designs of loops and swirls.

"If you were Mexican—and if you were a girl—this would be your quincinera," Cyril sighed. "Oh, well, there's always your eighteenth to look forward to."

Fox smiled. It was just Cyril being Cyril.

From then on, things got even better. School went well. Mr. Flores, his guidance counselor, called him in for a conference after the first report card. "Your grades in math are better this year," he commented after looking over the records in front of him.

"Yeah, I understand it more." Fox smiled. "Geometry and trig are more . . . I can sort of see them, the shapes and figures. I couldn't do that in algebra."

Mr. Flores nodded. "Your other grades are good, too. And I see you're on the staff of the literary magazine. That will look good on your college application."

Fox blinked several times in surprise. "College? But I'm only a sophomore. I'm not thinking about college yet."

"You should be. These things count—grades, extra-curricular activities, service. Your work with "Greener New York" is good. It shows environmental awareness and a desire to help. Keep that up. We'll talk more at the end of the year. Keep up the good work."

During the year three of Fox's stories were published in the literary magazine. Dad put those copies of the magazine on the living room shelf, right next to his own books. Fox looked at them every time he passed.

He still missed Mark, but not as much as he thought he would. He enjoyed the texts and IM's from California. They gave him a glimpse of college life, and Mark's descriptions of the professors and the other students were often funny.

Fox started dating. Real dates, not study plus make-out sessions, or movie and make-out. Dates where he talked to the other person. He didn't want sex, he wanted love. Most of the time he went out with girls, but he saw boys as well. He couldn't find the feeling that swept him up and joined him to another.

Most of his friends told him he was crazy.

Vijay's long, slender face was wrapped in a grimace. "Why're you trying to complicate it? If you like the person, go ahead. If not, say good-bye."

Clark looked at Fox through his dark-framed glasses. He had a serious take on it. "Most biologists agree that it's simply a matter of pheromones. You are either attracted or you aren't." But his eyes glinted mischievously.

Even his fathers chimed in. "You're fifteen," Dad said. "Give it time."

Papa nodded. "You'll know when it's right."

Fox wasn't convinced.

There was nothing from Sonia. As the months flew by and the anniversary of her father's death approached, her absence preyed on Fox's mind. All he wanted was to hug her, hear her say she forgave him, drive the sadness away for both of them. The futility of his dream hurt.

Dad's movie progressed. It meant he had to be in Hollywood a lot, but he came home as often as he could. Over Christmas vacation he flew Pop and Fox out to watch the filming. It was so exciting that Fox didn't even want to go up to Stanford although Mark was there.

When the film was released in the spring, Fox guilted the entire staff of the literary magazine into going to see it. They joined the science fiction crowd outside the theater. Fox led them inside, pointing proudly to the poster with Dad's name on it.

The girls emerged from the darkened theater teary-eyed, and the boys spent a lot of time clearing their throats. Even though Fox had read the story many times, he had to admit he was moved. They all proclaimed it a success, and he beamed.

The final report card came out in June. Fox's grades were high enough that he could take two Advanced Placement classes the next year, as well as the science fiction class. And he was accepted onto the swim team.

The world looked bright and colorful to him he flew out to Wyoming for his third summer with his mother. He felt like a frequent flyer as he navigated the security check and shoved his carry-on into the overhead compartment.

Marta met him at the airport. He saw her as soon as he walked down the hallway from the gates. It was a surprise. She never liked coming into Cheyenne, and actively hated the airport. Too many people. But she smiled and waved and Fox ran to her and swept her up in a huge hug.

"You've grown," she said, breathlessly.

Fox smiled down at her, drinking in her face. He missed the closeness of their relationship that went beyond the usual mother-son bond. But he also noticed the lines of pain starting to form around her mouth and eyes, the way they always did when they were in a crowed. He hurried them out of the airport as fast as he could.

When they were back in the quiet solitude of her house, Marta relaxed. The savory smell of stew made Fox's mouth water. He settled back in his chair as his mother dished out the salad fresh from her garden. As they ate, she outlined the events of the summer.

"I've got a show in Santa Fe next month. Joshua'll be there. He asked about you. Said he's looking forward to seeing you."

Surprised, Fox swallowed a mouthful of hot stew too fast. "I didn't think he liked me," he sputtered.

Marta dismissed the idea with a shrug. "Well, I guess he does." Then she went on to describe how she wanted to enlarge the garden and maybe get a cell phone.

Fox was enthusiastic about the second part of the plan. He'd been encouraging her to get a cell for a year, ever since they put towers on the butte near her house.

On the other hand, pulling weeds was way low on his list of favorite activities, so the thought of a larger area to maintain dimmed his excitement. When he worked in the garden the next week, he seemed to be sweating more than usual.

"Hey, Mom," he called, letting the screen door swing shut behind him as he walked into the kitchen.

"Don't slam—"

"I know, don't slam the door."

"But you keep on doing it. So don't." She looked up from the dried herbs she was cutting. "What's up?"

"Is it me, or is it hotter here than it used to be?"

Marta looked puzzled for a moment. Then she nodded. "Now that you mention it, maybe it is. I didn't use as much wood last winter. Global warming, you think?"

He accompanied Marta to Cheyenne to buy a cell phone, then taught her how to use it. She was delighted with it, like a little kid. Fox watched her stare intently at the device as she texted him. He smiled.

The show was a success, the garden got bigger, and the renovation started on his mother's studio. The workers were all men from the area. Lon was the boss, the one who drew up the plans and barked orders at the others. When his blue eyes got hard and steely and his gray moustache started to quiver, everyone knew to get out of his way.

Frankie and Adam were more easy-going. They were both younger, in their twenties, but they knew what they were doing.

"I started out helping my Dad build the extension on our house," Frankie told Fox. "I like the work, like doing stuff with my hands. Here, you wanna try?"

"I dunno," Fox answered. "I never built anything."

He looked at his mother, who shrugged and glanced over at Lon.

"Okay by me, as long as he helps. But," he said, glaring at Marta, "if he gets hurt or killed it's on your head."

Marta raised her eyebrows, but nodded her agreement.

"Likely to kill him myself if he slows us down," Lon added as he turned away.

At first all he did was haul lumber or nails for the others. When they finally let him use a hammer, he hit the wood, and sometimes his thumb, more often than the nail. But he learned, and actually got a few compliments from the guys. The frame went up, the rest followed quickly. Fox was surprised to find that he was proud of himself.

He stuck to his resolution and didn't use his power, except in very limited ways. So he *sent* his instructions to Tango or briefly *shared* thoughts with his mother, but otherwise kept his shields up.

At the end of the summer, Marta announced that she was going to teach Fox to drive.

"Mom, you're the coolest!" he said. He wanted to jump up and down. Then he stopped. "But I'm still only fifteen."

"If you're gonna be here every summer, you have to know how to drive," Marta said as though it was obvious.

"The cops—"

"If we stay to the back roads nobody'll bother us."

She was right.

At the end of the first lesson, they looked back at the dirt road. A track was etched in the dust that looked like a sidewinder's path, curving back and forth from one edge to the other.

Marta looked at him and raised one eyebrow. "Well, not the worst I've seen. We'll have you driving yet."

As they drove to the airport for his flight back to New York, he couldn't believe how fast the summer had gone. He didn't feel like the same person he'd been a year ago. Last summer he had been a hurt, confused kid. He was more in control now, far more mature. After all, now he knew how to drive, as well as plant a garden and pound a nail. Would he ever need this knowledge? It didn't matter.

Fox walked into the school cafeteria at the beginning of the year. He was smiling. He liked his classes. He had the two Advanced Placement classes he wanted, and science fiction. The swim team had set up a practice schedule.

All he needed to complete the picture was a lover. Not someone to just have sex with, but someone he could love, and who would love him. Maybe even a person he could talk to about his telepathic ability, and eventually tell about Sonia and her father.

His bright mood darkened slightly. Then he spied his friends at the table they had commandeered. They waved at him and he waved back. He was eager to tell them everything that had happened over the summer.

He paid for his lunch and was walking to the table when his phone vibrated. He fished it out of his pocket and looked at the screen.

And nearly dropped the phone and the food.

It was from Sonia. After almost three years, she was getting in touch with him. His smile broadened as he read the screen.

<Happy 16th b n nyc nxt mth email 2 follo>

What a birthday present, he thought, a huge grin spreading over his face. *We'll spend our birthday together.*

He made his way to the science fiction table. The usual group was there, Effie, Shawn, Vijay, Clark. Fox pulled out a chair and sat, still grinning. He couldn't stop.

Vijay stared at him. "Hey, dude, cheer up."

"Just got some great news." Fox felt like standing on the table and shouting it out to the world. "Heard from an old friend. I haven't seen her in a couple of years."

"She must be one helluva friend, she got you grinning like that," Effie smiled. Effie was one of the girls Fox had dated the year before, but there was no jealousy in her tone.

"She was my best friend when we were kids. Then she moved away. I didn't hear from her until now."

He wanted to tell them about running through Washington Square Park and combined birthday parties. He knew that he wouldn't. They couldn't understand and anyway it didn't matter.

Soon she'd be here.

He told his fathers when he got home. They were happy for him and started suggesting a combined birthday party at the end of October. Not as huge as the thirteenth, but larger than ordinary.

Fox flashed on memories of that party. The last time he'd been truly happy. Maybe he could recapture that feeling.

Time slowed, the way it always did when he wanted it to rush. The two months seemed an eternity. Most of his classes were okay, especially the science fiction class, but the work was hard.

Over and over, he imagined their meeting. She'd run to him and hug him and everything would be the way it was when they were kids. No, that couldn't happen.

They'd hug and she'd forgive him and say they could be friends again, but long distance. They could email and text and maybe see each other every once in a while. He would finally have someone his own age he could really talk to, who knew his secrets and understood.

At other times he felt down. He imagined that they could never be friends again, never be close, that she never wanted to see him or hear from him again, and that she wanted to tell him that face to face.

The images tumbled in his mind along with the memories of ice cream sodas and Harry Potter.

The days dragged on until the text message finally arrived. <@ Norrie cmon.>

He grabbed his coat. "Sonia's here! Goin' over to Norrie's," he called to his fathers as he dashed out the door.

They waved at him. "Don't be too late," Dad called.

—~

When Norrie answered the door, she said something about her parents were out for the evening. Fox barely heard. He saw Sonia as soon as the door closed behind him. She stood in the middle of the living room. A white silky blouse hinted at a voluptuous figure and black jeans hugged her hips.

She's even more beautiful than ever, Fox thought. He walked hesitantly toward her, not certain about her reaction. He tightened his shields to avoid the temptation of *searching* her mind. She would tell him how she felt.

At the last moment, she ran to him and threw her arms around his neck. "Oh, Fox, I missed you."

The joy and surprise weakened his shields for a moment and he *sensed* her. He hesitated before he hugged her back. There was a darkness in her, a whirlpool of sadness and . . . He couldn't penetrate it.

Norrie came over and put her arms around them. "It's so good to see the two of you. Y'know, together again. But c'mon, the rest of the gang'll be here any minute. We have so much to catch up on."

The crew arrived shortly. Fox didn't have a chance to say much to Sonia before Joey burst in. He wasn't "Fat Joey" any more. He was taller and thinner, even good-looking. Kim and Mercedes stood close to Joey, smiling up at him. Fox felt comforted, surrounded by his friends.

It was impossible to get near Sonia for a while. The other kids clustered around her, pumping her for information about her school and friends. Fox looked at her over his own circle of admirers, caught her eye. They stared at each other for a long moment.

Then they both excused themselves. They escaped to Norrie's room and sat facing each other on the bed.

Fox broke the silence. "I missed you so much, Sonia. There's so much to tell, about me, about my mother. It's been too weird."

She nodded and reached into her jeans pocket. She pulled out a small pill box, opened it and offered it to Fox. "Here, have one. It makes conversation easier."

"What is it?"

"Ecstasy. Just a small one. It's nice."

For a moment he couldn't talk. When he could, he said, "When did you start this?" He wanted her to explain, make him understand so he could help her. Instead, all he saw was the hungry half-smile on her face as she lifted the golden top.

Sonia took one of the pills and popped it in her mouth. "Mmm," she said, closing her eyes. "Give it a minute. It'll kick in and everything'll be righteous."

Fox stared at her. He couldn't believe she needed a pill to talk to him. He was so shocked by her behavior that he lost his shields. Her mind was a jumble of sensation and images. Underneath was the darkness, the sadness, the self-hatred, the guilt.

He wanted to *reach* inside her and erase the bad feelings he found there. To restore that sparkling, chocolate-flavored *scent* that was hers. But he couldn't. A stranger who looked like Sonia faced him.

"What are you doing to yourself?" Fox blurted.

Sonia stared at him. "It's just a little pill. Helps everything make sense."

"No, it doesn't. Sonia, you gotta . . ." Fox's frustration made him lose the words.

"I don't *gotta* do anything. Except try to be happy." Her eyes narrowed and her voice got harsh. "D'you know how hard it is for me to be happy? What I have to do—"

"You don't have to do *this*! You could—"

"What do you know about me? About my life now?" Tears ran down her cheeks. She stood, her back to him.

Fox walked over and put his hand on her shoulder. She turned.

Her pupils were dilated, and the muscles in her face went slack. The tears dried on her face and a smile that never reached her eyes parted her lips.

Fox stepped back. He felt helpless.

Sonia moved closer to him. Her voice was slurred. "I have lots of friends now. We could be friends again if you wanted to." Now she was right in front of him, so close that they were almost touching. "You're even better looking than when we were kids. Your eyes are so . . . I always had a thing for you, y'know. And I wouldn't mind at all if we . . ." She let the words trail off as she suggestively opened a button of her blouse.

He was so shocked that for a moment he couldn't move. Then her face was next to his, her breath in his ear as she kissed his neck. Her arms went around him and her lips traced a burning path to his mouth as her tongue pressed in softly, probing and caressing.

Unwillingly he felt himself responding. The tingle spread from his knees to his groin. But this wasn't right. He couldn't do this.

"No," he said. He pushed Sonia away more roughly than he intended. He grabbed her shoulders and shook her gently. "Don't do this, Sonia. Please."

"Why not? All the other boys like it," she said sulkily. She moved away from him.

"Well, I don't. Not like this."

"I'm not good enough for you, huh?" Her voice was accusing. "You don't like me?"

"I love you," he said simply. "I always have. I don't want anything like this, not if you need pills just to talk to me."

Her voice rose. "Well, I don't need you. I got others. They do things for me. They give me things. Not like you. All you ever gave me was grief."

Her words stung.

"I just wanted to make you happy," he said miserably. "Just keep you safe. I want to keep you safe now."

"Oh, yeah?" Sonia said, her voice shrill. "And who are you gonna kill this time?"

~

Fox didn't remember how he left the party. He walked the streets of his neighborhood the way he had three years ago, feeling the familiar gray fog wrap around him. Had he done this to her?

His mind told him that it wasn't entirely his fault, that it was her father's. But his gut said it was him, and he couldn't shake the feeling. Everything he touched turned to shit. He tried to help, and instead he hurt. He tried to love, and he was rejected. Was this why he had the power?

Was he going to be alone for his whole life?

It isn't fair! he howled silently to the universe.

He walked the familiar streets, trying to shake the feelings of failure and despair. *Okay,* he thought after a while, *that's the way things are. I can't let anyone love me, it's too dangerous. I can't love anyone, I'll only end up hurting them. I don't need love, I don't need anyone. Just enjoy the ride.*

CHAPTER 27

Fox fled to Wyoming that summer. He felt he had to *share* what had happened with his mother, sure that she would understand.

At the end of his second day, they sat on the porch in their usual chairs watching the sun set. He lowered his shields and *showed* Marta what had happened with Sonia.

When they returned to themselves, there were tears in his mother's eyes. "I'm sorry, hon. Really, really sorry."

He nodded.

"You realize it isn't your fault, don't you? You didn't make her that way."

"I know it in my head. But my gut tells me different."

"Guts are pesky, I know. But I trust you, Fox. You'll get it right."

"There's more, Mom. Look." He *showed* her the memories.

Pop is lying on the green couch in the living room. He has a compress over his eyes. He looks up and smiles. "It's only a headache," he says.

Impression of time passing. Fox walks down the hallway and hears his fathers talking softly. The conversation stops abruptly as he enters the room.

A night scene. In his bed. He lowers his shields and catches bits of thought. From Pop, "Don't say anything yet . . . too young . . . might put him back in the hospital." From Dad, "He should know . . . find out eventually."

"And they won't talk to me about it," he said pulling out of the contact.

"They love you, they want to protect you."

"I don't need protection!" The anger that was always close to the surface now sparked.

"I'd say you do. What's all this about *just along for the ride* and *not getting close*? What are you doing to yourself?"

That stopped him. Not only was it the same question he had asked Sonia, but he felt a curious reluctance about discussing this with his mother. How could he tell her that the short times he spent making love, sharing the orgasm of his partner, were the only times he could do without his shields? They were respites from the constantly nagging guilt, concern and frustration that were his companions.

As for his determination to stay out of people's minds, he rationalized. He wasn't going in deep. He was only skimming.

There was one thing he could say. "You gotta understand, Mom. I'm toxic. I hurt the people who love me."

"You never hurt me. Or your fathers."

"But I never tell my dads the whole truth. So I can't get close to them. Not like with you."

"Sweetie, you wouldn't consciously hurt someone. I know you."

"Yeah, well, conscious or not, I manage. I have to keep cool. I *have* to."

The next afternoon he was on Tango, slowly wandering along the river. Even though he could drive now, Fox preferred taking one of the horses out onto the grassland. Communing with the uncomplicated mind of animals was soothing. Checking briefly for the shadow, he *relaxed* his shields, and sent his mind out *searching* for the small thoughts of the inhabitants of the area.

Suddenly, he *sensed* the evil presence.

He clapped his shields up and rode back home trying to make sense of it.

His mother *sensed* his confusion when he walked through the door. "What's the matter?"

"I *felt* the shadow again." He tried to shake off the fear encounters with the shadow always brought. "It never bothers me in the city," he went on, speaking as much to himself as his mother. "And out here, only when I try to stretch out my thoughts. Why?"

"Like I said before, maybe there are just too many people in the city. It gets confused, or something."

"And it never bothers you—"

"—because I never *send*, and I can't *stretch* the way you do."

147

Fox nodded and followed Marta into the kitchen. She got out a large pot and started assembling the peppers, onions and rice for a vegetable chili. He took his usual station at the small island where the salad ingredients were already laid out.

Marta spoke without looking at him. "Have you thought about what I said? Y'know, about your fathers?"

"Yeah. I guess you're right." He tore the spinach leaves angrily. "But I don't have to like it."

They were both silent for a while. It was not quite the companionable quiet that Fox was used to with her.

Finally she stopped cutting. "And what about your . . . dating?"

"What about it?" He knew he sounded defensive, but he didn't care.

"Why don't we just open up—?"

"No. The shadow's too close." He was glad he had the excuse.

"Okay. I'm listening."

"I can't get involved. I explained that."

A soft grunt of disbelief answered him.

"Well, that's what *I* think. But as for seeing different people . . . I'm careful, Mom. I always use protection. And I only go out with people who feel the same way I do."

There was a puzzled frown on his mother's face. "What do you mean?"

"There're lots of kids my age who don't want commitment. There's this girl, Tiffani, we hook up every once in a while. And Sharif, a guy in my physics class. I'm not hurting anyone. And I'm not getting hurt."

His mother didn't speak for a while. Then she sighed. "Okay, Fox, I understand. I can't approve, but I understand. I just don't want to see you become that kind of man."

"What kind?" His tone was more defensive than he meant it to be.

"The kind that's given up on love. If you don't look, you'll never find it."

She didn't understand, Fox thought. *No one could.*

For the rest of the summer, Fox worked hard to the point of exhaustion. He hoped it would expel the negative feelings that stung him.

Instead, he flew back to New York in worse shape than he had left.

Fox walked out of the bright October sunshine into the dimness of the pizza place. It took a moment for his eyes to adjust. Then he saw his friends at the far table.

"Hey," he said as he walked over.

"Hey, yourself," Vijay said. His lanky form was sprawled in one of the metal chairs. "We were just comparing summer vacations."

Fox sat down and surveyed the group. The overhead lights picked out blonde highlights in Effie's long, brown hair, and Laurinda's dark skin almost glowed. They'd spent time in the sun. So had Vijay. His usually tan complexion was darker, and it looked as if he was trying to grow a moustache. Only Clark seemed unchanged. He'd obviously been locked in a computer dungeon all summer.

Laurinda started talking, picking up the story that Fox had interrupted. She went on about a trip to the Grand Canyon. As she described it in detail, Fox's mind wandered to his own problems.

Laurinda stopped talking. Fox snapped out of his reverie to find his friends looking at him.

"So, Casanova," Effie said. "How many hearts did *you* break this summer?"

Fox sat back in his chair, crossing his legs and pretending nonchalance. "None, sadly," he said. "Kinda slim pickin's there in the boonies."

Vijay and Clark chuckled, but Effie's face was serious. "Fox, you're getting a reputation, y'know. Love 'em and leave 'em Monroe. Shallow. They're saying you're toxic."

That word again. His temper flared. "What do *they* know? And why should I care?"

Laurinda's dark eyes were sad. "But it's not true. You're not like that."

"Maybe I am," Fox muttered. "And anyway, I'm just following advice."

"Who'd give you advice like that?" Effie scoffed.

"Them." Fox pointed at Vijay and Clark.

"What!" Vijay seemed puzzled, Clark merely amused.

"Remember last year, when I was looking for *true love*." He allowed his disdain to show. "And you—," he pointed at Vijay, "said something about not complicating it. And you—," pointing at Clark, "brought in pheromones and chemistry."

The two boys fidgeted in their seats.

"See," Fox spread his hands in demonstration and opened his eyes wide in pretended innocence. "Just taking advice."

"Whatever you call it," Effie said, "it's not right."

There was an uncomfortable silence.

Effie stood up. "I gotta go. See you tonight?"

Everyone nodded.

Laurinda looked at Fox. "Bernice'll be there. A new conquest." Her voice was hard.

The girls turned and hurried away.

"Dude, maybe they have a point," Vijay said quietly. His slender face was serious.

"No, they don't," Fox stood abruptly and walked out.

Once outside, his footsteps slowed. He was reluctant to go home. The apartment, that had always been his refuge, was now infused with secrets, worry and the underlying *sense* of pain coming from Pop.

He thought about what his friends had said. Barely submerged anger simmered under his skin. There was no one he could talk to.

He flirted with the idea of calling Doc Smallwood, but dismissed it. What could he say? *Hey, Doc, I can read minds and kill people long distance and everything I do turns out wrong.*

She'd have him back in the hospital in a New York minute.

No, he thought, *I'll have to figure this out on my own. Again. Not that my choices have been worth shit.*

⇛

Fox stayed in his room until dinner, and afterward retreated as soon as he could. He dressed quickly for his night of clubbing, and walked quietly into the living room. Pop and Dad were talking when Fox entered, but when they saw him their conversation ended quickly. Pop seemed withdrawn and he looked pale.

"You okay, Pop?" Fox asked softly looking at him closely as he sat down.

His father nodded but didn't speak.

Dad spoke up quickly as though trying to change the subject. "Where are you going tonight, Fox?"

"A club over in Gawannus. Just opened up."

Pop's voice was weak but he smiled. "Gawannus, huh? Was a time that was the most toxic place in New York."

The use of the word jolted Fox, stirring up the feelings of the afternoon with his friends. He said nothing.

"Who's going?" Pop didn't seem to notice Fox's discomfort.

"Science fiction crowd. New girl named Bernice. Seems nice." Fox knew he was being short in his answers, but he didn't want to be drawn into a discussion of his dating habits.

Dad looked hard at Fox. "What happened to Kareen? Or Brad?"

"Don't see them anymore." He glanced at the clock on the wall. "Look, it's getting late and I—"

Pop struggled slightly as he sat straighter. When he spoke his voice was stronger. "Fox, we have to talk. This business of seeing a different person every week . . . Your dad and I are worried."

Oh, great. They should worry about Pop, not me. Everyone should just leave me alone. I fuck up other people's lives and they worry about me.

He fought to control his anger. There was a vat of acid where his stomach usually sat. He stood. "I'm going." His voice was cold.

"Just wait one minute, young man." Dad's hazel eyes looked gray and hard.

The acid boiled over and sparked his rage. "No, I won't wait. I'm not a little kid anymore. You can't tell me what to do."

He grabbed his jacket and walked to the door. He turned to say good-bye, but his rage took control of his tongue. "Just because you're too old to remember what it's like, don't blame me."

He slammed out the door, ignoring Pop's weak call of "No. Fox. Wait. Please."

The chill air hit him as soon as he walked out of the building. Fox shivered. It was cold for September. Climate change showing again. Loose newspaper blew across the streets and black clouds reflected the city lights. It looked like a bloody bandage hanging over the buildings.

He fought to control his breathing, to keep the unintentional rage from breaking out. He felt that his head would burst.

I should end it, he thought. *If it were all over now everyone would be better off. They wouldn't have to worry or get angry.*

Instead he walked fast, trying to drive out the feelings that threatened to overwhelm him. The wind whipped his hair and stung his eyes. It didn't cool his temper. He couldn't meet his friends like this.

After a few blocks he stopped to call Effie. "Can't make it tonight," he mumbled when she answered. "Y'know, home things to do. They need me." It sounded lame in his own ears.

He heard her relay the news to the others. When she came back on her tone was sympathetic. "Sorry, Fox. Maybe next—"

"Yeah," he interrupted, and hung up.

He walked downtown to the Battery, through the deserted financial area. The narrow streets funneled the wind. Fox reveled in the chill, as though the suffering could make up for his behavior.

He turned east before he got to the waterfront. His feet seemed to move of their own volition over to the East Side where the more established upscale clubs were opening for the evening. He pushed past the well-dressed, jeweled couples without slowing down or apologizing.

The cold and exercise slowly drained his anger and he walked home, his footsteps slower. When he got home there was just one light on and his fathers were asleep. Breathing a sigh of relief, Fox walked quietly to his room.

The next morning he didn't want to wake up. He wanted to stay in bed all day. He didn't feel sick, just ashamed and worried.

It was after nine when he finally forced himself to get dressed and walk to the living room. Pop was lying on the couch, his eyes closed. The TV was on, but the volume was turned down. Dad was sitting in the easy chair not really watching. His gaze wandered over the room.

"Hey, Pops," Fox said softly. He was conscious of walking as quietly as he could, as though trying to make up for last night's harsh words.

"Shhh," Dad said. "Pop has another of those headaches."

"Sorry," Fox said. He walked over to the couch and kissed Pop on the forehead. "Does that make it better?"

Pop looked up at him. A small, pained smile crossed his lips. Then he turned to Dad. "Pete, don't do this."

"We have to," Dad answered. "He has a right to know."

"What's the matter?" Fox asked quickly.

"We didn't want to burden you with this, but *I* think it's necessary." Dad glanced at Pop and took a deep breath. "You know Pop has been having a lot of headaches and had a lot of tests. We got a text from the doctor. The results from the ones he took a couple of weeks ago are in. He wants to see us tomorrow."

Fox's heart raced. "When? Where? I want to be there."

Dad shook his head. "No, Fox. There's no need for that. You go to school tomorrow. It's probably nothing anyway."

But Fox's ability to detect a lie, even with his shields up, told him differently.

CHAPTER 28

"Earth to Fox. Come in, Fox," Effie said playfully.

"Huh?" Fox answered.

"Where *is* your head? Join the rest of us planet-bound folks, please."

"Sorry. I'm just kind of distracted."

Effie looked up into his face. She was so much like her older sister. Amy had been part of the original science fiction crowd when Fox had been a freshman, and Effie had her blue eyes and unaffected laugh. "What's the matter?"

"Nothing. It's just—no, never mind." Fox didn't want to talk about Pop now. He was too worried.

Effie shrugged and turned back to the group at the lunch table. They were talking about going to the next Comicon. Fox couldn't get his mind around it. The morning's classes had been endless. All he wanted was to go home. To find out about the tests. Pop *had* to be okay. He just had to be.

Fox went through his afternoon classes automatically. Even Mr. Weitzman's English class, the one he liked best, couldn't hold his interest. When he left, he felt the teacher's eyes on him, as though the man could tell he wasn't all there. He knew he would pay for it later, but he couldn't concentrate on anything.

After his last class he raced home.

Dad and Papa were sitting in the living room when he walked in. They sat next to each other on the green couch holding hands. Their faces looked grim.

Fox lowered his bookbag carefully to the floor and hung up his coat. Then he walked slowly to the easy chair and sat down. Suddenly, he was in no hurry to hear what his fathers had to say. He was afraid of the news.

Then Dad was telling him about a tumor in Papa Gerry's brain. A very aggressive, fast-growing cancer. It was inoperable but chemo would help. Everything would be okay.

Fox *sensed* the lie. It was like a red light flashing on and off above Dad's head. Chemo wouldn't help. Everything wouldn't be okay. Somewhere deep down he had known. It wasn't anything specific and he had tried to ignore it. Now he couldn't. Now the words had been spoken.

Dad went on for a while about plans, chemo schedules, but Fox wasn't listening. All he *heard* was the sorrow and loss. It was as if the pain was his own. He slammed his shields tight to avoid the feelings. But they were so strong they seeped through in spite of the protection.

When he felt that he could trust his voice, he looked from one to the other. "I want to be here for you guys, the way you've always been there for me. Anything I can do . . . I love you both so much!" His voice choked and he couldn't say anything else.

His fathers nodded. He could see tears in their eyes, too.

Fox went on, speaking around the lump in his throat. "And, Pop, what I said. Y'know, when you were talking to me about the people I dated. I'm sorry. You were right. And I'm gonna change. But I need you." Again, he had to stop.

"I know, dear," Pop said. He got up slowly and walked haltingly back to the bedroom.

Dad's face was pale and his eyes were red. "I know it's not fair, but we're going to lean on you now. From what the doctor said, it's going to get bad." He stopped to collect himself. "I didn't want this for you. *We* didn't want this for you. But we have to be hopeful. The chemo could work. Pop could get better." He sighed.

Fox walked to the couch and sat next to Dad, their arms around each other. "It'll be okay," Fox said through his tears.

"It has to be." Dad's voice was thick.

"I'll help," Fox said. "I'm not a little kid anymore. I'll help."

He and Dad didn't move for a long time.

Later that evening, Fox slipped into his parents' room. Pop was lying on the bed, not moving, but Fox forced himself to lower his shields and *feel* his father's thoughts. The pain and worry hung in the room like a bad smell.

Maybe I can help, like with Lucky, Fox thought. He had tried to do this with Joey, and failed, but that was many years ago. He was older, now, and stronger. Gently, he *fed* his mind into his father's, hunting for the root of the pain. But it was too difficult to follow the pathways, and the emotions were a barrier he couldn't get around.

He withdrew his mind, defeated.

Fox left the oppression of the apartment for a walk. He was numb. It was as though all emotion had been blasted out of him, leaving a dull ache where comfort and family used to be.

What remained was resolution. He had to be strong for his fathers. He didn't have to feel. In fact, it was better if he didn't. He simply had to do what needed to be done. Take care of Pop. Make sure that Dad didn't work himself to death. Just put one foot in front of the other.

As he walked, Fox felt determination like a thin, cooling breeze winding around the streets of the neighborhood. Other people were facing similar problems, dealing with hopelessness and sorrow, and dealing with it stoically. He could do it, too. And when he got too weak, he would be able to . . . borrow a little from the city. He could relax his shields and drink in the aura. The energy of so many people in one place could replenish his waning strength.

Like a vampire living off sips of blood from his pets, a voice in his head derided him.

No. Like a thirsty stranger getting a glass of water from a helpful farmer. Images of a raggedy man on horseback riding up to a cabin, drinking from a battered tin ladle replaced the bloody fangs. Yeah, that was it.

The mocking voice quieted, but didn't disappear.

It wasn't like he was going to drain anybody. All he had to do was lower his shields a little and allow a trickle of strength to enter, the way he did when he was fu—making love. Let a little feeling in. He could pay it back later. The shadow wouldn't bother him. It never did in the city, and he didn't *sense* it when he was the receiver, only when he broadcast.

Fox stood at the bathroom sink tipping dirty water out of the basin. He had been helping Dad give Pop a sponge bath. It had only been five months since the diagnosis, but Papa Gerry had deteriorated frighteningly fast. Now he couldn't even get up to use the bathroom and he had to wear a diaper. Most of the time he was out of it. He sang to himself, or stared off into space.

Fox spent hours sitting next to Pop's bed. He spoke, even though he knew Pop probably couldn't understand what he was saying. Sometimes, though, his father was lucid. One time, as Fox was sitting in the bedside chair, he turned and said, "I'm sorry, Son. You didn't sign on for this."

"Forget it," Fox replied. "You've done the same thing for me a gazillion times. Remember when I had that food poisoning real bad and I was puking and shitting like a machine and you—"

But Pop had drifted off into his own world again, and was humming tunelessly.

Now Fox looked at himself in the mirror. He knew that at some level Pop was embarrassed that his son had to help clean him, had to change his diapers. And Fox was tired. He tried to keep up with his schoolwork but his grades were plummeting. His teachers were understanding, granting him extensions on assignments or forgiving his absences. Mr. Weitzman had taken over the task of making sure his college applications were handed in on time, and had offered many times to listen if Fox needed to talk.

Fox found it difficult to care about any of it. His Papa was dying. Everyone knew it, even Dad, although he never said the words. There was a look of pain and hopelessness in his eyes that gave it away. There was the same look in Pop's eyes whenever he was lucid. Fox hated it.

One foot in front of the other, he reminded himself. Just keep doing what has to be done. Don't think. Don't feel. That had been his mantra for five months as life became more and more difficult. The whispers in the night from his parents' room, that seeped through his shields, battered him with pain and hopelessness.

The next morning he trudged off to school. Spring was taking over the city again. The irony of it wasn't lost on Fox. A time of renewal, of life triumphing over death. He noted it through the self-imposed fog that surrounded him.

If only everyone at school wasn't so fucking understanding! All his friends—Effie, Vijay, Laurinda, Clark—looked at him with pity and spoke in hushed tones, and his teachers treated him with kid gloves as if Pop had died already.

Fox got to school and stuffed his gear into his locker. First period was math—pre-calc. He hated it. He didn't understand it, any more than he'd understood any math he'd taken. But it was required, and he was squeaking through.

It was impossible to concentrate on the teacher's voice. Memories kept popping up. Papa Gerry scooping Fox up to his shoulders at the Pride Parade. Papa Gerry patiently explaining set theory to him. Papa Gerry listening quietly as Fox tried to figure out relationships and sex.

The bell finally rang, then another and another. Fox drifted from class to class. Seventh period was almost over when Fox's phone vibrated in his pocket. It was Dad, it was urgent.

He raised his hand. "I'm sorry, Mr. Weitzman. I have to go. An emergency."

He noted the concern in his teacher's eyes as he rushed out of school, the phone still in his hand.

The cab snaked through the crowded April streets to the hospital. Dad's text said that Pop had difficulty breathing, that an ambulance had taken him to Beth Israel. Fox's heart beat fast. He quietly cursed every red light.

He raced through the hospital to the room where Papa Gerry lay. Fox walked to where his dad was standing next to the bed. There were tubes in Papa's arms and a mask over his nose. Antiseptic smells barely covered the odors of despair. Dad put an arm around Fox and they looked down at the bed.

The figure on the white sheets was pale and shrunken. His skin stretched tightly over the bones in his face, his arms straight at his side. He looked a thousand years old, almost mummified. Fox could barely stand to see it.

Dad turned to him. "He suddenly couldn't breathe," he said, his voice shaking. "He was gasping. I didn't know what—I called 911. And now . . ."

Fox put his arm around his father. Dad's head came to just above Fox's shoulder. I'm about as tall as Papa, Fox thought distantly. He was thankful for the blessed fog that dulled everything. He lowered his shields a tiny bit, trying to find a *sense* of what Papa was feeling, but all he got was a blur of pain and confusion.

Dr. Wallenstein came in with a chart in his hand and a solemn look on his face. "I'm really sorry, Mr. Monroe, Fox." He nodded at them in turn.

"What's happening, doctor?" Dad asked.

"I'm afraid it's . . . not good," the doctor answered. "I think—look, shall we talk outside? Fox, you can stay here."

"No," Fox said firmly. "I want to hear this too."

Dad nodded and they walked outside the room. Fox couldn't understand why this was necessary. It wasn't as though Papa could hear them, or understand.

When they stood in the hallway, the doctor turned to them. "I don't think he has much more time," he said softly. "I'm really sorry. He was a good man."

"How much longer?" Dad choked out.

"A few days, maybe. We can make him comfortable here. There's a relatives' room at the end of the hall with some couches and chairs. Or you could go home, rest there, come back in a few hours. And here." He took a pad out of his pocket and wrote something on it. "A prescription for a sedative. Just a very mild one. It might help."

Mechanically, Fox took the prescription from the doctor's hand. He knew he would never use it, not after his experience with Zoloft, but Dad might need it. He muttered his thanks and led his father back into the room.

They both gazed down at the pale, motionless figure. Fox knew that Dad was trying to swallow around the lump in his throat, just as he was.

But Dad wasn't insulated by the friendly gray fog. Fox realized he had to take charge.

"Dad, let's go home," he said softly.

A slight shake of the head was the only answer.

"You have to. You're exhausted. You won't be any good like this. Not to Papa, or yourself . . . or me."

Dad hesitated, then nodded. He allowed Fox to help him into his coat and guide him downstairs, into a cab and home. Fox fixed him a cup of herbal tea and made him sit on the couch with the afghan covering him. Dad's hand shook slightly as he held the tea.

"I'll be back in a minute," Fox said, kissing Dad on the forehead. *The way he did when I was hurt*, Fox thought fleetingly.

He hurried down to the drug store and filled the prescription, then ran back. Gently, he fed one of the pills to his father. He watched as the older man lay down, then sat in the easy chair as his dad fell into an uneasy sleep.

The next few days would be hard. Very hard. One foot after the other.

They took turns at the deathwatch. He stopped going to school. It was April already, he'd gotten his acceptances to colleges, it was all over but the shouting. Not that he cared. He drew the friendly gray blanket around him and concentrated on his fathers. Nothing else mattered.

On the second day he sat by Papa's bedside. Dad was down the hall in the relatives' room, resting. He refused to stay home anymore, in spite of his exhaustion.

Fox talked to him about happy memories. He wasn't sure his father could hear him, but he spoke anyway. His father's hand looked different as it lay in his, not large and muscular as it used to be. The pain radiating from the figure on the bed penetrated the tightest shields. Fox stood up, still holding the hand, trying to stretch cramped muscles. He would get Dad to spell him for a while.

Suddenly, Papa's eyes opened. He gripped Fox's hand.

"Don't go. I'm so scared," he said in a raspy voice. His eyes looked pleadingly at Fox.

Fox tried to reassure him. "I know, Pop. It'll be okay. We'll get through this—"

"I'm so scared," Pop's voice repeated.

It broke through the gray envelope, through the fear of going into anyone's head again. He had to do something.

Carefully, he went into Papa Gerry's head, the way he had with his cat Lucky, looking for the alien thing, to make it go away. Carefully, slowly he traced the path of the pain. There! He found it. All he had to do was squeeze it off, kill it, gently, cautiously . . .

But he wasn't good enough, not skilled enough. He did something wrong, and he—

He killed his father.

CHAPTER 29

The loud alarm shocked Fox out of his chair. People burst into the room, doctors and nurses with machines and needles. A few seconds later, Dad ran in.

Fox retreated to the far wall, devastated by what he had done. For the second time, he had killed someone. He was a murderer, and the fact that no one would ever know didn't matter. Faintly, Fox could hear Dad saying something about DNR, telling them to stop. Then Dr. Wallenstein came in, and the activity and noise ceased.

The only sound Fox heard was Dad sobbing next to him. He put a protective arm around his father and spoke to the doctor. "Is he—" He swallowed. "Gone?"

Wallenstein's face was sorrowful as he replied. "Yes. I'm sorry."

Fox and his father walked to the bedside. They stood there for a few moments, leaning against each other.

"Would you like a minister to come in? A priest, or any religious figure?" the doctor continued.

Fox and Dad both shook their heads.

"Take your time," Wallenstein went on. "But there are some arrangements that have to be made . . ." He looked at them once more. Then he turned and left the room.

Dad bent down and picked up Papa's hand. Tears ran down his cheeks, but he didn't wipe them away. He stood there, not making a sound, weeping, as Fox looked on.

Murderer, Fox's mind screamed. You killed him. It didn't matter that he was going to die soon, that the disease was eating him up. You killed him.

"I'll go talk to the doctors," Fox whispered, giving his father's shoulder a squeeze.

Activity was good. If he was moving, he didn't have to think. One foot after the other, just keep going. He wasn't running away. He was taking action.

—

Fox stood in the corner of the living room he had established as his own. *This is the result of my great telepathic powers,* he thought. *Great for killing, or fucking. Get rid of what hurts me or double my pleasure. Maybe next time I'll try both at the same time.*

He looked out at the guests. Guests, not mourners. He and Dad had decided on cremation and a memorial gathering rather than a funeral. The invitations read, "We meet to celebrate the life of an extraordinary man." It was an assembly of those who loved him, and whom he had loved.

Earlier, people had come over to him, to whisper condolences and offer support. Fox listened politely and answered in a few sentences and saw them turn away. Mostly he watched in silence.

Everyone told a story about Gerry, something he had done for them or simply a time they remembered most vividly. Fox described briefly being held on Papa's shoulders to view the Pride Parade. Dad told about the day he first met Gerry and about the day Fox was born. Co-workers described patients he had helped, or encouragement he had given them. Neighbors talked about his generosity in helping them when they were hurt or in need.

Dad's fellow writers offered stories, too. About how helpful Papa had been to Dad. How supportive, especially at the beginning before Dad's career took off.

People cried and laughed as they explored and exchanged memories.

It was a release for them, Fox thought. A sense of closure. But not for him. He still felt the raw wound inside, the site of his father's death, a death he had caused. He fought to maintain the insulating blanket of non-feeling, but it was getting more difficult. The "one foot after the other" mantra was wearing thin, his footsteps faltering.

Fox's friends, both old and new, came to give what comfort they could. Norrie was there, and Joey (not fat any more), and Kim, Mercedes, Dennis—the old crew. His newer friends, too, his school chums. Effie,

Clark, Laurinda, Hakim, Vijay—even Mark, home for vacation. Mr. Weitzman was there also.

There were so many people. Papa had touched them all, and hundreds more who weren't here. People he'd helped in his career, strangers who had gotten into accidents on the street.

He flashed on the memory of Mr. Barkowski's funeral, and the hurtful things Sonia had said to him. He understood the grief and anger that had fueled that outburst. He wished he could talk to her, but after their last meeting he knew it was impossible.

His mother had sent him a special letter, offering what comfort she could. He longed to see her but he understood why she couldn't come. The city was always painful for her, and now with emotions running especially high, she had to avoid it. She was the only one who really understood what he was going through.

He looked at Dad standing in the middle of the room surrounded by friends and relatives. His father looked so tired. Aunt Georgia wanted Dad and Fox to stay with her for a few days. "Just get out of the house," she said. "A change of scene. Be good for you."

Gamma Rose, Dad's mother, had flown in from Maryland. She was pressing her son to come and stay with her, maybe even move there permanently. Dad said he wanted to get back to normal life, and that Fox had school.

As he stood there, purposely isolated, Fox realized that he couldn't stay here. There were too much guilt. He had to leave.

The insulating blanket dissolved and Fox saw clearly for the first time in months. They would be okay. Dad had lots of support and his work to keep him busy. The others had their lives. Dad would figure out his own life without having to worry about him. Everybody here would be better off.

He would write a letter to Dad, make a clean break. And after that . . . Whatever. But no matter what, he would never use his power again, not to help or cure or even just see.

It would be safer for the ones he loved.

━━

It took a week to arrange everything. Joey was very good at producing fake ID's, and Fox became John Marshall who held a GED, was nineteen years old and lived in Brooklyn. Fox took as much money from his bank account as he could without arousing suspicion.

At midnight of April 12th, he started to pack. Just a small duffel, only what was absolutely necessary. Lucky sat on the bed, watching Fox warily. She was silent as her eyes tracked Fox's movements from dresser to bed.

Then he wrote the letter to his dad.

That was the most difficult of all.

Fox tried to fit onto the page all his love, gratitude and grief. He included the pride he felt in being Dad's son. It wasn't enough, but it would have to do.

He ended with a plea to his father not to look for him.

"I'll get in touch with you," Fox wrote, "as soon as I can figure out who I am and what I'm supposed to do with my life."

He finished at three in the morning. He signed the letter and folded it into an envelope. Then he pushed back from the desk and went to the bed where Lucky had been watching him.

Fox zipped the bag and sat next to the cat. He stroked her head absently as he looked around his room for the last time. The desk where he'd done his homework. The DVD player where Sonia had shown him how to build his shields. The bed he sat on where Lucky had curled up over his heart and soothed him when he couldn't sleep. He sighed.

Fox sat down and lifted Lucky's now considerable weight onto his lap. "Take care of him," he whispered into the soft fur of the cat's forehead.

Lucky let out a quiet meow and jumped onto the floor. She padded silently across the room. Her gray-black head turned once, giving him a reproachful look. Then she walked through the half-open door.

Fox turned out the light and made his way to the kitchen, setting the letter on the table where Dad was sure to see it. He slipped out of the house.

He didn't cry.

⌐━

Fox chose at random, the first bus he could get out of Port Authority. He considered Wyoming, but he assumed it would be the first place his father would look for him. Besides, it was too expensive.

He headed north in the calm spring sunrise, breathing deeply as he tried to quiet his racing thoughts. He was completely on his own for the first time in his life. Exhilaration was quickly replaced by leaden guilt that settled in his gut. He was tempted to get off at the next stop and get a bus back home.

Strengthening his resolve, he rejected the idea. A clean break, lance the infection. In time the wounds he caused would heal. And everyone would be safe.

He plugged the earbuds into his phone and called up a jazz playlist. Maybe the soothing notes would calm him, let him relax. Accompanied by saxophones and guitars, he let the bus carry him toward western Massachusetts.

Fatigue caught up with him on the Thruway and he fell asleep somewhere after Peekskill. He didn't wake up until they pulled into Lee. It was half an hour out from his destination.

The scenery he passed was still wintry, although spring was firmly established in the city. Trees were bare and there was a rim of ice around a lake they passed. It wasn't like Wyoming where the flatness was suddenly interrupted by buttes. Here, the road wound through hills bordered by trees and fields. There didn't seem to be a flat surface.

When he arrived at the station in Pittsfield, he had no plan. He slung his duffel over his shoulder and walked slowly to the glass booth where the station manager sat.

"Excuse me," Fox said.

The man in the booth continued to sort through papers on his desk.

Fox cleared his throat. "Excuse me," he said, louder this time.

The manager looked up. "Yes?" he said in a bored tone.

"Um, I'm sort of new . . . I mean, I've never been here before. Is there a . . . shelter or something?"

The station manager stared at him for a moment. "How old are you, kid?"

"Nineteen," Fox said. It came out louder than he intended.

"Uh-huh. Sure." The man hesitated. "Look, go outta here, turn right to the main street. That's North Street. Go right to the circle. There's a church there. Reverend Jack'll help you."

The church was made of gray stone. Fox thought it looked cold and intimidating. A sign on the side directed him around to the back. A small house of the same gray stone sat behind a tiny garden.

Fox knocked on the red door. The man who answered was slight. His gray hair was neatly combed in thick waves away from his face. The jeans and plaid flannel shirt he wore seemed serviceable but not expensive. His gaze was politely inquisitive.

Fox shifted even though in the sunshine it wasn't a chilly day. "My name is John Marshall," Fox broke the silence.

A lie to start his new life.

"I'm Jack Smith. I'm the minister here." The man hesitated a moment. "Why don't you come in?"

CHAPTER 30

They sat at a round table in the tidy kitchen. The white stove shone. The yellow granite countertops were clean, toaster and other small appliances neatly lined up against the wall. Dark wood gleamed on the floor.

Fox was nervous but the older man slowly filled a pipe and lit it. Neither one spoke for a while.

Finally Reverend Smith took the pipe out of his mouth. "What can I do for you?"

"Well, I'm away from home for the first time. Trying to make my way, sort of find myself. And I need a little help right now."

Reverend Smith didn't say anything. He nodded, encouraging Fox to continue.

"I need someplace to stay. I don't have much money, so I thought that maybe a shelter . . ."

"Yes, there is one up at the north end of town. But it's intended as a temporary solution, you understand." He stared intently at Fox. "You don't seem to be the kind of young man who needs lodging like that . . ." He trailed off, inviting Fox to comment.

Fox gazed at the man trying to *sense* a motive without lowering his shields. Nothing sinister, he decided, no menace at all.

He tried to project honesty as he spoke. "I just want a chance to get a job and be independent. I know I can do it."

The reverend continued to stare for a moment more. Then he nodded. "I understand. If you would agree, I have a better idea. There's a small room in the basement." He gestured at the church. "I can let you stay there for a few days until you get on your feet."

Fox stayed at the church for two weeks while the minister helped him get an apartment at the local Y, and even arranged a job for him stocking shelves at Walmart. The pay wasn't much, but it covered his rent and food. "John Marshall" was getting established.

A sense of unreality surrounded him. It wasn't like he was dreaming, more like that time between waking and sleeping when he wasn't sure of what was true. For a while he hoped that he would wake up soon in his bed with Lucky on his chest and Pop calling him to breakfast. But by the beginning of June he gave up on that idea and sadly accepted his situation.

He wiped his tablet and phone, then sold them. He didn't want anyone tracking him. All traces of Fox Monroe would be gone, only John Marshall would remain.

Except for his memories. He wished he could wipe them, too.

⌇

Fox sat at the minister's small kitchen table sipping tea. Reverend Smith sat opposite him. The silence was friendly.

An open window let in a gentle breeze scented with lilacs and the chirping of birds.

Finally the older man spoke. "In all the time you were here I never asked you."

Fox's muscles tensed. There was so much the man had never asked him, so much that Fox had to hide.

"Do you play chess, John?" Jack said.

Fox breathed out. "Yes, I do, sir, but I don't want to build up your expectation. I don't play well."

"Neither do I, young man. But any game would be appreciated."

They sat in silence again for a short while.

Jack broke the quiet. "On your next day off, then? Say around five? You can stay for dinner."

Fox walked into the spring afternoon. He sincerely liked Reverend Jack and regretted that he had to lie. Sighing, he followed the street to the bus stop and made his way to work.

⌇

The night shift gathered slowly in the Walmart break room. Caroline, the shift supervisor, stood next to the candy vending machine holding a styrofoam cup of something hot. She looked tiny, almost fragile, but Fox had seen her heft fifty pound bags of potting soil with ease.

"Hi, Caroline," he said as he walked to the coffee machine. The beverage was barely tolerable, but it had caffeine.

Fox nodded to the others who sat at the long folding table in the middle of the room. Doris and Keila were chatting about the previous night's *Dancing With the Stars* and complaining about the unfairness of the judges.

Bill looked tired. He'd probably been up late writing again. His poetry was dreadful, full of the kind of teenage angst that only a nineteen-year-old could write. But he was determined to keep at it.

Fox poured coffee and sat next to him. "Late night?" he asked softly.

"Yeah. Had a fight with Jenny." He sighed. "She wants to move to New York right after she graduates and she's angry that I'm not earning enough money. I mean, graduation is just around the corner. How'm I supposed to get it together by then?"

Fox nodded sympathetically. He'd hoped that Bill could be a friend, someone he could talk to about literature and politics. But the young man was wrapped up in his own problems and ambitions. Besides, Fox couldn't stand to read another poem.

Dave sat half way down the table. His head was bent over a coffee cup. Fox didn't need to go *into* the older man's mind to see he was worried. Dave had been downsized from the plastics factory a year before and, at forty-five, he had few prospects. His three kids were nearing college age. His wife's income as a nurse at the hospital helped them stay afloat but wouldn't give them enough for college.

It wasn't a cheery group.

Shorty walked in, the usual goofy grin on his face. He stopped in front of Fox. "John-bo! Johnny boy! John-John! How's it hangin'?" He giggled, his eyes wide and bright.

Fox couldn't decide if Shorty was mentally challenged or just high all the time. It was tempting to go *into* the other boy's mind to check. Fox banished the thought. He would never go *into* anyone's mind again.

These are my companions, he mused. *The people I spend my time with now. It's funny how you can feel lonelier in a crowd than by yourself.*

In the middle of June he found an apartment in the city. As he was moving his few belongings out of the Y, Don, the manager, stopped him.

"I know you're moving, John," the earnest young man said. "But I wanted to show you this." He handed Fox a piece of paper.

The flyer wasn't at all prepossessing. Just a plain, black-on-white printed sheet. It advertised for a recycling program in Pittsfield.

Fox looked up, puzzled. "Don't we have a recycling program already?"

Don nodded. "But it's private. A lot of apartment buildings here don't subscribe to it. We wanted to get a bunch of volunteers who would go to those places and pick up the paper and cans and stuff."

Fox didn't even have to think. It was like the *Greener New York* that he'd joined some years back. "Yeah. I'm in."

The manager smiled. "That's great, John. I have your new address. I'll be in touch. By the way, do you drive?"

"Drive? Get rid of some dirt in the air by adding more?"

"Electric vans. Got 'em cheap. They're pretty beat up on the outside, but they work fine. So. Do you? Drive?"

"I know how. Don't have a license, though."

"That's okay. Just asking. I'll talk to you."

Fox walked out of the building feeling a little better about himself.

The apartment was small, just a studio, but it was in the city. The living room window looked out over North Street, so it was noisy. The tiny kitchenette, with the dinged-up stove and chipped sink, was enough for his needs. He found a futon and a coffee table in a consignment shop, and a bike as well. It was an old, beat-up thing. It suited his purposes. He used his employee's discount at Walmart to buy supplies and repainted it. Not a great job, he figured, but okay.

Three weeks later Fox sat at a round table in the Dunkin Donuts with the other members of *Recycle Pittsfield*. He was glad it was only a temporary name. It sucked.

"Well, we're off to a good start," Don said. "We have twelve buildings already and phone calls keep—"

"It's not enough," Petra interrupted, a frown on her dusky face.

The seven members of the committee looked at her.

"What d'you mean?" Warren asked.

"Didn't you read the Friedman article?" Petra looked from face to face. "I sent it to everyone last week!" She seemed shocked at the laxness.

"Not everyone has a lot of *leisure time*," Kathryn said disdainfully. "Some of us have to work, y'know."

Don sighed. "Why don't you just, uh, refresh our memories, Petra?"

"Friedman quotes scientists who believe we already reached the tipping point. That just recycling and fluorescent bulbs aren't enough. It's too little too late."

"So we should just give up?" Jody's blue eyes flashed. "Just do nothing?"

"No," Petra said. "We have to expand. Neighborhood committees like this one won't help enough. We have to form a nationwide movement, get the government to intervene . . ."

Fox tuned out. *Grandiose schemes*, he thought. *Get everyone together. Sing songs around the campfire. Yeah, sure.*

An hour later, depressed and angry, he rode to the state forest and hiked the tree-shaded paths. It was unseasonably warm, and very humid. The bugs were swarming, making the forest unpleasant. He gave up on that and returned to the parking lot to get his bike.

Even though he didn't consciously use his telepathy, he felt as though his power was growing. When he walked in the forest, he could *hear* the tiny animals and insects, even through his shields. The sounds of life were enticing. It was as though they begged him to relax and join his mind with theirs.

But he held back. He felt he didn't deserve the pleasure. How could he enjoy the presence of such abundance when Pop lay dead and Sonia ruined beyond help? And Dad was alone. Besides, the shadow was out there somewhere, waiting for him.

He pedaled slowly to the lake. Glad he had worn his bathing suit under his clothing, he dove into the chill water of the lake. He imagined how quiet it would be if he never came up. Just allowed himself to sink into the unlighted depths. Yet with his lungs hurting, he found himself swimming toward the brightness again.

He stayed locked in his own mind. It didn't seem to matter where he was, or who he was with, he was isolated.

≈

Every week he played chess with Reverend Jack.

The first time was difficult. Fox remembered afternoons playing the game with Dad. When he first learned, his father was very patient, and allowed him to take back moves that were obviously bad. An explanation of the mistake always followed. As Fox grew older, Dad wasn't so lenient. But no matter how good Fox got, Dad always seemed to be just a little better.

The memories were painful. But gradually they dulled, if only a bit, and Fox no longer saw his father sitting, ghost-like, on the couch.

The living room of the residence, like the rest of the house, was small but tidy. Three brown leather chairs sat opposite a matching couch. Heavy green drapes were usually drawn back to let in the sunlight that streamed from the back yard. The room always smelled faintly of furniture polish.

When they played chess, two of the chairs were turned to face each other with a small round wooden table in between. The chess set was beautiful, hand-carved of some exotic wood. Each of the pawns was individual, and the kings and queens wore different expressions on their faces.

The first few times they played, Jack won easily. Then Fox found the rhythm and was able to put up a better fight. They seldom spoke. Jack sat hunched over the board, a pipe in his hand, and Fox sat across from him, shields in tight to prevent any *peeking*.

Afterwards there was always a light supper and conversations that ranged from politics to religion to movies. The games and the talks were stimulating, but it only emphasized the separateness that was his constant companion.

⟳

In August he helped Jack and members of the congregation decorate the church for the wedding of Alan and Steven. The decorating committee showed up on Saturday bearing armfuls of flowers from their gardens.

"Oh, John," said Mrs. Houseman, her mellow voice contrasting with her gray hair and substantial figure, "it's so kind of you to join us."

Bird-like Miss Torrental chirped, "How nice to have a strong young man in the group."

All five ladies agreed that he helped a lot. They didn't seem to need much, as they arranged flowers they brought from their gardens. Between the frequent calls of, "John, can you move this?" or "Would you carry this please, dear," he leaned against the wall, watching. He knew they were perfectly capable of doing the work themselves. He was sure the requests were only make work. The ladies' movements seemed coordinated as they worked with and around each other, never interfering.

At the wedding Fox watched the two men as they exchanged vows. Tears stung his eyes as he remembered his parents' wedding. It seemed so long ago. During the reception the couple thanked him for his help, and other members of the community kept offering him glasses of champagne. Fox politely put them to his lips, but he didn't drink.

He was lonely.

Summer passed in a routine that was both dull and strangely comforting. Thought was unnecessary, he never had to use his powers. In spite of the solitude of his situation, he felt that he was healing. Colors returned and green no longer looked dusty, purple and gold sunsets glowed. Just not as brightly.

Then the days grew shorter. It got too chilly for the street fairs where the music and energy of large crowds buoyed him up, if only briefly. Hikes in the woods and swimming sessions at the lake stopped. Leaves changed color. With a final burst of reds and oranges the season was over and bare branches were outlined against the sky.

Fox spent Thanksgiving at Reverend Smith's church volunteering to cook for and serve people who couldn't afford their own feast. He was grateful to his friend for the opportunity to help. He didn't realize how much he'd missed simply being of use. For so long during the time Papa was sick he had assumed the role of caretaker. Then suddenly it stopped. Fox hadn't known he'd be so empty.

He leaned back against the wall of the large rec room that made up the space under the church. Happy feelings spread through the basement area. Just as at the fairs, the power given off by people enjoying themselves lifted his spirits. He watched people eat, for some of them the first really good meal they'd had in a long time. Laughter and buzzing conversation formed a pleasing background hum.

Reverend Smith walked over to him. "It's good to see them like this, isn't it?"

Fox nodded, unwilling to take his eyes from the cheerful scene.

The Reverend leaned next to Fox, both of them enjoying a well-earned rest. After a few minutes he clapped Fox on the shoulder. "Okay, John, time to get to work again."

Fox smiled.

⟋

December brought snow. That was bad enough, but the biting winds that accompanied it nearly drove Fox out of the Berkshires. Only his friendship with the Reverend anchored him to the place. He even gave in when the older man finally guilted him into coming to Christmas service.

Afterwards Fox walked home alone, his head bent against the wind. The service had been pleasant, the church decorated beautifully with garlands of pine boughs and poinsettias. As he sat through the prayers and the sermon he tried to feel part of the community, to recognize holiness. Trying to belong. But it was impossible.

No leap of faith here.

He opened the door to his apartment and walked to the table, taking off his coat and hat and slinging them on the bed. The cheap pay-as-you-go phone was in his pocket. He put it on the table and stared at it.

Finally he sighed and picked it up, punching in the familiar numbers. It rang. One. Two. Three. Four. Click.

"Hi, you've reached Peter Monroe. I can't take your call right now. Please leave a message, including your name and phone number, and I'll get back to you."

Fox pressed the phone tight against his ear, listening to the voice he loved. Then the tone sounded.

He didn't leave a message.

⟋

The snowy Pittsfield streets were deserted by ten o'clock on the night after Christmas. There were partiers in the bars and restaurants, mostly tourists or skiers. Christmas decorations brightened the darkness but did little to lift Fox's spirits.

Earlier that day he had walked to the bus station. For the third time in as many months, he checked the schedules for buses headed to New York City. And, as before, he had turned and walked out. He couldn't go back, couldn't put Dad in danger. The memory of all the harm he'd caused haunted him.

He was restless. He couldn't stay home and read, and he'd spent his monthly allotment of movie money already. He walked towards North Street, his breath steaming. He glanced at Patrick's Pub as he passed, the warm light and laughter spilling invitingly over the sidewalk. He moved on.

Soon people would be celebrating the new year. 2014, almost the middle of the decade. Fox didn't feel like celebrating.

At the corner a woman leaned against the ornate lamppost the city had installed last year. Her head was lowered, the light shining on dark curls that escaped from under her scarf. A lit cigarette hung from her ungloved fingers.

Fox couldn't see her face clearly, but there was a sense of sadness and loneliness around her that echoed his own. Pittsfield was not New York City, he knew, but it wasn't completely safe for a woman to hang out in the dark like this. And there was something almost familiar about her.

Fox walked over. "Are you okay?"

The woman nodded.

"Look, it's really cold. Don't you have someplace to go?"

She shook her head.

"Isn't there anything I can do? I hate to just leave you here like this."

She looked at him. Long bangs obscured her eyes. She seemed to hesitate, examining him for a moment. "I'm okay. But I could use some company," she said at last. Her voice was low and slightly hoarse. She spoke with a slight accent that Fox couldn't place.

"I'm afraid I wouldn't be very good company tonight," Fox answered. No malevolence seeped through his shields. No violence intended, he recognized, just loneliness.

"Neither am I. But sometimes two negatives can make a positive."

Fox smiled.

"Want to go inside for a drink?" She nodded toward the bar.

"I don't drink."

"How about just a drive then? My car's over there." She pointed to a spot on the street.

He hesitated. Something drew him to her, not just physical attraction, but something he couldn't define. He wanted to, and yet . . .

"Okay," he said suddenly.

They drove south toward Stockbridge without talking. The full moon shone on the snow-covered trees lining the sides of the road, brightening the night. When they came to a point in the road where it overlooked a meadow and the hills beyond, she stopped. The moonlight on the snowy meadow was as bright as day.

"I'm Elena Patterson," she said.

"John Marshall."

"So what's your story, John Marshall?"

And Fox told her John Marshall's story—growing up in Brooklyn, leaving to make his way in the world. It was easier now to become his alter ego. He barely had to think about it.

When he got to the part about leaving to find his way on his own, she nodded. "I got divorced three months ago. We'd been married nearly five years."

Fox made a sympathetic noise.

"It wasn't anything terrible," she said quickly as though reassuring him. "We just . . . grew apart. I wanted different things from life than I did five years ago."

"Like what?"

"I wanted to travel more. Explore the world, y'know? I needed time to . . . figure out where I should be. He wanted a pleasant home, a family. I hope he finds it."

"Really?" Fox's skepticism was obvious.

"Yes. Honestly."

The reflected moonlight illuminated the inside of the car. Fox looked at Elena Patterson. She kept her head bent, her long hair partly obscuring her face. In the confines of the car Fox could smell her perfume. It was something citrusy, light and sweet. He liked it.

They talked for hours, about literature, politics, relationships. Fox felt he could talk to her more honestly than he could to anyone he'd met since he left New York.

There was a nagging feeling of familiarity about her that encouraged him to talk. He found himself getting too near the truth, and pulled back. Staring hard at Elena he said, "I would swear I know you."

"Yeah. I guess I have one of those faces. Lots of people tell me that I look like someone they know."

"But you seem so damn *familiar*," Fox insisted.

"Maybe it's just that we're so much alike, y'know? No responsibilities, no commitments. Searching for something."

He shrugged, accepting her statements.

They never kissed, never even touched. When the sky began to lighten, Elena turned on the ignition and drove back to Pittsfield. Fox wanted to make the evening go on and on, but he couldn't find a way.

She dropped him off in front of his building. He got out of the car but kept the door open. "When can I see you again?" Fox asked, leaning in.

"I don't know," Elena answered. "I'm leaving tomorrow. Uh, I mean today." She gestured at the brightening sky.

"Where are you going?" He really wanted to continue their strange friendship.

"Somewhere else. Maybe somewhere warm. I have no idea. I'll know when I get there."

Her offhand comments struck him. She was rootless, could wander freely anywhere she chose.

As she drove off, Fox realized that he could do the same thing.

The gentle lamplight made Jack's living room a cozy, welcoming place. Fox stared at the chessboard, not really seeing it. His mind was filled with plans and calculations that had nothing to do with the game in front of him.

He was going to leave, and he had to tell Jack. No easy way out this time, no letter left on the table. He had to do the adult thing and face the situation, the way he had to with Lilah.

Jack's knight took his bishop. Fox looked up in surprise.

"Where's your mind this afternoon, John?" the reverend asked softly.

"It's noth—" Fox caught himself. "You're right, Jack. I'm no good today. Got a lot on my mind."

The older man nodded but didn't speak.

"Do you mind if we don't play just now? Could we just talk?" Fox asked.

"Sure, son. What's the matter?" Jack's face showed his concern.

Fox told him about the encounter with Elena the week before. When he got to the part where they didn't touch or kiss, Jack's eyebrows rose. "No, it's true. It wasn't that kind of thing. It was a kind of revelation."

Jack smiled.

"I realized that I'm just marking time here. That there was more I should be doing." Fox shook his head. "I'm not saying this right. I like it here. You, the community, even the church. But I feel that there's something out there, a place I could really belong."

"I think I understand," Jack said. "You have to leave."

"Yeah. But not like I'm running away from anything here. More like I'm heading *toward* something. Only I don't know where it is."

The reverend nodded. He looked sad. "I'll hate to see you go, John. I've enjoyed our friendship very much."

"Can we keep in touch?" Fox asked hesitantly.

"Of course!"

"And I'll come back when I can." The promise was sincere.

Jack held out his hand. Fox grasped it, then moved into a brief, warm hug.

He used the last minutes on his phone to call his mother. It rang three times before she answered.

"Hi, Mom. It's me," he said softly.

Silence on the other end.

"Mom? Are you there?"

He heard a smothered sob.

"Mom, please don't—"

"Fox, darling, how are you? *Where* are you?" The words came out in a rush. "We've been so worried . . ."

"I know. I'm sorry. But I had to. I couldn't tell anyone."

And then it all came out, about Papa's lying on the hospital bed and hurting so much and he had to do something.

When he finished they were both crying.

"You see, Mom. I had to leave, before I did something else." He wiped his cheeks. "I'm sorry I left like that. I didn't mean to hurt you. Or Dad."

He heard her blow her nose. "Okay, so you can't go home right now. But will you at least call your Dad? He's so worried."

"No, I'm not up to it right now. I couldn't do it."

"Then may I call him?"

"Sure, Mom. Tell him . . . tell him I'm thinking about him. Like all the time. And I love him."

A sigh on the other end. "But where are you?"

"That doesn't matter. I'm only going to be here a little while longer."

"Where will you go?"

"I don't know."

$\rightleftharpoons$

The bus headed west out of Pittsfield three days later. Fox's few belongings were stowed in the old duffel bag in the baggage compartment.

He watched the snow-covered landscape pass by and vaguely remembered words of an old song by James Taylor tumbled around his mind. Something about December being covered with snow, and the turnpike, and the Berkshires looking dream-like. The last line echoed, *With ten miles behind me and ten thousand more to go.*

But this time it wasn't where he was running from that was important. It was where he was going.

CHAPTER 31

Fox opened his eyes slowly. He tried to remember exactly what had happened. He was lying in a damp, dirty alley, and every part of him hurt.

The events of the previous evening revealed themselves to him in bits and pieces. Encountering four men on the street. In Tulsa. That's where he was. They decided they didn't like his looks, and they had beaten the crap out of him.

Oh, yeah. Hadn't he said something about their ancestry? Jeez, you'd think that after traveling around for five years he would be smarter than that. He knew he could handle himself in a fight. But there were four of them.

He groaned as he tried to get up. *Gotta give 'em credit,* he thought. *They knew how to hit.*

The wall behind him was only a bit cleaner than the ground. Fox pushed against it to stand up. It was the only thing that kept him from falling down again. Street lights glinted on the sidewalk at the end of the alley but did little to illuminate the spot where Fox leaned. The comfort of the brightness seemed miles away.

A figure blocked out part of the light. "Hey, fella, you okay?" a deep voice asked.

Fox looked blearily at the stocky outline that blocked the mouth of the alley. Short, maybe five and half feet tall. But broad shoulders. No bad vibes. Not like the four who beat him up earlier.

"Just need a few minutes," Fox mumbled. He tried to stand straight and nearly fell.

"Sure," the other man drawled. "Here, lemme help you." He walked to Fox and reached out an arm.

"Thanks." Fox grabbed the arm and groaned as he leaned on the man's shoulder.

"Where ya goin' to?" The stranger led Fox to the bright end of the narrow way.

"Don't know. I was gonna find a place to stay. But those bastards took everything. All my money." He didn't have much, just some old clothes in the duffel he'd carried on the road. A few dollars, enough to get a room for a night or two. He had ditched his temporary phone in Arizona, right after he called his mother. He called her every time he got ready to move on.

Through his bruised, half-open eyes, Fox could see the stranger more clearly. The streetlamps revealed the scars on his dark skin, and his broad nose bore evidence of having been broken a few times. But his voice was warm.

"My name's John," Fox said as they walked down the street.

"Louie," the man answered. "Full handle's Louisville Slugger. I'm pretty good with these." He held up a fist the size of a small dinner plate.

"Wish you were with me last night." Fox gave a short laugh but was stopped by the pain.

"You be quiet for a bit, John. Keep your strength for walking."

They went slowly, Fox leaning on Louie's shoulder. *Something about this is familiar,* he thought. *Like déjà vu. Can't place it.*

He smelled the wood smoke before they got to the encampment. A vacant lot was filled with tents arranged randomly in the area. Fires burned in front of many of them. People sat in small groups, eating and talking quietly. Under the pleasant scent of the smoke was the less pleasant aroma of unwashed bodies.

Heads lifted as he and Louie made their way between the tents. Some calls of, "Hey, Slugger, whatcha got there." Louie waved back with his free hand, but didn't stop.

Louie led Fox into one of the tents. Firelight from outside showed a sleeping bag and an open duffel.

"Lay down and get some rest." Louie settled Fox on the makeshift bed. "We'll talk in the morning."

Fox fell asleep immediately.

The morning sun woke him. He looked around the tent. Louie was asleep on a pile of blankets in one corner. Fox felt guilty that he'd taken the man's bed and promised to make it up to his new friend as soon as possible.

He sat up and found that movement and breathing were easier. Still not comfortable, though.

Louie opened one eye. "Feelin' better? Good. Got stuff to do."

Outside the tent, Fox sat on a log while Louie built up the fire. They skewered a couple of sausages on long sticks. When the food was done, they sat back and ate.

Louie said, "I been a lot of places. Started in Chicago, but worked all over. Oregon, Idaho, Utah. Not much to do in Utah. Real hard to find work. Been to New Mexico, too. Nice. Warm. Ever been there?"

Fox thought of the trip to Santa Fe with his mother when he was thirteen, the paintings, the gallery. He remembered Joshua. He didn't say anything, just nodded.

"You done some traveling, too?"

"Uh-huh. Started in Massachusetts, that's five years ago. Been to Ohio, Wisconsin, California, Arizona." Fox was used to the listing of places visited. It was routine among those who were roaming the country looking for something better.

Louie nodded. He was obviously used to the listing also. "Anyplace that looked good? Work easier to get?"

Fox shook his head. "It's all the same. Work hard to get, weather gone to hell. How about you? Any luck?"

Now it was Louie's turn to shake his head. "So what happened last night?"

"Met up with some guys. They took exception to my looks." Fox gestured at his eyes.

"Yeah." Louie smiled and pointed to his face. "I get that a lot."

Fox stared at his new friend. "I could swear I know you. Did we ever meet before?"

Louie stared back. "Nah. I'd remember those eyes."

Fox smiled. Louie's eyes were large and dark. Almost too large, like he wore contacts or something. But he'd never met anyone on the road who could afford contacts.

They finished their meal in a friendly silence. Louie stood up and helped Fox to his feet.

"You okay now? Feel up to job hunting?"

"Where do we start?"

"Oh, I got some leads."

Fox hesitated.

"What's up?" Louie asked.

"Do they look at your papers real close?" Fox's ID had stood up so far, but his jobs were low level, cleaning and grunt work. He'd never tried anything bigger.

Louie stared at him. "Look, government got more to worry about than papers, what with the weather and roads goin' to hell. No money to hire a lot of guys to check on people. 'Sides, nobody sneaks *into* this country anymore. Ain't enough jobs to go around. So don't worry."

Louie's friends steered them to a three month gig renovating old houses in the city. After they signed up Fox and Louie returned to the camp.

"Hey," Fox said as they walked between the tents, "what's with the big sticks?"

He pointed at two men and a woman walking around the encampment with clubs in their hands

"Enforcement," Louie answered.

Fox looked at him questioningly.

"You had a problem with bully boys, right? Well, these guys make sure those types don't come in here. The bastards won't tangle with armed folk ready to fight."

Fox stared at the guards for a moment. "Where do I sign up?"

Louie smiled at him and led him to a tent in the center of the camp.

After work the next day, Fox started putting together a shack out of junk lumber he found on the job. He got help from some of the people around him, and when they found out he signed up for enforcement, more hands drifted over. With so many working, the shack was soon finished. It wasn't great, but it would keep out the rain and give him a place to keep his belongings.

They didn't talk much. Fox wasn't surprised. People on the road didn't say a lot about their pasts. Some of them were running away from trouble, others were hurt or simply fed up with their old lives. The code dictated, *Don't ask, don't tell.* Fox was grateful that he didn't have to explain himself.

When the three-month gig was over, Louie said, "Well, I'm headin' west. Never been to California. It's nice there, right?"

"Yeah. But I'm going south. Texas. Maybe find a ranch that needs a hand." He paused, suddenly shy. "Look, Louie, I can never thank you. I guess you saved my life that first night."

"Hey, what're we here for but to help each other, y'know? You'll do the same thing for someone. I know."

They shook hands, and pulled each other into a brief hug. Then Louie turned and walked away.

Fox stared at the sandy high plains outside Cisco's ranch. It was so dry here you didn't even sweat, in spite of the heat. The moisture evaporated from your skin as soon as it formed. Dangerous. You didn't know you were getting dehydrated until you keeled over. It had happened to a few guys here.

The drought had been going on for almost a decade. Some brilliant politician had decided on the campaign slogan, *2020, A Year of Perfect Vision.* The news Fox was able to get from time to time told about coastlines under water and storms where there shouldn't be any. *Perfect Vision,* Fox thought. *The country needs glasses.*

Fox turned back to see Mr. Cisco hurrying over. The stocky figure was better suited to horseback than running.

"Clara's missing," the man said, worry evident in his voice.

His five-year-old daughter wandering in the desert. Fox pictured the child, round face framed by dark curls that reminded him so much of another girl whose black curls had floated in the breeze.

"We're getting a group together," Cisco continued. "Be ready in five." He turned to go, then looked back. "Glad you're here now. You're real good at finding the lost strays."

Fox didn't want to tell anyone that his talent was due to his telepathic ability. When a calf drifted away, he could usually find it by *listening.* It was good that the shadow never seemed to find him when he was only *receiving.* And, keeping his word to himself, he never *sent,* never even *scanned.*

He checked to make sure he had water. He drank before he saddled his horse, and gave the animal water as well. No sense in getting sick out there. The men had a job to do.

Nodding to the other men, he joined the group on horseback and rode into the scrub and dust. He relaxed his shields, searching for where the small animals, always wary, broadcast their fear that something was wrong. As the men spread out, he edged forward, subtly taking the lead, heading for the area that seemed to have the most activity.

After two hours, he found it. A blank spot in the desert that the mice and lizards steered clear of. Then he did what he avoided for six years.

Taking a deep breath, he *sent* into the middle of the spot. It was not a coherent thought, more like a strong jab. Enough to wake her up if she was asleep.

A thin, child-like cry sounded in the desert.

Fox whistled, loud and shrill. "Hey, guys, over here. I think I hear something," he called.

The men closed in on the location. Cisco jumped off his horse and ran to the rocks that shaded his daughter. He scooped her up in a smothering hug as she cried into his neck.

Fox watched with a small pang of jealousy. To love someone that much, and have her love you back, without worrying about killing her or hurting her. It was what he longed for. What he thought he could never have.

When they returned to the ranch, Cisco and his wife hugged Fox. "It was really you who found her," Cisco said. "We could've searched for hours more. She might have—" He choked.

Fox felt himself blush and hated the old reaction. "I'm just glad I could help," he said, as he scanned for the shadow.

An hour later it appeared. He barely got his shields up in time.

That night, as he cowered in his bunk, he felt the psychic tentacles of the thing probing the area around him. He *sensed* its intelligence, and it seemed human. It was similar to what he *felt* when he was mind to mind with his mother, but darker, dirtier. There was a malevolence about it.

During that long, sleepless night, Fox tried to analyze the shadow. It was obviously another telepath, or group of telepaths. Probably a group, because after a few hours the *feel* of it changed. It was like the bunch of men who had beaten Fox so badly back in Tulsa, like the other collection of bullies he had encountered in his travels.

One thing he had learned over the years was that if he, as a person alone, challenged the bullies, he lost. The best way to survive was to keep his head down, not look them in the eye, not flash his money. It was different in the camp in Tulsa where a lot of people together fought the predators.

Here, he was alone. There were no other telepaths around to help him if he got into trouble. From now on, he would rein in his talent. He wouldn't challenge the shadow. He would keep his head down.

Pursued by fear of the shadow and his own guilt, Fox felt that no place was home. He kept searching.

~~

The Sweetwater Retirement Home in Delray, Florida looked good from the outside. Fox stood for a moment, admiring the clean lines and pastel colors. He took a deep breath and walked inside to start his first day of work.

He looked around the hallway as he walked to the Human Resources office. The walls were painted a pleasant, inoffensive beige. A strip of burgundy floral wallpaper ran the length of the wall three feet from the bottom. The navy blue carpet on the floor was relatively clean, showing a little wear. It was a cheerful, soothing place.

The work would be difficult, but he could help people. And maybe he'd find a way to an even more responsible job. Become a nurse like Papa.

The thought brought a stab, an almost physical pain. He hadn't felt it that sharply in the seven years since he left home. *It must be the surroundings* he thought. *It reminds me so much of him. Of all of them.* He flashed on Sonia's face as she started to unbutton her blouse, on Papa's as he lay dying. Dad might be alone, but at least he was alive.

No one he loved was safe as long as he was around.

Ms. Rosen, the Director, wasn't in her office. Instead, a younger woman came forward as he walked in. "Hi. I'm Melodie. I was asked to show you around." Her smile was welcoming.

They took the elevator to the second floor and followed the sounds of talk and laughter to a large room near the nurse's station. Sunlight flooded through the windows Several elderly people sat in upholstered chairs. A few were in wheelchairs. Walkers and oxygen canisters stood inside the door.

A slim man with a thick mane of white hair said, ". . . and some of those Fokkers were Messerschmitts!"

Laughter erupted. The speaker smiled broadly.

"Hey, Kornfeld, you haven't lost it," said an African American man across the informal circle.

"You bet, Reynolds, and I never will," the other man replied. He looked suggestively at Melodie and raised his eyebrows. "Just ask this lovely young lady!"

Melodie led Fox to the group, laughing. "Everybody, this is John Marshall. He'll be joining us as the new orderly."

The residents in the circle turned bright, interested eyes toward Fox. He had lost a lot of his shyness during his travels, but he still felt uncomfortable as the center of attention. Shaking off the feeling, he smiled.

Melodie went around the group reeling off names. Fox couldn't remember them, but he figured he'd get to know the people in time. Then she dragged him away.

"Marshall," the man called Kornfeld shouted as they left, "the closet at the end of the hall is nice—if you got a pretty girl to share it with!"

Everyone laughed again. Melodie smiled, and it transformed her.

Fox grinned at her. "How'd he know about the closet? Personal experience?"

She nodded. "Probably. Wouldn't put anything past him."

~

Fox got an apartment in a rental development. There were many vacant properties because most people had been frightened away by predictions of coastal flooding and water shortages. It was easy to persuade the management company. All he had to do was show them his pay stubs.

A car was too expensive, he decided, so he rented a bicycle from one of the companies that had sprung up. He opened a bank account, got a debit card, a non-driver's ID card, and he was set.

CHAPTER 32

F ox was friendly toward everyone at Sweetwater, but some of the residents were special. Mr. Kornfeld had been a computer analyst who was now over ninety years old. His memory was starting to go and he could be cantankerous and loud, but Fox could calm him down. When the older man was lucid, he was kind and interesting. He had lived in places all over the world and, if he could be believed, had a very checkered past.

"I was sent to Australia once," the old man said as Fox helped him out of bed. "Yup. Back in the sixties. Y'know, computers took up a whole building then."

"Yeah, I've seen pictures," Fox answered, settling Kornfeld into his wheelchair.

"Yup. Was in Sydney for a whole year. Did some traveling around the Outback, too. Ever been there?"

"No. Wanted to."

"You're young. You'll get the chance. Anyways," Kornfeld continued as Fox pushed him to the common room, "I was in the Outback. And there was this beautiful Aborigine girl. She had a body on her . . ."

The story of the seduction of the beautiful maiden by the older American went on. Kornfeld went into detail. Fox sat on a couch next to the old man, fascinated, as the tale unfolded.

"And in the end she thanks me," Kornfeld concluded. "Said she was happy and she would have a beautiful baby!" His laugh was loud and infectious.

Mrs. Gentera was younger than most. She was only seventy-three and had Alzheimer's. It was a sad case. She had been an artist. Not like Marta,

188

nowhere near as good, at least in Fox's estimation. Now she just sat most of the time, staring into space. Sometimes she hummed quietly, like Papa did at the end. Her paintings hung on the walls of her room like old friends gathered trying to give comfort.

There were others he saw regularly. Mr. Castleman was a retired teacher who spoke about teaching in the New York City high schools for thirty years. His stories, like the one about the boy who threatened to smash a chair over his head, were sometimes frightening. But then he talked about how his students gave him a surprise party when they found out he was going to be married. His face lit up when he told that one.

Ms. Francis used to be an actress and at first appeared snobby. After Fox got to know her, he found a gentleness that was endearing. She was different when he was around. Her southern accent was lovely.

Mrs. Borstein complained. "My legs are hurtin' a lot today," she'd say. Or, "My kids never come to see me." She was diabetic. The pain of the neuropathy sometimes made her cranky.

He got to know their problems and became quite a favorite among them. He tried to help them as much as he could, *sensing* when they needed a bedside water pitcher refilled or had to go to the bathroom.

He never went *inside* their heads in spite of the temptation, and never tried to cure their bodies. The risk was too great. But sometimes after his shift was over he listened to Mr. Kornfeld's stories of a wild bachelor life lived in exotic places, or sat with Mrs. Gentera and held her hand. She always hummed when Fox was with her.

Although he occasionally hung out with people from work, he thought of the residents as his friends.

He'd been working at Sweetwater a year when Ms. Rosen called him into her office. Fox felt anxious as he walked down the hall. His work was good, or at least he thought so. What could she want?

Ms. Rosen came right to the point when Fox sat down. "You've been working here for a year. And you've done really well."

Fox nodded his thanks.

"I think you're capable of more. I think you should get your CNA license."

Certified nursing assistant. He hadn't considered that. It would mean more money, and more responsibility. He could help even more than he did now.

"Here's the application," Ms. Rosen said handing him a stack of papers. "There's also information there about the courses you have to take and the other requirements."

"Thanks," Fox said, genuinely grateful.

She smiled at him. "I hope you take this opportunity, John. I think you're capable of a great deal more than simply being an orderly."

He left the office feeling a flush of pride. It was good to be appreciated.

But reading the information packet showed a problem. *Damn, they wanted a background check. Would Joey's papers hold up?*

He argued with himself for two days. If he applied and his false identity was revealed he'd be fired at least, maybe thrown in jail. But news reports told about government agencies in disarray, budget cutbacks forcing overworked people to make mistakes, cut corners. If he was real lucky . . .

As he walked onto his floor he saw Mrs. Borstein get out of bed and fall. He ran to her, stopping only to pull the cord for the nurse. He checked quickly to make sure she was breathing. There was no blood. He was tempted to check *inside* her, but avoided it. He *sensed* a wrongness in her blood.

When Clementine arrived, he said, "Her blood sugar's too low. She got dizzy and fell. I think she—" He caught himself before he said too much. "—might have broken something."

Clementine kneeled down and ran her hands over the woman's legs and hips. Then she shook her head. "I think we be lucky," she said, her Island accent more pronounced. "Nothing seems broken. I'll check her sugar. Get you some help and we put her in the bed."

When Fox and another orderly had placed her gently on the mattress, Clementine grabbed the testing kit. Carefully she took a drop of blood from Mrs. Borstein's finger, then looked at Fox, amazed. "How you know her sugar be too low?"

Good question, he realized. How *had* he known? He had *sensed* it, that's how. But he couldn't say that. "Um, by the way her breath smelled sweet. You know, the way a patient's breath gets in ketosis."

Clementine looked at him. "You *are* good, John Marshall."

After they had made sure that Mrs. Borstein was okay, Clementine pulled Fox out of the room. "I hear Ms. Rosen think you could be a CNA. You should. You a natural."

He filed the papers the next day. Luck was with him. Either officials were too busy, or someone fouled up, or Joey was a lot better than anyone thought, because the background check went through with no problem.

Fox started on the coursework. It wasn't as hard as he thought it would be. Of course, after pre-calculus at Stuyvesant, what could be? He was on his way to something better. A way he could really help people without using his power.

⚡

On his way to lunch, Fox saw an unfamiliar figure walking the hall. He couldn't see any visitor's badge, and he knew no one was supposed to wander through the halls unescorted. "Excuse me, sir," he said, stopping the man. "Can I help you?"

"Sure can, son." The man turned a tanned face toward him. His white hair was thick and carefully styled and his sunglasses were expensive. "See, I'm looking for a place for my uncle. He can't take care of himself . . . Well, you know the story. So I'm investigating."

For a moment Fox hesitated. He wondered how someone could have gotten in without being stopped, but he didn't want to insult someone whose relative might be staying here.

"There are regular tours of the place, you know," Fox said quickly. "I could arrange—"

"Nah, those things, they only show you what they want you to see. I wanna be able to see what really goes on."

"I could bring you to—"

The man didn't seem to hear him. "Hey, you work here. You could show me around."

Fox couldn't see his eyes behind the sunglasses, and it bothered him. Still, he got no bad vibes from the stranger.

"Well, maybe I could answer some questions," Fox said. "But I'm on my lunch break. Only got an hour."

"Great." The man put an arm around Fox's shoulder. "I'll buy you lunch. What's your name, kid?"

They got food from the nearby Popeye's and sat outside at a plastic table as they ate. "M'name's Ezra," the man said. "My uncle, he's about 90. I'm checking out places. Heard this one was good. You know how it goes."

Fox nodded, his mouth full of fried chicken.

"So tell me, this a good place?" Ezra took a huge bite.

Fox swallowed his food. "Yeah. The residents are well cared for. We have a top medical team. You saw, the place is clean."

Now it was Ezra's turn to nod. "Y'like working there?"

Fox described some of the residents on his floor. He was careful of their privacy and didn't give names. Ezra had an uncanny way of pulling information out of him, and he found himself telling the older man more about his own life than he intended to.

At one point Ezra asked him, "So where you from, kid? I mean, no one down here is *from* here, y'know?"

"Brooklyn," Fox answered, hoping the shortness of his reply would keep Ezra from asking more.

"Oh, yeah? I'm from Queens, myself. We were almost neighbors!" He laughed. "What brought you to sunny Florida?"

Fox searched for an answer. "I heard there was work here. Not like most other places."

Ezra attacked his cole slaw. "You been a lot of other places?"

Surprised by the question, Fox was prepared to refuse an answer. Instead, he found himself listing the places he'd been, just as he did on the road. He even started telling Ezra about leaving home, but he caught himself before he went too far.

At the end of the hour Ezra wiped his face with the napkin. "Thanks, kid. You helped a lot. This looks like a good place. It's definitely on the list."

"Then I look forward to seeing you again, with your uncle. You should bring him in so he can see it for himself."

"Okay," Ezra said, waving good-bye.

He didn't come in again. Fox figured he had decided against Sweetwater. Or maybe his uncle had gotten worse. He soon forgot about it in the press of everyday responsibilities.

One day as he came on duty he glanced into Mrs. Gentera's room. It looked different. The bed was stripped and boxes filled with her belongings lined the walls. Puzzled, Fox walked quickly to the nurse's station. Jeannette sat behind the counter, a large stack of papers in front of her.

"What happened to Mrs. Gentera?" he asked.

Jeannette looked up and frowned at the interruption. When she recognized Fox her expression changed to one of pity. "Oh, Fox, I'm sorry. I guess no one told you. Mrs. Gentera died last night. Peacefully, in her sleep."

Fox didn't say anything. He was sad. He would miss her, in a way. He realized that no one could have helped Mrs. Gentera. He started to walk away, then turned around.

"Jeannette, what happened to her paintings?" he asked.

"I dunno. Probably just taken downstairs to the cellar. She didn't have any kids, no relatives we knew about. If no one claims them, they'll be tossed."

"D'you think anyone would mind if I took one? Just to remember her?" Fox didn't love her paintings, or even feel very close to Mrs. Gentera. He simply felt it was a shame that she should pass from the world and leave nothing behind, no trace she existed.

Jeannette smiled. "Check with Admin first. I doubt anyone'll care."

Fox nodded and went off to finish his shift. At least *he* would remember Mrs. Gentera.

CHAPTER 33

When he got his CNA license, Fox decided to treat himself to a new minicomp. He was glad he didn't have to carry around a laptop, and the screen of the smaller model was easy to read. Then he rode to the only Barnes and Noble still open and functioning. Even after two years, he still enjoyed riding his bike rather than driving. It was much cheaper and gave him a greater chance to see his surroundings, to be a part of the city. He could have ordered the items he wanted online, but he treasured his few visits to the bookstore.

The smell of coffee lifted his spirits as he walked through the door. There weren't many printed works, mostly best-sellers and self-help. The majority of the area was taken up by computer kiosks. Today, half of them were occupied by people checking out the titles of the most recent offerings.

Fox sat in an empty chair and called up the science fiction listings. He went through them quickly, pausing every once in a while at one he remembered. The authors were listed alphabetically, with Brian Aldiss heading the list.

He ran down the list. When he got to the "M's" he stopped. There it was, a whole page to itself. Peter Monroe. They seemed to have all of Dad's books there. He read through the familiar titles and stopped at two he'd never seen.

Syncing his new comp to the store's mainframe, he paid for and downloaded the two books. It put a considerable dent in his discretionary spending for the month, but it was worth it.

Fox stared at the screen as though he could conjure his father through it. Tears prickled his eyes. He sat there for a moment, resting his fingers on the machine, before he stood and walked away.

Shaking off the melancholy, he rode to the Morikami. Fox enjoyed the manicured, Japanese-style park with its gravel paths and secluded nooks.

It threatened rain as he pedaled to the parking lot. Only a few cars. That was good. Fewer people in the garden meant more chance to be alone and quiet.

He hurried by the muted chatter from the restaurant and stepped onto the path that wound around bushes and over a bridge. A mild breeze swayed the branches of the trees. Farther on, he could see the bamboo moving gently back and forth and hear the creak of their trunks.

There were no people nearby.

It was perfect.

Lowering his shields a crack, Fox *checked* for the shadow. Detecting nothing, he vanished the shields altogether, leaving only the brick wall to stop the ever present whispers.

For the first time in months he was able to relax. At work and even in his apartment on a secluded street in Delray, there were too many people around. He had to keep his shields up or the psychic noise was unbearable, but maintaining them was draining.

Even through his protection, there were times when Fox felt the earth itself cry out to him for help. The need of people in pain or trouble battered his shields. He usually ignored it, but recently it had been getting to him.

He sighed. There was nothing he could do about humanity or the problems of the planet.

The meditation garden was empty. The sun filtered through the trees onto tiny tan stones and shone directly on the mossy boulder.

Fox centered himself on the deep wooden bench and crossed his legs in front of him, lotus position. He assumed the stance that should indicate to any passers-by that he was meditating. Maybe he could avoid any interruption.

He sank into the murmur of insects, the slow life of trees and flowers. He *shared* the joy of lives that didn't have to die or hibernate because it was always summer here. For a moment, the psychic tumult threatened to overwhelm him. He managed to turn down the volume, and relaxed into the sounds.

Fox didn't know how long he sat, basking in the relative quiet of undemanding whispers. Then he heard the crunch of footsteps, and reluctantly raised his shields.

The intruder walked to the bench and sat down on the end opposite Fox. Maintaining his stance, Fox looked sidelong at the young woman.

She appeared to be about twenty-five, maybe five years younger than he was. She sat, unmoving, in a pose that mirrored his, breathing rhythmically. Her small breasts rose and fell slowly under a yellow tee. Brown hair framed her face in waves as the sun picked out red and gold highlights.

Fox liked the way she looked.

His concentration ruined, he straightened his legs and moved forward on the bench and got up.

She looked at him. "I'm sorry. I didn't mean to interrupt your meditation." Her voice was low-pitched and soft.

Fox was reluctant to leave. "I was just about finished anyway—" he started.

A group of older women chattered their way into the garden. They stood at the entrance commenting on the precise wavy lines in the gravel, the placement of the boulder, and how it all came together to produce an atmosphere of peace. They chattered loudly about the aura of serenity, unaware of the disruption caused by their entrance. When they walked away after a few minutes, they left a welcome silence.

Unfolding her legs, she rose gracefully from the bench. "I guess neither one of us was destined to meditate today."

Fox hesitated. "Are you going to continue around the garden?"

"Yes," she answered, looking at him shyly.

For a moment they stood, looking silently at each other.

"I'm going this—" Fox said.

"Well, would you like to—" she said at the same time. Her cheeks turned pink.

They laughed.

"I mean, we could walk together," she said.

"That would be good," Fox answered.

"My name is Delores," she said as they wandered along the path.

"I'm John. John Marshall."

"Hello, John John Marshall." Delores' dark eyes sparkled.

Fox felt his cheeks warm and cursed silently. Then he smiled back.

"So what do you do here in Florida?" she asked. "Or are you just visiting?"

Fox liked her gentle but unabashed curiosity. "I'm a nurse at a retirement home. Here in Delray. You?"

"Office manager for a pediatrician in Boca. We're in the same business." The delight in her voice was obvious.

"If you'll pardon my saying so, maybe not so unique here in Florida."

She giggled. "Let's walk up the hill. Look at the koi pond. I love that spot."

"Me, too," Fox said, pleased that there was something else they shared.

When they came down the hill, Delores stopped and pulled out her cell. "Damn. I didn't realize it was so late. I have to run." She gave Fox an apologetic look

"Oh, yeah, of course." He felt awkward. "But, look, if I gave you my phone number you could call me. If you wanted to." Would he *ever* learn not to blush?

She handed him her phone and he entered his number. "Please call," he said.

She smiled and hurried off down the path.

Fox wandered into the bonsai display and found a bench. The contorted shapes of the miniature trees were somehow calming, even though the presence of several people meant he had to keep his shields up. He was almost happy for the first time in years. Delores would call, he was sure.

—

When his phone rang two days later, Fox opened it immediately.

"I'm gonna be downtown day after tomorrow," Delores' voice came through. "You wanna meet for lunch?"

He was glad she couldn't hear his rapid heart beat. "There's this great Italian place," he said, trying to sound cool. "I eat there a lot."

"Great. Around twelve thirty?"

Delores was waiting outside the restaurant when Fox walked over. She was eyeing the tiny storefront. "Doesn't look like much."

"Yeah, it looks like a hole in the wall. But the food's good. You'll see."

The interior was dim after the bright outdoor sunlight. Franco, the owner, greeted them as they walked in, and ushered them to what Fox considered "his" table.

"You alone today?" Fox asked him as they sat. Often Mirabella, Franco's teenage daughter, waited tables.

Franco nodded. "Not busy today." He gestured at the other tables, only two of which were occupied. "Something to drink for your lovely young lady? For you, of course, I have the sparkling water." His accent was slight, but noticeable.

Delores shook her head. "I have to drive. I'll have the water, too, please."

"Okey dokey," he said and left.

Delores picked up her menu. "So what's good here? You obviously know the place."

"Everything I've tried has been good. The food's fresh and the cook has a way with spices. But . . ." He grinned at her. "You trust me?"

She cocked her head and looked at him, a mischievous glint in her eyes. "Yes, John Marshall, I think I do."

"You like chicken?"

She nodded.

Franco returned with water and breadsticks. He looked at Fox inquiringly.

"Can you make us that special chicken you do? And the spaghetti with pesto?"

"Sure thing, John. Just like you like it." He walked away.

Delores took a sip of her water. Her movements were graceful and unhurried, a kind of dance. Fox was enthralled.

"Why are you staring at me?" she asked. "Did I dribble or something?"

Embarrassed, Fox looked down. "No. You just . . . Your movements are so graceful. Are you a dancer?"

"No. But I did study for a while when I was a kid. Did you ever dance?"

Fox smiled. "Ever seen the animation *Bambi*? Y'know where he's on the ice, slipping around all over the place?"

She nodded.

"That's me. Can't get my feet under me."

"So what do you do? When you're not working."

I read people's minds and kill them, Fox thought, but quickly stepped on the idea. "I used to do some writing. Short stories. But I haven't in a long time."

She did the head-cocking thing again, waiting for him to continue, and he had to smile. She was lovely.

"I was on the road for a long time," he continued. "Didn't have much time for writing."

"How come? Not how come you didn't have time. I understand that. But how come you were on the road?"

Fox decided to stay as close to the truth as possible. "My Pop got sick when I was senior in high school. I had to drop out to take care of him. And then he died." It still hurt to say that, even after twelve years. "I couldn't stay there. So I left. Tried to find a path."

"How about your Mom?"

"She lives in Wyoming. Left when I was a baby. I'm in touch with her a lot. We're close." That was true. He called her at least once a month. "But how about you? Why didn't you keep dancing?"

"My folks really wanted me to go to college. Actually, I did, too. But I had to earn some money first. So I worked for a couple of years after high school. Then . . ." She looked down and fiddled with her silverware, turning the knife this way and that. "Well, in college I met a boy. And I got pregnant."

Franco brought out their meals and conversation stopped for a few minutes. Delores took a bite of chicken and pronounced it "Extraordinary." Franco looked pleased, then hurried to another table.

Fox wanted Delores to continue speaking, but he *sensed* that she needed time to frame her words. They ate in silence for a few minutes. She ate in quick, dainty bites. Fox kept his head bent as though looking at his plate, but his eyes were on her.

Finally, Fox couldn't wait. "What happened?" he asked, raising his eyes.

She looked back at him, a smile playing on her lips. "I kept the baby. My Lily. She's almost three now, and she's beautiful." Delores took out her wallet and opened it, handing it to Fox.

A sweet-faced little girl smiled out at him. Dark eyes danced above creamy, pudgy cheeks. Her head was cocked slightly to one side in the same gesture her mother often used.

"She's lovely," Fox said. "And her father . . . ?"

"Not in the picture." Delores picked up her fork again. "Hasn't been since before she was born."

"Nice guy."

"No biggie. I didn't want him involved. Lily's mine and I like it that way." A shadow crossed her face and she was quiet for a moment.

"What?" Fox prompted.

"She has asthma, and it gets bad sometimes. I worry about her."

He nodded sympathetically. "Lily. It's a good name."

Delores smiled. "I got it from the Harry Potter books. I used to read them all the time—"

"Me, too," Fox said, excited. "Did you ever—"

They reached for breadsticks at the same time.

"Expelliamus!" Fox cried.

"Protego!" Delores answered simultaneously.

They laughed.

"I read all of them," Fox said. "I had a best friend, Sonia." It still hurt. "We used to play at it all the time."

"Yeah. My buddy, Sammy, we did, too."

"She would say, Fox, you never—"

"Fox?"

"That's what they called me. Red hair, pointy nose, yellow eyes."

She tilted her head and examined him. "Yeah. Suits you."

They lingered over coffee until Fox *sensed* Franco's impatience. They shared the bill. Fox was grateful.

Outside the restaurant, they paused. Fox didn't want to leave, and he *sensed* that Delores was equally reluctant.

"I really enjoyed this," he said. "Do you think we could do it again?"

"I'd like that," Delores answered.

⸺

Fox and Delores saw each other two or three times a week, but he didn't meet Lily until three weeks later.

"How about dinner here this weekend?" Delores asked when Fox called. "You can see what a great cook I am. And you can meet Lily."

Fox was nervous as he pedaled to Delores' apartment complex. In the basket of his bike were a bouquet of flowers and a bottle of wine. The flowers weren't roses and the wine wasn't champagne. But the wine store clerk told him it was a good, inexpensive bottle.

Delores answered the door when he rang. Her cheeks were flushed. The wonderful aromas coming from the kitchen hinted that she'd been hard at work making dinner. He handed her the wine and flowers, first extracting one from the bunch. As they walked into the short hallway, a little girl ran up. She half hid behind her mother's leg and looked shyly at Fox.

He squatted in front of the child. "I bet I know your name."

She stared at him from the safety of her mother's shadow.

He reached behind his back and brought out a tall flower. He held it out to her.

Lily looked up at her mother, asking permission to take the gift. Delores nodded, smiling. The child stepped hesitantly to him and held out her hand.

"Do you know what kind of flower it is?" Fox asked.

Lily shook her head.

"It's called a lily."

"Like me!" she squealed.

"Is that really your name?" he teased.

She nodded.

He looked at her, wide-eyed with pretended surprise. "Then the flower must be for you!"

She retreated behind her mother, the flower clutched tightly in her chubby fist. But she was smiling.

"I think you've made a hit with her," Delores whispered as they walked to the dining room.

"I hope so," he said.

They dated for two months, sharing good-night kisses, but nothing beyond that. Fox wanted to wait. He wanted to make sure it was right. And he *sensed* a shyness in her that echoed his own misgivings.

Two months later, they drove back to her apartment after dinner. When she turned off the car, Delores smiled and said, "Lily's staying with her grandparents tonight."

As the door to the apartment closed behind them, they turned to each other. The kiss was explosive. Fox had never been so shaken, even by that first kiss with Mark. He *knew* she felt the same. They made their way to the bedroom, stopping to kiss and shed their clothing, one slow piece at a time.

He tasted wine on her tongue as the waves of desire mounted in her. His hand cupped her small breast and his fingers brushed the nipple. She moaned. They fell onto the bed, their hands exploring each other's bodies. When she slipped the condom on him, he almost came, but managed to hold back.

He ran his hands over her slender body, enjoying the feelings of pleasure that rose from her. He *sensed* what she wanted and let her excitement add to his. The sensations rolled and tumbled in his mind as they rode the waves of combined desire, swirling in passion, until together they climaxed and lay entwined in exhaustion.

"Wow," Delores said breathlessly.

"Yeah," Fox answered.

CHAPTER 34

F ox walked into the Sweetwater building the next morning whistling. Jeannette looked up from the desk.

"Someone got lucky last night," she said drily.

"Jealous?" he said.

"Huh. You wish." She turned back to her computer.

Fox smiled.

The shift went rapidly. Fox lowered his shields very slightly and *shared* the happiness of the elderly residents of his floor. It added to his own in a marvelous feedback.

Mr. Kornfeld regaled the people in the hall with a risqué ballad he had learned in Sarajevo. His translation, he claimed, toned it down a lot. Fox couldn't believe he was about to celebrate his one hundred and fifth birthday.

Everyone in the room laughed and clapped when he finished. Their eyes were bright. The mood was lively.

"Hey, Kornfeld," called Mr. Roberts, a grin spread across his dark face. "How come *you* ended up here? You been all over."

"I wanted to be with people like me," Mr. Kornfeld said.

"Y'mean white and rich?" Mr. Roberts baited.

"Nah. I mean kinda wrinkled on the edges and flabby in the middle!"

The crowd laughed again.

Fox left the lounge and walked past Ms. Francis's room.

"Hey, John, got a minute?" she called. She was sitting in her chair with a large book in her lap.

"For you, darling, any time," he said, walking in.

"C'mere. Look at this." She showed him the cover of the book, *Starlets of 1957*, then opened to a page about half way through.

He looked at the picture. The girl who stared out at him was beautiful. She had wavy blonde hair and huge dark eyes. Her breasts were improbably high and pointed, her waist trim.

The caption read, "Miss Laura Francis, of MGM Studios, whose movie credits include . . ." There followed a list of movies Fox had never heard of.

"You were a real looker, Ms. Francis," Fox said, and he meant it.

Her eyes lit up. Fox could see a hint of the girl in the old woman who sat in front of him.

"You still are," he continued. "You must have been some movie star."

"Aw, g'wan with you," she said, her soft southern accent more pronounced than usual. "Ah was nevah a *star*. But Ah did meet some of the greats."

Fox spent a pleasant fifteen minutes with her as she told stories about the movies in the 50's. He was sure much of it was made up, but he didn't mind. He *sensed* her happiness at being able to talk about it.

As he walked out that evening, he gave a sigh of satisfaction. He made his people feel better. He knew that he couldn't make them well. There was no cure for old age.

His cell buzzed in his pocket. A text from Delores.

<Dinner tmw?>

<@ 8?> he sent back.

<My place> came the message a few seconds later.

A flutter of happiness bubbled in Fox's stomach. Then he sobered. He was entering dangerous territory. He would have to control himself, be very careful not to get too close. Memories of his past threatened to erase all the joy he felt.

"I think you should move in here," Delores said six months later.

It was after dinner and Lily was asleep in her room. The apartment was quiet.

Fox turned his head and looked into Delores' eyes. "Are you sure about this?" he asked.

She nodded. "Definitely."

"'Cause I . . . Hell, it's such a cliché. I never felt like this."

Dee cocked her head and grinned mischievously. "You're here almost every night anyway. It's impractical to have two households."

He smiled in response. "And the bike ride from my place to here is so long."

"It just makes sense," she giggled.

"Only sensible thing to do." He laughed softly.

The next evening, as they ate hamburgers and French fries, Delores said to Lily, "How would you like it if Fox came to live with us?"

Lily stopped nibbling on her fry and looked from one adult to the other. Then she grinned and clapped her hands. "That'd be the best thing in the world."

"Better than chocolate cake?" Fox asked.

"Yeah," the little girl said, planting a ketchup-stained kiss on his cheek.

That night, Fox had trouble falling asleep. He kept going over how he could tell Delores about himself. He'd finally found a home and he didn't want to ruin it.

On a day off they took Lily to the zoo. She danced and skipped ahead as they moved from cage to cage. She stopped abruptly in front of the bonobo chimpanzees.

"They're unhappy," she said staring solemnly at the animals.

"What makes you think they're sad?" asked Delores.

"They just are. They're not playing."

Fox relaxed his shields. The minds of the apes were murky and it was hard to *see* anything specific. He *sensed* a general unhappiness but nothing more.

Lily turned to him. "Make them happy, Fox. Please!"

The pleading look on her face pierced him. He checked briefly for the shadow. He hadn't seen it in a long time, but still . . .

He swooped her up in his arms. Her solidity always surprised him. "I'll try, Lily Flower, but you have to help."

"How?"

"Think really happy thoughts."

Lily closed her eyes and grimaced in concentration. Suggestions of ice cream and bedtime stories floated from her. An image of forming a snowball helped him concentrate the feelings behind the blurry pictures. Then he *threw* the ball at the caged animals.

They perked up.

Lily wrapped her arms around his neck. "You did it, Fox! You did it!"

He smiled at her, trying to hide his confusion.

Did he really do something? He was trying to figure it out when a keeper rounded the corner wheeling a cart heaped with fruits and vegetables. The chimps gathered around a door on the back wall, jumping up and down and jabbering excitedly at each other. The door opened and huge trays of food were shoved into the cage.

"Well, I guess they were just hungry," Fox said.

Then the large female chimp turned around and stared at Fox. She winked.

Fox was astonished. He had never influenced anyone before, at least not consciously. He thought about his residents at Sweetwater, how they reacted to him. Was he doing the same thing to them even though he didn't realize it? He would have to be more careful.

That night he tucked Lily in and kissed her good-night. She looked up at him. "I love you, Daddy Fox," she whispered.

A thrill ran through him, but it was quickly tempered by fear. He was a father now, the way his fathers had been to him. Could he do this? Could he hold this little life in his hands without messing it up?

"I love you, too, Lily," he said.

Later he and Delores sat on the couch. Her feet were tucked up and her head was on his shoulder. Fox had never felt so happy, and so solid. He had a family of his own that he was responsible for. Soon he would tell Dee all about himself, and everything would be in place.

"I love the way you are with Lily," Dee said. "Y'know, the way you encourage her to make up stories. I never had that with my folks."

Fox kissed her forehead.

"It's just . . . You will be sure to tell her it's just stories, right? That it's not real? I mean, no one can really read minds or send happiness to someone else."

He took her hand, holding it gently. "If that's what you want, of course. You know I would never do *anything* to hurt Lily. Or you."

He turned her head so she looked at him. He held her gaze until it softened. He kissed her and the fire ignited.

Later, as he drowsed toward sleep, he felt the barrier again, the separation between him and "normal" people. How could he tell Delores about his talents in a way that she would believe him, and still love him?

~~

Fox nursed his old car north along Federal Highway. He had been driving for three months. Delores' brother, Ray, had helped him find the fifteen-year-old 2012 Ford, and together they fixed it so it ran. The hybrid engine was an antique, but there were enough stations left so he could get gas. He wanted one of the new solar powered cars, but Ray argued that the technology was too new. No one knew how often they needed repairs. Besides, they were too expensive.

The days had started getting longer. Palm trees were outlined against an orange-pink sky instead of being shrouded in darkness as they had been for months. He was happy. Spring gave him a feeling of renewal.

For once, he found a place in the development's parking lot that was not too far from the building's entrance. He ran up the three flights, too eager to wait for the elevator.

As he opened the door, he was hit by thirty pounds of squealing four-year-old.

"Fox! You're home! Mommy! Fox is home!" Lily seemed to live her life at high volume.

Fox picked the child up and kissed her cheek. "Yes, *I'm* home. But who are you?" he teased.

"Silly!" she said and squirmed out of his arms. "C'mon. Dinner's almost ready and I'm hungry. An' we're gonna eat *outside!*"

She grabbed his hand and pulled him toward the kitchen. Delores came into the hall, her cheeks flushed from the heat of the stove. He kissed her lightly on the lips, surprised at the electricity that flared. She smiled.

They sat at the round glass table on the tiny balcony of their apartment. Fox loved this time of year, February shading into March. So did Delores. It was still cool enough to be pleasant, and the air was filled with springtime scents of growing things. Delores tucked a napkin around Lily's neck and put some chicken and green beans on her plate. Fox smiled, enjoying the scene.

He turned to the little girl. "So what did you do in school today?"

Lily had started pre-school in September and was very proud of her new status. She wasn't in day care anymore, she announced proudly to everyone. She was too grown up for that.

The child rattled on about pictures and songs and a boy who had thrown up after lunch. Big news. Fox and Delores smiled at each other over her head.

Lily interrupted her stories. "Hey, Fox, y'know what?"

"No, what?"

"Y'know what?" she insisted

"Okay. What?"

"It's my birthday!"

"Today?" he asked in mock surprise.

"No, silly. In two days." She held up two pudgy fingers.

"Really? Imagine that. How old are you going to be?"

Lily started to answer but Fox interrupted. "No, wait, let me guess. Let's see . . . You're going to be—fifteen!"

She shook her head.

"Uh, thirty-seven? A hundred and nineteen?"

She put on her *don't you know anything?* look. "No. I'm gonna be this many." She held up five fingers.

"How much is that?" Fox asked, going along with the game.

"Count 'em," the girl ordered.

"Oh, Lily, you know I can't count that high," he said, looking helpless. "You count for me."

The child continued the game, counting on each of her fingers. "One, two, three, four—*five!*" she piped triumphantly.

"Nah, you can't be five. I bet you're only three and a half."

Delores suppressed a smile and Fox had a hard time keeping a straight face.

"I'm gonna be *five,*" Lily insisted. "And Mommy's gonna make me a special cake. And we're gonna go somewhere for supper. Right, Mommy? You said so, right?"

"Yes, darling, I said so," Delores agreed, looking fondly at her daughter. Then she put on her serious face. "But we're not going anywhere if you don't finish your green beans."

"Aw, Mom," Lily complained, but started putting the beans in her mouth one at a time.

Delores turned to Fox. "How was work today?"

"Good. Very good, in fact. Old Joe Kornfeld actually told a story no one had ever heard before. And Laura Francis sang for us. She has kind of a nice voice for an old lady."

Fox didn't tell her that the activity was the result of the tactic he had discovered at the zoo. As he *fed* a little bit of his strength into his people a drop at a time, they reacted. Mr. Kornfeld got more rational, Ms. Francis became more energetic. They all "woke up" in a way. It was very satisfying.

He smiled at Delores. He used this particular ability when they were making love, too. He found that if he *trickled* his pleasure into her and *sipped* a small amount from her, he could keep the feedback loop going until they both lost themselves.

He reached over and took her hand. "How about you, hon. Good day, bad day, in between?"

"It was pretty horrific, as a matter of fact. I'll tell you later."

After Lily was asleep, they sat on the couch.

Delores said, "A little boy came in, Joey, about—" Her voice thickened and she had to pause. "About Lily's age. We'd given him a lot of tests. Turns out he has leukemia. There are treatments, but they're expensive, and with the cutbacks . . . His mother can't afford them, and Medicaid won't pay."

Fox squeezed her hand. He saw the tears in her eyes.

"He's going to die, Fox, and there's nothing I can do."

Fox *fed* some comfort to her through their joined hands. He felt depleted when he finished. He was using himself up but he had to help her. He didn't have to be a telepath to know what she was thinking. Lily was asthmatic, and Delores worried about her. Fox didn't understand how she could work with sick kids.

"You give them comfort, Dee," he said, remembering Daddy saying that to Papa in similar circumstances.

She nodded, but looked unconvinced, just as Papa had been unconvinced. Giving comfort was fine, but making people well was what counted.

And that was something he could never trust himself to try again.

That night he held her, their bodies pressed together in the bed, as she cried over the little boy who was going to die. He was exhausted, both physically and emotionally. *Giving* strength to so many people was getting to him. But he couldn't help himself. They needed it.

When she quieted, Fox whispered, "I love you, Dee."

"I love you too," she muttered sleepily.

He still hadn't told her about his power. They'd been living together for nearly two years, and he still couldn't bring himself to say the words. He never loved anyone the way he loved Dee, not even Sonia or Mark. It bothered him to keep such an important secret.

Then he remembered the words, "Daddy Fox." The thrill he'd felt. He wanted that. Needed that. He would tell her. Not tomorrow, but soon. And he'd ask her to marry him. They could be a family.

He would call Dad, introduce him to the new additions. Dad. He couldn't believe that ten years had passed since he left New York. Guilt crashed down on him again as he imagined his father sitting alone in the apartment.

But he was safe, Fox reminded himself. He was still writing. That was why Fox left, to remove the danger. It had worked.

And now, with Dee and Lily. Wasn't he jeopardizing them? Everyone he ever loved ended up hurt, or dead. He argued with himself that he was older now, his judgment was better, and there hadn't been a problem in years. But still . . .

Phrases bounced back and forth in his brain.

"I love you, Daddy Fox," in Lily's childish whisper.

"Who are you gonna kill this time," in Sonia's voice.

"I'm so scared," in Papa's weak rasp.

When he finally drifted off, his dreams were troubled. Just as when he first *heard* the whispers, the sounds of children crying penetrated his sleep. He tossed and turned, tightening his shields, but the *sounds* crept in.

Fox woke the next morning feeling as though he hadn't slept at all. Delores commented on it as they ate breakfast.

"You really look sick, hon. Maybe you're coming down with something."

"Nah, I'm fine," Fox replied. "Really. I'm okay."

"Take the day off," Delores said, her eyes narrowed in worry. "Just rest up."

"I never get sick, remember?" he said. "Don't worry."

He walked into Sweetwater. Henrietta was at the desk, reading the newsfeed on her tablet. She shook her head.

"Bad news?" Fox asked.

"There be flooding again. Hollywood and Dania. Bad."

"Anyone die?" It had become a normal question.

She scanned the words once more and shook her head before she looked up. She pursed her lips. "You look terrible, John. You sick?" Her Island accent was thick with concern.

"Nah, I never get sick. Just tired. Bad night."

"Too much kissey-kissey with that pretty woman of yours," Henrietta teased. "You gotta take it easy. 'Sides, I heard on the news that there be a flu bug goin' around. Nasty one, I heard."

Fox nodded and turned to go.

"Oh, John, water restrictions again. Men only shower today. Women tomorrow."

Fox waved wearily and went off to start his shift.

CHAPTER 35

The flu was a bad one, and it made the rounds quickly. The evening news was filled with statistics of the number of dead. It drove out the usual reports of coastal flooding and highway closings.

Mr. Delacruz, the head of the facility, called a morning staff meeting two weeks into the epidemic. "I know this is a difficult time for you—for everyone," he said, shifting from foot to foot nervously. "This bug is very contagious and very debilitating, especially for our people who are frail to begin with. We all have to do everything we can to help them through this."

He went over the usual precautions of washing or disinfecting hands before going into a resident's room, disposing of used tissues and sharp paraphernalia properly, encouraging those who were sick to cough into their elbows rather than their hands. Fox knew it was all stuff they'd heard before, but it didn't hurt to go over it.

"Anything about a cure?" Lisa asked when he finished.

"Nothing yet," Mr. Delacruz answered. "It's viral, so antibiotics don't help. And it seems to be resistant to all the stuff that's available now. We just have to try to get them to eat and drink, to stay strong so they can fight the infection naturally."

He ended the meeting with suggestions to get as much rest as possible, and to take care of themselves. "Remember, you can't help if you're sick yourself. Be smart. Be well."

Fox made the rounds when he had time, going to the rooms of all the residents he could. He sat at the bedside of each person, *transmitting* strength through his touch. It was seldom enough, and most of them died.

He was fighting the battle by himself, and it was impossible. He thought about his childhood hero who would always go it alone. With some initial help from Hermione and Ron, of course, but when it came to facing the evil, Harry was always the solitary figure. Fox felt that *he* was battling evil, too. It was an amorphous evil, though, not embodied in one man but in billions of microscopic bugs that invaded bodies and killed. How could he fight that?

Mr. Kornfeld was in bad shape. A feeding tube snaked into his nose and a small canula under his nostrils pumped oxygen into him. He seemed to be asleep when Fox came into his room one afternoon. His pale skin was stretched tight over the bones of his face. His shriveled hands occasionally plucked weakly at the bedcovers.

Fox pulled a chair over to the bed. The scene reminded him painfully of Papa Gerry at the end. He took Mr. Kornfeld's hand, looking at the age spots and the raised blue veins. He wanted to *give* some strength to the old man, but when he tried he found he had almost nothing in him. He was exhausted.

"Please, Mr. Kornfeld," he whispered. "You can get better, but you have to fight."

The figure on the bed moaned softly. His eyes fluttered, but didn't open. Then, suddenly, Mr. Kornfeld spoke, although his eyes remained shut.

"John." His voice was soft and hoarse. "You. Have. To. Help." There was a pause between words as Mr. Kornfeld struggled to speak.

"I know, Mr. Kornfeld. I'm trying to help you. But you have to help me. You have to—"

"No," the raspy whisper interrupted. "Help. Everyone."

Fox was stunned. "What do you mean? How can I help everyone? I can't even help you!"

But there was no answer. The old man's eyes fluttered again and the sound of his labored breathing filled the room.

The administration wanted to send Mr. Kornfeld to the hospital, but all the hospitals in the area were restricting their admissions to those "who stood a good chance of recovery." The elderly, the very young, those who had other medical issues that complicated their condition, were turned away.

He died two days later.

Fox went home every evening weary and depressed. There was nothing he could do. His *strength* was almost gone and the evening news was terrible. Neither he nor Delores wanted to watch the reports, but it was impossible to avoid them. The talking heads were blathering about how the country never really recovered from the recession twenty years before, and now this epidemic was making it worse.

They said it was decimating the population. The disease was attacking everywhere but the most deaths were in the poorer parts of the globe, as always.

Some of the newscasters blamed America's situation on the government for letting too many people into the country. Because of the economy there was mass immigration, so it didn't matter where the sickness started, they claimed. Others blamed the government for cutting back on health care, so the people who were ill couldn't afford to see doctors and they spread the disease further.

There was no cure, at least not yet, and no one was able to figure out where it came from. It spread rapidly. Every TV station had an expert who showed the audience charts comparing it to the flu of 1917 that spread around the planet and killed millions. Whatever you called it, it was horrible, and Fox hated the microscopic germ that caused it.

A month into the epidemic, Fox sat at the dinner table. He was tired, more tired than he'd ever been. Almost all the residents at Sweetwater were sick, and he tried to help them as much as possible. He went from one to the other, doling out strength where he could. But he was only one person, and he couldn't get to everyone.

Delores put out the food without talking, a sure sign to Fox that it had been a bad day. Even Lily wasn't chattering away as she usually did.

"Hey, Lily Flower," he said, smiling down at her. "What's up?"

"Nuthin'," Lily said.

"What exciting stuff happened in school today?" he tried again.

"Nuthin'."

"Gosh, Flower, I bet something—" He stroked her cheek. It was warm. Her forehead, when he put his hand to it, was hot.

He looked up at Delores. She felt her daughter's forehead and gasped.

"I'm sure it's nothing," Fox said reassuringly. "Probably just a cold."

Delores nodded. Fox picked Lily up and carried her to her bed, whispering nonsense about a boring day where nothing happened and going to sleep early would help. His heart beat faster with worry. She had to be all right. She just had to be.

The adults didn't get any sleep that night. Lily's temperature went up during the night and her breathing was labored. Fox had seen one asthma attack since he'd been living with them, and it had been terrible. Now, Fox sat near one side of the bed holding her hand while Delores sat on the other. But he had little strength to *feed* into her as she struggled to breathe.

He knew he should try to reach inside her, the way he had with his cat Lucky so many years ago. He could help her breathe until she was strong enough to do it on her own.

He held back. Every time he went inside a person, that person died. He hadn't helped anyone since he saved his kitten. He couldn't trust himself.

Fox forced himself to sit next to the bed through the long night. He watched the tears snake down Delores's face as the child got weaker. When the sky grew lighter, Delores stood up.

"I'm taking her to the hospital."

Fox looked up at her. "It won't do any good. There are no places—"

"I don't care. I'm taking her anyway. There has to be somewhere that can help."

They bundled Lily into the car and raced to DiMaggio Children's. Fox screeched to a halt and grabbed the little girl from the back of the car. They burst into the emergency room.

"She's sick," he gasped to the triage nurse.

The nurse was wearing a sterile mask over her nose and mouth. She left the booth and stepped out to look at Lily. Fox saw her take in the flushed, sweaty cheeks and labored breathing.

Finally she looked at him with pain in her eyes. "I'm sorry, sir. You'll have to wait." She pointed to the hard plastic chairs that lined the room. Several other adults sat in them holding children who gasped and fretted.

"But—" Delores tried to protest.

"I'm truly sorry, ma'am. You'll have to wait."

Fox didn't need to *look* into the nurse to see how it hurt her to have to say it. Cradling Lily in one arm, he led Delores to the chairs.

Hours later they saw a tired and harried doctor in one of the curtained cubicles. Dr. Farber's face was unlined, so he was young—probably an intern. His eyes, though, were old. He took Lily's temperature, listened to her lungs, all the usual gestures doctors make.

Finally he looked up. "I'm afraid—"

"It's the flu," Fox interrupted.

"Yes," the doctor sighed.

"Well, do something! Give her fluids, something to keep her strong enough to fight off this thing herself."

"We can't. We don't have the equipment left. We're swamped. We can't help them. There are just too many." The young man's voice choked.

"Please," Delores sobbed. "Please help my baby."

Dr. Farber gestured for Fox to follow him to a wall cabinet. He took out a bottle and pressed it into Fox's hand. "All we can do is lessen the pain. It'll make it easier." He spoke in a low voice, glancing at Delores to make sure she didn't hear.

The doctor left the cubicle. Delores bent over the examining table, her breath catching in the sobs that wracked her body.

Fox went to work in a daze. Sweetwater was becoming a hospice where the elderly were admitted for a few days until they died of the illness.

Lily lingered for a week. Fox sat by her bedside every night, *feeding* what strength he had into her. But he was tired and there was very little to give. Delores didn't go to work. She sat next to her daughter, motionless, staring at the small body as it labored to breathe. Sometimes she wandered restlessly around the apartment. She refused to go to bed.

Delores' family came to help. Angelina, her mother, tried to get Delores to eat, while Robert Uguchi stood, stoically looking on. Their presence was a comfort to Fox.

They all tried to feed the little girl, spooning soup and ice chips into her mouth, but she became too weak to swallow. They rubbed alcohol on her hot skin and put cool cloths on her forehead. Nothing helped.

On her last night Delores sat in her chair and cried. She and Fox were both exhausted. Fox was afraid Delores would get sick herself. He was tempted to go inside that small body and help her breathe, make her lungs pull in the air she needed. All he had to do was find the way in . . .

Carefully, he went under Lily's skin, then into her blood. There was so much wrong, and Fox didn't know where to start. He tried to *see* her lungs, her heart, but the pathways were so complex. He tried clearing something *there*, but the child's breathing faltered and he drew back. Maybe *this*. Her heartbeat speeded up alarmingly.

He couldn't do it. Defeated, he pulled back.

Lily took her last breath at four a.m. Delores was sitting at her side, eyes closed in exhaustion. Fox *felt* the life leave the small body and ran into the room just as Delores woke.

She collapsed. Fox carried her to the bedroom and laid her carefully on the bed. She didn't move, didn't even open her eyes. It was as if she had died, too.

Fox tried to *feed* strength into her, to rouse her. But there was nothing left to give.

Mechanically he did the necessary. He called EMS to confirm the death, then phoned the funeral home. One foot after another. No feeling, no reaction.

Once again, his great talent, his wonderful ability, showed that it was only good for fucking or killing. The guilt pounded at him but he refused to acknowledge it. He had to be strong.

Delores didn't get out of bed the following day, or the next. Fox called the office of the doctor she worked for and explained the situation. He said he didn't know when Delores could return. Then he called Sweetwater and told Ms. Rosen what happened.

"I don't know when I'll be back. It'll probably be a week. I know you're very busy, and I don't mean to hang you up," he apologized.

"I'm really sorry for your loss, John. You should take all the time you need." She hesitated.

"What is it?"

"Things are really bad here. We're getting swamped with people who have the flu. They—Well. they don't last long. There's paperwork and . . . It's a mess. Mr. Delacruz is talking about shutting the facility down."

Fox was speechless. It was one more grief he had to shoulder on top of everything else.

"But I shouldn't be burdening you with this now. I'm sorry, John, it just came out. Look, take your time and call when you're ready. And—I'm really sorry."

Fox hung up feeling empty.

⌐

Fox took care of the endless official documentation and the funeral arrangements the way he had for Papa Gerry. He was dead inside, as dead as Lily. Delores seemed dead, too. She didn't get out of bed unless he physically moved her. She didn't speak to anyone or take an interest in anything.

Her family was very supportive.

"Give her time," Angelina said in her soft Spanish accent. "She has just lost her child. You must show her love, and make her eat."

"We're here for you, son, and for her," Robert told him. "Stay strong."

Ray was at the apartment every day. Delores was his favorite sister, just two years older than he was. They had been very close as kids and they remained that way as adults.

Fox liked Ray, not just because Ray knew cars and helped him fix his old rattletrap Buick whenever it broke down. Ray was pragmatic, but he was never afraid to show his emotions. They would sit for hours over cups of tea. Ray was a recovering alcoholic and Fox was grateful that he didn't constantly say, "Drink something, it'll help you."

Two weeks after the funeral the two men sat at the glass table. Neither one said anything for a long time.

Finally Fox said, "I can't do anything for her, Ray. She just stays in bed. She won't talk, and she only eats when I put food in her mouth. I'm at the end. I don't know what else to do."

Ray put his hand on Fox's shoulder. "She has to see a doc, bro. We don't know enough."

Fox remembered his sessions with Doc Smallwood. He thought about the gray life he was living before he saw her, and how it improved afterward.

He nodded.

⌐

They got Delores into a psych hospital the next week. Their connections with the medical profession helped, and so did the fact that she wasn't physically sick. Most hospitals weren't accepting new patients for medical issues. There was still no cure for the illness. The death toll kept climbing.

Fox went back to work at Sweetwater. He needed to keep busy, to put one foot after the other. He didn't know what else to do.

Henrietta was at the desk as he entered the building. "Hi, John. I'm really sorry to hear about what happened. We all were. How's Delores?"

"Not good," Fox answered in a choked voice. "We had to put her in the hospital."

Henrietta nodded in sympathy. "It'll get better, dear. Just wait. You'll see." She shook her head sadly. "Can't get much worse."

Fox gave a sad smile and went off to start his shift. He hoped, rather than believed, that Henrietta was right.

During his break he wandered into the staff room. He wasn't hungry enough for lunch. He just needed the company. But the talk around the table was even more depressing.

"I hear they're gonna close Sweetwater down," Jasmine said in hushed tones.

"Yeah," Tomas said. "I hear there ain't enough old people left down here. Either they died off or they're strong. Don't need no assisted living."

"So what're we gonna do?" Fox asked.

Head shakes and shrugs were his only answer.

"Y'know, I got into this profession 'cause everyone said it was the way to go," Jasmine said. "People get older, they need special help. But what I hear, ain't too many old people left."

"Not just down here," Andres said. "It's all over. This fuckin' flu thing done damage even up north."

Tomas nodded. "It's all over the world."

"Yeah," Jasmine said. "I bet it was those illegal aliens slippin' in. Y'know, since security stopped workin'."

"You can't know that," Fox argued. "Maybe it started here in the good ol' USA."

"Hey, I know what I know," Jasmine said.

"The whole world's going crazy," Andres said. "Storms, flooding—y'know whole islands disappeared. It's not just this."

"Well, they should do something about it," Tomas said.

"Who should?" Fox asked, even though he knew better.

"You know. The government," Tomas answered.

"Huh," Jasmine said. "They can't even fix the damn roads."

Fox went to the hospital as soon as he finished his shift, just as he had every evening since Delores was admitted. He held flowers in one hand as he always did, hoping that tonight Dee would respond to them.

Tonight, Delores was sitting up in bed, staring at the television. He smiled. Maybe she was getting better.

But the eyes she turned on him were hard and cold.

Confused, Fox tried to keep the smile on his face as he walked toward the bed. "Hi, hon, I'm glad to see you—"

"Don't talk to me. And don't smile at me." Her voice was flat.

He stopped halfway through the room. He didn't understand. What had happened?

She pushed back the covers and slowly turned her body so her feet dangled over the edge of the bed. Her narrowed eyes never wavered from his face.

"Dee, I don't think you should try—"

"It's your fault," she said, her voice rising. "She's dead and it's your fault." She rose shakily and staggered toward him. "If you never came into our lives this wouldn't have happened. You killed her. You—"

Her voice had risen to a shriek. The floor nurse and an orderly burst into the room. They caught Delores as she fell to the floor weeping.

Fox rushed forward to help, but he was waved off by the nurse.

"Wait outside," she said.

"But I can help. I know—"

She moved him gently out of the way.

Fox felt as though he'd been punched in the gut. Almost doubled over in pain, he staggered into the hall and collapsed into the plastic chair against the wall. The flowers fell, unnoticed.

The orderly came out and asked Fox to wait for a few minutes. Soon Dr. Gomez appeared. His shoulders were slumped as he took the chair next to Fox. They sat in silence for a moment. Then the doctor said, "I heard about it. I'm sorry. It was unexpected. She hadn't given any indication before this."

Fox nodded. He couldn't speak.

When he saw that Fox wasn't going to respond, the doctor continued. "Sometimes patients have this kind of inappropriate response. I'm sure she'll get over it," he said kindly.

Fox wasn't so sure. He *was* responsible. If he hadn't been such a coward, if he had used his powers to help Lily . . .

He thanked the doctor and walked away. The familiar, comforting gray cloud began to gather around him. But clinging to the hope that she would get better, he returned to the hospital every evening for the next three days. Delores's reaction was the same. She screamed at him, shouting terrible cutting accusations.

On the fourth visit, the orderly stopped him before he could enter Dee's room. "I'm sorry, Mr. Marshall, but the doctor thinks you shouldn't see her any more."

"Why?" Fox got the words out around the lump in his throat. "I'm her fiancé. I love her. Why—"

Dr. Gomez walked quickly down the hall and laid his hand gently on Fox's arm. "Come talk to me."

They went to the family room and sat on the uncomfortable plastic couch. Fox slumped in the seat, his head down.

"There's a problem, John," Dr. Gomez said softly. "Delores seems to be getting steadily worse, losing touch with reality. I think we'll have to start her on an anti-psychotic."

Fox nodded without looking up. He couldn't speak.

"Try to understand. When patients are delusional, they often can't distinguish between reality and imagination. To her, this belief is very real. There's nothing you can do to change it. We can only hope that one of the medications, or a combination, can bring her back to reality."

"Yeah," Fox managed to get out.

"In the meantime, I suggest that you don't visit. It upsets her."

"But—"

"Please, John. For her sake."

Dr. Gomez patted Fox's arm and left the room. Fox was devastated. He wanted to believe that Delores would get better, that they could have a relationship made even stronger by trauma.

He could go *into* her mind, change things, make her better.

No, he wouldn't do that. He didn't know what he was doing, it could kill her. There was nothing to do. He was just causing everyone pain.

Fox dragged himself home. It wasn't home any more, not without Delores and Lily. Night was falling as he walked into the apartment. He sat on the couch without turning on the lights.

Ray came over an hour later. He visited every night since Delores went into the hospital. He said he needed a quiet place to get his head together. Fox *sensed* that Ray was checking on him, making sure he was okay, but he appreciated the company.

"I went to the hospital today," Fox explained to his friend. "They told me that Delores doesn't want to see me. That she blames me for Lily's death."

"That's rough, bro," Ray said softly.

Fox stayed silent.

"Look, people say stupid things when they feel that way. It's not Delores talking. It's the depression."

"But she's right, Ray," Fox blurted out. "I *am* responsible."

"Hey, hey, hey. You ain't responsible. You didn't kill Lily. And you didn't make Dee the way she is. You keep this up, you won't be any good for anyone."

Fox couldn't say anything. He wanted to admit everything to Ray, but he knew he couldn't.

Ray shook his head. "Don't carry around extra weight, bro. Look, in AA we say the Serenity Prayer. Y'know, God give me the serenity to accept the things I cannot change, the courage to change the things I can, and the wisdom to know the difference."

Fox remained quiet, sitting on the couch with his head bowed and his hands dangling between his splayed legs.

"The wisdom to know the difference. You're smart. You can figure it out. Don't give in to it."

Fox stayed silent.

"John, you gotta be the strong one here. I know it ain't easy. But Dee needs you. I can help, but you're the one she loves. So please, don't give in."

At the sound of Ray's obvious worry, Fox looked up. He forced a smile on his face and nodded.

Despair washed over him after Ray left. He saw their faces in his mind—Dee and Lily, his fathers, Sonia, even Sonia's father. The guilt threatened to drown him. If he had been stronger he could have helped them. All his fault.

━━

Two months later the prognosis was no different.

Fox sat in the family room surrounded by Delores's relatives. Her parents and Ray shared the orange couch. Her sisters, Sandra and Helena, whom Fox had never really gotten to know, sat on chairs to one side.

Dr. Gomez stood facing them. "The anti-psychotics seem to having an effect."

Fox felt a small smile start to form.

"Except for one thing." The doctor turned to face Fox. "She is still holding on to the false idea that you caused her daughter's death."

Fox's stomach fell. He didn't understand. If the meds were working . . .

The doctor's voice was gentle. "I'm sorry, John. We're trying, but she seems to be clutching this psychosis and we can't dislodge it."

The green walls of the room closed in on Fox. He couldn't accept this. There had to be something he could do.

"In all other respects, Delores is ready to be discharged," the doctor continued. "She behaves rationally and is capable of taking care of herself."

Fox found his voice. "But she'll get better, right? I mean, she'll get over this?"

A shadow crossed Gomez's face and he dropped his gaze, as though afraid to look Fox in the eye. "We can't guarantee anything. We hope she will, but . . ."

The lump in Fox's throat dropped into his stomach like a lead ball. It was difficult to breathe. He tried to speak, but all that came out was a strangled grunt.

Gomez continued in the same soft tone. "Even when she comes through this, she probably won't be the same person as before. You'll . . . you'll have to build your relationship over from the beginning."

Through tears that made everything blurry, Fox looked around the room. The pain and fear on the faces of people he'd grown to love, to think of as possible family, was too much to bear.

If he stayed around, he'd only bring more heartache. He couldn't do any good. Once again, everything he touched turned to shit.

⌒

The next day Mr. Delacruz called the entire staff together. "It's official now," he said after a few brief words of welcome. "The facility is being closed, and probably will be sold to a developer."

There were murmurs all around, but most of the staff had been expecting it.

"The corporation wants to do right by you, though," Mr. Delacruz continued. "You'll each be given a full month's wages as severance, and letters of recommendation. We all hope you'll do well."

Fox sat on the wooden chair and felt the message wash over him. A sense of unreality surrounded the scene and filled his whole life. Now there was truly no reason for him to stay.

That night he wrote a letter to Ray, and another to Angelina and Robert, explaining that there was no life for him here any more.

He could imagine the looks on their faces, a combination of sorrow and relief. They would build a life without him, a better life. He wouldn't be around to remind them of the pain. They could recover and move on.

He tried to call his mother, but what he heard was mostly static. He tried to tell her about Delores and what he planned to do, but he wasn't sure that anything got through. He heard a few words that sounded like *your grandmother* and *Pete*. But nothing he could make sense of. Then just static that indicated a dropped call.

Fox stamped the letters and sealed the envelopes. He resolved to call Ray as soon as he got to his grandmother's. After taking one last look around, he turned off the lights.

Then he ran.

CHAPTER 36

Fox set off up the East Coast, not at all certain the old Ford would hold up. He was lucky. He made it to Maryland, to his grandmother Rose's. He hoped Daddy Pete was still living there, or Gamma could tell him where he was. The thought was a dim beacon of hope, but the only one he had.

It was after nine and full dark when he pulled up in front of the neat red brick house and rang the bell next to the varnished oak door.

Fox was relieved when he saw her familiar face. For a moment, her eyes were guarded and didn't show any recognition. Then, "Oh, my god, Fox! Oh, my! Oh, come in, boy, come in!"

She led him into the long hallway and down to the living room. "What do you want? Ice tea? Coffee? Something stronger?"

"Just water, Gamma."

He was so tired. He had been driving straight through, for about twenty hours. All he wanted was a place to sleep and news about his father. Then he could figure out what to do.

Rose came back with the ice water and set it down in front of him. "I guess you want to know how it happened."

Fox froze. "How what happened?"

"How—Wait. You don't know, do you? Oh, god, I didn't want to be the one . . ."

"What? Gamma, tell me."

For a few minutes, Gamma sat silently in her chair, looking at her hands. When she looked up there were tears in her eyes. "Oh, Fox, your Daddy Pete is—" Her voice caught. "He's dead." She took a deep breath. "It was that horrible disease. It killed him."

225

Fox's mind went blank. It was too much to take.

"After your Papa died, Pete was never the same. It was like he didn't want to live. He gave up the apartment and moved down here. He kept on writing, though." A note of pride entered her voice. "Even made some movies. You probably saw them."

Fox nodded. Every time an ad appeared in the paper for a new movie *written by Peter Monroe, who gave you . . .* , he found a theater and bought a ticket. It was as though he was showing support for the father he left behind. Just seeing his father's name on the screen was somehow comforting, a tie to a former life.

Gamma continued, her voice choked. "He got sick about two weeks ago, and he didn't last long. We buried him down here. I hope you don't mind."

Fox shook his head. He couldn't trust himself to speak.

They sat in silence for a while. Then Gamma led him to the guest room and made sure he was comfortable. Fox was grateful that she didn't ask any questions about where he'd been or what he'd been doing.

That night Fox didn't sleep well. He dreamt about Papa Gerry as tall as he had been when Fox was young. Papa held out a hand to him as though asking him to help with something, but Fox turned away. Then Dad was there. He looked disappointed. They both turned around, and Lily ran toward them as she always had when Fox came home. But when she saw Fox she stopped and went to hug Papa and Dad instead.

The dream shifted to the prairie outside Mom's house. Countless people wearing heavy black veils milled aimlessly on the brown grass. As Fox stepped forward, they turned to face him. They called his name, their tones accusing. He turned around to go back into the house, but the building had disappeared. He tried to get away from the crowd, but his feet wouldn't work properly, he couldn't run, they were walking toward him their arms outstretched . . .

Fox woke up, a cold sweat drenching his body. It was morning and Gamma was knocking on his door.

"Do you want some breakfast, dear?" she called.

Fox grunted yes. He threw on his bathrobe and went to brush his teeth. His reflection in the mirror seemed alien. His eyes weren't gold, but rather a pale gray, and there were dark circles under them. His cheeks were hollow.

"Oh, my, you look as though you hadn't slept well," she said when he walked into the kitchen.

He poured a cup of coffee. "Bad dreams."

"Eat something. You'll feel better. Then we can talk."

Gamma's answer to everything, Fox thought. Food, rest . . . love. She seemed to think they could fix everything. He forced down some eggs and toast that curdled around the lump of guilt in his stomach but did nothing to make him feel better.

After breakfast they sat in Gamma's comfortable living room, the furniture old but well cared for. Fox sank into the sofa, a cup of coffee in his hands. He was grateful for the numbness that enveloped him.

Gamma sat primly in the chair opposite him. "There are some things we have to talk about."

Fox glanced at her questioningly.

"Pete—your dad—" Her voice caught on the words. She straightened her shoulders. "He had quite a bit of money by the end. You know, his book sales and the movies he wrote. Some of it came to me. He was very specific in his will. But most of it he left in trust to you."

Fox looked up in surprise. "But what—I mean how can that be?"

"I guess he figured you'd come here eventually. I wrote to Marta to tell her, in case she saw you first. I just want to make sure you get it. That you're a little safer. He wanted that."

Fox hadn't spoken to his mother in over a month. He bent his head and tears ran down his face. He thought about how he had treated his father, how he had deserted him years ago. Yet his father worried about giving him a better life. He loosened his shields, expecting to *feel* anger and bitterness from his grandmother. But his *senses* were weak, and all he picked up were vague wisps of love and concern.

"I shouldn't have left him like that," Fox choked out.

"No, I guess you shouldn't have. But he understood. He read your letter and figured you had to go off and find yourself."

Gamma fell silent. Fox looked up. She stared at him.

"Well, have you?" she asked gently.

He wiped his cheeks. "Have I what?"

"Found yourself."

"No. But I'm working on it," he said meeting her gaze squarely.

"Good."

Gamma got up from the chair and straightened her dress. "Go take a shower and get dressed. We have to see a lawyer."

⌇

The law offices of Bradley C. Trent were in an older part of the city. The brown stones and tall windows of the façade were imposing. They rode an old fashioned elevator up to the third floor where a polished wood and glass door bore the name "Bradley C. Trent, Attorney at Law."

The receptionist led them to a large book-lined room. The large table and green leather chairs indicated that Mr. Trent was doing well, even in this economy. They were obviously meant to impress.

The lawyer entered the room, a tall gentleman impeccably dressed in a three-piece suit. His thick white hair was neatly combed back from his face, his mustache neatly trimmed. Fox stood and shook hands with him. Rose remained seated, and just smiled.

"I'm glad to meet you at last, Fox," Mr. Trent said taking a seat. He gestured for Fox to be seated.

Fox sat, but didn't speak. He looked at the other man inquiringly.

"I knew your father at the end. Not well, but enough to think that he trusted me."

Fox nodded. The lawyer's deep voice inspired confidence.

Mr. Trent went on, "He was very specific in his will. He gave your grandmother enough so she won't have to worry. He also left a nice amount to your mother out in Wyoming. We can go over the specifics shortly. But the greatest part of his estate went to you. My firm has invested it. The books are available to you whenever you want them."

"How much are we talking about?" Fox asked.

"He was worth close to a couple of million when he passed," Mr. Trent said matter-of-factly.

Fox was stunned. He had never thought that Dad was so rich. If only he could think straight. Depression slowed him almost to the point of paralysis. He had to force himself to concentrate.

Three hours later Fox and Rose walked out of the building. Gamma was smiling.

"I think you made all the right decisions, Fox. Keeping the money with Mr. Trent, getting the downloadable credit card. You won't have to worry about money."

Fox took her arm as they crossed the street to the parking garage. He agreed. The card would give him more freedom, allow him to go wherever he needed to.

"Now all we have to do is see about getting you settled," Gamma went on. "Maybe we can find a nice little house somewhere nearby. You don't want to just rent . . ."

Fox stopped listening. She expected him to stay here. He couldn't do that, it was too dangerous. Everyone he loved died, didn't she realize that? Couldn't she see he was like that virus that had killed off so many people?

He would have to tell her. Gently, of course, but firmly. He had to be on his own. Just like when he left New York, Fox was running away. He had no real plans, no goals. He knew only that he had to be where he felt secure.

He ran home.

CHAPTER 37

Fox stepped out of Grand Central Station and breathed deeply. The smell of home, the familiar combination of odors, swirled through his brain evoking memories. *Just like Proust*, he thought. *Yeah, sure.*

It was April, but, as usual, it was hard to tell here in midtown. There was no brown snow, no slush, and the wind that occasionally gusted down the street wasn't bitter cold. The gray fog that had enveloped him for months thinned. It felt like home.

He hoisted his backpack higher onto his shoulder and started walking. The city looked the same. Tall buildings, gray sidewalks. He relaxed his shields to *taste* the tempo of the city. It was there, as fast as he remembered, but weaker. And there was something more, a desperation that he *sensed* only dimly. It bothered him.

He walked to a small hotel on the east side that he'd found online. The man at the desk took his card.

"Yes, Mr. Monroe, we have your reservation. Welcome to New York."

Fox smiled. It was a relief to have his real name again.

The clerk continued as Fox signed in. "We have to apologize in advance, though. Electric service has been a bit spotty. Especially during peak hours. We work around it as best we can. Well, you know how it is, what with the flu and the weather and all."

No, Fox didn't know how it was. He was shocked. Here, in the middle of the City? He knew things had gotten bad, but he never imagined . . .

"It's all right," Fox said. "I'll manage."

The room was small but Fox didn't intend to spend much time in it. He wanted to explore his city, taste the essence of home. He didn't realize how much he had missed it. Maybe here he would be able to get a night's sleep.

Before he started out, he put in a call to Ray. The connection was spotty, the static making it difficult to understand the voice mail greeting. Fox left a short message telling where he was and asking Ray to get in touch if there was anything to report.

He washed his face in the small bathroom sink. When he looked in the mirror above it, he noticed his eyes. They still looked gray instead of gold. Colorless, like he felt.

He dried his face quickly. Then he began his tour of home.

He took the subway to Battery Park. He would start at the tip of the island and work his way up.

Leaving the station, he looked around. The park hadn't changed. The benches, the fence along the sea wall, it was all familiar. In his memory he saw the gang, Sonia, Fat Joey, Norrie, and all the others, running through the park, laughing. The picture warmed him against the slight chill of the breeze that blew off the water.

He walked to the edge and looked out over the harbor. The water seemed higher than he remembered. The oily wavelets splashed close to the top of the wall.

An old man in a thin overcoat stopped next to him and stared at the water. "Yup, it's higher than it used to be." The man's voice was cigarette rough.

Fox nodded.

"Five years ago it never touched the top. Now it's almost there."

They stood in companionable silence for a moment.

The man continued, "Another five years and the water'll be washing over the ground we're standing on. Just like it did in the hurricane last year. Wonder what the city'll do then?"

Fox turned to face him. "You sound like you lived here a long time."

"Yup. Lived in the city my whole life. I worked down here, too, before things fell apart. Now . . . Well, I get by."

Fox tried to relax his shields slightly, and was shocked to discover that he hadn't raised them since he left Grand Central. Why wasn't he inundated with voices and feelings? What had happened to him?

Even without his ability he felt the resignation in the man, the hopelessness. "Yeah, well, good luck, man," he said, and turned away.

Another person he couldn't help.

He walked slowly up to Washington Square, trying to shed some of the grayness that had grown over him. Dammit, this visit was supposed to help him get over the depression, not make it worse. This was supposed to be home.

The Square was almost deserted in the weak afternoon sun. Even the students from NYU who usually populated the park were gone. A few young women pushing baby strollers wandered along the paths but no one was sitting at the fountain. There was no music or laughter.

The City felt quieter than it had ever been. Not the physical noise, but the psychic tumult. It was as though he had water in his ears. Everything was blunted, fuzzy.

The temperature fell as the sun went down. *I need to be around people,* Fox decided. It was Friday. He'd have some dinner and hit the clubs. That would cheer him up.

He treated himself to a fine meal at a restaurant in midtown. It was interesting that the high-end places were still doing well. The restaurant was crowded but not noisy. Fox ate slowly and lingered over coffee until he figured the clubs would get going.

The clerk at the hotel had told him that the club scene had moved to the South Bronx and had given him the names of a few. "You should take a taxi if you're going up there, sir. The area is a lot safer than it used to be, but the public transportation at night can be a little tough."

Fox decided he would chance it. His city senses were returning, the almost Spidey-like tingle that told him when someone was walking behind him. When he left the train at 149th Street, he was glad he hadn't taken a cab. He felt stronger than he had in a long time.

Maybe this was working. Maybe his city was helping him.

The Millennium was a converted warehouse south of the subway station. A glaring neon sign advertised its location. The bouncer at the door stopped him.

Fox knew what he looked like. He hadn't slept well in months, and he hadn't eaten much. He was skinny and exhausted. But his clothes were good, and he slipped a twenty into the large tattooed hand.

The bouncer gestured him inside with a grunt.

A wall of noise greeted him as he stepped through the doors. A central dance floor, strobing lights, the smell of sweat and burning marijuana. Shit, he should have brought some of those nose filters that had come out lately. Well, he'd just have to manage. He hoped he didn't get too heavy a contact high. He wanted to *feel* the excitement of the club but he didn't want to lose control.

He walked to the bar and ordered a seltzer with lime. A young man sat down next to him. Fox noticed the long, slender arms and carefully combed black hair.

"Hi, I'm Sidney," he said, his words slightly slurred.

"Fox."

He smiled. "Strange name."

"It's a nickname."

"Oh. Yeah."

"Can I buy you a drink?" Fox asked.

Sidney moved closer. "Sure." He leaned over and spoke in Fox's ear. "Then you wanna take a room upstairs?"

He stepped back and looked at Fox, his dark eyes sparkling in the club lights. Fox looked back. Behind the reflection of the lights the man's eyes were dead and his smile was empty. Fox wasn't ready for this. He didn't want an anonymous hook-up with a stranger in a room that was rented for five minutes.

He tried to *feel* Sidney's mind, but the images were indistinct and fragmented. It was a swirl of drugs and alcohol, a kaleidoscope of sensation. There was no emotion. He felt sick.

"Thanks for the invitation, Sidney, but no." Fox paid for the drinks and left the club.

The walk back to the subway cleared his head. So far his return wasn't working. The gray fog was getting stronger.

There was only one place left to go.

Half an hour later, he was back on his home turf in the Village. He walked the familiar streets ending up on his old block. The lights on their tall poles made the shadows seem to push into the street. He stepped into a doorway to get out of the cold breeze that sprang up.

Everything seemed familiar, but it wasn't home anymore. From his shelter, he stared out onto the street. The dark shapes made him feel uneasy.

A young woman strolled slowly past his hiding place. She didn't seem to be bothered by the chilly searching wind, in spite of the short shorts she wore, or the flimsy blouse that barely covered her voluptuous breasts.

She glanced at Fox's refuge, and stopped.

"Hey, guy, you better move. This is my corner." Her voice was light, almost childish. Fox looked at her. Then he unfolded himself from the doorway.

"Sonia?" he said softly. "Sonia? That you?"

As he stepped into the light, the girl stared at him. Recognition slowly dawned. "Fox? Fox Monroe?"

Fox nodded.

"Oh my God. I don't believe it!" She peered at him closely then she drew back. "You look like shit, man. What happened? We all thought you were dead or something."

"Yeah," he said, tonelessly. "Maybe I was for a while."

He stared hungrily at her high cheekbones, her uptilted eyes. The streetlights leached the color from her café-au-lait skin, but he remembered its color perfectly. He'd often fantasized about it when they were in school.

The combination of the cold, the tug of memory, the fatigue, all weakened his control. He felt as if he was drowning.

"Look, Fox, you gotta move. Mario could show up. He doesn't like anyone hanging around my corner. He can be mean, Fox. So, please. Go." She held out a small plasticene bag. "Here."

Fox looked at it and despaired. "Thanks, Sonia. I don't do that shit."

"Okay. Look, you need money? Here's a couple of bucks. It's all I have. Mario doesn't let me have much."

"No. I don't need any money." He reached into his pocket and took out a hundred. "Here. For you. Please."

Sonia hesitated for a moment, then took the bill. "Fox, you have the money. I can give it to Mario. Then if you wanted to we could . . ." She let her voice trail off.

By putting out a great deal of effort, he *glimpsed* Sonia's mind. There was nothing there, no joy, no hope. This was what his help had done to her.

"No, Sonia. Listen. Come have something to eat with me. We can sit and talk, just for an hour or so. Please!"

She looked around. A large man was crossing the street and walking toward them. "No. I can't. Now go—please!"

He turned and shuffled down the street, shoulders hunched. The old fashioned all night diner on 12th Avenue beckoned to him with a promise of temporary warmth and something to eat.

The vinyl bench at the booth was cracked and stained, but the diner was warm. He sat, cold and exhausted, surrounded by the smells of old grease and stale coffee. The harsh fluorescent lights emphasized the drabness of his surroundings.

With half his cheeseburger and tea inside him, Fox realized that coming back was a mistake. It was so much easier to keep his mind in focus among strangers, in unfamiliar surroundings. If only he could rest!

But memories made the tears stream down his face. His parents, Sonia, Dee, Lily, the friends he never helped.

He had to go, somewhere, anywhere. Just keep moving. Stay away from anyone who mattered to him. He was lethal.

Fox dried his eyes and tilted his head back to drain the last of his tea. A man stopped abruptly at his booth, staring at him.

"Franklin? Franklin Monroe? Is it really you?"

The man's piercing gray eyes sparked Fox's memories. The salt and pepper beard was new, but the face was unmistakable. Mr. Weitzman's classes at Stuyvesant High School had always been interesting, the discussions far-ranging and stimulating. The teacher had been especially good to him during that last year, when Papa was so sick. He made sure Fox's college applications were in on time, and made sure the other teachers knew the situation.

"Hi, Mr. Weitzman. And it's Fox. Remember? Everyone calls me Fox."

"Hm," Weitzman nodded. "Still suits you. May I join you?" Weitzman was always polite, always correct.

Fox signaled agreement, but didn't hold out his hand to shake. Touch always let in other people's thoughts, forced him into their heads to read what was there, to try to change—

He slammed down the thought.

"I must say, Franklin—"

"Fox, please, Mr. Weitzman."

"Okay. Fox. You have to acknowledge how difficult it is for a teacher to refer to his former students by anything but their legal names." Weitzman chuckled. "But what have you been up to, uh, Fox?" Weitzman pronounced the name carefully. "I must admit we expected great things from you. But after your father died, you ran away—didn't even finish your senior year, didn't graduate."

"Shit happens, Mr. Weitzman," Fox muttered, looking down at the remnants on his plate.

"That's no answer. I thought I'd taught you better than that." The remembered voice had always induced trust. "I know it was hard for you, your father's death. You were only seventeen. But it wasn't your fault, Fox. It was the disease. Nothing you could have done—"

Fox broke in. "You don't understand. It *was* my fault. I—I killed him." Now the tears were running down Fox's face again.

Mr. Weitzman didn't say anything for a moment. Then he took a deep breath. "Look, Fox. You need time. A place to stay. Rest up a bit, gain strength."

Fox stared at the half-eaten food and stayed silent.

The same judging look, that always seemed to ferret out whether a student was lying about missed homework, assessed him now. "Look, I have a nice little apartment, not too far from your father's—I'm sorry, I mean from where you grew up. It has a guest room that is quite comfortable. Or so I have been told. You could stay there, for as long as you like. No commitments. Just a place to crash."

Fox looked up at the older man. He was hungry for respite, just a temporary harbor. He had the money to stay at the hotel, but a place with someone who cared about him but that he didn't have to fix . . .

He saw only compassion and the real desire to help in his teacher's eyes. It would be so wonderful to be able to rest, to not worry about what had happened to his power. Some time to stop obsessing about the darkness in the other minds invading his. Perhaps a place where he could really sleep.

Mr. Weitzman reached out in a gesture of comfort. He touched Fox's wrist.

With the last of his power, Fox *sensed* the abyss in Mr. Weitzman's mind, the yawning emptiness that no job or field of study or trip abroad could fill.

The anguish cried for Fox to help, to reach inside and fill it. It was the same cry he heard over and over again, that wouldn't let him rest.

The *connection* ended abruptly. Fox felt as if he had suddenly gone deaf. The whispers that he had heard his entire life, that had alternately plagued and comforted him, were gone. His powers had disappeared.

Fox muttered a few words to Mr. Weitzman, whose confusion was written on his face.

Then Fox ran.

CHAPTER 38

"Hi, Mom," Fox said, dropping his bag on the front step.

"Oh, darling, you're here!" She hugged him tightly and pulled him into the house. He just had time to grab his suitcase and drag it in after him.

Marta stared up at him. Then she nodded.

"You'll tell me everything later, after you've had time to rest. Meanwhile, get settled. You know where everything is. I'll make tea."

Grateful for the lack of questions, Fox carried his belongings to the room that had been his for so many years. He didn't bother to unpack, just took off his coat and hung it up. Then he joined his mother in the kitchen.

"I'm glad you called me," she said as soon as he entered the room.

Fox nodded. Suddenly he couldn't speak. He was afraid that if he uttered a single word the whole story would come out, he would tell her everything about Dee and Lily, about the shadow that followed him, about Sonia and Mr. Weitzman. About the terrible guilt he felt because he was never able to help. And that his mind reading ability was gone.

Marta seemed to sense his reluctance. She kept up a patter of trivia, detailing what had happened in the area. "The flu didn't hit us too hard. I guess all of us are kind of stronger here and we're so spread out the bug couldn't get to everyone."

Fox grunted agreement and sipped his tea. He was glad it gave him an excuse not to speak.

"And those new cell towers are working out fine. They're hooked up through Cheyenne, so we only get service in the area. But it's good to be able to stay in touch with neighbors. With the turbines and panels, we even have electricity a lot of the time. Just not enough to recharge cars."

She waited for him to speak. He took a large gulp of tea to cover over his silence.

"Biggest problem we have now is that there are no tourists anymore. No way for cars to get around. Good thing you have the solar." She ignored the fact that Fox's wasn't speaking. "Well, we get by in other ways."

Fox mustered some interest. "What do you mean?"

"We barter. I did some of that before, but now everyone is doing it. Mr. Taunton can't run a dude ranch any more. No one's coming out. So he rents out his horses to the farmers for food or help in the stables. Everybody has something to trade, even if it's only grunt labor."

"Sounds to me like a good way to live," he sighed.

Marta looked at him as if she was measuring him. "Um-hm. Sounds to me like you need rest. Do you want something to eat first?"

Fox shook his head. "I grabbed a bite in on the road."

Smiling, Marta said, "Go to bed. We'll talk in the morning."

Fox undressed quickly and slid into bed, wrapping the quilt around him. The nights were always chilly here. He closed his eyes and waited for the nightmares to come, the crying children and accusing, faceless people. There was nothing.

He lowered his shields, expecting a barrage of *sounds* and *images*. There was nothing but the terrible silence that had followed him since he left New York.

It was like a part of him had been cut off. He wanted to examine it, explore the problem. But exhaustion took him and he fell into a deep sleep.

～

He woke up late the next morning with the sun shining through the gap in the curtains. He stayed in bed trying to figure out where to go, what he should do with the rest of his life. He couldn't go back, not to Florida or Maryland or New York. Someplace else, where people wouldn't depend on him to save their lives.

When he finally wandered down to the kitchen, it was almost noon. Marta wasn't there. He called out and she answered from her studio.

239

"Well, about time you re-entered the world," she greeted him when he joined her.

Fox looked around the room. There weren't as many finished paintings as there had been and the ones he could see were darker, less colorful.

Marta noticed his attention. "Yeah, I know. I haven't been working as much. Been busy making medicines and growing herbs to trade for food. Not much call for paintings in trade." She hooked her arm in his and guided him to the kitchen. "We have to talk, hon, and I think it's best to do it over food."

She made a huge omelet with peppers and onions fresh from the garden and bread she had baked herself. The aroma made Fox's mouth water. He started eating as soon as the food was in front of him.

Marta picked up her fork but didn't eat. "Fox, what's wrong?"

He paused with his fork halfway to his mouth. "What do you mean?"

"It's more than just mother's intuition. Something's very wrong. There's this cloud of unhappiness around you. It's more than learning about Dad's death. Now spill it."

He hadn't intended it. In fact, he had promised himself that he wouldn't burden her with his troubles. But as he studied her face, noticing the lines that hadn't been there before and the gray hairs sprinkled in the auburn, he felt a terrible need to confide in someone. Not just anyone, but someone who could understand what he had been through.

But once he started talking about Florida, it all came out. He talked about Delores and Lily and about the pain of finding out about Dad's death. The encounter with Sonia came spilling out along with his meeting with Mr. Weitzman.

He paused for a moment. "What I didn't want to tell you when I called you yesterday . . . I seem to have exhausted my powers. I feel like for months I've given away pieces of myself. Now there's nothing left. My shields aren't even up. And there's nothing—nothing coming in or going out."

Marta looked stricken. "Oh, darling. I'm so sorry. Look, I can *give* you a little of my strength, just like you described, and then—"

"No," Fox interrupted. "I don't want it. Maybe this is for the best. If my abilities are gone I can be normal, live a regular life. I'll be happier."

Marta stared at him. "Yeah, right. Tell that to your face."

"It's a shock. It'll take getting used to. Maybe this is a sign that I should begin a new life. Maybe I can do that here. This is a good way to live." He looked down at his plate so he wouldn't have to meet his mother's eyes.

She was quiet for a moment. Then she sighed. "Okay, if that's how you want it. I admit it'll be good having you around. Your old room is ready—"

Fox shook his head. "Mom, I love you, but I don't want to live in this house. I need a place of my own. I need space."

He looked up and saw the worry in her face. It was difficult to deal with the *silence*, to be blind and deaf to the feelings of others.

"I understand," Marta said at last. "I'll see what I can do."

Mr. Taunton still stood tall and straight, in spite of his seventy plus years. His hair, held back in a pony tail, was completely white now, and so was his bushy mustache.

"So, boy, you want to move in around here?" he asked.

"Yes, sir," Fox answered. He looked straight into the older man's blue eyes and wished he could *read* him.

Mr. Taunton nodded. "Well, I think we can come to an agreement."

He led Fox to the stables and brought out two horses. Fox noted that they were older animals, but still strong and healthy. The two men arranged the saddles and equipment and mounted up.

Mr. Taunton didn't speak as they rode. Fox appreciated the silence. He allowed it to surround him like warm, healing water. His muscles relaxed and his jaw unclenched.

As they came around a bend in the butte Fox saw the house. It was in surprisingly good shape. The roof looked sound, the walls were straight. The glassless windows stared out at the world but the doors were closed tight. A single-family wind turbine stood in the front yard. It looked undamaged. There was a glint of water where the river curved around half a mile away.

"Good fishing in that river," Mr. Taunton said. "Used to go there a lot when I was a kid."

They rode to the house and dismounted. Fox examined the peeling clapboards and the windows that gaped wide. It would need work.

"This was the original house for the ranch," Mr. Taunton explained. "Almost a hundred and fifty years old. But things were built to last then."

Fox nodded, but didn't speak.

Mr. Taunton went on. "Then around the beginning of the century, around '07 or so, before the bust, a guy came out here, put a down payment on the place. Started to fix it up. There's solar panels on the roof, and you got the turbine, so you got some electricity. And you got water. Don't know how well the pipes held up."

They went inside. It was better than Fox had imagined. Water had gotten in the damaged windows, but there didn't seem to be any leaks from the roof. Stairs up to the second floor were in good shape. He thought he could manage.

"Well, you interested?" Mr. Taunton asked.

"Depends on the terms," Fox answered.

Mr. Taunton smiled. "Smart kid. Your mama probably told you money don't mean much around here. We barter. What you got?"

Fox made a muscle in his right arm. "And you know I'm good with animals."

The older man nodded. "Okay, you exchange labor for the place and materials, if you need them. You know it'll take you a good while to work it off?"

"Yeah. That's okay. I'm not going anywhere for a while."

They shook hands.

Fox finished painting the last clapboard and stepped back to look at the house. His house. He felt a real sense of accomplishment. He had done this with his own hands. Well, all right, he acknowledged to himself, his and the other guys.

Jim Benson came around the corner. He was the building guru, the leader of the four men who helped him. They were the real builders and Fox just followed their lead. He liked the way the men worked, speaking rarely and then only to ask for a tool or more nails. Each one seemed to know where the others were. They danced around each other in a sort of ballet and miraculously never got in another man's way. It was almost like they could read each other's minds.

Fox smiled. They had the benefits without the problems.

"Well, kid," Jim said clapping him on the shoulder. "Looks like it's done. Took all summer but it's worth it, right?"

Fox nodded. He had fallen into the habit of speaking only when necessary, like the men he'd worked with. "Couldn't've done it without you guys."

Bo Hubert joined them. "Yeah. Specially since you didn't know which end of a hammer to hold 'til we showed you."

Frank and Verne laughed as they walked over.

"Was I *that* bad?" Fox asked.

They nodded.

"Good thing you had that old solar powered Jeep. Couldn't've finished so fast without it," Jim said, mercifully changing the topic.

The five men gathered around to look at their handiwork. They were all proud.

"Beer?" Fox asked.

They nodded and he walked into the kitchen. The refrigerator was humming. He was amazed at the amount of power generated by the turbine and solar panels. It wasn't enough for air conditioning in the summer or heat in the winter, he realized. But open windows when the weather permitted was fine, and the wood stove he'd put in would keep things toasty.

He came out with the covered bucket and ceramic mugs to find the four others sitting on the edge of the porch, their legs dangling. He joined them and passed the glasses, then the bucket.

"This Miz Johnson's brew?" Bo asked.

Fox nodded.

"Yep," Frank said, "she makes the best."

They sat and drank their beer watching the sky darken as evening fell. The wind sighed gently across the grassland and Fox was at peace.

When they finished, the four others stood up. Fox followed.

"Well, time to go," Jim said. "You got a good house. How about food? How you fixed for eating?"

"My mom'll supply me." He was embarrassed not to be self-sufficient.

"Yeah, good vegetables and stuff. But what about meat? Can't live on greens," Verne said.

"Some people do," Fox defended.

"Not around here," Jim said.

243

"Look," Bo offered, "it's gettin' on autumn. We're goin' huntin' next week. Come along."

Fox looked down. "Well, I don't know . . ."

"You never been huntin' before?" Verne asked, amazed.

Shrugging, Fox said, "City kid, y'know? Never found the need."

The other men looked at each other. Then Bo nodded. "You're comin' with us next week. You gotta learn."

They all shook hands and the others piled into Jim's wagon. Jim climbed into the front and picked up the reins.

"You take care," Jim said. "Good working with you."

Fox watched them drive off. He looked at his house once more then turned to stare at the sun as it set behind the butte. He had been tired ever since he came to Wyoming, but it was a good tired. He slept deeply. No dreams troubled him.

So why was he still upset about losing his powers? He never wanted to be able to read minds, always wanted to get rid of the ability. And now, when it was gone, he missed it. There was no explanation.

He went inside and got the package of cold roast chicken and vegetables that his mother had made for him. He took it outside and ate it on the porch as he watched the last of the sunset. The peace enveloped him.

This would be a good place for Delores to come. The serenity of it might help her, and without his powers, Fox could be a better companion to her. He could be totally open with her, hold nothing back. The visions of the life they might share lifted his spirits even more.

—

That night the whispers started again. It was like when he was six and he heard them for the first time. There were no distinct images or recognizable words, like the sound of voices just out of earshot.

Fox woke at sunrise trying to decipher the words. He got out of bed and went outside to the pump. The cold water running over his head washed away the cobwebs and allowed him to convince himself that it wasn't starting all over again. It couldn't be, he told himself. His abilities were gone. He didn't even remember how to raise his shields.

The work of the day drove the memory of the whispers out of his mind. He rode over to Marta's. She had promised him some seeds so he could start a vegetable garden. He wanted to get started on it as soon as possible, maybe get something in before winter.

Marta ran to meet him as he rode up to her house. He jumped off the horse and she hugged him.

He *sensed* her.

The feeling made him tense for a moment. Marta stepped back.

"What's the matter, hon?" she asked.

Fox shook his head as if scattering raindrops. "It was—No it wasn't anything. Just for a minute there I thought . . ."

"What?"

"Nothing."

It wasn't coming back, he thought. *That's impossible. I don't want it. It's not coming back.*

"Let's eat something," Marta said. "Then I'll give you the seeds and you can start being a farmer."

As they ate, she went over the steps to start the seeds. Fox smiled. She had been giving him the instructions for two months.

"Yes, Mom, I know. You told me a hundred times." His tone was gentle and he grinned broadly.

"I just worry about you, living all alone out there."

"Oh, yeah, like you live in the city!"

"I'm a mother. I have a license to worry, it comes with the hormones."

They laughed, and Fox left feeling good. It was as though he could *feel* the love coming from his mother—

No! It wasn't happening. His denial was fierce. He had lived his entire adult life saddled by this curse, this ability he had never asked for. Now it had gone, and he was just getting used to the silence. It wasn't fair if it came back.

CHAPTER 39

After three days Fox had to admit that his powers were returning. He worked himself mercilessly, trying to force himself into a dreamless, whisperless sleep at night. It didn't work. He was a telepath again.

He resurrected his shields. It wasn't as difficult as the first time because he knew what to do, what to expect. As the shields grew stronger the noises subsided but, like before, they never completely disappeared.

By the time Jim and the others came to take him hunting he had planted a small garden. They rode up to his house on horses borrowed from Mr. Taunton. The price of the loan was a portion of the meat they hunted.

The men sat easily in their saddles. They were dressed for the chillier weather they expected in the hills. Each one had a rifle barrel sticking up from his saddle.

Jim had two. "Figured you wouldn't have a gun of your own. This is my son's. He said you could borrow it. You can get your own later."

As they ambled into the foothills the temperature dropped. They went in silence, the only sound the clop of the horses' hooves and the wind. After an hour they reached a spot that Bo said was a good one. They dismounted, tethered their horses and walked a little ways off.

"Seen elk around here," Bo whispered. "Bear, too, but most of them're probably in their dens by now. Deer, rabbits. We'll see."

They crouched down behind a fallen tree. Jim showed Fox how to line up the sights on the rifle. "Just like that, see? Then you pull the trigger back real easy and hold on. There's some recoil but not much. Good beginner's gun."

Fox nodded. He was nervous. He had never killed anything on purpose before. He wasn't sure he could do it.

After an hour a buck wandered into the clearing in front of them. Bo took the first shot, got him straight through the heart. The noise was deafening and the smell of gunpowder clogged Fox's nose for a moment. They hauled the carcass away to drain the blood and left it hoisted into a tree while they tried for another one.

Almost as soon as they were settled in another clearing a second buck came into view. It was a magnificent creature, larger than the first. He didn't want to kill it, but he knew he had to. It was his survival.

They had decided that the second attempt was Fox's. He was breathing fast as he sighted the gun and his hands shook slightly. Then, without thinking, he lowered his shields and sent his thoughts to the deer in front of him. He *urged* the animal to stay still, calmed its mind.

He shot.

The deer fell.

Fox's heart was beating fast but he forced his breathing to slow as he raised his shields. He got up with the others to examine the dead animal. Stunned by what he had done, he stood and looked at the pool of blood spreading under the head.

"Damn, a head shot," Verne said. "First time out and the little fucker makes a head shot."

Fox made himself respond. "Beginner's luck is all."

Jim snorted. "Let's just haul these two back and cut 'em up. We'll eat good for a while."

Fox *felt* the shadow pass overhead.

⸻

Alone at home that night Fox lit a big fire in the fireplace and poured a glass of Buzz Hammond's still whiskey. It burned like hell but took the edge off. The liquor didn't make a dent in the mental defenses he'd put up, probably because he was so upset. It worked on his nerves but not his ability.

Gloom settled over him. He had used his powers to kill a defenseless animal. Oh, he squashed his share of roaches and ants, and set mouse traps, but this was different. He remembered the rifle's recoil, the deer collapsing. He had *felt* the shock in the animal's mind at the moment of impact. His hands started shaking and he took a sip of the whiskey to calm himself.

This was going to be his life from now on, he realized. He would have to get used to it. No more going to the supermarket to buy his food or paying for a meal at a restaurant.

He breathed in to stop his trembling, so he could think rationally. As much as he feared his ability to read minds, having it back made him feel whole again. To add to that, he had friends, people who were willing and able to help him. And there was a whole community he could help.

He could do more than just survive. He would use his ability to hunt deer and elk, and maybe even the buffalo that had started coming back into the plains. He could *urge* the animals toward the hunters and hold them steady. He would be helpful, but not essential. After all, these guys had been taking care of themselves for a long time. But he could help.

He was an executioner. It wasn't a role he wanted, but it was necessary.

⌒

The winter snow was only about a foot deep in the mountains as Fox made his way to a clearing. The hunting group had decided to split up so he was on his own. He preferred it that way. This was the third expedition for him. All of them had been successful.

He walked quietly and settled behind a log. Keeping an eye on the clearing, he watched for the shadow. He had often felt it over the past two months but today it was nowhere around. Then he *called* the deer.

A huge elk walked slowly and majestically into sight. This was the first one he'd seen up close. He was enormous. The obvious layers of fat on him indicated that he had fought off smaller animals for the last of the autumn leaves and plants. His meat would be a definite asset to the neighborhood.

Fox stayed in the elk's mind as he calmed him and *urged* him to stay still. He remained there as he took aim and fired.

He *felt* the elk's death.

Staying in the animal's mind as it died was his penance. Reassuring the animal was his atonement.

He whistled for the other men after the elk died. He couldn't handle something this big on his own.

Jim was the first to join him. "Damn, you *are* good luck for us. Nice fat elk like this'll feed a bunch of us."

Bo, Verne and Frank entered the clearing. Bo was smiling. "Good job, kid. You're gettin' to be real good at this."

"I had good teachers," Fox answered. He was worried that it was getting so easy.

⌁

That night Fox *felt* the shadow passing by. He knew it was looking for him, but he couldn't figure out why. Avoiding it had become a reflex by now. He kept his shields tight until it passed.

His *sense* of the shadow returned every time he came back from a hunt. No matter how quickly he slammed his shields into place after *calling* an animal, the shadow seemed to find him. It was nerve-wracking.

He set about to figure a way to hide himself. The memory of that evening when he was thirteen. He and Marta were at the gallery and he tried to protect her by enlarging his shield. It hadn't worked then, but he was older now.

Visualization. A dome. A forcefield, like in the old Star Trek. Shimmering. Nothing getting in or out.

And there is was, a glittering curtain surrounding him completely. Pleased, he *nudged* the structure. It moved easily, without losing its strength.

Encouraged by his success, he tried to keep his shields in place and *send* to the horses in the barn at the same time. But no matter how he tried to reconfigure the shelter, he had no success. All he got was a headache.

He worked on it for two weeks as winter blustered outdoors. The headaches were horrible. It was as though the wind was blowing his brain around in his head.

On a frigid morning in January, as the thermometer hovered around zero, Fox sat cross-legged on the living room floor in front of the fire and concentrated on his shield.

He formed a tiny chink in the top. A sliver of his thought escaped. Instinctively he closed the chink. Part of his consciousness remained outside. It floated to the barn. Lightheaded. Two places at once.

Success, of a sort.

Fox *called* the sliver back and collapsed the dome. The room spun. Working through the dizziness, he tried to figure out what he had done. He had been in his house, in his living room, yet out in the barn at the same time. He rehearsed the steps, first opening the small hole in his shield, then dividing his consciousness.

Finally, he was convinced he could do it again. He would have to work on the vertigo, though. It wouldn't be a good idea to faint when he was out hunting.

His next hunt, two weeks later, showed the results of his effort. He split his consciousness and *called* the elk. There was just a bit of dizziness that he ignored, and it quickly passed. But that night he *felt* the shadow again. He would need to refine the process.

For the next two months Fox practiced broadening his shields. Each day he nudged them out further. It was like building up his muscles, the way he had during his first summer in Wyoming.

At first the headaches landed him on his couch with a cold compress over his eyes. But the more he repeated the drill, the easier it got. By the end of winter he had expanded his shields enough that the entire house was under protection. And on the first hunt of the spring he was able to protect the whole area that he and his friends surrounded. He *calmed* the bison while Bo shot it. As always he stayed in the animal's mind as it died.

That night there was no sign of the shadow.

The snow melted and the sun warmed the earth. He planted the seeds and, using the technique he had worked on during the winter, Fox split his consciousness and left part of it to watch for the shadow. Then he *sank* into the ground.

He was surrounded by the densely packed dirt that was thawing out from its winter freeze. He *urged* the nematodes and burrowing beetles to churn up the soil so that the tiny rootlets could find their way down. He *encouraged* the tiny seeds to send out tendrils seeking the nourishment of the earth. He *felt* their strength as they enjoyed the richness of the composted soil.

Yeah, he thought. *This is good. This'll work.*

CHAPTER 40

May. The first farmers' market of the season, the first one he'd ever been to. Fox knew it was early and there wouldn't be much out there yet. He certainly didn't have lots of vegetables to barter.

He decided to go anyway. He had some produce as well as smoked venison from the last hunt. And it would be good to see other people. Much as he enjoyed his solitude he was at a point where he wanted company.

It was a glorious day. The smell of sun-warmed earth drifted up as Fox loaded the Jeep. He saw the horses in the distance cropping the new grass and *caught* their feelings of enjoyment. Then he took a moment to admire his house and barn. They might need some minor repair, maybe some repainting, but they had survived the winter well enough.

He jumped in the car the headed for his mother's. The electric motor was a soft hum in the background. He was glad that he was living some distance away from Marta. She was an independent person, that was good. He didn't want to be responsible for anyone.

When he pulled up she was waiting outside, the herbs and vegetables she had harvested neatly boxed and sitting in front of her door.

"Hey, Mom," he called, jumping out. "You're ready. I thought I could help you. Did you *sense* me coming?"

"Just logic," Marta answered. "First market of the season, first time you'll be displaying your gardening prowess. Figured you'd be here." She stared at him. "You trimmed your beard," she said. "Looks good."

Fox smiled back. "Might meet a pretty lady. Besides you, of course."

Marta snorted and they carefully placed the cartons in the car. She looked appraisingly at the boxes already there. "You've done well, darling. These look very good. They'll fetch a high price."

He shook his head. "You really think so? Look at this." He pointed at the ragged edges of some of the leaves.

"Yeah, you're gonna have to do something about that," Marta said. "Set traps for rabbits, do things to get rid of snails. That sort of thing."

Fox nodded but his mind was busy trying to devise ways of using his talent to drive pests away. He hated the idea of killing more things than he absolutely had to.

Marta examined the produce more closely. "How did you get them to grow so large?" she exclaimed. "They really look wonderful."

Instead of answering, Fox grabbed her hand. He *showed* her how he sank into the soil and *encouraged* the growth.

I even call the soil churners to help out, he added.

His mother stared at him. "That's amazing," she said, falling back into speech. "You're getting stronger, you know. What you've accomplished, what you told me about the hunting and everything . . ."

Fox was embarrassed by his mother's admiration even while he was pleased by it. "I can't really take credit for a natural talent. It's a matter of working with what you've got."

Marta snorted. "You worked hard, I know. No more false modesty. Accept that you're extraordinary. And let's go."

She climbed into the jeep and gestured for Fox to do the same. Acknowledging that she had won the argument, he followed.

Chugwater displayed a festive air. Bunting hung from storefronts and across the main street. Flowerpots with the first hardy blooms of spring lined the sidewalks. Fox hadn't seen it look this good in a long while.

The farmers' market was set up in the park just outside of town. It was crowded even though the sun was still climbing over the eastern hills. Fox made a note to himself that they would have to get there earlier in the future.

Marta greeted her friends as they drove slowly to the edge of the field. Everyone was dressed up, as though for a party. It *was* a kind of party. The local musicians were setting up near the trees to the south. People had brought out the best of their early yield. There were boxes of vegetables, jars of preserves. Buzz Hammond even had jars of his homemade liquor. He didn't see anyone objecting to it, or calling it illegal.

Tables shaded by awnings lined the perimeter of the park, with hand-made signs advertising their wares. Some people had simply lowered the tailgates of their trucks and placed cartons in neat rows. Everywhere neighbors laughed and talked excitedly, while the trees, with their new leaves, waved gently above.

He drove slowly. A tall, slender woman with two children was busy setting up a table at the end of the row. The little boy looked to be about six, the girl a little younger. They struggled bravely as they lifted heavy boxes from a truck behind them. Fox was impressed with their attempts.

Marta tapped him on the arm. "Let me out here—I want to say hello to Randy."

He stopped to let his mother off, then drove to the empty spot next to the threesome. He parked and spread a blanket on the ground. As he unloaded cartons, he glanced at the booth next to his. The woman was good-looking. Her brown hair was caught loosely behind her head and she smiled often at the children, working with them and encouraging them.

Fox quickly emptied his jeep. Then he walked over to the neighboring booth.

"Hi. I'm Fox."

The woman nodded at him. Fox was pleased to see she didn't have to look up. They were the same height.

"Veronica," she responded.

They smiled.

"And this is Grant," she said, pointing to the boy, "and this is Beatrice."

"Hi, Grant," Fox said. "It's good to meet you."

The boy solemnly shook hands with him.

The little girl stood behind her mother, glancing at him curiously, her head cocked to one side like a bird. Her eyes were a brilliant blue.

"Hello, Beatrice," Fox said softly.

He looked at their truck. There were three more boxes to unload. "Look, I'm just about finished. Can I help you?"

"Thanks," Veronica said.

Fox took one of the boxes from the truck. He looked around, trying to find a place to set it.

"Over here," the girl said, pointing to a spot on the table.

"Okay, Beatrice," Fox said, following her directions.

"You can call me Bea," she piped. "I have three names." She followed Fox back to the truck. "Most people call me Bea, some Beatie. My teacher calls me Beatrice."

He lifted another box. "Your teacher, huh? Where do you go to school?"

She looked at him as if she couldn't believe how stupid a grown-up could be. "Over there, of course," she said, pointing back to the town.

"So what should I call you?" he asked.

She stared at him intently, then seemed to come to a decision. "Call me Bea," she said walking back to the truck. "I like you."

"I like you, too, Bea."

Fox hefted the last box and placed it beneath the table, as Bea ordered. Veronica thanked him softly and he walked back to his blanket. He took two folding chairs out of the jeep. Opening one, he sat down and surveyed the scene.

Marta joined him in a few minutes. "Randy's doing much better," she informed him. "Remember? She had a bad cold last week. I gave her some echinacea and rose hips. Worked real well, she said."

She sat down with a contented sigh. He opened the other chair. They sat without speaking for a while.

Fox said, "I'll take the first shift if you want to circulate."

"Thanks, hon, but I saw some of the stuff already. Why don't you go around?"

Fox walked from booth to booth. Some had collapsible canopies that shaded the vendors, while others, like Veronica, just had folding tables. Most showed vegetables or herbs, the first ones of the spring harvest. He was searching for household things—plates, glasses, pots. There were several displays of these things, but he was being particularly choosy.

He got back to the blanket without making any deals. Three people gathered around, inspecting the display. Frank, one of the guys who helped Fox with his house, was looking at the winter squash.

"Hey, Frank," Fox said, sauntering up to the blanket.

"Hey, yourself. Got some good-looking stuff here. Might want to make a deal."

Fox ended up with a new hat and three fewer squash. It was going to be a good market, he decided.

By the end of the market all the venison was gone, and almost all the produce. Fox had developed a reputation as a fine hunter who returned with meat that was sweet, not gamy. Most of Marta's medicines were sold, too. They had both done very well. In addition to the hat, Fox had two finely carved wooden plates and a couple of goblets. He'd commissioned a wooden rocker from Jim in exchange for a promise of the vegetables that would grow later in the season.

Fox looked over at Veronica's table. Most of her produce had gone, as well as her knitted goods. Instead, the boxes held wooden platters and glasses. She and the children were having a hard time lifting them into the truck.

He walked over to them. Without talking, he picked up one of the cartons and carried it over to them. "Where do you want it?"

Veronica gestured at the empty space in the truck bed. "Thanks for all your help."

Bea pulled her arm.

Veronica squatted next to the little girl and Bea whispered in her ear. Then the woman stood up. Bea looked at Fox, smiling.

"We'd like to repay you for your kindness," Veronica said.

"No need," Fox murmured.

"We'd like you to have dinner with us." She spoke quickly as though she hadn't heard. "Would next Saturday be okay? Around six?"

Fox hesitated for a moment. "Thanks. That would be great."

They exchanged phone numbers, "in case anything should change," and Fox walked back to his mother, a thoughtful look on his face.

"Looks like you made a friend," Marta said laughingly.

"I don't know, Mom," he answered. "I . . . don't know if I'm ready for this."

"Why? What did she say?"

"She invited me to dinner." Now that he said it out loud, he felt foolish that he was making a fuss.

"It's only dinner, Fox. Don't get ahead of yourself."

Fox nodded and they finished loading the Jeep in silence.

⌒

Dinner was a success. The four of them laughed a lot and the food was excellent. The children were the focus of attention for most of the meal, and Fox was willing to let the conversation revolve around them. Grant was a bright kid who was just getting into a practical study of bugs and snakes. He spent a lot of time collecting and examining them, and he proudly showed his collection to Fox.

"That's a good display you have," he said. "You must have done some research to identify them. How long did it take you?"

Grant was glad to talk for a while about his hobby. Fox actually learned a bit about the helpful insects and reptiles, information he could file away to help in his farming.

And Bea—Bea was just starting to get into, of all things, Harry Potter. Her mother had some "old books" from when she was a kid. Veronica had started reading them to her daughter as bedtime stories. Bea loved them. She went on at length about Harry and magic and flying on broomsticks.

Fox looked down at the little girl, her bright blue eyes shining, the firelight glinting in her brown hair. In his mind he saw the other girl, whose cloud of black curls and sweet dark eyes had entranced him when he was eight, and the smaller one who ran squealing to him when he came home. He looked up at the mother smiling softly at her daughter's enthusiasm.

Behind the eyes, there was a sadness. Fox relaxed his shields. He *felt* the loss and sadness, softened by time. She seemed to be an interesting woman, one he would like to get to know better.

After the children went to bed, Ronnie and Fox sat in the living room. The fire was warm and his stomach was full. He relaxed.

"Your kids are wonderful," he said.

She nodded. "They're amazing. Grant is so smart. And Bea has a fantastic imagination. It's just—"

He waited for her to continue. When she didn't, he asked, "Just what?"

"I don't know what kind of world they'll have when they grow up. I mean, everything is so messed up. The weather, the country. When people drive through here they tell stories about what it's like in other places. I worry."

"Yeah. I was in Florida for a while, a couple of years back. It was pretty bad there. Folks were moving out of the state because the flooding was so bad. And then the flu came."

Ronnie stared at the fire. "When the flu started . . . Two years ago. Tom, my husband, died. And . . . so did Rafe. My baby." There were tears in her eyes. "He was five weeks old. I . . . there was nothing we could do."

Fox reached out and touched her arm. He *allowed* a trickle of sympathy and warmth to flow into her. "I know," he said.

She looked up and smiled sadly. They were quiet together for a while.

That summer Fox experimented further with his farming talent. One blisteringly hot day, more suited to Florida than Wyoming, he tried to find ways to discourage snails and small animals from invading the patch. He really didn't want to set up traps.

He found some snails making their slow way toward the plants. *Sensing* their attraction, *feeling* what made them come toward him, he planted in them the signals of *danger* and *avoidance*. They turned away.

Now all he had to figure out was how to make the signals permanent.

It took him two solid weeks of work, but he finally got it. A sort of wall, a permanently resonating shield of air, surrounded the garden, but only from the ground up. He didn't want to discourage the worms and soil-churning beetles from helping him.

He sat on the warm, dry grass and *sank* his thoughts into the earth. The bugs and worms were busy at work. The vegetable rootlets stretched out in search of water. It was excellent. Except for one thing. A stone sat in the way of a root trying to creep toward water. That was wrong.

He *reached* out toward the stone. It shifted.

Interesting, he thought. *Did I do that?*

He reached out again. The stone moved farther away.

Fox brought himself out of the ground. He had to experiment with this power. What more could he move?

A huge tree stump sat at the edge of the field. He had been meaning to get rid of it for a while. He *stretched* his mind toward the dead wood and followed its dead roots into the earth. If he *pushed* at that point it might tip over, saving him hours of back-breaking work.

Suddenly he was jolted by a feeling of being *watched*.

He catapulted his consciousness back into his body. The presence seemed to be almost directly overhead. He slammed his shields into place.

That had been close.

The nightmare visited him again. Throngs of people, most of them faceless, crowded him, arms outstretched, begging for help. But this time he recognized the figures in the front. Sonia, not as a little girl but as he'd seen her last, tight-skirted and hollow-eyed; Papa, pale-faced and sweating; Daddy, shrunken and alone; Mr. Kornfeld, Dee, Lily.

And behind him was a presence. Afraid, he turned toward the grasping hands. He tried to see what was urging him on, but he couldn't force himself to look.

He jerked awake, his mouth opened in a silent scream. There were so many, too many. He couldn't do it. He couldn't help them all.

Fox lay down again and pulled his shields tight. He turned, trying to get comfortable, but his dreams kept him awake.

CHAPTER 41

Fox looked at the scudding clouds and grimaced at the cool breeze on his cheeks. He'd been at this for five years but there'd never been a winter this warm. More rain than snow, and the thermometer hadn't gone below zero for the entire time.

Frank and Bo were talking about it when Fox joined up with them to hunt. "Haven't even burned up half my wood, and it's February already," Frank said.

Bo nodded. "Y'know, last year, Mrs. Henderson put in *peaches*. Can you believe it? Fruit, here in Wyoming!"

"Yeah," Jim said, sauntering up to the group. "I'm right pleased with it."

Fox wasn't. He feared the change. He knew what it meant, and how the earth itself was protesting.

He liked his neighbors, though. They were an independent group, yet gave assistance if it was needed. There was no one who relied completely on him, not even Veronica. His mother seemed content to keep a certain distance as well. They had agreed they wouldn't *send* to each other unless they were in the same room. Both of them were afraid of the shadow.

For years now Fox had been able to help the community, but they could get along without him if they needed to. And if he occasionally sneaked a couple of rabbits onto the porch of an ailing neighbor—well, others did, too.

He was doing well and the bad dreams hadn't bothered him for years. If he wasn't ecstatic, at least he wasn't unhappy.

At the beginning of April Fox sat cross-legged on the chilly ground in the middle of his field. It hadn't yet been warmed by the sun, but he made himself as comfortable as possible. He didn't intend to be here long.

He *established* his forcefield and *extended* a tiny bit of his consciousness outside to keep watch. He had to be careful. The shadow had been around more often in the past few months than ever before.

Then he laid his hands flat on the bare soil. Slowly he *sank* to where he could *summon* his helpers, the tiny insects and worms that churned the earth, making it easier for him to plow. The seeds he broadcast could find purchase, sending tender rootlets into the loosened bed. Effortlessly, he *moved* a few pebbles out of the way to allow easier passage.

Finished, he was about to *recall* his thoughts. But something beckoned to him, pulled him down. He *descended* slowly, past the fertile loam of his farm into the bedrock. He *felt* the slow movement as the stones rubbed against each other, dissolved over the millennia by rain, worn away century by century. He settled into the unhurried atmosphere.

And then he *fell* further into the unbearable heat of the magma as it bubbled and ran beneath the crust. The power in it momentarily threatened to overwhelm him. He gathered his strength to pull himself out.

Only to be *drawn* slowly into the molten core of the planet itself.

He *felt* it seething around him and through him, filling him, swelling within him until he thought he would burst.

Instead of exploding, he expanded, his mind encompassing the planet.

The stones groaning under the weight of population. The fish drowning in polluted water. The whales and dolphins disoriented by waste and sonar, washing up on sand and rocks. And the people—so much pain, so many sorrows. Yet pleasure, too. Joy. Hope.

He reached out further, narrowing his search. He found Mark's *scent*. Faintly, he *sensed* Norrie, Dennis, Joey. Then Delores, her mind still dark and confused. He pulled away quickly.

But nowhere could he *find* Sonia.

Liquid heat washed into him, strengthening him. He knew he could lose himself in the immensity of the feeling, never return to the surface.

A warning from above alerted him to the shadow hovering above his physical body. He withdrew and plunged back into his own head. For a moment he was disappointed by the limitations of his body and perceptions, disoriented by the change of perspective.

Then he *reached* up through the tiny hole in his shield and seized the shadow. It felt greasy. He wasn't able to hold it, didn't even want to. It slithered out of his mental grasp and fluttered away leaving behind what felt like a slick of oily dirt in his mind.

Disgusted he wiped his hands on his pants, trying to rid himself of the pollution. But he couldn't clear it from his mind. He was sickened.

He had never challenged the shadow. In fact, he tried to run from it whenever he felt it. Now it almost felt as though the presence was calling *him* out, urging him toward a duel.

The disgust he felt when he touched the thing made him certain that he didn't want to have anything more to do with it. But this time he didn't know it he could avoid it. When he had *touched* the shadow, it had also *touched* him. He worried that it knew where he lived.

His dinner that evening sat in his stomach like a dirty rock.

The nightmare came back as he tried to sleep that night in spite of his shields. It was worse than ever. This time he was surrounded by a crowd of people who came at him across an endless, featureless plain, faceless figures morphing into people he knew and loved. But their faces were like the undead, gray and scabbed. They shambled toward him, forcing him back to where the shadow hovered like a saw-toothed maw waiting to swallow him.

He woke, sweating and shaking, and couldn't get back to sleep.

Fox pushed himself to finish his chores the next day. He worked like an automaton, unthinking. He thought he should examine his dream, figure out what it meant, especially since it had come so soon after his encounter with the shadow in real life. But he couldn't bear to relive it.

Instead, he did his best to forget it. He drove himself harder than ever, hoping that exhaustion would give him a dreamless sleep.

It didn't work.

A week later he rode his horse to his mother's back door. He knew what he looked like. He had circles under his eyes, his hair was a tangled mess, and he had lost weight.

The rising sun glinted from the bright metal of a low-flying jet speeding across the sky. A few seconds later the noise of its engines split the silence. The sound made him flinch. Fatigue and worry were playing havoc with his nerves.

He knocked on the door and waited. He knew it would have been okay with Marta if he just opened the door and walked in, but he never did that. Their relationship was special, tighter even that the usual mother-son bond. He was skittish, though, afraid of too much closeness, too much informality.

When he got too close, people got hurt. That's how it always was.

It took a little longer than usual for his mother to come to the door and unlock it. That was unusual. They never locked their doors. He fidgeted as he waited, too nervous to stand still.

Marta's robe was wrapped around her, and her hair was sleep-tousled. Her huge smile of welcome was quickly replaced by a worried frown. "Oh, sweetie, you look like hell. C'mon in. Sit down. I'll make coffee. You talk."

As she bustled about the kitchen, Fox told her about what had happened—delving into the earth, the shadow, the nightmare. When he described the chase, his hands started to shake. He clenched them in his lap and closed his eyes.

Wordlessly, his mother circled the table and hugged him from behind. Then she kissed the top of his head. "I'll fix something up for you. Some herbs."

"But what does it mean, Mom?" he asked, turning to face her.

"I don't know—"

A raspy voice from the doorway interrupted her. "Maybe I can help with that."

Fox whipped around, his heart hammering. The figure leaning against the doorjamb was as tall as he remembered, although his hair was all gray now. But Joshua wasn't wearing sunglasses now, and the ever present smell of marijuana was missing.

The eyes staring at him shone gold.

For a moment, Fox's mind went blank. Joshua's eyes were gold. Like his, like his mothers. Unlike any he'd ever seen on anyone else. The fog of fatigue and stress kept him from thinking clearly.

"Who are—No, *what* are you?" Fox yelped.

Joshua gave him a pitying glance and shook his head. "Waddaya think?"

Fox started to stand, fists balled at his side, ready to fight. Nerves vibrated in his body. Another telepath, like the shadow.

Marta stroked his shoulders and forced him back into his chair. "It's okay, hon. Joshua is here to help. He came—"

"How do you know?" Fox shot back. "I told you years ago that the shadow was other telepaths. He's a telepath." He jabbed a finger at Joshua. "Do the math." He shook off his mother's hands.

"But this is different, dear." Marta's voice was almost pleading.

Fox stared at his mother, and then at Joshua, and for the first time took note of their appearance. Both looked as though they had just gotten out of bed. An unexpected anger filled him and he shot out of his chair.

"Just because you're fucking him doesn't mean I have to trust him," he shouted.

Joshua pushed himself straight. "Watch your mouth, boy," he spat.

Fox looked from Joshua to Marta. The stricken expression on her face stopped him cold, and he breathed deeply in an effort to calm down. "I'm sorry, Mom. I shouldn't have said that." He slumped into his chair.

Joshua's cold voice broke the temporary silence. "Okay, boy, you wanna check? Scan me. I'm open."

Fox didn't hesitate. He opened a chink in his shield, waited the few seconds for the disorientation to pass, and let the small piece of his consciousness go *into* Joshua. There was no hint of deception or malice, just concern and a touch of . . . fear?

Resetting his forcefield, Fox settled into his seat. There was no immediate danger. "So? Explain."

Joshua took a deep breath. "You probably already figured there's more of us—telepaths. I can't tell you the whole story right now."

Fox tensed again and started to stand up.

Joshua raised a hand, flat palm facing out. "Not 'cause I don't want to. Just that I don't tell it so good. There's others better at it."

Marta sat in a chair next to Fox and took his hand. "Joshua wants us to go with him, hear their story. I think we should."

Fox stared at his mother and scanned her lightly. No sign of tampering or coercion. Then he looked back at Joshua. "And what about this shadow thing? I know it's real. I *felt* it."

A look of disgust crossed Joshua's face. "It's real, all right. Not very nice, though."

"Yeah, I kinda got that," Fox said.

"We think maybe they're planning something. Something big. They're sort of attacking the lone telepaths, tryin' to drive 'em crazy or something."

"And you want us to . . . ?" Fox let his skepticism show plainly.

"Come with me. You and your mom. Hear us out."

Fox stayed silent.

"Just for a day or two. Listen to what we have to say."

Fox glanced at his mother, then turned back to Joshua. "And then?"

"You can stay. Or go. No one'll stop you." Now it was Joshua's turn to glance at Marta and turn back to Fox. "We hope you'll stay. We need you."

Fox *sensed* that Marta believed Joshua, and he couldn't *feel* anything evil in the man. "Okay. But I need a couple of days to settle things here."

Joshua nodded. "Great. Just don't take too long, okay?"

CHAPTER 42

F ox rode the horse slowly back to his house. The concoction his mother had made for him was stowed safely in his saddlebag. Joshua suggested that he strengthen his shield as much as possible, and between that and the sleeping medicine, Fox could last a little while.

They planned to start in three days. That way Fox would have enough time to complete some unfinished business, like saying good-bye to Ronnie and closing up the house.

He didn't relish the idea of breaking the news to Veronica. Fox didn't know how she'd recovered from the death of her husband and infant son, but she told him it was because of the other two kids. They depended on her, so she had to hold up even when it felt impossible.

He admired Veronica a lot. She was a strong woman, but sweet and generous. They fit together well. Neither one was looking for a great love, or even a lifetime commitment. She was grounded in the present and focused on the practical, but with none of the dullness that Fox always associated with those sunk in depression.

She kept him sane.

Every once in a while, though, Fox caught her sitting in a chair with the "thousand yard stare" he'd seen on women who had lost a child. His heart ached for her then, even as he knew he couldn't help. He wondered if his father had ever sat like that, eyes focused on something no one else could see.

He went to Ronnie's house the next afternoon. They sat in the living room, the adults on the couch, the two children on the braided rug in front of the fireplace. The flames were comforting, although the day was warm enough that it wasn't really needed. The three looked at Fox as he told them the news.

Ronnie's gaze was placid as she asked him, "When do you leave?"

"Day after tomorrow," he said.

"When will you come back?" ten-year-old Beatrice asked plaintively.

Fox looked her in the eye. He wasn't going to lie. "I don't know, Bea. I'll be back when I can."

"Does that mean you're never coming back?" Grant, at twelve, was more worldly-wise than his sister.

Fox smiled. "Never is a very long time, Grant. I don't know about never."

Ronnie glanced at him over the heads of her children. She smiled sadly. He *felt* that she understood it was something he had to do, and she was cool with it. Not happy, but resigned.

That night they lay in bed, their naked bodies close. The sex, as always, had been good. There were no fireworks or shooting stars, but sparklers were enough.

"You have the key to the house," Fox said as he stroked her back. "There's meat in the freezer, and vegetables in the cellar."

He pulled back slightly to look at her. She raised her head and their gazes locked for a moment.

"You know the house is yours for as long as you want it," Fox said.

She nodded. "But I probably won't use it. Too isolated."

He kissed her then, and said, "I'm sorry to leave you alone like this. But—"

"I was alone before I met you," she interrupted, her voice soft. "I managed then. I'll manage now. Don't worry about me."

One more thing to feel guilty about, Fox thought as he listened to her steady breathing. He was glad that at least he could leave her with something.

Because he didn't know if he would be back—ever.

~~

The sun was rising as Fox drove his solar powered Jeep to his mother's front door. His fingers drummed nervously on the steering wheel. He honked the horn.

Marta came out. "Is this the way you come to pick up your mother?" she asked in mock anger. "You could at least come up and ring the bell."

He couldn't help smiling. He *sensed* her nervousness, which echoed his. "I know, I'm an ungrateful son. I never call, I never write."

They both laughed, but it was forced.

"I just want to get this over with," he said.

She went back inside and reappeared with a knapsack. Fox mentally *took* it from her and *lifted* it into the back seat.

Joshua came out of the house as Fox settled the bundle in the car. He dropped his duffel and stood, mouth open. "Who did that?" His voice was loud.

"Me," Fox answered. He *lifted* Joshua's bag and added it to the pile.

"How long have you been able to—"

"Long enough." Fox's words were clipped. "Look, are we going or not?"

He and Marta looked at Joshua, who nodded. His mouth was a thin line.

"I'll drive the first leg," Fox offered. Then his tone became sarcastic. "Oh, by the way, where are we going?"

Joshua looked intently at both of them. "May I?"

They nodded, and he *sent* the destination to them.

Marta stared at him. "You *gotta* be kidding," she said.

Fox had a compass in his head, pointing him in the right direction. The top was down with the warm spring sun shining on their heads. Every hour or so, a car passed on the opposite side of the road, and they saw only six cars going their way. The Jeep bumped over cracks in the highway. Weeds grew tall on either side.

It would have seemed they were going on vacation, except for the small cloud of dread in his heart.

With three drivers they ate up the miles. Marta took over in the late afternoon, then Joshua drove through most of the night. By mid-morning of the next day, with Fox again at the wheel, they came to the exit.

The sign read, "Roswell, N.M." Joshua was asleep in the back seat. Fox and Marta looked at each other.

"Are you sure about this?" Fox asked one last time.

Marta nodded.

"Okay. But I'm not going in there without protection."

He brought up his shield, the forcefield he had developed. Marta's eyes widened as he extended it to surround the two of them. They both looked up. A slight shimmering in the air was visible only if you knew where to look. Even to his psychic sense, Fox noted, it was barely there.

"I'm keeping it up until we're certain they're the good guys," he said.

"I don't think we'll need it. But if you want to . . ."

Shrugging, Fox drove on.

Joshua woke up as they pulled up to a diner outside of the city. They didn't talk much as they ate lunch. Fox was fighting his fear and trying to figure out where Joshua was leading them.

I'll put my faith in my shield, he finally decided. *It can protect both of us.*

A few hours later they pulled onto a long dirt road. It wound past a mile or so of neatly laid out rows of green. Fox couldn't tell what the plants were, but he saw his mother nodding several times as though she recognized them. Every once in a while he saw a solitary figure in the field, but mostly it seemed deserted.

The compound itself consisted of several adobe houses, their pink tile roofs shimmering slightly in the heat. They stopped in front of the largest of the houses. It had a square brown adobe front, an arched oak door, a few elegant cacti planted in the yard. Nothing ominous. There were three cars parked in front of it, but there was room in the driveway for the Jeep, as though they had cleared the way.

Fox was first out of the car. He walked quickly to the door and raised his hand to knock. His heart was beating faster than normal.

Before he could bring his fist to the wood, the door opened. A tall, slender woman with dark skin stood in the entryway. The blue dress that covered her willowy figure looked like one piece of material that draped from one shoulder to her knees. It was a lovely cool color that contrasted with the red, beige and gray of the landscape.

Her golden eyes shone, and her voice was low but scratchy. "I'm Belinda. We're expecting you." She stepped out of the way to allow them to enter.

She waited until they passed her, then closed the door and led them down the cool, dim hallway to the living room. Marta slipped her hand into Fox's. He squeezed it for reassurance. Reflexively, he *checked* his shield around the two of them. Joshua followed them, footsteps loud in the narrow space.

An older woman sat in a large wooden chair. It was unadorned, just upright dark wood, yet it had the look of a throne. Her gray hair was pulled straight back in a severe bun, but her sparkling gold eyes were welcoming.

Fox *felt* the welcome, even through his shield. He fought against the warmth and acceptance. It was too easy to slip into it, and he needed to keep his mind clear, to maintain the shimmering protection around Marta and himself. Yet he couldn't *feel* any hurtful desire in the woman in front of him.

"Welcome, Fox, Marta." Her voice was level but had the same raspy edge as Belinda's. She gestured at two easy chairs that faced hers.

They sat. Fox remained upright rather than relaxing into the cushions. Marta allowed herself to sit back, more at ease.

Joshua went through a doorway, returning a moment later with four glasses of clear liquid. Fox heard the ice cubes clink.

"Why are we here?" he asked, as he accepted a glass from the large man.

"You don't waste any time, do you?" the woman said. A small smile lifted the corners of her mouth. "My name is Joanna. I am the . . . leader, I guess you'd say, of a group of people like you."

"What d'you mean, like me?" The questions came from Fox more aggressively than he intended. He thought he knew the answer, but he needed to hear it.

Joshua's shook his head, his mouth turned down in disgust. "What d'you think? We can *see* into people, read their minds. I thought you were supposed to be smart."

Joanna resumed. "We have a favor to ask . . . or perhaps more precisely, a job opportunity to offer."

Fox gave a snort to indicate his disbelief.

"I would like to explain." Joanna's voice was soft and reasonable. "But I would appreciate it if you would walk with me as I do." She looked inquiringly at Fox.

He shrugged. "Okay, I guess. Mom, you want to . . . ?"

Marta wasn't sitting in the chair. She was standing at the entry to the kitchen talking to Joshua. Their heads were bent together as they whispered.

Fox felt a surprising pang of jealousy. *Why should I be jealous*, he thought. *She's entitled to her life. She probably had a lot of . . . friends.*

He couldn't maintain the shield around the two of them if he left. He *sent* a warning to mother, and she nodded. She was on her own. He had to trust that she'd be okay.

He stood up abruptly. "Let's go," he said to Joanna.

They walked out the back door onto a gravel path. The compound was neatly laid out. Small adobe houses were separated from each other by neat graveled plots. An occasional cactus or hardy tree grew, giving shade to the bench or chair placed under it. The sun beat down from a cloudless sky. Fox was thankful for the relief of the shadows cast by houses and trees.

They meandered along the paths not speaking for a while. As they passed one of the houses, Joanna stroked a white chain hanging from the roof to a barrel.

She looked at Fox. "Chains are useful, you know. This one, for instance, allows the little rain we have to be collected. Yes," she nodded, "very useful."

Fox shrugged.

"What do you think of chains, Fox?"

He glanced at her, surprised by the question. "They're good for imprisoning you. Weighing you down."

"Nothing positive?"

Fox shook his head.

"The chains of family, of community. Are they bad?"

She was beginning to sound like Doc Smallwood. He remembered the sessions with the psychologist as she probed, making him rethink his life. Joanna was doing the same, and he could no more ignore her than he could his doctor.

"They bind you," he answered at last. "Even when you know you should get away."

She nodded, just as Doc Smallwood had. "If you don't mind my asking, what about your life in Wyoming? Do you feel imprisoned?"

Don't mind her asking. Of course I mind.

But he answered anyway. "No. They don't need me."

"And if I asked you to stay here, because we needed you. What would you say?"

"I'd say no fucking way."

Joanna sighed. "Shall we return to the house?"

The couches in the living room were both filled when they returned. Six people of varying ages and skin tones sat quietly. His mother sat in one of the easy chairs and Joshua leaned against the kitchen entry. All of them turned golden eyes to Fox and Joanna as they entered.

Fox glanced up and was reassured by the barely perceptible sparkle of his shield. He took his seat but, just as before, didn't relax.

"We're all here now, I see," Joanna said as she sat. She turned to Fox. "So. What do you want to know?"

Fox took a deep breath. Now that he was here, a million questions swarmed in his head. "Okay. What do you do here?"

"You certainly cut to the chase, don't you?" The gruff, cool voice, with its slight Boston accent, came from a middle-aged woman on the couch. The brown curls were grayer, and her eyes, no longer hidden by glasses or a woolen scarf, sparkled gold.

"I know you," Fox said.

She nodded.

"You're . . ." It took him a moment. "You're Elena. From Massachusetts."

She nodded again.

Memories flooded in. The dark snowy night. Moonlight through the windows of the car partially illuminating her face. Talk that went on until the sky lightened.

Other faces in the group struck memories. "You." He pointed at a man with white hair "You're Ezra! And you." He pointed to a woman about his mother's age. "You're the woman I met when I was a kid. When I got punched out. Ms. Rigby."

More remembered scenes. Finding Ezra in the hall of Sweetwater and the lunch where the older man asked question after question. Much earlier, lying hurt and cold on the ground when a pair of soft hands helped him up and took him home.

He looked at the others, at other faces he recognized. The homeless guy in Oklahoma, Louisville Slugger, who helped him find the "hobo camp" near the railroad tracks, then stuck around looking for pickup work. He thought of the night the two of them had faced down a group of drunken rowdies who objected to a white man and a black man traveling together. Had Louie gone *into* their minds and changed them?

Then there was Celeste, who picked him up in her car on the turnpike in Nevada and invited him to dinner. Fox had been mesmerized by her curly mop of blonde and her quick speech that showed vestiges of her New York City roots.

Telepaths' eyes stared at him.

"Why were you following me?"

"Only to make sure you were alright," Francine Rigby said.

"We just wanted to be there if you needed us," Ezra said.

"So you were spying on me!" Fox stood up, ready to walk out.

"No," Joanna said, her low voice a calming influence. "Just trying to help. To keep you safe."

The words struck an uncomfortable chord in Fox's memory. He wanted to keep Sonia safe, and Delores. He knew that motives could be misunderstood.

Joshua interrupted his thoughts. "Of course we were there, looking after you, and your mother."

Joanna said, "There are others, you see. Groups that would use you for different reasons. We wanted to keep you away from them." She puffed a sigh of frustration. "It's really easier if we *show* you."

Fox shook his head, but he sat down.

"We've all been there, Fox," Celeste said. "We know about keeping our talents secret. And all of us were scared when we finally got here. It took me a long time to trust anyone."

Joanna's tone was earnest. "But what's going on now is really important, and we need you. What can we do to help you understand our problem?"

Fox thought quickly. "Lower your shields. Let me *see*."

Joanna glanced around the circle of faces. One by one they gave their agreement. Then she turned to Fox. Her eyes were open, her face calm and unafraid.

He *felt* the relaxation of their defenses and allowed a chink in his shield so that a small part of his consciousness escaped. The momentary disorientation that followed being in two places at once passed quickly. He *glanced* into Joanna's mind. Just a quick look. He didn't want to risk going in too deeply.

There was no menace, no malicious intention. He couldn't see much in his brief intrusion, just enough to reassure him that what she said was true.

There was no reason to keep her out. But no one had ever been *inside* but his mother. The thought of allowing access to a stranger was frightening. But maybe necessary.

He took a deep breath and relaxed his defenses. Her *essence* flowed into him like runoff from the mountains, cool and refreshing. He lived her memories.

He relives her awakening talent with her. Her story is similar to Marta's, and he *sees* the doctors' visits and *hears* the psychiatrists talking. But her talent is stronger than Marta's and she quickly learns to build a defensive wall.

Riding in her mind, he follows her journey around the country. Her path echoes the one he took, but her landscape is different. Not as broken, much greener, more positive.

He comes with her to New Mexico, following an unspoken and barely understood invitation. He *sees* her hand raised to knock on the same door he and his mother found. He shares her fear and reluctance and her resolve to find the reason for the summons.

The group she enters is different from the present one, older, more guarded. He *senses* them open their minds to her and he joins her in the exploration of their memories. They are a defensive group, gathered together to protect each other and any other telepaths they can find.

He follows her life. Her reflection ages as she looks in the mirror. One by one, the older members of the original group are replaced by younger faces. Then the group selects her as leader. That's when their mission changes.

Fox came back to himself.

"That's why we invited you here." Joanna said. "You see, we need you if we're going to help."

"Help who?" Marta spoke up. Her voice was accusing.

"Everyone," a young man said.

A woman on the other side of the circle said, "We can cure people. Not all the time, but often." Her flat features and straight black hair indicated her Native American heritage. "You appreciate that, Fox. We can show you how."

"Yes," Joanna said. "But there's more. We have a grander mission. We want to save the planet."

CHAPTER 43

F ox and Marta stared at Joanna.

After a moment, Fox spoke. "What do you mean *save the planet?*"

Francine Rigby's girlish voice answered. "Fox, you know what shape the world is in. Climate change, political disruption. We think we can help."

"If all of us work together we can physically change things," Joshua said. "But we need everybody. That's why we asked you two."

"You're all crazy." Fox's voice was loud. They had followed him, spied on him, no matter how they rationalized it. And now they wanted him to join in on some grand idea that was sure to fail. Like his attempts to help Sonia, or Papa. Anger clouded his mind.

His mother put a hand on his arm. "Wait." She turned to the others. "Can you *show* us?"

Joanna nodded. "Of course. But it's getting late." She gestured at the window.

Fox was surprised to see that the rapid desert twilight was descending. They had been there for hours. He was hungry.

"We've set aside a house for you in the compound, if you're willing to stay here. And dinner will be ready in the dining room in half an hour," Joanna said.

"What if we don't want to stay?" Fox asked. It was happening too fast. Decisions were being made for him.

Joanna's eyebrows rose in surprise. "Why, of course you can go. No one will stop you. We just hoped . . ." Her voice caught.

Elena took over. "Hoped you would stay and hear us out. Consider joining us. Please."

Fox looked at his mother.

"You could go to a motel," Elena added softly. "But you would be more comfortable here."

Marta shook her head. "We'll stay here, of course." She stared at Fox. "Of course," she said more firmly.

Belinda led them to a cottage on the edge of the compound. A soft light illuminated a small living room. Three partly opened doors hinted at two bedrooms and a bath.

As soon as she left, Fox turned to his mother. "What do you mean, of course?"

"Give them a chance, Fox," his mother answered. "They're . . . Oh, I don't know. They're our people."

He grudgingly agreed to stay for one more day. They dropped their bags in the bedrooms and went off to eat.

The dining room was in a long, low building that housed a huge kitchen as well as a separate eating area. Five tables flanked by benches stretched the length of the room. There were very few vacant seats, yet the room was silent.

Fox noticed latecomers picking up trays from a stack near the door and taking them to a pass-through from the kitchen. Food was served from there. Some diners looked up as Fox and Marta entered and nodded, then turned to their neighbors. But no one spoke.

"Oh my God," Marta said to Fox. "They're *sending*. No wonder it's so quiet."

He relaxed his shields and the murmur of mental conversation flooded in. He suddenly realized why everyone's voices seemed rusty when they spoke to him. They weren't used to actually talking!

The two of them filled a tray and found a table with empty chairs. The others *sent* a welcome to them as they sat. Fox responded, but kept his shields loose around him. He concentrated on the spicy chili with bits of tender meat and the fresh salad. A contented sigh escaped his lips when he finished. There had been no sign of the shadow all day.

Fox fell asleep easily that night. He expected to lay awake. But the warm welcome he and Marta had been received and the absence of the dark presence made him feel free. It took all of his will to remain objective. He wasn't going to make up his mind based on an initial impression.

He woke up to a pair of golden eyes staring at him. The eyes were surrounded by a small brown face and a mass of black curls. They didn't blink.

Fox sat up quickly. "Who are—? Where did—?" he sputtered.

The girl he faced was about five years old. She smiled and peace flooded into him. He smiled back, and she placed a perfectly ripe peach in his hand. Then she turned and skipped out of the room.

He had locked the door the night before, hadn't he? He couldn't remember. And even if he hadn't, how had such a young kid . . . ? Even if she could read minds, could she unlock a door?

He showered quickly and dressed. When he finished he passed the door to his mother's room. It was open and she was gone. His stomach told him it was time for breakfast. He went out.

The door had been locked.

The dining area was almost empty. He saw his mother immediately, seated next to the group he had met the previous day. He filled his tray slowly, somehow reluctant to join them.

Marta kissed his cheek when he sat, but it was Ezra who spoke. "We understand that you don't want to allow *real* contact all the time." His emphasis on the word told Fox what he meant. "So we'll use words. Slower. Not as precise." The gravelly voice indicated impatience. "So. You have questions, kid. Fire away."

Without hesitating, Fox asked, "Who are you?"

Joshua leveled a *how stupid are you* look at him that was so much like Lily's or Bea's that Fox smiled. But all he said was, "Who do you think we are?"

Unabashed, Fox continued. "Yeah, I know. But why are you *here*? And if you want to save the planet, why aren't you shouting it from the rooftops?"

Joanna spoke up. "It's much easier if we *show* you. Okay?"

He hesitated, but nodded and lowered his shield.

Scenes flashed through his mind so quickly he could hardly keep up. *People dressed in skins leaving a cave to follow a man with golden eyes who lead them to a herd of deer. He calls the deer. They come and are killed.*

A primitive hut. A woman with golden eyes tends a child on a straw bed as other adults look on. She lays her hand on the child's forehead. He stirs and opens his eyes.

It's the history of his people, Fox realizes, his real family. Other images flash by, men with golden eyes being worshipped, women being honored.

Then the images stop.

"There came a time when we were no longer trusted," Joanna said aloud. "People locked us in insane asylums, or killed us. That was when we started to retreat."

"Retreat?" Marta asked.

"We formed communities, towns of people like us. We hid from the rest of the world, didn't interact. Until—" Joanna's voice choked off.

Fox waited patiently until the older woman regained her composure. He *peeked* into her thoughts. Her anguish was real.

Finally Joanna took a deep breath and continued. "It was about seventy years ago, during the Vietnam war. We kept our boys out of the draft in any way we could because we didn't want their talents discovered.

"But the ones outside of our enclaves. Those we couldn't help. One of those was Kevin."

She *sent* a picture of a small, slender boy who looked about fifteen. He was very pale and the shadows under his eyes told of a person who wasn't sleeping well. His dark hair was plastered to his skull with sweat, his feet dragged as though he barely had the strength to walk. His eyes were golden.

"We don't know how he found his way here. We didn't send anyone for him the way we did you. He was exhausted by his journey and keeping what he called *the shadow* away. He said he was running from a shadow and found his way here. We're just glad he came because the story he told was horrible."

A worry niggled at Fox's mind at this but he was too caught up in the story to examine it.

"He was older than he looked—about eighteen," Joanna continued. "He'd been drafted into the army and chose not to run or try to avoid his duty as others did. They discovered his talent.

"You see, he could do the same thing you can, Fox. He was able to throw energy and make things move. And he was strong. He could *read* and *manipulate* from a distance.

"At first he thought they were training him to spy, to get information from the enemy. Unfortunately, that wasn't all they wanted.

"They wanted him to kill with his mind." Joanna's shoulders slumped and she closed her eyes.

Joshua took up the story. "His mind was pretty much blasted by the time he got here. We pieced together his story as best we could. Far as we can tell they sent him to a special area. Probably not the army, but some private group. The training they put him through was horrible. Really shook him up. See, he was willing to go into battle for his country, to kill the enemy that was trying to kill him. He didn't count on being an assassin, murdering civilians." He grimaced as though swallowing something nasty.

"When he figured out what they wanted, he freaked," Joshua continued. "Just let his powers loose on his trainers. Doing to them what they wanted him to do to others.

"Of course, they couldn't have that. But they didn't want to kill him. He was a valuable asset." Joshua's tone was bitterly sarcastic. "So they sedated him, big time. What they didn't know was that meds like that only made it harder for him to control himself."

Fox and Marta both nodded, remembering. Joshua noticed and gave a small smile.

"Yeah, you know what I mean. Well, somehow he got here, and we've been taking care of him ever since. His mind isn't what it was. I mean, his talent is half burned out and so's his brain, so in a way he's still a kid. At first we tried to help him remember what happened, then we figured it was better for him to forget."

"What gives you the right to decide that?" Fox spat.

"We're his family," Elena answered. "We're closer than any blood relative. Unless . . ." she gestured at Marta, "the blood relative is also a telepath."

"No one else can understand," Joanna said. Her voice was weak, but composed. "Who else could make that choice?"

Marta frowned. "So you want to force us—"

"No one is forcing anyone to do anything," Joanna said. "But we would like you to join us."

"And if we decide not to?" Fox asked.

Francine's girlish rasp. "As we said before, no one will force you to stay."

"No one's gonna force you, kid," Ezra said. "But if you stay here for a bit . . ."

"You have plenty of time to make up your mind," Joanna said.

All at once pieces came together in Fox's mind. "This shadow. What does it *feel* like?"

The others turned to each other, puzzlement on their faces.

"Shit," Fox said. "Look. Did this . . . group . . . agency . . . whatever it was that was training Kevin. Did it ever *send* nightmares to people?"

"Yeah," Ezra said. He looked at Joanna. "Anthony. Remember? Came here about three, four years ago?"

Joanna nodded.

"What happened to him?" Fox insisted, panic rising.

"He had the same nightmare a week in a row. Then someone came to see him, said they could get rid of the dreams. But he didn't trust the guy, ran away before they came back."

Fox put his head in his hands. "Shit," he repeated.

"What's the matter?" Marta asked.

"We don't have time, Mom," Fox answered. He looked at the others. "That shadow thing you talked about. I think I met it."

Fear and concern rushing from the others assaulted Fox's mental senses and he reflexively tightened his shields. But not completely. He gathered the memory and *showed* them. Starting with sinking into the earth, *sensing* all the multilayered life on the planet, finding the *traces* of his friends. Ending with his encounter with the shadow.

"It knows me now." He fell back into speech. "It may have followed me here."

He wasn't prepared for the flurry of psychic activity that followed his words. He *sensed* warning messages flowing from Joanna and Joshua, and saw the tension in the faces of the others.

After a few seconds, they all relaxed.

"The spotters report all clear," Joshua said. "No sign of the damn thing."

Fox looked at the group, the question in his eyes. And they *showed* him.

A dim room. Ten figures on beds. Their consciousness focused on the area around the compound. Searching for an enemy. Projecting enough harmless chatter to seem normal.

Fox took it in, and wondered why they didn't put the kind of permanent shelter he had established around his house, or his fields. He filed the thought away in a corner of his mind.

When he came back to himself, the others were regarding him with a mixture of awe and envy.

"You went into the earth?" Joanna asked wonderingly. "By yourself? No assistance?"

Fox nodded.

"And you found—" Ezra lost his words for a moment. "You *found* people all over the world? Marta didn't help you?"

Fox shook his head.

"My god," Joshua whispered, "how strong *are* you?"

Fox shrugged.

Everyone was quiet for a moment. Fox couldn't even detect mental contact. Which was good, because his own mind was in turmoil. Was he so much stronger than the others? And the way they looked at him, like he was some kind of savior or something.

"You can see what we're up against," Joanna said. "You could be just what we need, someone powerful enough to bring us all together—"

"What do you mean?" Fox kept his voice level.

"There are enclaves like this one all over the world," Elena explained. "We're in contact with each other, but it's spotty. You . . . With you in the lead, we could all work together."

"And the others, these shadow people, will just let us be?" he said sarcastically.

"No," Joanna said quietly. "We'd have to go up against them first. They have their own agenda. They want the chaos to continue, to use it for their own ends. We'd have to stop them."

Fox shook his head. "I need some time alone," he said walking to the door.

From the corner of his eye he saw his mother get up and motion to the others to stay. She walked out the door with him.

"What's the matter, Fox?" She laid a hand on his arm.

He turned to her. "I don't know if I can do this, Mom."

"Do what?"

"Join them. Lead them."

She looked at him, head cocked to one side.

"You know me. I've been a loner most of my adult life. And when I haven't . . ."

Marta still didn't speak, just continued to look at him.

"Okay, when I haven't, I killed people, or hurt them so much they'll never recover." Images of Sonia in a skimpy outfit, of Papa lying stiff on the hospital bed, of Delores yelling, crowded in on him.

"It doesn't have to be that way, hon." His mother's soft voice broke through the nightmarish scenes.

"I just have to be alone for a while, okay? I have to think."

She shrugged and walked back into the house.

Fox wandered through the compound. It was quiet. He hadn't tightened his shields, so the background whisper of human thoughts and animal life came through. He filtered it out of his consciousness. His feet crunched on the gravel as scattered ideas cascaded through his mind.

Suddenly he came face to face with an elderly man and the same little girl who had woken him. Startled, he stared at them.

The man flinched backward, as though afraid. But the little girl smiled and the picture of a perfectly ripe peach surfaced in Fox's mind.

"Yes, I recognize you," he said. He squatted in front of her. With a pang he realized she was the same size that Lily had been. "Thank you for the fruit. And would you tell me your name? Just so I know what to call you the next time you wake me up."

Now there was a picture of a pink rose.

"Rose?" Fox asked.

The girl nodded.

"My grandma's name is Rose. I think it's a beautiful name."

"Thank you," said a soft voice behind him.

Fox turned quickly. A pair of golden eyes looked at him from a pretty brown face. The woman's lips were turned up. He looked from the girl to the woman and returned her smile. "Your daughter is lovely. Also an excellent delivery person."

Rose giggled. She looked at her mother, then ran off in the direction of childish laughter and shouts.

"The other kids are out of school now. We can relax for a while." She indicated the bench. "Oh, my name is Melina, by the way. And this . . ." She put an arm around the man who had been walking with Rose and urged him forward. "This is—"

Fox recalled what he'd been shown. "This is Kevin."

The man's expression lit up in a sunny, completely innocent smile that made his face look like a child's. "Yeah, that's me. I'm Kevin. Everyone knows me." A puzzled look appeared for a moment. "Don't remember why, though."

Melina took Kevin's hand and led him to the bench. "That's okay, hon. This," she pointed to Fox, "is someone new. His name is Fox."

Kevin turned to look at Fox. "Are you famous, too?"

Fox shook his head.

Melina settled Kevin onto the bench as she sat down. Then she gestured Fox to sit. "No, he's not. At least, not yet. We're kinda hoping he will be."

Her words returned Fox to his dilemma. He sat on the bench next to Melina and Kevin. "So, Kevin, you like it here?"

The other man jumped slightly as though startled. "Yeah."

"Kevin, are you afraid?"

Now Kevin smiled again. "Nope. Not afraid of nothing. Don't have to be, not with Joanna and Melina and everyone around." He sounded proud.

"We take care of each other here," Melina said.

"And the children?" Fox asked.

"We're all born here. There're about thirty of them now." Her face became animated. "And it's wonderful to see them. You should visit the school, Fox."

He raised one eyebrow skeptically.

"No, really. It's not just that my husband is one of the teachers. But what the kids can do! I'm amazed by them every day."

"Yeah," Kevin said. "They're real smart. They can do lots of stuff."

"Like what?" Fox asked.

"They are learning awesome things," Melina said. "They can all talk mind to mind as well as out loud. Among themselves, they switch from one to the other without any effort. They even have their own shorthand. Sometimes they don't *send* in words, just images." She smiled fondly at the high-pitched giggles that came from behind the nearest house.

Kevin nodded. "Yup. Sometimes we talk in pictures."

"And some of them are like you," Melina continued. "They can move things, change things."

"How did you know I can move things?" A second later, he realized. They were all telepaths. If Joshua knew, they all did.

Melina's eyes glowed in understanding. She gave Fox a moment to digest it before continuing her story. "See, they grew up here. They never had to hide their abilities."

Fox blinked fast. *Never had to hide. No secrets. They're growing up free.*

At that point the group of children exploded from behind one of the buildings. They ran, skipped and danced to Melina, who laughed out loud.

"They want their afternoon snack," she told Fox. "I have to take them to the dining room. But first . . ." She turned to the group and they quieted down. Looking straight at the children, she said, "I'm going to speak out loud and I want all of you to listen."

Thirty pairs of gold eyes went wide and focused on her face.

"This is Fox," she said, holding her hand towards him. "We hope he'll stay here with us."

A sudden warmth enveloped him, like being wrapped in a soft blanket. It felt as though thirty pairs of small arms hugged him.

He had never outgrown blushing. "Thank you," he managed to say.

Melina took Kevin's hand and together they led the children to the dining room. Fox sat, transfixed, on the bench. For the first time in his adult life he could imagine a future for himself free of concealment, where he wouldn't have to explain.

Fox rose from the bench and crunched along the path. He saw the rain chains that Joanna had pointed out earlier. The chains of community and family, she'd said.

Responsibility. He'd always run away from it. When he couldn't face up to what he'd done, he vanished. The group thought he had more power than any of them. But with power comes responsibility. And with family comes responsibility.

He picked up one end of the chain. It was light, as weightless as one of Lily's hair ribbons. He remembered Delores braiding the colorful bit of silk into the child's hair. Ribbons that connect and interweave, but don't bind.

He knew he couldn't go up against the shadow by himself, or solve the problems of the world on his own. Now he didn't have to. There was a whole community that had his back. People working together could protect a large group, could lift a one-ton elk and bring it home. Could challenge the shadow and go on to help everyone.

A frozen knot that lodged somewhere deep inside him, one he didn't even know was there, started to thaw.

If they succeeded, there would be no more Kevins, wounded beyond healing. They could restore the damage done to the planet, maybe even find cures for diseases so there wouldn't be any more Lilys. Or Papas.

It would take time. First they had to find the shadow and get rid of it. Then, bit by bit, the work on the Earth might begin. One foot after the other, not dragging this time like they had in that gray time when Papa was sick. But slow, careful steps toward a glowing promise.

He stood up, the tears in his eyes blurring the shapes of the houses. He lowered his shields and *found* his mother's *trace*. She and the others were in the large house. Was it only yesterday he had come here?

The door was unlocked. He walked in without knocking and headed to the living room. The golden eyes turned to him as he entered. The question hung in the air.

I want to help, he sent.

He *felt* relief and joy.

I don't know if I can do it, though.

The response that came from all of them didn't need words.

You're not alone.

Fox looked at the group seated in the dimness. The *feeling* of solidarity surrounded him. *My family*, he thought. *Where I belong.*

His memory painted another scene, a transparent overlay on the one in front of him. A green couch and dark wood parquet floors and two men, one small and slender, the other larger and darker. Next to them a girl with curly black hair, a tall dark-skinned boy, a woman with oriental eyes, a little girl in a frilly dress, so many others. He breathed in deeply. It was the smell of home.

Fox had stopped running.